Nora Roberts, writing as J. D. Robb, explores the hidden connections among friends and lovers, enemies and strangers in the #1 *New York Times* bestselling series.

STRANGERS IN DEATH

In 2060 New York, some murders still get more attention than others, especially those in which the victim is a prominent businessman, found in his Park Avenue apartment, tied to the bed—and strangled with cords of black velvet. Fortunately, homicide cop Lieutenant Eve Dallas's billionaire husband, Roarke, happens to own the prime real estate where Thomas Anders's sporting-goods firm is headquartered, giving her some help with access. Before long, she's knocking on doors—and barging through them—to look for the answers she needs.

But some things don't add up—and everyone's alibi checks out, from the wife who was off in the tropics to the nephew who stood to inherit millions. Was this a crime of passion—or a carefully planned execution? It's up to Dallas to solve this sensational case in which those who seem to be intimates sometimes guard secrets from each other—and strangers may be connected in unexpected, and deadly, ways. . . .

"Robb's strong, hard-nosed heroine once again generates the kind of heat that keeps fans turning the pages."

—*Publishers Weekly*

Nora Roberts

Nora Roberts & J. D. Robb

REMEMBER WHEN

J. D. Robb

STRANGERS IN DEATH

J. D. Robb

BERKLEY BOOKS, NEW YORK

THE BERKLEY PUBLISHING GROUP
Published by the Penguin Group
Penguin Group (USA) Inc.
375 Hudson Street, New York, New York 10014, USA
Penguin Group (Canada), 90 Eglinton Avenue East, Suite 700, Toronto, Ontario M4P 2Y3, Canada
(a division of Pearson Penguin Canada Inc.)
Penguin Books Ltd., 80 Strand, London WC2R 0RL, England
Penguin Group Ireland, 25 St. Stephen's Green, Dublin 2, Ireland (a division of Penguin Books Ltd.)
Penguin Group (Australia), 250 Camberwell Road, Camberwell, Victoria 3124, Australia
(a division of Pearson Australia Group Pty. Ltd.)
Penguin Books India Pvt. Ltd., 11 Community Centre, Panchsheel Park, New Delhi—110 017, India
Penguin Group (NZ), 67 Apollo Drive, Rosedale, North Shore 0632, New Zealand
(a division of Pearson New Zealand Ltd.)
Penguin Books (South Africa) (Pty.) Ltd., 24 Sturdee Avenue, Rosebank, Johannesburg 2196,
South Africa

Penguin Books Ltd., Registered Offices: 80 Strand, London WC2R 0RL, England

STRANGERS IN DEATH

A Berkley Book / published by arrangement with the author

PRINTING HISTORY
G. P. Putnam's Sons hardcover edition / February 2008
Berkley mass-market edition / August 2008

ISBN: 978-0-425-22289-8

BERKLEY®
Berkley Books are published by The Berkley Publishing Group,
a division of Penguin Group (USA) Inc.,
375 Hudson Street, New York, New York 10014.
BERKLEY® is a registered trademark of Penguin Group (USA) Inc.
The "B" design is a trademark belonging to Penguin Group (USA) Inc.

PRINTED IN THE UNITED STATES OF AMERICA

10 9 8 7 6 5 4 3

Sin has many tools,
but a lie is the handle which fits them all.

—OLIVER WENDELL HOLMES

One cannot be in two places at once.

—SEVENTEENTH-CENTURY PROVERB

Chapter 1

Murder harbored no bigotry, no bias. It subscribed to no class system. In its gleeful, deadly, and terminally judicious way, murder turned a blind eye on race, creed, gender, and social stratum. As Lieutenant Eve Dallas stood in the sumptuous bedroom of the recently departed Thomas A. Anders, she considered that.

Only the night before she'd caught—and closed—a case dealing with the homicide of a twenty-year-old woman who'd been throttled, beaten, then chucked out the window of her nine-story flop.

The rent-by-the-week flop, Eve mused, where the victim's boyfriend claimed to have slept through her *demise,* smelled of stale sex, stale zoner, and really bad Chinese food. Anders? His Park Avenue bedroom smelled of candy-colored tulips, cool, clean wealth, and dead body. Death had come to him on the luxurious sheets of his massive, silk-canopied bed. And to Tisha Brown it had come on the stained mattress tossed on the floor of a junkie's flop. The header to the sidewalk had just been the flourish.

The point was, Eve supposed, no matter who you

were—sex, race, tax bracket—death leveled it all out. As a murder cop going on a dozen years for the NYPSD, she'd seen it all before.

It was barely seven in the morning, and she was alone with the dead. She had the first officers on scene downstairs with the housekeeper who'd called in the nine-one-one. With her hands and boots sealed, she walked around the edges of the room while her recorder documented.

"Victim is identified as Anders, Thomas Aurelius, of this address. Male, Caucasian, age sixty-one. Vic is married. Spouse is reported to be out of town, and has been notified by Horowitz, Greta, domestic who discovered the body at approximately oh six hundred and placed the nine-one-one at oh six twelve."

Eve cocked her head. Her hair was a short, somewhat shaggy brown around a face of angles and planes. Her eyes, a few shades lighter than her hair, were all cop—sharp, cynical, and cool as they studied the dead man in the big, fancy bed.

"Anders was reputed to be alone in the house. There are two domestic droids, both of which were shut down. On cursory exam, there are no signs of forced entry, no signs of burglary, no signs of struggle."

On long legs, she crossed to the bed. Over her lean body she wore rough trousers, a plain cotton shirt, and a long coat of black leather. Behind her, over a gas fireplace where flames simmered gold and red, the view screen popped on.

Good morning, Mr. Anders!

Narrow-eyed, Eve turned to stare at the screen. The computerized female voice struck her as annoyingly perky, and the sunrise colors bleeding onto the screen wouldn't have been her choice of wake-up call.

It's now seven-fifteen on Tuesday, March eighteenth, twenty-sixty. You have a ten o'clock tee time at the club, with Edmond Luce.

As the computer chirpily reminded Anders what he'd ordered for breakfast, Eve thought: *No egg-white omelette for you this morning, Tom.*

Across the room in an ornate sitting area, a mini-AutoChef with bright brass fittings beeped twice.

Your coffee's ready! Enjoy your day!

"Not so much," Eve murmured.

The screen flipped to the morning's headline news, anchored by a woman only slightly less perky than the computer. Eve tuned her out.

The headboard gleamed brass, too—all of its sleek, shiny rungs. Black velvet ropes tied Anders's wrists to two of them, while two more ropes bound his ankles by a length to the footboard. The four matching ropes were joined by the fifth that wrapped around Anders's throat, pulling his head off the pillows. His eyes were wide, and his mouth hung open as if he was very surprised to find himself in his current position.

Several sex toys sat on the table beside the bed. Anal probe, vibrator, colorful cock rings, gliding and warming lotions, and lubricants. The usual suspects, Eve thought. Leaning down, she studied, sniffed Anders's thin, bare chest. Kiwi, she thought, and angled her head to read labels on the lotions.

Definitely the kiwi. It took all kinds.

As she'd noticed something else, she lifted the duvet from where it pooled at Anders's waist. Under it, three neon (possibly glow-in-the-dark) cock rings rode on an impressive erection.

"Not bad for a dead man."

Eve eased open the drawer in the nightstand. Inside, as she'd suspected, was an economy pack of the top-selling erection enhancer, Stay-Up. "Hell of a product endorsement."

She started to open her field kit, then stopped when she heard approaching footsteps. She recognized the clomp of boots as her partner's shit-kickers. Whatever the calendar said about the approach of spring, in New York that was a big, fat lie. As if to prove the point, Detective Delia Peabody stepped through the door in an enormous—and puffy— purple coat, with a long, striped scarf that appeared to be wrapped around her neck three times. Between that and the cap pulled over her ears, only her eyes and the bridge of her nose were visible.

"It's freaking five degrees," somebody who might have been Peabody said against the muffle of scarf.

"I know."

"With the windchill, they said it's, like, freaking minus ten."

"I heard that."

"It's freaking March, three days before spring. It's not right."

"Take it up with them."

"Who?"

"The *they* who have to go mouthing off about it being freaking minus ten. You're colder and pissier because they have to blabber about it. Take some of that shit off. You look ridiculous."

"Even my teeth are frozen."

But Peabody began to peel off the multiple layers covering her sturdy body. Scarf, coat, gloves, insulated zippy. Eve wondered how the hell she managed to walk with all of it weighing her down. With the hat discarded, Peabody's dark hair with its sassy little flip at the nape appeared to frame her square face. She still sported a pink-from-cold-tipped nose.

"Cop on the door said it looked like sex games gone bad."

"Could be. Wife's out of town."

"Bad boy." Down to her street clothes, sealed up, Peabody carted her field kit to the bed. Scanned the nightstand. "Very bad boy."

"Let's verify ID, get TOD." Eve examined one of the limp hands. "Looks like he had a nice manicure recently.

Nails are short, clean, and buffed." She angled her head. "No scratches, no bruises, no apparent trauma other than the throat. And . . ." She lifted the duvet again.

Peabody's dark brown eyes popped. "Wowzer!"

"Yeah, fully loaded. Place like this has to have good security, so we'll check that. Two domestic droids—we'll check their replay. Take a look at his house 'links, pocket 'links, memo, date, address books. Tom had company. He didn't hoist himself up like this."

"*Cherchez la femme.* It's French for—"

"I know it's French. We could also be *cherchez*ing the . . . whatever 'guy' is in French."

"Oh. Yeah."

"Finish with the body," Eve ordered. "I'll take the room."

It was a hell of a room, if you went for a lot of gold accent, shiny bits, curlicues. Besides the big bed in which Anders had apparently died, a sofa, a couple of oversized scoop chairs, and a full-service sleep chair offered other places to stretch out. In addition to the AutoChef, the bedroom boasted a brass friggie, a wet bar, and an entertainment unit. The his and hers bathrooms both held jet tubs, showers, drying tubes, entertainment and communication centers within their impressive acreage. The space continued with two tri-level closets with attached dressing areas.

Eve wondered why they needed the rest of the house.

She should talk, she admitted. Living with Roarke meant living in enough space to house a small city with all the bells and whistles big, fat fists of money could buy. He had better taste—thank God—than the Anderses. She wasn't entirely sure she could've fallen for him, much less married him, if he'd surrounded himself with gold and glitter and tassels, and Christ knew.

But as much *stuff* as there was jammed into the space, it all looked . . . in place, she decided. No sign or sense anything had been riffled through. She found a safe in each closet, concealed so a child of ten with dirt in both eyes could have found them. She'd check with the wife on those, but she wasn't smelling theft or burglary.

Walking out into the main bedroom again, she took another, hard look around.

"Prints verify ID as Anders, Thomas A., of this address," Peabody began. "Gauge gives me three thirty-two as time of death. That's really late or really early to be playing tie-me-up, tie-me-down games."

"If killer and vic came up here together, where are his clothes?"

Peabody turned toward her lieutenant, pursed her lips. "Considering you're married to the hottest guy on or off the planet, I shouldn't have to tell you that the point in the tie-me-wherever game is to be naked while you're doing it."

"One of the other points is to get each other naked. If they came in here together," Eve considered, "if they came up here for games, is he going to strip down, *then* hang up his clothes or dump his shorts in the hamper? You got that on the menu"—she gestured to the sex toys— "you're not thinking about tidy. Clothes get pulled, tugged, torn, yanked off—fall on the floor. Even if this is an old game with a usual playmate, wouldn't you just toss your shirt over the chair?"

"I hang up my clothes. Sometimes." Peabody shrugged now. She angled her head to study the scene again, absently tossed back the hair that fell over her cheek. "But, yeah, that's going to be when I'm not thinking about jumping McNab, or he's not already jumping me. Everything looks pretty tidy in here, and in the rest of the house I got a look at on the way up. Vic could've been a neat freak."

"Could. The killer could've come in when he was already in bed. Three in the morning, surprise, surprise. Then things got out of hand—accidentally or on purpose. Killer comes in—the probability's high the vic or another household member knew the killer. No sign of break-in, and there's a high-end security system. Maybe this is another part of the game. Comes in after he's asleep. Surprises him. Wakes him up. Trusses him up, works him up. Toys and games."

"And went too far."

Eve shook her head. "It went as far as he or she meant it to go. The erotic asphyxiation oops doesn't play."

"But ..." Peabody studied the body again, the scene, and wished she could see whatever Eve could. "Why?"

"If it was all in fun, and went wrong, why did the killer leave the noose around Anders's neck? An accident, but you don't loosen it, try to revive when he starts choking, convulsing?"

"Maybe in the throes ... Okay, that's a stretch, but if it happened fast, and she or he panicked ..."

"Either way, we've got a corpse, we've got a case. We'll see what the ME thinks about accidental. We'll go interview the housekeeper, let the sweepers in here."

Greta Horowitz was a sturdy-looking woman with a long rectangle of a face and a no-nonsense 'tude Eve appreciated. She offered coffee in the big silver and black kitchen, then served it with steady hands and dry eyes. With her strong, German-accented voice, direct blue eyes, and Valkyrie build, Eve assumed Greta handled what came her way.

"How long have you been here, Ms. Horowitz?"

"I am nine years in this employment, and in this country."

"You came to the U.S. from ..."

"Berlin."

"How did you come to be employed by the Anderses?"

"Through an employment agency. You want to know how I came here and why. This is simple, and then we can speak of what is important. My husband was in the military. He was killed twelve years ago. We had no children. I am accomplished in running households, and to work I signed with an agency in Germany. I came to wish to come here. A soldier's wife sees much of the world, but I had never seen

New York. I applied for this position, and after several interviews via 'link and holo, was hired."

"Thank you. Before we get to what's important, do you know why the Anderses wanted a German housekeeper, particularly?"

"I am House Manager."

"House Manager."

"Mr. Anders's grandmother was from Germany, and as a boy he had a German nanny."

"Okay. What time did you arrive this morning?"

"Six. Precisely. I arrive at six precisely every morning but Sunday, which is my full day off. I leave at four, precisely, but for Tuesdays and Thursdays when I leave at one. My schedule can be adjusted as needed, and with sufficient notice."

"When you arrived at precisely six this morning, what did you do? Precisely?"

Greta's lips twitched, very slightly. It might have been humor. "Precisely, I removed my coat, hat, scarf, gloves, and stored them in the closet. Then I engaged the in-house security cameras. Mr. Anders disengages them every night prior to retiring. He dislikes the sensation of being watched, even if no one is in the house. My first duty in the morning is to turn them on again. After doing so, I came in here. I turned on the news, as is my habit, then checked the communication system. My employers most usually leave their breakfast orders the night before. They prefer I prepare them, rather than using the AutoChef. Mr. Anders ordered sliced melon, an egg-white omelette with dill, and two slices of wheat toast, with butter and orange marmalade. Coffee—he takes his with cream and one sugar—and a glass of tomato juice."

"Do you know what time he put the order in?"

"Yes. At twenty-two seventeen."

"So you started breakfast?"

"I did not. Mr. Anders would have breakfasted today at eight-fifteen. My next morning duty would have been to reengage the two domestic droids, as these are shut down every evening before Mr. and Mrs. Anders retire, and to give them the day's work schedule. The droids are kept in the security room, there." She gestured. "I went in to deal with them, but I noticed the security screens—the in-house. I saw Mr. Anders's bedroom door was open. Mr. Anders *never* leaves his door open. If he's inside the room, or has left the room, the door is closed. If I'm required to be in the room, I'm to leave the door open while I'm inside, then close it again when I leave. It's the same for the domestics."

"Why?"

"It's not my place to ask."

It's my place, Eve thought. "You saw the door was open, but you didn't notice the dead man in bed?"

"The bedroom camera screens only the sitting area. Mr. Anders programmed it that way."

"A little phobic, maybe?"

"Perhaps. I will say he's a very private man."

"So his door was open."

"Nine years," Greta continued. "The door has never been open when I arrive in the morning, unless my employers are not in residence. I was concerned, so I went upstairs without booting up the droids. When I got to the bedroom, I saw the fire in the hearth. Mr. Anders will not allow the fire when he sleeps or when he is out of the room. I was more concerned, so I went into the room. I saw him immediately. I went to the bedside, and I saw that I couldn't help him. I went downstairs again, very quickly, and called nine-one-one."

"Why downstairs?"

Greta looked puzzled. "I thought, from books and plays and vids, that I was not to touch anything in the room. Is that wrong?"

"No, it's exactly right. You did exactly the right thing."

"Good." Greta gave a brisk, self-congratulatory nod. "Then I contacted Mrs. Anders, and waited for the police to come. They came in, perhaps, five or six minutes. I took the two officers upstairs, then one brought me back down to the kitchen, and waited here with me until you stepped in."

"I appreciate the details. Can you tell me who has the security codes to the house?"

"Mr. and Mrs. Anders and myself. The codes are changed every ten days."

"No one else has the codes? A good friend, another employee, a relative?"

Greta shook her head, decisively. "No one else has the codes."

"Mrs. Anders is away."

"Yes. She left on Friday for a week in St. Lucia with some female friends. This is an annual trip, though they don't go to the same place necessarily."

"You contacted her."

"Yes." Greta shifted slightly. "I realize, after thinking more clearly, I should have waited, and the police would have notified Mrs. Anders. But . . . they're my employers."

"How did you contact her?"

"Through the resort. When she goes on holiday, she often shuts off her pocket 'link."

"And her reaction?"

"I told her there had been an accident, that Mr. Anders was dead. I don't think she believed me, or understood me initially. I had to repeat it twice, and I felt, under the circumstances, I couldn't tell her when she asked what kind of accident. She said she would come home immediately."

"Okay, Greta. You have a good relationship with the Anderses?"

"They are very good employers. Very fair, very correct."

"How about their relationship, with each other? It's not gossip," Eve said, reading Greta perfectly. "It's very fair, and it's very 'correct' for you to tell me any and everything you can that may help me find out what happened to Mr. Anders."

"They seemed very content to me, very well suited. It

would be my impression that they enjoyed each other, and their life together."

Enjoying each other wasn't what the crime scene transmitted, Eve thought. "Did either, or both of them, have relationships outside the marriage?"

"You mean sexual. I couldn't say. I manage the house. I've never seen anything in the house that would lead me to believe either, or both, engaged in adulterous affairs."

"Can you think of anyone who'd want him dead?"

"No." Greta eased back slowly. "I thought—I assumed—that someone had broken in to steal, and that Mr. Anders was killed by the thief."

"Have you noticed anything missing or out of place?"

"No. No. But I haven't looked."

"I'm going to have you do that now. One of the officers will take you around." She glanced over as Peabody came in. "Peabody, get one of the uniforms. I want Mrs. Horowitz escorted while she looks around the house. You're free to go afterward," Eve told Greta. "If you'd give my partner or me the contact information where you'll be."

"I prefer to stay, until Mrs. Anders arrives, if this is allowed. She may need me."

"All right then." Eve rose, signaling the end to the initial interview. "Thanks for your cooperation."

As Greta went out, Eve walked to the room off the kitchen. Inside two droids, disengaged, stood. One male, one female, both uniformed and dignified in appearance. The security screens Greta had spoken of ranged over a wall, and as she'd stated, the master bedroom camera showed only the sitting area.

"Dallas?"

"Huh?"

"House security was disengaged at two twenty-eight, reengaged at three twenty-six."

Eve turned to frown at Peabody. "Reengaged before TOD?"

"Yeah. All security discs for the twenty-four-hour period before the security was reset are gone."

"Why, I'm shocked. We'll get EDD in here to see if they can dig something out. So Anders's night visitor left him hanging, and still alive. That doesn't sound like sex games gone wrong."

"No," Peabody agreed. "Sounds like murder."

Eve pulled out her communicator when it signaled. "Dallas."

"Sir, Mrs. Anders just got here. Should I bring her in?"

"Bring her straight back to the kitchen." Eve switched off. "Okay, let's see what the widow has to say."

Turning back to the screens, she watched Ava Anders sweep through the front door, her sable coat swinging back from a slim body dressed in deep blue. Her hair, a delicate blond, was pulled severely back from a face of high planes. Fat pearl drops swung at her ears, shaded glasses masked her eyes as she crossed the wide, marble foyer, through ornate archways, in skinny-heeled boots with the uniform at her side.

Eve stepped back into the kitchen, took her seat at the sunny breakfast nook seconds before Ava strode in. "You're in charge?" She pointed a finger at Eve. "You're the one in charge? I demand to know what's going on. Who the hell *are* you?"

"Lieutenant Dallas, NYPSD. Homicide."

"Homicide? What do you mean 'Homicide'?" She pulled off her sunglasses, revealing eyes as blue and deep as her suit, tossed them onto the counter. "Greta said there'd been an accident. Tommy was in an accident. Where's my husband? Where's Greta?"

Eve got to her feet. "Mrs. Anders, I'm sorry to tell you your husband was killed this morning."

Ava stood where she was, her eyebrows drawing together, her breath coming in short little bursts. "Killed. Greta said... but I thought." She braced a hand on the counter, then slowly walked over to sit. "How? Did he... did he fall? Did he get sick, or..."

Always best to stab quick and clean, Eve thought. "He was strangled in his bed."

Ava lifted a hand, pressed it to her mouth. Lifted the other to cross it over the first. Those deep blue eyes filled, and the tears spilled as she shook her head.

"I'm sorry, but I need to ask you some questions."

"Where's Tommy?"

"We're taking care of him now, Mrs. Anders." Peabody stepped over, offered a glass of water.

She took the water, and when one hand shook, gripped the glass with both. "Someone broke in? I don't see how that can be. We're secure, we're very secure here. Fifteen years. We've been here for fifteen years. We've never had a break-in."

"There weren't any signs of a break-in."

"I don't understand."

"Whoever killed your husband either knew the security code, or was given access to the house."

"That can't be." Ava waved a hand in quick dismissal. "No one other than Tommy and myself and Greta has the code. Surely you're not suggesting Greta—"

"I'm not, no." Though she'd be doing a thorough check on the house manager. "There wasn't a break-in, Mrs. Anders. Thus far there's no sign anything in the house was taken, or disturbed."

Ava laid a hand between her breasts where a rope of luminous pearls rested. "You're saying Tommy let someone in, and they killed him. But that doesn't make sense."

"Mrs. Anders, was your husband involved with someone, sexually or romantically?"

She turned away immediately, first her face, then her body. "I don't want to talk about this now. I'm not going to talk about this now. My husband is dead."

"If you know anyone who could gain access to the house, to his bedroom—while you were out of the country—it could tell us who killed your husband, and why."

"I don't know. I don't. And I can't *think* about something like that." The anger slapped out at Eve. "I want you to leave me alone. I want you out of my house."

"That's not going to happen. Until we clear it, this house

is part of a homicide investigation. Your husband's bedroom is a crime scene. I suggest you make arrangements to stay elsewhere for the time being, and to stay available. If you don't want to finish this now, we'll finish it later."

"I want to see my husband. I want to see Tommy."

"We'll arrange that as soon as possible. Do you want us to contact anyone for you?"

"No." Ava looked out the sunny window. "I don't want anyone. I don't want anyone now."

Outside, Eve climbed behind the wheel while Peabody sat shotgun. "Rough," Peabody commented. "You're soaking up tropical drinks and rays one minute, and the next, your husband's dead."

"She knows he was screwing around. She knows something about it."

"I guess they probably always do. The spouse, I mean, of the screwing-arounder. And I think a lot of times they can just block it out, pretend it's not happening hard enough so they start to believe it."

"Would you be shedding tears for McNab's dead body if he'd been screwing around on you?"

Peabody pursed her lips. "Well, since I'd've been the one who killed him, I'd probably be shedding tears for me because you'd be arresting me. And that would really make me sad. Easy enough to verify Ava Anders was out of the country when Anders died."

"Yeah, do that. And we'll check her financials. They've got plenty of dough to roll. Maybe she cut off some to hire somebody to kill him. Paid his playmate to do it."

"Man, how cold would *that* be?"

"We'll run friends, business associates, golf partners—"

"Golf?"

"He had a golf game scheduled this morning with an Edmond Luce. Maybe we'll shake loose something on who he played other games with when the wife was off with the girls."

"Wouldn't you like to do that? Have a girl trip?"

"No."

"Ah, come on, Dallas." The very idea brightened Peabody's voice. "Go somewhere with girlfriends, hang, drink lots of wine or fussy drinks, get facials and spa treatments, or lie on the beach, and talk about stuff half the night."

Eve glanced over. "I'd rather be dragged naked over jagged glass."

"Well, I think we should do it some time. You, me, Mavis, maybe Nadine and Louise. And Trina—she could do our hair and—"

"If Trina comes on this mythical nightmare, I get to drag *her* naked over jagged glass. That's my bottom line."

"You'd have fun," Peabody muttered.

"I would, I probably would. I'd feel bad about dragging her over jagged glass ten or twenty years later, but at the time, I'd have fun."

Giving up, Peabody huffed out a breath, took out her PPC, and began to do the checks and runs.

Chapter 2

It was interesting, but not surprising, that Anders Worldwide's New York headquarters were housed in the sleek black tower on Fifth. Roarke Enterprises' New York headquarters also housed its base there and owned every inch of that sleek black tower.

"Do you want to stop by and see—"

"No."

Peabody rolled her eyes at Eve's back as they stepped into the huge, glossy lobby with its rivers of flowers, its moving maps, its busy shops. "I just figured since we were right here—"

"Why are we right here, Peabody? And if you roll your eyes behind me again, I'm going to poke them out with a stick."

"You don't have a stick."

"There's a tree right over there. I'll get one."

Peabody sighed. "We're right here because we're investigating a murder."

"And do we think Roarke killed Anders?"

"No."

Eve stopped at Security, started to badge the guard on duty. And he smiled toothily. "Lieutenant Dallas. You can go right up."

"I'm not going there. Anders Worldwide."

He tapped his computer screen. "Twenty-first and -second floors. Reception on twenty-one. You'll want the first bank of elevators. Do you want me to call up?"

"No, thanks."

Eve called the car, stepped on, ordered the twenty-first floor.

"Do you think Roarke knew Anders?"

"Probably."

"Could be handy."

"Maybe." Eve had nearly reached the point where having Roarke know so many damn people wasn't completely annoying. "The run said Anders is worth about half a billion including his controlling interest in Anders Worldwide." Hooking her thumbs in her pockets, Eve tapped her fingers on her thighs. "That's a lot of motives for murder. Add sex, you've pretty much got it all. Greed, jealousy, gain, revenge."

"The guy was practically asking for it."

Eve grinned. "Let's find out." Her face sober again, she walked through the open elevator doors.

Behind a long red counter, three receptionists wore headsets and appeared very busy. Even so, the center one, a dark-skinned brunette, offered a beaming smile. "Good morning! How can I help you?"

"I need to see whoever's in charge."

"Which department are you— Oh." She broke off, blinking rapidly at Eve's badge when it slapped on the slick red counter.

"All of them. Who's the top dog under Thomas A. Anders?"

"This is my first week. I don't know what I'm supposed to do. Frankie!"

"What is it, Syl?" The man at her left glanced over, then down at the badge. "Is there something I can help you with, ah . . ."

"Lieutenant. I need to speak with Thomas Anders's second-in-command, or whoever's highest in the pecking order and in house now."

"That would be Mr. Forrest. Benedict Forrest. He's in a meeting, but—"

"Not anymore."

"Right. If you could give me a minute to contact his admin. He'll come down and escort you upstairs."

"I can get upstairs myself. Tell the admin to get Forrest out of the meeting." Eve got back in the elevator, rolled her shoulders. "That was fun."

"Pretty bitchy."

"That's what was fun about it."

As Eve stepped off again, a stick-thin woman in high, stick-thin heels came bolting through a set of glass doors. "Ah, officers! If you'd come with me."

"You're the admin?"

"No, I'm the AA. Assistant administrator. I'll take you to Mr. Walsh's office."

"Who would be the administrative assistant, rather than the assistant administrator."

"Exactly."

"How does anybody get business done when they have to translate all these titles?"

"Ah, Mr. Walsh is letting Mr. Forrest know you're here. Apparently Reception didn't get the nature of the business you're here to discuss."

"No, they didn't."

The AA opened her mouth, obviously thought better of it, and closed it. They wound their way through a busy hive of offices and cubes, then made a forty-five-degree turn into the efficient space of—his name was engraved on a small onyx plaque beside the door— Leopold Walsh.

His workstation was a long, free-standing counter in

sleek black holding the usual necessities of comp, data and communication unit, and little else. A second counter ran along the wall to support a laser fax, a secondary computer. A third counter served as a refreshment center with AutoChef and friggie. A trio of visitors' chairs ranged together, backless cubes in pristine white.

The only color in the room came from the showy plant with its vivid red blossoms spearing up from the middle windowsill of the generous triple glass.

Supplies, she supposed, and any necessary paperwork would be tucked away in the cabinetry built into the wall.

Altogether she preferred the miserly space and tattered style of her office at Central.

"If you'd like to have a seat, Mr. Walsh should be—" The AA glanced at the door with obvious relief lighting her face. "Mr. Walsh."

"Thank you, Delly." He stepped in, an imposing man with dark chocolate skin in a pin-striped suit. His hair formed a skullcap that set off a striking face of sharp angles. Deep-set eyes, the color of good, strong coffee, flicked over Peabody, fastened on Eve. "Leopold Walsh. Lieutenant…"

"Dallas." For form, Eve presented her badge again. "And Detective Peabody. We're here to see Benedict Forrest."

"So I'm told." He handed her badge back to her. "As you were told, Mr. Forrest is in a meeting."

"Badge trumps meeting."

"It would be helpful if you told me what this is in regards to."

"It would be helpful if I told Mr. Forrest what this is in regards to."

He wanted to stonewall—she could see it. And couldn't blame him, as she'd have wanted to do the same.

"Mr. Forrest—" He broke off, holding up a hand as the ear-com he wore blinked blue. "Yes, sir. Of course. Mr. Forrest," he began again, "is available. This way, please."

Benedict Forrest's office was only steps away from

his admin's, but a world away from it in style. Here, the workstation held the necessary and the efficient, crowded together with what Eve thought of as guy toys—an autographed baseball on a pedestal, a handheld golf game, a couple of trophies, a sponge-weight toy football. Photographs and posters of sports figures or sports products juggled for space along the wall.

Chairs were leather, deep, and looked comfortably worn.

Forrest himself stood about three inches under his admin's height. He wore a shirt open at the collar, casual khakis, and trendy gel-skids. There was a friendly, just-one-of-the-guys look about him with his tousled sandy hair, easy smile, cheerful hazel eyes.

"You've been waiting. Sorry. I had to wrap things up. Ben Forrest." He crossed the office as he spoke, shot out his hand. Eve shook, studying him as he offered his hand to Peabody.

"Lieutenant Dallas, Detective Peabody."

"Have a seat. What can we get you? Coffee, bottled water, a sports drink?"

"We're fine. We're hear to speak with you about Thomas Anders."

Humor danced over Forrest's expressive face. "Don't tell me Uncle Tommy's in trouble."

"Uncle?"

"My mother's brother. Please, sit." He gestured, then dropped down into a chair. "More, really, as he basically raised me after my mother died."

"How did she die?"

"Eaten by a shark."

Intrigued, Eve sat. "Really?"

His grin flashed. "Yeah, really. I was about six, and don't remember her that well, so it's more interesting than tragic for me. Scuba diving off the coast of Madagascar. Anyway, what about my uncle?"

Sticky now, Eve thought. "I'm sorry to have to tell you Mr. Anders was killed this morning."

Amusement snapped into shock that leached the healthy color out of his face. "What? Killed? How? Are you sure? Wait." He rose, dug a 'link out of his pocket.

"Mr. Forrest, we've just left your uncle's home, and his widow."

"But . . . we're going to the Knicks game tonight. We— we played golf on Sunday. He . . ."

"Ben." Leopold moved across the room. After taking the 'link out of Ben's hand, he laid a hand on Ben's shoulder, eased him down into the chair. "I'm very sorry. So very sorry. I'm going to cancel the rest of your appointments for the day." He walked to a cabinet, tapped the door. When it opened, he took out a chilled bottle of water, unscrewed the top. "Drink some water."

Like a puppet, Ben obeyed. Eve made no objection when Leopold ranged himself like a guard behind Ben's chair.

"What happened?"

"He was strangled."

"That can't be right." Ben shook his head slowly from side to side. "That just can't be right."

"Do you know anyone who wished him harm?"

"No. No."

"Where were you this morning between one and four A.M.?"

"Jesus. Home. Home in bed."

"Alone?"

"No. I had . . . a friend." He rubbed the cold bottle over his face. "Gatch Brooks. She was there all night. We got up about six, worked out together. She left—we both left around eight. You can check. Just check. I wouldn't hurt Uncle Tommy. He's like a father to me."

"You were close. How would you describe Mr. Anders's relationship with his wife?"

"Great. Good. Ava's . . . you said you'd talked to her. Told her. God. Leopold, get the number where she's staying. I need to—"

"She's home, Mr. Forrest," Peabody told him.

"She...Oh, she came home. She came home when you told her..." Ben pressed his fingers to his eyes. "I can't think straight. I need to get over to the house, to Ava. I need to—Where is he? Is he still home, or..."

"He's been taken to the morgue." He didn't bother to fight the tears, Eve noted. He let them come. "You—your family—will be able to make arrangements as soon as we finish our examination."

"Okay." Now he pressed the heels of his hands to his eyes, leaning forward to brace his elbows on his thighs. "Okay."

"Who was your uncle sexually involved with?"

"Huh." Ben's eyes, already rimmed with red, lifted to Eve's face. "Well, Jesus, Ava. I mean they were married for Christ's sake."

"Outside of marriage."

"Nobody." Anger and insult snapped through the grief, brought color back to Ben's face. "That's a hell of a thing to say. He didn't cheat. He wasn't a cheater. You don't know the kind of man he was. He believed in honesty, in good sportsmanship, in playing to win, but playing it straight."

"Who stands to gain from his death?"

"Nobody," Ben replied. "His death diminishes all of us. You mean financially. I would, Ava would." He let out a long breath. "I don't know how things were set up. There are probably charitable organizations, there'd be something for Greta—the house manager. But what you're talking about, that would be me and Ava. I need to get over there."

Even as he rose, the 'link Leopold still held signaled. After a glance at the display, Leopold offered it. "It's Mrs. Anders."

Ben grabbed the 'link, turned his back. "Privacy mode," he ordered. "Ava. God, Ava, I just heard... I know. I know. It's all right. Yes, the police are here. Yes, that's right. I'm coming right over. I—" His voice cracked, then firmed again. "I can't believe he's gone. I can't take it in. I'll be there as soon as I can."

After ending the transmission, Ben turned back to Eve. His expression was simply shattered. "She needs family. I have to go now."

"We'll need to see Mr. Anders's office," Eve told him. "And we'll need to access his electronics."

"All right. Yes, all right. I have to go. Leo, whatever they need."

Eve waited until they were heading down. "Funny, isn't it, how Anders's office—like his nephew's—is all casual guy, even a little toward man cave with the trophies and the sports equipment everywhere. Nothing polished, fashionable, or edgy. Nothing like where he lives."

"Well, he sells the sports stuff. And lots of houses more reflect the woman's taste than the guy's. Or one partner's taste over the other's."

She thought of herself and Roarke. When it came to decor, she . . . never gave it a thought, she admitted. Yet, she had her home office, her somewhat shabby—by comparison with the rest—home office that fit what could be called her style.

"Didn't notice a man cave at the house," she commented, and shrugged. "How'd Forrest play for you, Peabody?"

"Forrest wins actor of the century award, or he was sincerely shocked when you told him his uncle was dead, and was sincerely and deeply broken up. There just wasn't a false note. I believe him."

"Seemed straight enough. We'll verify his alibi. If Anders stood as Daddy since Forrest was six, that's twenty-five years or so. Funny that Ava said they didn't have any children."

"Well, *they* didn't."

"She didn't even mention him, and doesn't call to tell him for hours after the house manager notified her. Maybe a false note," Eve speculated, "maybe just shock and confusion. Forrest comes off as a nice guy—and a nice, well-off kind of guy. Now he's a really rich kind of guy."

"I'll start a run on him. You didn't mention really cute kind of guy," Peabody added as they rode down to the underground garage. "He had that easygoing, athletic thing happening. But the admin?" Peabody hissed air in between her teeth. *"Sizzling."*

"Sure, if you're another guy."

"Huh?"

"Gay, Peabody."

"Uh-uh. Why?"

"Could be bi." With another shrug Eve leaned against the wall. "Either way, he's got a serious man crush on his boss."

"I didn't get that. I did not get that."

"Because you were too busy being sizzled. Myself, I was practically buried in the unrequited love/lust vibes. Sizzling Leopold had them in check, until Forrest fell apart. Must be tough."

"Maybe the love/lust isn't unrequited?"

Eve shook her head. "Forrest is clueless to that part of it. Didn't even notice Leopold's quick flinch when he mentioned sleeping with the alibi. Let's run the sizzler, too." She pushed off the wall as the doors slid open. "Love makes you do the wacky."

Yes, indeed it did, she thought a moment later when she saw Roarke leaning casually on her we're-on-a-budget police vehicle. Tall, lean, with a mane of black hair framing a face blessed by the gods, he shifted those killer blue eyes toward her. It was ridiculous, she thought, to feel that burn in the belly, that thump of the heart over a look—but no more ridiculous than a man who owned a fat chunk of the known universe passing the time on his PPC while he loitered in a parking garage.

He slipped the PPC into his pocket, smiled. "Lieutenant. Hello, Peabody."

"Shouldn't you be upstairs buying Alaska?"

"I did that last week. I got wind cops were in the house. What can I do for the NYPSD that I haven't already done?"

Oh yeah, she thought, the voice was another killer, hinting of Ireland's misty green hills. And she supposed she should have known he'd *get wind*. Nothing got by Roarke.

"This one isn't on you, since you're alibied for the time in question."

"Pretty solid," Peabody put in, "sleeping with the primary." At Eve's cool stare, Peabody hunched. "Just saying."

Roarke grinned at her. "And the primary was up and out early as duty called." He looked back at Eve. "So who's dead then?"

"Thomas A. Anders of Anders Worldwide."

The grin faded. "Is he? Well, that's a shame."

"You knew him?"

"A bit. Liked what I knew well enough. You've been up to his office then, seen Ben—Benedict Forrest."

"Points for you. How well do you know Forrest?"

"Casually. He's a casual sort of man. Agreeable, and smarter than a lot take him for."

"How about the widow?"

Roarke cocked his head. "Seems we're having ourselves an interview after all. You should've come up, and we'd have done this in more pleasant surroundings."

"I have to get to the morgue."

"How many men are married to women who say that routinely, I wonder? Well." He glanced at his wrist unit. "As it happens, I have some business downtown. You could give me a lift, and question me ruthlessly along the way."

The idea had its merits. Eve uncoded the car. "You can ride as far as the morgue, then you're on your own."

"Again, how many are as blessed as I?" He opened the door for Peabody, but she waved him on.

"I'll take the back. I've got work anyway."

"Track down Forrest's alibi first," Eve ordered, then took the wheel.

"How was Anders killed?" Roarke asked her.

"Give me impressions first. The vic, the widow, anyone else who applies."

"Anders would've been the second generation of the company—taking it over from his father, who I believe died a year or so ago. A bit longer maybe. It does quite well, good quality products at a reasonable price point."

"Not the business," Eve said as she wound through the garage. "Not for now."

"One influences the other. Lived fairly quietly, I believe. Sports mad—both him and Ben—which fits with the fact they sell and develop sports equipment. He enjoyed golf, particularly, I believe, and various other games that feature whacking or hurling a ball about. I gather he preferred, when possible, to conduct his business on some court or green rather than in the office. My impression would be he enjoyed his work, and was good at it."

Eve streamed through traffic, cutting around a maxibus, then began to hack her way across town. "How about the spouse?"

"Attractive, well-spoken. Ah, involved in some charity work, it seems to me. Anders sponsors sports camps for underprivileged children. I believe she beats the drum for funding. I can't say I've seen them out and about together more than a handful of times, but he had a reputation for avoiding the social scene ... as some do."

She slid her eyes in his direction. "I go to stuff. Impressions of their relationship?"

"Hard to say, as we weren't chummy. They struck me as a team, appeared affectionate. In sync, I suppose I'd say."

"Any mumbles about him screwing around on her?"

Roarke's brows lifted. "None I've heard, though I don't know as I would, either way. Is that basic cop cynicism, or is there reason for you to believe he cheated on his wife?"

"At the time of death, the wife was out of town. That's verified. Anders's housekeeper—house *manager*," Eve corrected, "found him this morning just after six. Naked, hands and feet bound with black velvet rope. The kind the bondage shops sell by the yard. Another length was wrapped around his neck in what would appear to be an erotic scarfing session gone bad. There were numerous sex aids and toys on the nightstand, and the corpse still sported an impressive hard-on when the primary began her investigation. There was no sign of forced entry, no sign of struggle, no additional visible signs of trauma or violence on the body."

Roarke was silent a moment. "People have their secrets, and the appetites they hide from the rest. Still, I wouldn't have thought him the sort for sport of that nature. It's the kind of salacious details the media will salivate over. Difficult for the family he leaves."

"Anybody you can think of who might want to do him, and set it up so the media salivates?"

"For what point? If you're thinking a competitor, killing Anders doesn't kill, or damage, the company. And a scandal like this? It wouldn't hurt stock or sales—not appreciably. In fact, it might give them a temporary boost. People are odd creatures. I need a new pair of track shoes, one might say. I think I'll buy some by that guy who died with a boner."

"If he lasted, so will they."

"Exactly. They could use it as a bloody slogan."

"Forrest's alibi checks," Peabody said from the backseat. "I tagged EDD, and they've got a geek squad on scene. Another will be transporting Anders's office electronics. First report verifies my findings. Security shut down at two twenty-eight, rebooted at three twenty-six. Security was dark for nearly an hour."

"Had to be remote." Eve glanced at Roarke. "Have to have the passcode or system specs to avoid the auto alarm."

"There are ways. There are always ways."

"You wouldn't need ways unless it was premeditated. Randy Tom's going to entertain, he doesn't need to shut down his security. His wife's out of the country, and for several days yet. So he lets them in, or he gives them the passcode. This way? It's too elaborate, it's too fucking *careful*."

"With a side of mean," Roarke added. "There are ways, always ways, to kill a man. Why choose to kill this way? Intimately, and in a manner that smears the victim and his family?"

"We'll find out. First stop." Eve pulled over to double park in front of the morgue. "Peabody, I'll take this. Head back to Central, start the runs. See if you can locate the vic's golf partner, and run him. I want EDD to start evaluations on what type of remote was used. Let's start a time line on the vic's day yesterday."

Ignoring the furious blast of horns, she shifted to Roarke. "This is your stop, ace."

He glanced through the window at the morgue. "Not for some time, I hope. Good luck, Peabody," he added as he slipped out of the car to join Eve on the sidewalk. "I could make some inquiries. I know people who knew him, people who did business with him."

"You could." Considering that, Eve stuck her hands in her pockets, and surprised herself by finding gloves in them. "Word's spreading by now, so it couldn't hurt. Do you really have business downtown?"

"I do. But even if I didn't, it would've been worth the trip."

She looked at him in the stubbornly frigid, blowing wind. "Murder talk makes it worth the trip?"

"As entertaining as that invariably is, no. This would make it worth the trip."

He grabbed her—she should've seen it coming—and his mouth covered hers. The instant blast of heat slammed right through such matters as late winter freezes and wind-chill factors. The sudden power and punch of the kiss rocked her back on her heels, and made her wonder if little beams of sunlight were shooting out of her fingertips.

He caught her chin in his hand, smiled down at her. "Definitely worth it."

"Cut it out."

"Nice work, stud."

They both glanced over at the sidewalk sleeper huddled in a nearby doorway. The woman—or Eve thought it was a woman as she was bundled in so many mixing layers she resembled a small, patchwork mountain—offered a grin and a thumbs-up.

Eve jammed a finger into Roarke's chest to dismiss any notion of an encore. "Go away now."

"Absolutely worth the trip. Good hunting, Lieutenant."

He strolled off, and she peeled away to the entrance of the morgue. But when she couldn't resist a glance back at him, she saw him stop and crouch down to speak to the sidewalk sleeper. Curious, she slowed her pace to keep him in view a moment longer, and wasn't surprised to see him dig something out of his pocket and pass it over.

Credits, she supposed, and probably more than the sleeper generally pulled in over the course of a week. She'd probably buy brew with it instead of a bed out of the cold, Eve thought. He had to know that, and still . . .

And still, she thought, pleased to love a man who'd toss a handful of credits into the void, just in case. Thinking of that, she walked into the house where death always had a room.

Chapter 3

In a room of white tile and bright steel, Chief Medical Examiner Morris stood unruffled and stylish over Thomas Anders's corpse. He'd teamed a rust-colored shirt with a dull gold shirt, and mirrored those tones with the thin rope worked through his long, dark braid. His clever face with its long eyes and hard planes was half covered with goggles while his skilled fingers gently lifted out the liver Anders no longer had any use for.

He set the organ aside on the scale, then offered Eve a welcoming smile. "A traveler stops by a farmhouse to ask for shelter for the night."

"Why?"

Morris wagged a bloody finger. "The farmer tells the traveler he can share a room with the farmer's daughter, if he keeps his hands to himself. The traveler agrees, goes into the room, and in the dark slips into bed beside the farmer's daughter. And, of course, breaks his word. In the morning, guilty, the traveler offers to pay the farmer for the hospitality, but the farmer waves this off. So the traveler says he hopes he didn't disturb the daughter in the night. 'Unlikely,' the farmer replies, 'as we're burying her today.' "

Eve let out a snort. "Sick death humor."

"A specialty of the house. And it seemed apt under the circumstances." He gestured toward Anders's stubborn erection.

"Yeah, how about that?"

"Somehow sad and enviable at the same time. I'm running tox, but unless your dead is a medical marvel, we can presuppose he was loaded with happy cock aids. Then after he achieved liftoff, the strategically placed rings trapped the blood supply at the—sticking point."

"Gee, Morris, I'm just a cop. You're confusing me with all these complicated medical terms."

He laughed, then removed a thin section of the liver. "We see death erections fairly routinely, particularly in stranglings or hangings, as the blood in the torso tries to obey the laws of gravity and travels down. The erectile tissue fills with it, and expands. But once the body's moved, as our friend's here was, it dissipates."

"Yeah, and people noticed guys got boners when they were publicly hanged, back in the good old days, and thought: Hey, maybe if I choke myself during sex I'll make really good wood. People are really stupid."

"Difficult to argue that point, as you and I often see them at their most terminally stupid. So, as to our current guest: Erotic—or autoerotic if you're going solo— asphyxiation decreases oxygen, and pumps up the endorphins to heighten sexual pleasure. It's responsible for a considerable number of accidental deaths annually, and many deaths that are officially termed suicide."

"This wasn't suicide."

"No, indeed." Morris looked down on Anders. "I believe it took him between fifteen and twenty minutes to die, slowly choking. Yet, there's no bruising on his wrists or ankles. However cushioned the rope, when a man slowly chokes to death he'll fight, he'll struggle, and velvet restraints or not, there would be ligature marks. Even here." He gestured again, then offered Eve a pair of microgoggles. "Here, where the rope tightened, cut in, cut off his oxygen, there's no evidence he fought against it, writhed, strained. The bruising here is almost uniform."

"So he just lay there and died."

"Essentially."

"Even if a guy wants to self-terminate, the body fights it."

"Exactly so. Unless—"

"It can't. How long for the tox?"

"I flagged it. But I can give you something now. Look here."

She bent over Anders again, scanning the bruising under the right ear until she saw it. The faint, circular mark was nearly obscured by the more traumatic bruising. "Pressure syringe."

"Yes, my bright young student. An odd place for self-medicating—especially by a right-hander—which he was."

Shoving up the goggles, Eve put herself back in Anders's bedroom. "Killer comes in, crosses to the bed. Sealed up, all sealed up, booties over the feet to muffle any sound. Lots of thick carpet anyway. Tranqs Anders while he's sleeping. Quick, clean. Guy could've slept right through that—even if he started to wake up, a good tranq would take him under in seconds. Then you truss him up, set the scene, walk out, and leave him to die. Pick up the security discs. You've already shut down the system, but you take the discs. You're either anal or hoping we're just incredibly stupid and that'll throw us off and make us think it was an accident."

"Incredibly stupid we aren't."

"Either way, he's dead." She paced away, among the steel and comps, back again. "If you're going there to do the guy, why just tranq him? Why not load him up so he ODs? Okay, you don't slit his throat or beat him to death with a bat because maybe you're squeamish, or you prefer more passive methods. But why the elaborate and de-meaning when a lethal dose of barbs or poison or any number of substances would've done the job?"

"It was too personal for that."

She nodded, appreciating a like mind, and her grin was fierce. "See? Incredibly stupid we aren't. As soon as you get the tox back, Morris."

"As soon as."

When she strode into the Homicide bullpen at Cop Central, Eve saw Peabody sucking down something from a mug the size of the Indian Ocean while she worked at her desk. It reminded Eve that she was probably about a quart low on coffee. She signaled her partner, jerked a thumb toward her office, and turning, nearly plowed into one of her detectives.

"Make a hole, Baxter."

"Need a sec."

"Then fall in line." She moved through to her office with its single, stingy window, battered desk, and sagging visitor's chair. And hit the AutoChef for coffee.

Taking the first slug, she studied Baxter over the rim. He was slick, savvy, and smart enough to wait to have his say until she'd kicked in some caffeine. "What's your deal?"

"Case I caught about a couple months ago, it's stalled."

"Refresh me."

"Guy gets his throat slashed and his works sliced off in a rent-by-the-hour flop down on Avenue D."

"Yeah." She flipped through the files in her head. "Came in with a woman nobody remembers, and nobody remembers seeing said woman leaving."

"Maid service, and I use the term loosely, found him the next morning. Custer, Ned, age thirty-eight, worked in building maintenance for an office building downtown. Guy left a wife and two kids."

"Cherchez la femme," Eve said, thinking of Peabody's comment that morning.

"I've been *cherchez*ing the damn *femme*. Got zip. Nobody remembers her—not clearly. We dug, found the bar—using that term loosely, too, where they hooked up, but other than her being a redhead with a sense she was a pro, nobody can paint her picture. Guy was a player. A little pushing with his friends and associates got that much. He screwed around regular, cruised bars and clubs once or twice a week to score—usually paying for it. The kid and I," he continued, speaking of his aide, Officer Troy Trueheart, "we've put in hours trolling dumps, dives, and dens of iniquity. We're stalled, Dallas. It's going stone-cold."

"What about the wife? Did she know he was dipping strange?"

"Yeah." Baxter blew out a breath. "It didn't take more than a poke to get her to cop to it. And to admit they fought about it. He tuned her up now and then, too. She copped to that, and neighbors verified."

"Maybe *she* should've cut his dick off."

"Yeah, yeah, women always go for the jewels. She didn't though. When he didn't come home by midnight, she tried his 'link, left messages until nearly three. TOD was about one-thirty, and we've got her tagging him from her home unit at one-fifteen, again at one-forty. Pissed off, crying, and nowhere near Avenue D. She's better off, seems to me. But I hate to lose one."

"Hit the flop again, push the street LCs who use it, or work the bars in the neighborhood. How about transpo?"

"No cabs letting off fares on that block, and nothing popped on the underground surveillance. We figured they hoofed it, and that's how we zeroed in on the bar."

"Make the rounds again, get meaner. Any chance he was into something nastier than banging strange?"

"Nothing's popped. Blue-collar asshole, pissing it away on cheap brew and loose women with a nice wife and a couple of cute kids at home. The thing is, Dallas, it was a cold kill. One slice." Baxter mimed cutting his own throat. "From behind. Then the bastard drops, but he's still alive, according to the ME, when she cuts off his dick. She had to be freaking covered with blood, but there's no trail, not out the door, not out the window and fire escape. Not a drop."

"Cleaned up after."

"No blood in the sink, no trace in the tap, the pipes. It reads like she came prepared, like she maybe sealed up, or changed. Like she had this in mind from the jump. I've knocked on women he's known to have dicked around with, who might be pissed off, but that's nowhere."

"Give it another push. I'll take a look at the file as soon as I get a chance. Fresh eyes."

"Appreciate that."

When he left, Eve stepped over to her desk. Her 'link indicated she had eight messages. A chunk of them, she knew, would be from media hounds. A rich guy buys it in his own home, it started the trickle that often became a flood. And the details of how would leak; she knew that, too. Nobody's finger was big enough to plug the hole in the dike when the flood was that juicy.

"All clear?" Peabody asked from the doorway.

"Yeah."

"Baxter wanted to talk about the Avenue D case? True-heart's run some of it by me," Peabody continued. "Nothing's gelling."

"They'll go back around, work it again. What've you got for me?"

"Benedict Forrest—whose mother really was eaten by a shark. Or severely chewed on by one. He was six at the time, and living in New York under the care of a nanny and numerous servants. Mother was quite the adrenaline junkie, from what I've got. Name the life-threatening activity, she gave it a whirl. Thirty-five at TOD, twice divorced, one child. When she ended up the main course for Jaws, Anders applied for custody and guardianship, and as the biological father didn't contest, same was granted."

"How much did Anders pay him? The bio dad?"

"Five million, apparently. The guy spends most of his time cruising around hot spots in Europe, hadn't seen the kid since the divorce—four years plus before the mother died. He's been married three times since, and is currently living in the south of France. Just doesn't feel like he plays into this."

"How much of a financial interest did the mother have in the company?"

"None. She took a buyout from her father in lieu. And she was smart enough—or vindictive enough—to arrange her trust and assets so even if the father took the kid, after her death, he couldn't touch a penny of the kid's take. Anders took the kid, supported, educated, and housed him on his own nickel."

Pausing, Peabody glanced down at her notes. "Forrest came into a nice chunk of change when he turned twenty-one, another portion at twenty-five, another at thirty. He has an MBA from Harvard, where he also played baseball and lacrosse. He worked his way up the ranks at Anders from a junior exec to his current position as Chief Operating Officer."

"Any criminal?"

"Nada. Pretty regular hits for speeding, and a shitload of parking tickets, all paid up."

Eve sat back, swiveled in her desk chair. "Give me the wife."

"Ava Montgomery Anders, who I confirmed was in her hotel suite on St. Lucia when contacted about trouble at home. She booked a shuttle after the transmission. There's no record of her leaving the island by any mode prior. Born Portland, Oregon, in 2008, upper-middle-class all the way. Previous marriage to one Dirk Bronson in 2032, ended in divorce in 2035. No offspring. Earned degrees in business and public relations from Brown—scholarship—which she put to use as the PR rep for Anders Worldwide—Chicago base, where she relocated after her divorce. Then she transferred to the New York office in 2041. She and Anders married in '44. She currently serves as the company's goodwill ambassador, serving on the board of Everybody Plays, Anders Worldwide's organization founded to provide facilities, training, and equipment for children, ah, worldwide. And serving as chairman of Moms, Too, a program that offers educational seminars, workshops, networking opportunities, and so on to mothers of kids in Everybody Plays. No criminal on her, either, and she's worth about ten million in her own right."

Peabody lowered her notebook. "I could give you Greta Horowitz, but everything she told us runs true. I was about to start on Leopold Walsh, but I must find food. I can find you food, too." Peabody smiled hugely. "How about a nice sandwich?"

"How about we find out where the hell some of the reports are, and why they're not on my desk? I want—" Eve broke off as her computer signaled an incoming. "Morris comes through," she murmured.

"And while you're singing the praises of our ME, I'll go hunt and gather."

"Computer, display incoming on screen, copy to open file, and print."

Multitask acknowledged. Working…

As the computer hummed, Eve scanned the toxicology report. "Well, Jesus, Tommy," she stated, "you didn't have a snowball's chance, did you?"

While it printed, she engaged her 'link to harass the sweepers for a preliminary, and because her mind was elsewhere, answered her 'link when it signaled a few minutes later.

"Dallas."

"You don't call, you don't write."

"Nadine." Eve didn't bother to curse herself as she stared into the sharp green eyes of the city's hottest reporter. The fact that they were friends made it convenient—or inconvenient, depending on the circumstances. "Gosh, I'd just love to chat, but I'm about to do lunch. Then maybe I'll have a manicure."

"That's so cute. You caught a hot one, Dallas, just the kind of case we love to spotlight on *Now*. Tomorrow night. You'll lead off, a full ten-minute segment."

"Again, gosh, but I have to have my eyes put out with a hot poker tomorrow night. Otherwise . . ."

"Thomas Anders's murder is big news, Dallas."

"We haven't determined or announced the death as murder."

"That's not what I hear. Strangled, in bed, with considerable kink attached. If not murder, was it accidental death during sex games?"

So the trickle was already a flood, Eve thought. "You know better, Nadine."

"A girl's gotta try. He was a nice guy, Dallas. I'd like to cover this right."

"You knew him?"

"I did a few features on him, his wife, his nephew over the years. That's not really knowing someone, but what I did know, I liked. Tabloid media—and a lot of other media—is going to pump up the sex, you know this. I can't avoid it, but I want to be evenhanded. So help me."

"Not this time. But I'll give you Peabody. You won't screw with her, or the investigation. And she needs to develop her media chops. So you help her."

"That's a deal. I'll have my people get in touch with her, but tell her I need her here, at the studio, by five tomorrow."

"Nadine, in five words or less, sum up your take on the relationship between Anders and his wife, and Anders and his nephew."

"With the wife, affectionate and proud. The same for the nephew, but even more so. I remember asking Anders what he considered his finest accomplishment. He turned a photo around that he kept on his desk—one of his nephew. 'You're looking at him,' is what he said. I ended the piece with it."

"Thanks." Eve clicked off, glanced over as Peabody clomped in with an armload of food.

"We got your pretend-I'm-turkey wraps, soy chips, and these cute little tubs of veggie hash. I got you a tube of Pepsi."

Eve watched while Peabody set food on her desk, tidily organizing debris to make room. "What are you angling for, Peabody?"

"Angling? Just making sure you don't forget to eat. You're always forgetting to eat, which is why you're skinny as a snake. Which looks great on you." Peabody's gaze darted up and away while she added a napkin and plastic fork. Then her breath huffed out as Eve continued to give her the fish-eye. "Okay, okay. Maybe I was hoping, if we're not on the tail of some hot lead or whatever, you could find it in your big, generous heart to—"

"Cut the crap."

"I want to leave early, take an hour's personal time. McNab and I have a date."

"You and McNab live together."

"Yeah, well, see, that's kind of the point." Peabody dragged the visitor's chair over, picked up her wrap, and chowed down. "We realized we didn't want the cohab thing to take the romance out of things. The spark. So we instituted Date Night. Tonight's the first, so I really want to get home in time to buff myself up. Special, you know? Kick him in the balls special."

"If you want to kick him in the balls—and I often want to myself—you should stay home."

"Dallas."

"Yeah, yeah, yeah. Take the hour, buff and polish, kick him in the balls."

"Thanks. We're going to this club, and not one of those bump-and-fuck joints," Peabody added, gesturing with a soy chip before popping it into her mouth to crunch. "But where you actually go to listen to music and dance with each other and stuff. I really want to look extreme, so you know, need that hour."

"Fine. You'll be making it up tomorrow. You need to report to Nadine's studio at Channel 75 at seventeen hundred."

"Whafo?" Peabody asked with a mouthful of veggie hash.

"She'll interview you on the Anders case, so make sure you're—"

"What? On the air? Me?" She choked, whistled out a breath while her eyes wheeled, then glugged down Diet Pepsi. "No."

"You'll be representing the department, and this division, so don't screw it up."

"But . . . But people watch *Now*. Practically everybody. I can't—"

"Screw it up. Exactly." It was small, it was mean, but Eve couldn't deny Peabody's reaction made the pretend turkey almost tasty. "Nadine has respect for cops, and for the process, but she's still a reporter. She's sneaky. Don't forget that. You give the facts I'll clear you to give, and the feel, your own take, but when she presses you—and she will—on investigative details, you block. Standard, I'm not at liberty."

Faintly green now, Peabody pressed a hand to her belly. "I think I'm going to be sick."

"You boot on my desk, I'll throw your gagging body out my window. You won't have to worry about going on screen."

"Can't you do it? You're used to it."

"No, I can't do it, and you need to get used to it."

"I don't know what to wear."

"Oh sweet, suffering Christ." Eve pressed her fingers against the twitching muscle beside her eye. "Window, Peabody. Headfirst."

"You couldn't fit me through that stupid window."

"Let's find out."

"Okay, okay, okay. Now my head's all screwed up."

"Unscrew it. We've got a few matters just a smidge more important than your date night and on-air debut. The vic was tranqed *twice*."

"What—who. Wait." Closing her eyes, Peabody took several deep breaths. "Anders. Okay, I'm back. Anders was tranqed?"

"Pressure syringe." Eve tapped her finger on the side of her neck. "Heavy dose of barbs, enough to knock out a horse. There were also traces of a sleep aid, standard over-the-counter. Preliminary take is this was ingested, probably three to four hours before TOD. The combo dropped him out. The killer could've performed brain surgery on him, and Anders wouldn't have noticed."

"Why not just give him a fatal dose? Why the big show?"

"Good question, and one of the reasons I haven't yet thrown you headfirst out the window. The show was as important as the murder. Disgrace? Revenge? A discarded lover who wanted him to pay? Is it smart, or is it sloppy?"

Peabody considered that over another chip. "If you wanted it to come off as it looked on the surface—accidental death due to erotic asphyxiation—you don't load him up with barbs. Maybe a mild tranq, sure, to disorient him while you do the bondage. Take your time after that, set the scene, let the tranq wear off some. If you're going to go to all that trouble, it seems like you want him to suffer. If you want him to suffer, why knock him out so he can't?"

"More good questions. You're redeeming yourself. I'm going to send the file to Dr. Mira. I'd like her profile and opinion on this. Could be the killer overdid the barbs. He had a massive dose of erectile enhancer in there, too.

"It feels personal, but let's run it through IRCCA for like crimes. We'll start trying to run down the restraints, the tranq. And we'll do a second level on financials. Forrest and the widow are the most likely to benefit financially. They've both got a solid base on their own, but who doesn't like more? And let's look for old and current lovers. Guy waits until he's well into his forties to do the marriage thing, he probably didn't say 'I do' without banging a few prospects first."

"I can give EDD another goose, see if we've got anything there."

"I want copies of any transmissions between the vic and his wife, his nephew. Have them round up the 'links from his office."

"Lieutenant?" Trueheart, Baxter's young and studly aide, tapped lightly on the doorjamb. "Sorry to interrupt your lunch, but there's an Edmond Luce out here. He wants to talk to you regarding the Anders case. Seems pretty worked up, and . . . a lot British."

Eve dumped the remains of her wrap onto Peabody's plate, shoved her own into the recycler. "Give me a minute, then send him back."

"Yes, sir."

"Ditch this stuff, Peabody, then goose EDD, and give one to the lab while you're at it. Minimum, I want a report of any and all medications and enhancements taken from the scene."

"On that." Gathering up the rest of the remains, Peabody headed out.

"Computer, standard bio run on Luce, Edmond, British, with business or personal connection to Anders, Thomas A., of Anders Worldwide. Display only."

Acknowledged. Working . . .

While she waited, Eve sent the case file and a quick memo to Dr. Charlotte Mira, the department's top profiler.

Task complete. Data displayed.

Eve scanned quickly, looking for the quick overview. Luce, London-born, was seventy-six, and served as Anders Worldwide's CEO, Great Britain. Oxford education, homes in London and in New York. Married, with one previous divorce, three children. One from first marriage.

"Copy data to file," she ordered when she heard approaching footsteps. "End display."

Acknowledged. Tasks complete.

She swiveled to face the doorway as it was filled with a big, burly bear of a man with a shock of hair the color of good sterling and eyes of nearly black that sparked off something approaching rage.

He wore khaki trousers with pleats sharp enough to draw blood and a navy V neck over a white shirt. Upscale golf clothes, Eve decided. Anders missed tee time.

"You're Lieutenant Dallas?"

"That's right. Mr. Luce, what can I do for you?"

"You can tell me why the bloody hell you're smearing the reputation of a good man. Why you're spreading these salacious and scandalous lies about Tommy. The man's dead, goddamn it all, and can't defend himself against this slander."

"Mr. Luce, I can assure you I haven't as yet given any statement, officially or unofficially, to the media regarding the investigation into Mr. Anders's death. Nor have I authorized anyone to do so."

"Then why in hell is it all over the bleeding screen?"

Eve leaned back. "I'm not responsible for what the media digs out and chooses to air. It may piss me off, but I'm not responsible. You suffered a sudden and shocking loss, so I'm going to cut you a break for coming into my office and blowing off steam. Now that you have, sit down. I have some questions."

"I suggest you take your questions and—"

"Careful," Eve said with enough steel in the word to have Luce pausing, narrowing those furious eyes on her face.

"What are you going to do? Lock me up?"

Casually, Eve swiveled back and forth in her chair. "I like the word *detain* myself. Would you care to be detained, Mr. Luce, by the NYPSD for refusing to answer questions in a homicide investigation? I'd be happy to put you in holding until your attorney arrives. Otherwise, you can sit down and you can settle down. I figure you and Anders were more than business associates. You might be upset, sad, surprised by his death if that's all you were. You might be surprised again, and shocked, fascinated, or angry with the media attention. But rage and grief come from more personal associations. So this is your second, and last break. Clear enough?"

He turned and walked away, but to her window, not out the door. She said nothing as he stood there, his rigid back to her. "I can't settle down. How could I settle down? Tommy . . . we've been friends for nearly fifty years. He's godfather to my son. I stood up for him when he married Ava. He was my younger brother, in every way but blood."

"I'm very sorry, Mr. Luce, for your loss."

He glanced back at her. "How many times have you said that to someone, to strangers?"

"Too many. Entirely too many. It doesn't make it less true."

He turned now, pressed his fingers to his eyes. "We were to play golf this morning. The indoor nine at Tommy's club. He's never late, but I didn't think anything of it when he was. Traffic is so brutal, and I'd run into an acquaintance. We ended up chatting for some time, until the caddy interrupted to ask if I wanted to cancel or reschedule the tee off."

"Did you try to contact him?"

"On his mobile—his personal mobile, but it went to voice messaging. So I tried his house." He did sit now, big shoulders slumping. "Greta, the house manager, told me there'd been an accident. Told me Tommy was . . ."

"When was the last time you saw him?"

"Three weeks ago. He and Ava were in London briefly. Tommy and I had a meeting, and we all went to the theater. We played golf at my club—he loves golf—while our wives went shopping, or something. Maybe salon. I don't remember."

"When did you get into New York?"

"Yesterday afternoon. My wife and I arrived about two. Our son, Tommy's godchild, works for the New York branch. We had dinner with Harry and his family. They've just remodeled their brownstone, and wanted to show it off, of course. It's quite lovely, our daughter-in-law..." He trailed off, looked back at Eve. "I have no idea why I'm telling you that."

"When did you last speak to Mr. Anders?"

"On the flight over. We confirmed our golf date. The last thing I said to him was: Brace yourself, Tommy. I'm going to clean your clock."

His face reddened, his eyes filled. For the next few moments, he sat breathing hard as he struggled for composure. "Why are they saying such horrid things about him? Isn't it enough he's gone, that a good man is gone?"

"No, it's not, and it won't be until we know why. That's my job. Who wished him harm?"

"I don't know. He could be tough in business, but he was never unfair. He watched the competition, of course, and was a competitive man. But he played by the rules. He believed in rules."

"And in his personal life? Did he play by the rules?"

The wide face reddened again, but with temper. "I won't have you implying—"

"I'm not implying anything. Obviously you know something of the circumstances of his death. If you know who had access to his home, his bedroom, I need a name. Or names."

He leaned forward, fierce as a lion. "Tommy would not cheat on Ava. On anyone."

"A great many people engage in affairs and sexual activity outside marriage. And a great many of them don't consider it cheating." She shrugged. "Just sex, means nothing. Nobody's hurt."

His mouth tightened, pure derision. "Perhaps you can live your life by those *standards*. Tommy didn't."

"Then who might want me to think he did?"

"I don't *know*. If anyone harbored such violent feelings toward him, if anyone had threatened him, he didn't tell me."

"Would he have?"

"I hope he would."

"To your knowledge, did he fire anyone, rebuff anyone?"

"By rebuff, you're speaking of a sexual proposition." Luce let out a short laugh. "I can't imagine a woman approaching Tommy that way. But I suppose . . . He was fit, charming in his way, wealthy. I suppose. But he never mentioned that sort of thing, either. Of course, it's possible he didn't mention it in order to spare the other party the embarrassment and not to open the door to teasing. I would have teased him," Luce admitted, "unmercifully.

"As to firing, most terminations would be up to the individual department heads and supervisors. I don't know of any major dismissals, not recently. Ben would have a better handle on that."

"Can you tell me who benefits financially?"

"I can and I will because this wasn't about money. What was done to him . . . couldn't have been about money. Both Ava and Ben will receive Tommy's shares of Anders. Ben will hold the majority, as Tommy did after his own father's death. Ava will get the house in New York, the estate in the Hamptons, and the pied-à-terre in Paris, and all contents therein unless specifically bequested to others. Ben will inherit Tommy's yacht, a number of his personal possessions—his collection of golf clubs, but for an antique set he left specifically to me. There's a house on the coast of South Carolina that will go to him, and the London townhouse. They'll also divide, in equal shares, his portfolio, after other bequests are made."

"You know the details."

"Yes, I know the details. I witnessed the paperwork, and he insisted I read it through first. If you don't read, you don't sign—that was Tommy. Lieutenant, I visited both Ava and Ben at the house this afternoon—after . . . Believe me, they're in deep mourning. He was loved. Tommy was loved."

Chapter 4

To satisfy herself, Eve detoured to the Anders house on the way home. The traffic, as Luce had said, was brutal, but she didn't mind. The stops, starts, stalls, gave her time to think. The bad-tempered blare of horns, the occasional fist or middle finger shooting out of a window, the snarling or desperate faces of fellow drivers all reminded her why she loved New York even when it was frozen in the bitter, bitter grasp of endless winter.

Glide-cart operators, bundled up like Arctic explorers, worked with their fingerless gloves over smoking grills, and the smoke—if she cracked her window enough to catch it—smelled of chestnuts and soy dogs and grease.

Animated billboards, as they had been all winter, hyped tropical getaways where scantily clad models frolicked in the surf, or families so bright and happy they struck Eve as just a little terrifying built elaborate castles in the sand.

YOU DESERVE IT!! was the battle cry.

To Eve's mind, people all too often didn't get what they deserved.

Thomas Anders certainly hadn't after he'd tucked into bed for the last time, so it was her job to make sure he got what he deserved now. Justice. Maybe he was the paragon of decency his friend and family described, or the secret sexual perv his style of death portrayed. More likely, he'd been something in between. Wherever he landed on the human scale, he was due justice.

She hunted up a parking spot, and hoofed it the half block crosstown to the Anders home. Since the wind bit at every inch of exposed skin, she wondered why Peabody was so juiced about getting dressed up and going back out again. Once home, Eve thought, nobody was prying her out of the warmth.

Outside, she gave the security system another gander. Palm plate, she noted, key swipe, voice recognition, full perimeter camera scans. Basic standards for a high-end system. And the code, she recalled, changed every ten days. No signs of external tampering.

When the door opened, Greta stood on the other side. "It's after one," Eve commented.

It took Greta only a moment. "Yes. Yes, it is usually my half day. Mr. Forrest asked if I would arrange to stay through the afternoon, perhaps into the evening. Mrs. Anders needs me."

"I assume she's in."

"She is. She and Mr. Forrest are in the family parlor. If you could wait here, Lieutenant, I'll let them know."

"Fine. Greta, who else has been here today?"

"Many police."

"Other than."

"Mr. and Mrs. Edmond Luce. Ms. Plowder and Ms. Bride-West, both friends of Mrs. Anders who'd traveled to St. Lucia with her. Naturally, they cut their trip short to come back, to be here for her. There have been many calls of condolence, of course, but Mr. Ben— Mr. Forrest and I are screening those. Several reporters attempted to gain admittance, or to contact the family. They were sent away or refused."

"Good on the last. You should keep doing that. I'll wait here."

Greta moved through the wide room off the foyer, through an archway. Alone, Eve glanced up the stairs. The master suite and some of the second level would be sealed. No one other than a cop with a master could enter the bedroom or adjoining room by any access until Eve cleared the scene. She wondered why the widow didn't opt to stay with a friend, or even in an anonymous hotel suite until that time.

Ben came through the archway, crossed to her. Sorrow coated him, Eve thought, like oil that might stain anyone he brushed up against. Eve thought if grief had a face, his fit the bill.

"Lieutenant. Is this necessary? Ava's . . . she's having a very hard time of it."

"I understand this is difficult. I'm afraid NYPSD will be in and out of the house for some time yet, and several areas will remain sealed. You may want to try to persuade Ms. Anders to stay with friends for the next few days."

"I'm working on that. I think she feels she's deserting him somehow, if she doesn't stay here. Brigit—a friend— offered Ava her guest suite for however long she needs it. I think I've nearly convinced her to go. They called from . . . the morgue. They told us we can't have him yet."

"It takes time."

"We can go there and see him. I thought, if she's up to it, the sooner we do that, the better."

"You're probably right."

"I'd take her. She needs to . . . We both need to . . ." He trailed off, shook his head. "Do you know, can you tell me, if you know . . ."

"It's very early yet, Mr. Forrest. We're actively pursuing all lines of investigation."

"It seems like days. I know it's only been hours, but it seems like days. Sorry." He rubbed his fingers over exhausted eyes. "I looked you up. There was something familiar, but I couldn't think. I just couldn't think clearly this morning. But I looked you up. Roarke's cop."

"The NYPSD considers me their cop."

"I didn't mean—"

"It's all right."

"I mean to say, you're supposed to be the best there is. You solved the Icove case, and you caught that maniac who was kidnapping and mutilating those women. You'll find who did this to Uncle Tommy." Now, riding with grief was a plea. "You won't give up."

"I don't give up." Eve looked past him as Ava came into the room.

"Can't we have a few hours? Can't we have any time alone? Must you people be here?"

"Ava." Ben rushed to her side, took her weight when she slumped against him. "The police are doing their job. We need them to do their job."

"They've made him a joke. They've made his death a joke."

"No." Ben turned her into his arms, stroked her back. "Ssh, now."

"Take me to Brigit's, Ben. Take me away from here. I can't bear it. I can't stay here."

"All right. That's what I'll do." He glanced at Eve, who pointed to herself, then upstairs. Nodding, he led Ava away.

Though she'd have preferred an empty house, Eve walked back to the front door. She imagined the dark, the quality of it in the odd blue glow of the security lights. An efficient killer would have already sealed up, hair, hands, shoes. Extra protection, extra soundproofing with booties over the shoes. No chance of leaving any sort of print.

Directly upstairs, she thought. Down to business—priority business, she decided as she climbed the stairs. No squeaks, she noted, no creaks. Solid construction. Straight to the master bedroom, no detours. The door would be closed, as it was now. Not sealed though, she thought as she used her master to uncode the police seal.

She turned the knob, eased the door open. Again, it was

soundless. Privacy shields over the windows, she recalled, and heavy blackout drapes over that. Tommy liked to sleep in his snug cave.

Pitch-black. It would be pitch-black. Even someone knowing the room intimately couldn't be sure how the victim would be positioned in the bed. A pin light would be enough, she mused. Just a thin beam to show the way.

Because she didn't want to be disturbed, she closed and locked the door behind her. "Lights on," she ordered, and took the time to arrange the room as it would have been for the killer. "Lights off," she ordered when she stood back at the door, and flipping on a pin light, used it to cross to the bed.

Syringe first. Knock him out. Did he stir? Feel that quick little nip over the skin? Count to ten—it doesn't take long—count to ten, slow and steady.

What are you thinking? she wondered. Excitement, fear? Not rage, can't be rage. He's already beyond you, you saw to that, so it's not rage.

Turn the lights back on now. No need to work in the dark. "Lights on, fire on," Eve ordered.

Did you bring the rope, or did he have that tucked away?

You brought it. Have to be sure, can't screw up now. You have to have all the tools at hand.

Was he nude already, or did you strip him? If you stripped him, where did you put the sleep clothes. A trophy?

Wrists first. Do you feel his breath, his heavy, drugged breath on your skin when you bind his wrists? They're limp, deadweight. He's already helpless, but you have a stage to set. Wrists first.

Then the ankles.

Set out the toys.

Time for the next dose. You want him hard. Slide the rings on his cock. How do you feel, fondling him when he's helpless? Enjoyment or disgust? Or neither. Is it all just the next step now?

Takes time, all this window dressing. Takes time, and effort. Have to get into bed with death now to finish it.

Eve hitched up, braced a knee on the bed. Not enough leverage, she decided, and climbed on until she knelt beside her mind picture of Anders, imagined tying the last rope, winding it around his neck. Heavy head. Secure the second end of the rope and the head falls forward. It practically does the work for you.

She eased off the bed again, smoothed out any depression. Study the work, she mused, go over your checklist. How's his breathing? Is it already changing? Is his system already sending out alarm signals his mind and body can't answer?

Pack up the light, the syringes, walk away. Leave the door open.

Unlike the killer, Eve locked and sealed it. When she walked downstairs, her mind still walking alongside the killer, she saw Greta sitting stiff-spined in a chair in the foyer.

"Mr. For asked if I'd stay, in case you needed anything. He's taken Mrs. Anders to Ms. Plowder's home."

"No, I've got all I need. You should go home."

"Yes, I should go home." She put on the serviceable coat draped over her arm.

"Greta, what did Mr. Anders wear in bed?"

"I beg your pardon!"

"There were pajamas in his drawer. You supervise the laundry, correct?"

"I— Yes, of course. Mr. Anders wore sensible pajamas. A fresh pair daily, pressed. No starch."

"How many pairs did he have?"

"At last count, which would have been Monday last, Mr. Anders owned ten pairs of all-cotton pajamas."

"Ten pairs. Did Mr. Anders routinely use sleep aids?"

"I wouldn't know. I'm sorry. I have purchased them from time to time, as I do the marketing, the shopping. I can't say if either Mr. or Mrs. Anders used them, or if that was routine use."

"Okay. You've been very helpful."

Greta fit a gray hat over her head. "Being helpful is what I do."

When the door closed behind Greta, Eve stood where she was and let it settle around her. The quiet, the sensation of empty. Turning, she walked through the foyer, took the left hall. Rooms, she thought, the more money somebody had the more rooms he needed to keep the stuff he spent his money on.

And the more money and more rooms and more stuff, the more security to stop somebody from coming in and robbing you blind.

Anders's security room was off the kitchen, another locked door requiring its own keypad or code. Eve used her master, opened it. Inside were the screens for inner security, and those for outer. All ran now. Figuring security could afford a quick breach with a cop in the house, she checked the code EDD had given her, keyed it in. The current disc for the exterior front ejected.

She tapped it back in, glanced over at the empty disc file.

Load 'em up, she thought. Cover all contingencies. Go out, lock the room. Why? Just being orderly?

She strode back to the front door, took a last glance around. Stepping out, she relocked, resealed. Then looked at her wrist unit. Taking time out for the three-minute conversation with Greta, from entry to exit, the reenactment had taken just under forty minutes. Adding in time to strip the victim out of his sensible pajamas, she'd make it a comfortable forty-five minutes.

Not enough time to hunt up the security room and bypass the code, not in a house this size. Not enough to hunt up the bedroom. The killer knew the layout. Not just where the master slept, but where to find the security discs.

Closed the security room door, she thought, striding back to her car, but left the bedroom door open. Turned the lights out, but left the fire going.

In her car she ordered the heat on blast furnace, then took out her book to make some notes while they were fresh in her mind. And, only ninety minutes past the end of her shift, she bulled her way into traffic and headed home.

Speaking of a ridiculous number of rooms, she thought after driving through the big iron gates and winding up the drive. Nobody held a candle (whatever that meant) to Roarke. The house was a stunner, lording over sky and city, windows blazing hot, cold stars dripping overhead. A couple of years before, she never would have believed she could live in a place so...spectacular, much less live there comfortably.

But she did. And pulling up in front of that vast stone beauty, leaving her cop's ride out in front where Roarke's majordomo, Summerset, would sneer at it, rated as one of the favorite parts of her day. Any day.

She climbed out of the stuffy car, jogged through cold air, and into the light- and warmth-drenched house.

He was there, of course. Lurking. The bony beanpole in a black suit who ran the house, and kept her mildly irritated like a sand-covered pebble in a shoe.

"Lieutenant," he said in a tone that scraped along the back of her neck like nails over a blackboard. "You're late, as usual."

"You're ugly, as usual. But I've learned to make allowances."

As she stripped off her coat, the fat cat Galahad gave Summerset's skinny ankle a last body rub, then padded over to Eve. She tossed her coat over the newel post, bent to give the cat a quick scratch between the ears. Duties done, she headed upstairs, with Galahad at her heels.

In the bedroom Roarke was stripped down to trousers and holding a black sweater. "Now there's timing," he said. "Maybe I shouldn't bother with this." He wagged the sweater. "And see how fast I can get you half naked instead."

Eyes narrowed, she pointed a finger at him. "How long have you been home?"

"About ten minutes, I'd think."

"See that! See!" Now she pointed a finger of both hands. "Why am *I* late according to His Boniness, but you're only minutes ahead of me and don't get sneered at."

"How do you know I wasn't sneered at?"

"Because I know. Were you?"

"I wasn't, no. But then I did have a message sent home that I'd be a bit late."

She sniffed. "Suck-up."

He smiled. "Come over here and say that."

"I'm not bouncing on you now. I've got notes to organize." She pulled off her weapon harness, draped it over the back of a chair. "Media shit's hit the public fan over how Anders died. I need to try to plug some holes."

"I made a statement myself."

"You what? A statement? What? Why? Why didn't you run it by me before—"

"I knew the man, and his corporate headquarters is in my building. I know how to make a statement, Eve. I had some experience in the process before I met you."

"Right. Right." She rubbed a spot between her eyebrows. "It's just. The whole thing smells."

"Of?"

"Overkill. I gotta..." She twirled a finger in the air. "Until something settles into place for me."

"You can"—he mimicked her gesture—"with me. I suppose you can bounce on me later, and for now we can have a meal at your desk."

"I could use the ear." She studied him as he pulled on the sweater. It was kind of a shame he needed one. "Are we supposed to date?"

"Date what?"

"Each other."

He sent her a look that combined amusement, charm, and bafflement. She wondered how he managed it. "As in I take you out, there is some form of activity, then I drop you off at the door with a long, hopeful good-night kiss?"

"No." She frowned. "We never did that anyway."

"I knew I forgot something." He skimmed a finger down the cleft in her chin. "Should I ask you out on a date, darling Eve?"

"Look, I just wondered about it, that's all. Peabody started this whole thing about could she take an hour's personal to get polished up because she and McNab had this date-night deal going so they wouldn't lose the juice."

"That's very sweet. Are you wondering if we're low on juice?" He took her hand, drew it to his lips.

"No." Why such a deliberately romantic gesture caused tingles straight up her arm, she didn't know. "I just wondered if that's the sort of thing you're supposed to do when you're married awhile. And you spend a lot of evenings with work."

"We like work, don't we?"

"Yeah, we do." She moved in, grabbed his hair with her fists and pulled his mouth to hers. She put some heat behind it—it was the least she could do—and felt the tingle up her arm arrow to her belly. She ended the kiss with a quick, light nip.

"Plenty of juice in reserve," she decided. She laid her hands on his cheeks a moment, then stepped back. "And I always hated dating."

Kicked back at her desk, sharing a bottle of wine and the comforting goodness of homemade chicken potpie struck her as just about perfect. Summerset might be a pain in her ass but the man could cook.

As they ate, she rewound the facts and impressions in her head, and played them out for Roarke.

"So on one hand, you've got a guy who appears to dick around on his wife of nearly sixteen years, likes the kink, and when things go wrong, the kink partner runs. But that's bogus."

"Because he was drugged."

"That's the big one, but it's not all. Accident, even

if the killer was hired sex, there would have been some attempt to revive. The very least, you take the rope away. Then there's the pajamas."

"There is?"

"Greta—who strikes me as spookily efficient as the Nazi downstairs, states the vic wore pj's. And had ten pairs. Count is nine. Where's pair number ten? I have to figure the killer took them, either for a trophy, or to dispose of them away from the scene. If he's expecting company, he either has them on so the company can undress him, or he leaves them folded in the drawer where the other nine pairs were. If he's wearing them, and it was an accident, why grab them up when you run? Doesn't follow."

"Maybe the killer worried there was DNA or other forensic evidence on them."

"The sweepers didn't find anything anywhere else in the room. Doesn't follow. Killer was sealed. Had to be sealed. The only prints in the room were Anders's, the wife's, and the housekeeper's. The few stray hairs in the bed were all his."

"Putting that aside for a moment, and given it's long odds considering what I know of Anders, there are some who get off on the idea of rape. Some who might enjoy the idea of being taken, forced, while they're unconscious. The ultimate submissive."

"People are sick in all kinds of ways," Eve commented. "But even if he was sick that way, would anyone in their right mind go into that kind of liaison without complete trust in the partner? And with that kind of trust, would the partner leave him choking to death? He was still alive when the security booted back up. I don't see it. But on the other hand..."

She paused to scoop up more potpie. "The other hand is premeditated murder. Someone who's been in the house, or had access to the setup. The killer knew where Anders slept, where the security room was, knew how to override the security. I timed it, and there wasn't room for hunting around."

She walked Roarke through, step by step, as she had done. "It's cold, vindictive, ugly—you don't just want him dead, you want to mess him up after he's dead. But something's missing in that. Where's the springboard? You're that vindictive, there has to be anger or hate. If you're controlled enough to strap those down, why aren't you controlled enough to handle the details? The hefty dose of barbs—it's off. You want to humiliate him, but you don't have anything to say to him. You're alone in the house—a light tranq would be enough, give you enough to wrap him up. Don't you want him to hear why—don't you have something to say, don't you want him to *know*?

"So that's the third hand. The sham. The killer didn't care if the stage fell apart after the curtain. The killer had nothing to say to Anders. But that's missing something. Why put on the show if you can't take the bows with a captive audience? What do you gain? What's the damn point?"

"He's dead. Whatever the window dressing, mission accomplished."

"Yeah." She nodded, gesturing with her fork. "And what have I got? A devoted nephew, a loving wife, steadfast friends, the efficient housekeeper. Somebody's hiding something. That somebody knew he'd be alone in the house that night. Had to be sure of it. So...I dig deeper into financials—see if Anders was paying for it, or if I can find he paid for a subscription to *Bondage Weekly*. See if the wife, the nephew had any money troubles. Gambling, illegals. Sports betting's big," she considered. "Maybe Ben got in too deep."

"It won't be Ben."

"Doesn't feel like Ben. Doesn't mean it won't be connected to Ben." Eyeing him, she polished off her wine. "You want to sign on, expert consultant, civilian, and poke into some bank accounts?"

"I live for these moments."

"Take the wife. I'll take Ben. Then maybe we'll split up Anders."

"Assignments, always exciting. I've one for you. Tend to the dishes. I'll get the coffee."

It was hard to argue, especially since he'd come up with the potpie idea. She carted the dishes, stacked them in the little washer in her office kitchen, then turned and found him studying her.

"What?"

"Awfully domestic, isn't it? A moment. Dish duty, coffee fetching, the two of us in the kitchen after a meal."

Eve glanced down to where Galahad was sniffing his bowl, obviously hoping for seconds. "That would be the three of us."

"Ah yes. Our little family." Reaching out, he brushed the tips of her choppy hair. "A nice settled moment between the business of the day and the puzzle of the evening. It occurs to me these are moments I live for."

Her heart simply melted. "I always wonder why they're enough for you."

He laid his lips on hers, soft, sweet. "You shouldn't."

The cat bumped between them, shot a leg up in the air, and began to wash his butt. With a laugh, Roarke shook his head. "And so the moment ends. Your coffee, Lieutenant," he said and handed her a mug.

She sat at her desk, and waited to settle as Roarke walked into his adjoining office. It remained an amazement, her personal miracle, that he loved her. Loved her because of or in spite of everything. In all the world, with all its misery, after all the pain, they'd found each other. He was right, of course. It was more than enough.

"Computer," she began, and ordered the next layer in the search of Anders's financials.

The rich were complicated, Eve thought, with all their many pockets inside which they tucked their booty. Stocks, bonds, trusts, tax-deferred, tax-free, liquid money, futures. Long-term, short-term. Subsets and arms and divisions.

But under it all, somehow, someway, even the rich paid bills and bought toilet paper.

She scraped and she dug, searching for something to tie her victim to a lover or to licensed companions, running a secondary search for medications and/or sexual aids.

"Eve."

"What?" She looked away from the data crowding her wall screen. "I've barely started. You can't have found something already. It's not natural."

"I have, and I don't think you'll like it."

"What?"

"In Ava Anders's financials. There are regular bimonthly payments, going back for eighteen months."

"For what?" Her eyes narrowed. "To who?"

"To Charles Monroe."

"Charles." As it slapped at her out of left field, Eve dragged a hand through her hair. "Son of a bitch." This was the trouble, she thought, this was the damn problem with making friends. It came back and bit you in the ass. "*She's* getting her pipes snaked twice a month by a licensed companion?"

"One would assume she wasn't paying for a bridge partner."

"And it just damn well has to be Charles." She sat back, let it simmer. "Why does a woman who claims to love her husband need to diddle or be diddled by an LC every two weeks?"

"You're not that naive. You know there are endless reasons for it."

"Maybe, maybe, but I'm only interested in *her* reasons." She rose, thinking she was about to be pried out of the warmth after all. "So I'll go ask him what they are."

"Now? Eve, it's after ten."

"LCs have flexible hours."

"And he's very likely to be out with a client."

"Or in with one."

"If you contact him first—"

"He'd have time to prepare. I want him off guard."

And she had a point. "I'll drive."

Chapter 5

"If he's in, isn't with a client, but with Louise?" Roarke stepped into the elevator in the elegant lobby of Charles's apartment building.

Eve shrugged. "It's not like she doesn't know what he does for a living." While she didn't have any problem seeing how the smart, dedicated Dr. Dimatto fell for Charles—and he for her—she couldn't quite work out how Louise so easily accepted his work.

"Why doesn't it bother her? Seriously, it doesn't. She's not putting on a front. She's in a serious relationship with a guy who has sex with other women for a living, and it doesn't matter to her."

"I married a cop." Roarke smiled at her. "We all have our levels of acceptance. He was an LC when they met, just as she was a doctor, and one who often works in dangerous areas of the city."

She shot him the same easy smile. "So . . . if I'd been an LC when we met, you wouldn't have any problem with me banging other guys. Professionally."

"None at all, as I'd kick your ass and murder all of them. But that's just my level of acceptance."

"Yes." Pleased, she jabbed a finger into his chest. "*That* makes sense to me."

"Which is why we're suited, darling Eve, and neither of us with Charles or Louise. If Louise is here," he added when the doors opened, "would you like me to take her off somewhere for a bit?"

"Let's see how it plays."

"And if he's with a client—as I believe he only takes females—I'd be happy to engage her elsewhere while you work."

"Sure, no problem. Remembering those acceptance levels, how suited we are, and how much you like having your balls kicked up to your throat."

He put an arm around her waist for a sideways hug. "It is true love with us, isn't it?"

"Hearts and flowers, every day." She pushed the buzzer on Charles's apartment door. In less than a minute, she saw the security light blink, flicked her gaze up to the camera. The light steadied to green; the door opened.

"This is a nice surprise. Roarke. Lieutenant Sugar."

He stepped back in welcome. Charles Monroe was vid-star handsome, with a sheen of urban polish even in the casual at-home loose pants and sweater. His apartment with its strong colors, bold art, and deep cushions, reflected his easy sophistication and affection for comfort. Music, what Eve thought might've been vintage jazz, flowed through the air.

"What can I get you? Some wine? Or how about some Irish coffee?" He glanced around the room as he spoke, as if checking for something he'd misplaced. "God knows it's cold enough out there."

"We're good. You alone, Charles?"

"Yes. Louise is doing a run with the medi-van tonight. These kind of temps make it rougher than usual on street people."

"No client tonight?"

Something came and went in his eyes, but his smile stayed easy. "Actually, I had a cancellation. So it's especially nice to see friends. Have a seat."

"It's police business, Charles."

"I was getting an inkling."

"About your client, Ava Anders."

"Is she all right?" Concern, and hints of alarm sounded in his voice. "She's not—"

"No, but her husband is." Eve angled her head. "It's been all over the media since this morning. You hadn't heard?"

"No." He closed his eyes a moment. "No, I hadn't. I've been busy today, and had . . . things on my mind. I haven't turned on the screen or looked at any reports. Thomas Anders is dead? Murdered since you're here. Surely you don't think Ava's responsible."

"Let's backtrack. Ava Anders is a client."

"Did she tell you that?"

"Her financials did."

"Then, as you have the information already, yes, she's a client."

"And the services you provide her?"

"Dallas, you know I can't. You know there has to be confidentiality between me and a client. I can't discuss the arrangement without her consent. Sit down, will you?" He said it wearily. "I'm getting a drink. Do you want anything?"

"We're fine, Charles." Roarke nudged Eve to a chair while Charles crossed to a sleek wet bar.

"How was he killed?"

"In bed, in what appears to be a sexual bondage and erotic asphyxiation accident."

"Oh Christ." Charles dropped ice into a short glass, poured whiskey over it. "Ava—"

"Wasn't there," Eve finished, and waited while he took the first sip. "It doesn't seem to surprise you—the manner of death, that his wife wasn't there. Would that be because she wasn't into the kink, or was too good at it to mess it up?"

"You'll want to ask her that. You're putting me in a position, Dallas."

"How many did you put Ava in?"

He laughed, quick and amused, and the tension in his face dissolved. "You'll have to ask her that, too."

"How about this? How did she come to be a client?"

"Referral." With the whiskey, he crossed back over, slid into a chair. "And no, I'm not going to tell you who. Not without consent. Dallas, my reputation and integrity hinge on consent, and on trust."

Eve sat back, debated different angles. "You'd be, arguably, an expert on relationships." When he laughed again, shook his head, she lifted her hands. "What? You trade in relationships. You told me once it's not only the sex, but the relationship the client pays for."

"True enough." And the strain was back on his face. "Yes, that's true enough."

"Charles, it's not my business," Roarke interrupted, "but as a friend I'll ask if everything's all right between you and Louise?"

Charles looked at Roarke. "Yes, thanks. Everything's very all right between me and Louise."

"Now that we cleared that up," Eve said, "let's try it this way. Hypothetically, why would a woman, in a long-term, ostensively happy marriage seek the services of a licensed companion? And seek them on a regular basis."

"Hypothetically." Charles nodded. "It might be that the woman has needs, desires, even fantasies that aren't or can't be met within the marriage."

"Why?"

Now he blew out a breath. "It might be that a woman isn't comfortable seeking those needs and so on from her spouse, or the spouse isn't comfortable or able to fulfill them. It might be by satisfying those needs with a professional, safely and confidentially, the marriage partners are more content. Not every marriage, however successful, gives both partners complete emotional or sexual satisfaction."

"So what, they stay together to have conversation over dinner?"

"It might be as simple as that, but it's usually considerably more complex. The fact is, sex, particularly a certain type of sex, is only one part of a relationship. I can't give you details, Dallas. Not without Ava's consent. If you get it, I'll be happy to talk to you again."

"Okay." That would have to do. "Don't contact her, Charles. If she tries to contact you, I'd appreciate it if you'd dodge until I've had a go with her on this."

"All right. I can do that."

"Good enough." Eve rose. "I'll be in touch. Hi to Louise and all that."

"I'll tell her." He stood, leaned over to kiss Eve's cheek.

"I don't get it. I don't get it." Eve frowned through the windshield as Roarke drove home. "I know he's right, I know it's true, but I don't *get* it."

"Precisely what would *it* be?"

"How you can have the sex outside marriage, and that's just hunky with everybody involved? Why bother with the marriage thing?"

"Finances, companionship, habit, security, status."

"Bullshit, bullshit, bullshit."

"You really should learn to form more definite opinions."

"And the other thing, that she can't get all her jollies from within the marriage? Okay, true—I hear this all the time, especially after he kills her or vice versa, but what crap." Sheer annoyance had her slumping down in her seat. "If you didn't have the sex buzz, you shouldn't have hooked up."

"Sometimes the buzz changes frequencies for one of the partners."

"Okay. All right. Say I want to change frequencies. I

decide I want you to suck your thumb and call me Mommy while I paddle your cute ass." She shifted her gaze to his profile. "What do you say?"

"I would probably suggest a reasonable compromise, such as I'd like to suck on something else, preferably something attached to you, and I'll call you whatever you like. If spanking must be involved, we'll just have to take turns there."

"See." She poked his shoulder. "That works for me."

"I sincerely hope not, but we can see."

"No." She snorted out a laugh. "I mean it works for me that you'd say let's modify a little if I came up with something weird."

"Remember that the next time I want to tie you up with your own underwear and slather your naked body with raspberry sauce."

She slid her eyes toward him again. "Was there a first time?"

"Could be."

The man, she mused, continued to surprise her. "Back to the point. I can't see a marriage staying solid if one or both partners enters into an intimate relationship elsewhere. And profession aside, the LC–client relationship is intimate." She considered, mulled, as Roarke drove through the gates. "Maybe, for instance, you're married to this guy, everything's frosty, then he turns out to be gay as an Easter basket. You got a problem. Maybe you stick it out because of those reasons you named—money, habit, whatever. And maybe you go to a professional to get off. But is that a marriage or just an arrangement?"

"Is there love? Your view on this is narrow. That's how you're built."

It didn't *feel* narrow to her. It felt right. "Marriage is a promise. That's one of the ways you talked me into it. If you break one part of the promise, it's going to crack other parts."

"Even if both parties agree?"

"I don't know." She got out of the car. "But I'm interested to hear how Ava Anders explains it."

Inside, they started upstairs together. "It seems to me," Roarke said, "that if she'd wanted to hide the payments to Charles, she'd have paid in cash. And speaking of Charles, did he seem distracted tonight? Even before he understood why we were there?"

"Yeah, something. Maybe some trouble in paradise, even though he said everything was fine."

"That would be a pity. They work together very well."

When she started to turn toward her office, he took her hand, tugged her in the opposite direction. "What? I've got work."

"We both always have work. Now, it's nearly midnight, and you've had a very long day."

"I just want to—"

"So do I. I'm thinking of ordering up some raspberry sauce."

"Funny guy. You're a funny guy. Look, I just want another hour to—"

"I have other plans for your next hour." Shifting position, he began to back her into the bedroom. "Here's that compromise. That . . . modification." He depressed the release on the weapon harness she'd strapped back on to go out.

"Maybe I'm not in the mood."

"Then . . ." He trailed a finger down her throat, flipped open the first button of her shirt. "I suppose you're going to be bored. Fire on." He opened the next button as the flames flashed in the hearth. "Lights off."

He continued to back her toward the platform, and the lake-sized bed it held, watching her eyes when her harness and then her shirt fell to the floor. "Step up," he warned when they reached the platform. "And again." Then he gave her a light shove so she fell back on the bed.

"I guess I'll just lie here and take it."

"You do that." He lifted her leg, pulled off her boot.

"Don't take it personally if I nod off."

"Of course not." He tossed the second boot aside. He ran his hands up her legs, smiling at her quiver when they stroked over her center on the way to the hook of her trousers. He drew them down her legs, let them drop.

Eve faked a yawn, tapped her hand over her mouth. "Sorry."

He cocked a brow. There wasn't another woman in the world, he thought, who could amuse, challenge, and arouse him as she did. He pulled off his sweater, tossed it aside, then sat on the side of the bed to remove his own boots. Behind him, she made exaggerated snorting sounds until he pinched her.

"Oh, sorry. Was I snoring?"

He stood, unhooked his trousers, stepped out of them. "Go back to sleep," he said as he slid onto the bed, slid onto her. "This won't take long."

She started to laugh, and the sound strangled when he closed his teeth over her breast through the thin tank she wore. "Okay then." She cleared the huskiness out of her throat. "I guess I can give you a few minutes."

"Well, now, I appreciate that." He caught her nipple, exquisite control, while he trailed a fingertip up her inner thigh, traced it at the edge of the simple cotton.

He heard her breath catch, and felt her muscles twitch, then the quiet moan when he slid just under the cotton. Slipping toward the heat and away again, teasing while her heart kicked to gallop under his relentless mouth. All that strength, all that wit, all that will melted into need beneath him.

His mouth found hers, took, as he stroked her up, still up, up to the quivering edge.

Then he rolled off. "Well, that ought to do it."

Her body all but screamed in denial.

She levered up, straddled him. He was hard as iron, and his gorgeous face covered with humor. "Funny guy," she said again. Crossing her arms, she tugged the tank up and off, then crooked both her index fingers. "Hands on, pal."

"Well, if you insist."

He cupped her breasts, brushed his thumbs over her nipples. She planted her hands on either side of his head, and leaning down, feasted on his mouth. The taste of him. She loved the taste of him, would never have her fill of it. The way his lips fit to hers, the glide of his tongue. She could spend hours, days, on his mouth alone, on the magic she found there.

With her breath quickened, her skin already hot, she flipped away, flopped onto her back. "*That* ought to do it."

They lay where they were a moment, then turning their heads, grinned at each other. And dove.

She laughed, and groaned, she gasped and giggled. The sheer fun and foolishness added bold, bright color to the deeper tones of desire. His hands were quick; her mouth avid. Together they moved recklessly over the big bed, under the cold stars gleaming through the sky window.

He drove her over, and her cry was of cheerful pleasure. This, he thought, this, the unity, the adventure of it, would always delight him. Sustain him. Even when he was inside her, when the need pounded them both, the utter joy of what they'd found, what they'd made, rushed through him. She was the happiness he'd searched for all of his life.

Her eyes, gilded by firelight, stayed on his; her lips curved. When they sprang over that shining edge together, his heart simply soared.

Under him, limp, her heart still pounding, she sighed. "Now, that," she said, "should definitely do it."

In the morning, she glugged down coffee to spark her brain into handling the basic chore of getting dressed. Roarke, already dressed, alert—as was his irritating habit—scanned the stock reports while he drank his coffee in the bedroom sitting area.

"Warmer today, if you're interested."

She spoke from the depths of the closet. "Warmer than what?"

"Than a witch's teat."

Considering that, she buttoned on a plain white shirt. "I'm going to work here this morning, have Peabody meet me. Easier to go from here to the address Ava's staying at. Do you know a Brigit Plowder?"

"Socialite, married to Peter Plowder—architect. Her family builds—bridges and tunnels most particularly. She's a respected philanthropic figure. Puts her money where her cause is. Would this be where the widow's staying?"

"Yeah." Eve came out, sat down to put on her boots. Then narrowed her eyes at Roarke's long look. "What? It's a jacket. It's just a damn jacket. I don't care if it goes with the pants."

"Pity then, as it goes very well. I was thinking how stylishly professional you look, which is probably a happy accident. But nonetheless."

"Stylishly professional." She sniffed, leaned over to steal a wedge of melon from his plate. "I've got to get my stylishly professional ass to work."

"Eat."

"I'll get a bagel or whatever in my office. I need to hit those financials, since somebody interfered with police business last night."

"I should be arrested."

"Pal, that goes without saying." She leaned over to kiss him. "Later. Oh, nearly forgot. Peabody's going on *Now* tonight."

"Is she? She must be . . ." He thought of Peabody. "Terrified."

"Yeah. She'll get over it."

In her office, she tackled the financials. She remembered the bagel, then forgot it again. When she heard the clump of Peabody's winter boots, she rubbed her already blurry eyes.

"You take over here."

Peabody stopped, blinked. "Take over where?"

"These stinking financials. Give them another fifteen minutes, then we'll take Ava."

"Okay." Peabody draped a bag over the back of Eve's sleep chair.

"What's that?"

"It's an outfit. For tonight. In case I spill something on what I'm wearing, or in case what I'm wearing's stupid. McNab liked it, but he wears Day-Glo half the time." Peabody pulled off her outerwear to reveal a ruby-red suit with small silver buttons running down the front. "What do you think? Does it look right?"

"Why are you asking me?"

"I don't know. I really don't know." Nerves pumping, Peabody brushed at her hair. "And I got stupid hair day going. They fix that, right? They fix that sort of thing. Nadine hired Trina to do hair and makeup so..." Peabody trailed off, pursed her lips. "You look all good and everything today. Seriously up."

Eve shook her head. Gray pants, white shirt, navy jacket over her weapon harness. What was the *deal*? "If we've finished our fashion consultation, maybe you could spare a minute for the damn financials."

"Okay. What do you think about the earrings?"

Eve gave the silver drops a passing glance. "About you wearing them, or about me ripping them off and stuffing them up your nose?"

"Okay," Peabody said again, and hotfooted it to the desk.

"The computer hasn't popped out anything from standard searches," Eve told her. "One more shot, then I'm thinking to pass it on to Roarke. He popped something straight out of the widow's in about ten minutes last night."

"He's got the knack."

"He popped Charles out."

Peabody's head jerked up. "Our Charles?"

"In a manner of. Ava's been a regular bimonthly client of our favorite LC for a year and a half."

"Shit. We're going to have to interview him."

"We went over there last night. He is, as expected, coy about the details. We need Ava to clear him for that. But he did tell me that she was a referral."

"If she was fooling around with a pro it might go to motive."

"It might. Hitch is she wasn't hiding it, at least not well. There were straight payments out of her personal debit account. No cover."

As she considered, Peabody played with one of the short dangles at her ear. "So, she doesn't think to hide the payments. The husband finds out, they go around about it. Fight, divorce is threatened. And she kills him, sexual overtones."

"She was out of the country."

"Right. Hired hit?"

"Too elaborate." Just too damn fussy, Eve thought. "Unless, it plays out like that, and she hired someone who tailors the hit to the client's specifications."

"Fantasy Hits R Us."

"There's a way to make money, people find it. I'm going to go over her financials and have Roarke comb them. But so far, nothing's popped there, either. No suspicious withdrawals, no payments that don't jibe." She paced. "Good-looking woman. She's got style, power. The sort that could talk a lover, if he's stupid enough, into doing her dirty work for her."

"But then if she had a lover," Peabody pointed out, "why is she paying Charles five thousand a bang, twice a month?"

"Exactly, so..." Eve turned back. "How do you know what Charles charges a bang?"

"Ah." Peabody fussed with her hair, pulled at the silver buttons on her suit jacket. "Maybe, being curious, I looked up his rates when we were sort of dating."

"Uh-huh. Well, I can agree that if a woman's getting strange for free, she's unlikely to pay ten grand a month for a couple thrills. See what you can find."

Moving away again, Eve pulled out her 'link to schedule an appointment with Mira, and to put a hold on an interview room.

"Ladies." Roarke spoke from the doorway of their adjoining offices. "Peabody, you look ravishing."

"I do?" She nearly squealed it. "But in a screen-friendly, trustworthy, public servant kind of way?"

"Yes, indeed. The color's wonderful on you."

"Jesus," Eve said under her breath, and earned a mild stare from her husband.

"Breakfast?" he said.

Peabody watched as Eve scowled, shrugged. Then Roarke lifted his brows with those dreamy eyes steady. Her lieutenant rolled hers, but stomped off to the kitchen.

"You guys don't even have to talk." Resting her chin on her fist, Peabody sighed. "You just know."

"It does come in handy from time to time. How was your date night?"

"It was mag. Really. Mostly because we both agreed we like noisy, crowded clubs better than grown-up, sophisticated ones. But it's good to try something new."

"Stop socializing with my partner," Eve called out from the kitchen.

"Financials," Peabody mouthed.

"Ah, yes." Casually, Roarke strolled over, gave a quick glance at the data on screen. He winked at Peabody and sent her pulse scrambling, then continued on to the kitchen where his wife was taking an annoyed bite out of a bagel.

"Breakfast," she muttered at him.

"Such as it is. Why don't I go over the financials? I can do it in considerably less time than you or Peabody, which frees you up to go out and browbeat suspects."

She frowned, chewed. "You'd have to do it straight. No unregistered, no illegal hacking."

"You underestimate the skill of an honest man."

"Yeah, but I'm talking to you." She grinned over another bite of bagel. "I could use the help, if you've got the time between schemes of universal financial domination."

"I'll work it in. Now." He brushed a crumb away from the side of her mouth, kissed her. "Go protect and serve."

"Good idea. Peabody," she said as she headed out, "with me."

"I haven't really started on—"

"The civilian's got it. Let's go take a few kicks at the grieving widow."

"That's lots more fun." Peabody jumped up, grabbed her garment bag. And because Eve was already out of earshot, turned back as Roarke came out of the kitchen. "Do you like the earrings?"

He stepped closer to give them a good study. "They're charming."

"But in a—"

"In a professional and intuitive police detective sort of way. You'll be wonderful and look the same."

"Thanks." She grabbed her coat, scarf, hat. "I—"

"Peabody! Move your damn ass!"

"Gotta go," Peabody finished on the heels of Eve's shout. And fled.

With his fresh cup of coffee, Roarke sat behind Eve's desk. He could spare twenty minutes now, he mused. "So, let's see what we have here."

Chapter 6

An elegant, old, lovingly restored building on the Upper East Side housed the Plowder's apartment. The quiet, rosy brick boasted a portico entrance with wide, beveled glass doors granting passersby a peek at the polished marble lobby. A doorman, in blue and silver livery, stood guard should any of those passersby need a little move-along.

Eve noted he gave her police issue the beady eye when she pulled up to park at the carpeted curb. She didn't mind a bit. She didn't just eat bagels for breakfast, she also enjoyed a good bite of doorman.

He strode across the swatch of red carpet, shook his head.

"Cop rides never get any prettier," he commented. "What house are you out of?"

She shifted her feet, and her prepared tone. "You on the job?"

"Was. Put in my papers after I did my thirty. My brother-in-law manages the place." He jerked his head toward the entrance. "Tried golf, tried fishing, tried driving the wife crazy." He flashed a smile. "Better pay, better hours on this door than doing the security guard thing. Dallas," he said, shooting a finger at her. "Lieutenant Eve."

"Yeah, that's right."

"Shoulda made you sooner. Getting rusty, I guess. I didn't hear about anybody getting murdered inside."

"Not yet." They exchanged quick cop grins. "Your tenants the Plowders have a guest I need to speak with. Ava Anders."

"Hmm. Husband got dead yesterday. Didn't know she was upstairs. She must've come in after I went off. She and the dead husband came around now and then. Her more than him, but he was friendlier."

"Was Mrs. Anders unfriendly?"

"No. Just one of the type who don't notice who opens the door for her 'cause she expects somebody to. On the snooty side, but not bitchy or anything. Him, he'd usually stop a minute going in or out, have a word, maybe ask if you caught the game—whatever the game was. Sorry to hear he got dead. I gotta call up. Worth my job if I don't."

"That's no problem. What was your house?" Eve asked as they moved to the doors.

"Did my last ten at the one-two-eight. Cold Case Unit."

"That's a tough hitch. The cold ones can haunt you."

"Yeah, they can." He pulled off his glove to offer a hand. "Frank O'Malley, formerly Detective."

"Nice to meet you, Detective."

"Peabody, Detective Delia," Peabody said when they shook. "I knew a uniform in the one-two-eight back when I was on patrol. Hannison?"

"Sure, I knew Hannison. He's all right."

Inside the lobby with its subtly fragrant air, Frank turned to an intercom screen. "Plowder penthouse," he ordered, then waited until the screen shifted from waiting blue and the image of a woman with short brown hair swam on. "Morning, Agnes."

"Frank."

"I got a Lieutenant Dallas and Detective Peabody in the lobby. They'd like to speak to Mrs. Anders."

"I see. Hold a moment, Frank."

"That was Mrs. Plowder's personal assistant, Agnes Morelli. She's okay."

"How about the Plowders?"

"Seem like solid types to me. Not on the snooty side. Call you by name, ask after the family they got time for it. Don't skimp on the tips."

A moment later, Agnes flowed back on screen. "You can send them right up, Frank, lower parlor entrance."

"Will do. Thanks, Agnes. First elevator," he told Eve. "Thirty-nine East. That'll take you straight to the lower parlor. It's a hell of a space they got up there. Three floors, river view."

"Appreciate the help, Detective."

Inside the elevator, the hammered silver walls boasted a long, built-in bench, in case your legs got tired of riding up, or down. Since the trip took under thirty seconds, Eve couldn't imagine the bench got much use.

The doors opened straight onto a wide room in pale and pretty colors, opening to a spectacular river view through a wall of glass doors and windows. Agnes stood, in a severe black suit given unexpected charm by the full-blown red rose on the lapel.

"Good morning, I'm Agnes, Mrs. Plowder's PA. If you wouldn't mind showing me some identification. We trust Frank, of course, but—"

"No problem." Eve took out her badge, as did Peabody.

"Thank you. Please come in, have a seat. Mrs. Anders will be right down. Can I offer you some refreshment? Coffee?"

It was knee-jerk for Eve to refuse, but she decided coffee in the parlor could lend a tone of female intimacy that might be helpful. "Coffee'd be great. Black for me, coffee regular for my partner."

"Make yourselves comfortable. I'll just be a minute."

The minute they were alone, Peabody let her eyes pop wide. "Can I just say: Woot, some digs. They've got a terrace out there bigger than my entire apartment."

"I bet your apartment's a lot warmer than that terrace right now."

"Yeah, there's that." But unable to resist, Peabody started across the parlor to the glass. "It's the kind of place that makes you feel you need to glide. I don't glide very well. It must relate to my center of gravity, which would be my ass."

"It's the kind of place where birds probably splat their tiny birdbrains on the windows regular."

"That's an image, boy." And Peabody took a couple cautious steps back. "Still, it's a totally uptown view. Don't you want to see?"

"I can see fine from here." To Eve's mind, lofty heights should be left to the birdbrains. In any case, her interest centered on what and who lived in the space, not what spread outside.

A moment later, Ava made her entrance. The widow wore black in a snugly fitted, high-collared shirt with slim pants and heels. Her hair coiled at the nape of her neck, pulled tightly back from a face with shadowed, exhausted eyes. Beside her, an arm supportively around Ava's waist, Brigit Plowder conveyed boldness and challenge. She topped off at about five feet, with her tiny frame tucked neatly into a plum-colored sweater and stone-gray pants. Her hair, a pure white cap, set off laser-sharp green eyes and the arched black brows that framed them. Her mouth formed a deep bow Eve assumed could be charming when it smiled, but at the moment those lips clamped together in tight disapproval bordering on anger.

"I'm going to say this straight off." Brigit's voice was a throaty boom worthy of a woman twice her size. "This is outrageous."

"I agree. Murder is always outrageous."

A quick spark fired in those keen eyes. It might have been approval. "I understand you have a job to do, Lieutenant, and from everything I've been told about you and this one," she said with a gesture toward Peabody, "you excel at your work. That's admirable. However, bombarding

Ava at such a time shows a distinct lack of sensitivity and compassion."

"It's all right, Bridge."

"It's *not* all right. Why can't you give us all a few days, just a few days to grieve?"

"Because then I give Thomas Anders's killer a few days." Eve shifted her gaze back to Ava. "I apologize for disturbing you, Mrs. Anders. The investigation requires it."

"I don't see why—"

"Look, Mrs. Plowder, I'm a murder cop, and any murder cop will tell you time's the enemy. The more time that passes, the cooler the trail. The trail goes cold, the killer can walk. When killers walk, it pisses me off. If you want to blame somebody for me being here, blame the killer. Now, the more time you stand there complaining, the more time we're going to be here."

Brigit's chin jutted out, then angled as she inclined her head. "You're absolutely right. I don't like it, don't like any of it, but you're absolutely right. Come on, Ava, let's sit down now. I'll apologize, Lieutenant, Detective," she continued as she led Ava to a thickly cushioned sofa in deep blue. "I'm rarely rude to guests in my home, even uninvited guests. I'm not altogether myself today. None of us are. Please, sit down."

As Eve and Peabody took wide-armed chairs, Agnes rolled in a tray. "I've got chamomile tea for you, Ava. You'll do better with that than coffee."

"Thank you, Agnes." Ava took the cup, stared into it.

"I'll see she drinks it this time," Brigit stated.

"Thanks." Eve accepted the coffee Agnes offered. "Since you're here, Mrs. Plowder, can you tell me when you and Mrs. Anders made your travel plans?"

"Travel? Oh. That seems like years ago already. We go away every year. Ava, Sasha—Sasha Bride-West—and myself. A week somewhere warm, a restorative at the end of winter."

"This particular restorative. When did you make the plans? The dates, the destination."

"Oh...Three months ago. About?" she added, turning to Agnes.

"Nearly four, actually. I booked the arrangements in November, just before Thanksgiving."

"Agnes knows all, remembers all," Brigit said, and Eve saw she'd been right. The smile was charming.

"We had such a lovely day." Ava's voice dripped like tears. "Such a lovely day on Monday. Breakfast on the terrace. Mimosas. We had mimosas, and we got just a little drunk. At breakfast, remember, Bridge?"

"Yes, honey, I remember."

"We laughed like idiots. Everything was so funny. And later, when I called Tommy later, I cut it all so short. We were going to have massages on the terrace, where we'd gotten a little bit drunk at breakfast. So I cut it all very short. 'I'll talk to you later, Tommy,' that's what I said to him. 'I'll talk to you later. I want my massage.' That's the last thing I said to him, because there wasn't any later."

"Sweetheart." Brigit brushed her fingers over Ava's cheek. "Don't do this."

"I don't know about trails going cold; I just know Tommy's dead. I saw him myself when Ben took me to him. I saw Tommy dead."

"Mrs. Anders." Peabody shifted forward. "This is a terrible time for you. We're here to help. You've lost your husband. Don't you want to know why? Don't you want to know who?"

"I don't know." Ava lifted her gaze, aimed those wet blue eyes at Peabody. "I should. I know I should. But he'll still be gone."

"He'd want you to know," Peabody said. "He'd want us to find those answers."

"I don't know them. How could I?"

"You knew him best. You were his wife. There are

things you know, things you may not realize are important, are relevant. That's why we're here. We will know."

"Your husband's date book," Eve began. "Did he make the entries himself?"

"His date book? Yes."

"And the autosystem in the bedroom, the wake-up program and so on. Would he have programmed that personally?"

"Yes." Ava straightened in her seat. "He enjoyed that, hearing his first appointment of the day, being reminded of what he'd ordered for breakfast."

"The two of you must have gotten up at the same time routinely."

"Oh, if he had an early appointment, and I didn't, I'd wear earplugs. And have Greta wake me."

"Do you take sleep aids?"

"Oh, occasionally." She waved a hand. "Now and then."

"Did he?"

"Now and then. Everyone does, don't they?"

"He had very specific routines. The bedroom door always closed, the internal security cameras shut down at night, no cameras in the sleeping area of the master bedroom."

"Yes, he was very private."

"Even in hotels," Brigit put in. "We all traveled together quite a bit. Tommy always instructed housekeeping to keep the bedroom door closed, and tipped them in advance to insure they did."

"He'd have been very careful regarding home security," Eve commented.

"He had the system checked and evaluated every quarter." Ava lifted her teacup, sipped. "And upgraded whenever upgrades became available. It wasn't just security, though of course that was the priority. But Tommy liked . . . toys, if you know what I mean."

"I do."

"He just got such a kick out of all the bells and whistles. He liked to play," she said wistfully.

And playing was the next line of questioning. "Mrs. Plowder, my partner and I need to speak with Mrs. Anders privately."

"Oh, but can't Brigit stay?" Ava fumbled for her friend's hand. "I feel so much better with her here."

"There are some sensitive questions. If, after we've concluded, you opt to share them with Mrs. Plowder, that's your privilege. If you'd excuse us, Mrs. Plowder, Ms. Morelli."

"We'll be right upstairs." Brigit patted Ava's arm. "You only have to call if you want me."

As her friend left the room, Ava set down her teacup, gripped her hands together in her lap. "This is about how Tommy was found. Brigit knows. Everyone knows."

"Was your husband involved in sexual relationships outside of your marriage?"

"No."

"Was your husband aware you procured the services of a licensed professional twice monthly for the last eighteen months?"

The prominent bones of Ava's cheeks seemed to push against her skin. Her lips trembled, even as she clamped them tightly together. When she reached for her tea again, her hand shook. "Yes. Yes. God. Do you know what people will say about him, about us if all this gets out?"

"In your previous statement you claimed to have a solid and happy marriage."

"It wasn't a claim. It's the truth."

"Yet you sought sexual gratification from a professional."

Ava closed her eyes a moment, let out a breath. When she opened them, her eyes were hard and angry. "You're very smug, aren't you? Sitting there, judging me by your lofty standards and morals."

"I'm not judging you. I'm asking you."

"Of course you're judging me, and Tommy. So will others. Even Bridge, if she knew. She's the most generous, open-hearted person I know, the most loyal of friends, but she'd never understand this. She'd never understand."

"Make me understand."

"Tommy and I loved each other. We enjoyed each other. We were devoted to each other. He used to say he made me laugh, and I made him think. Our marriage was very solid, very fulfilling to us both. A couple of years ago, a little more than that, I suppose, he felt, began to feel, he wanted more experimentation in bed." She took a long drink of tea. Embarrassment or the heat from the drink flushed color into her cheeks. "We were neither of us children. Even when we married we were mature, experienced people. My husband wanted more...variety in our sexual relationship, and I tried to meet that. But, I wasn't comfortable with some of his..."

She pressed her lips together. "In short, I wasn't able to provide him with what he wanted, and he wasn't satisfied with what I wanted in that one area of our marriage. It began to erode our relationship, to peck away at our foundation. We both felt it. Why should we allow that to destroy the rest?" she demanded. "We decided that we would take that off the table, so to speak. That sex wasn't as important as we were, what we were to each other. We would simply obtain that aspect elsewhere. Discreetly. We would use professionals, and would never engage those professionals in any of our homes."

"Did you both adhere to those terms?"

Ava looked away. "I did. Over the last few months I suspected...I thought Tommy might have been bringing women into the house while I was away. I found some lingerie in my drawer, another woman's lingerie Greta must have laundered and put away believing it was mine. Some of my perfume went missing. Little things."

"Did you confront him?"

"No. I was hurt, I admit it. Hurt and disappointed. Angry, too. I'd decided to take the time during this trip with my friends to decide how to handle it. He let someone into our home, and now he's dead." Her hand fisted in her lap.

"I'm so angry with him, so angry with him for leaving me over this."

"Do you know the names or the agencies of the professionals he used?"

"No. We'd agreed not to bring that up. It was outside. It wasn't us. It was outside of us."

"But your payments to Charles Monroe came out of your debit account where your husband could see them."

She let out a half laugh. "Tommy never looked at my personal accounts."

"Did you look at his?"

Color rose into her face again. "Yes, I did. I did when I suspected he was bringing women home. I couldn't find anything there. I'm not sure what I'd have done if I had."

"How did you select Charles Monroe?"

"My friend Sasha recommended him. She knows. Unlike Brigit, Sasha's very open. Even a little wild, by some standards. She told me he was very smooth, very skilled, and very discreet. I was a nervous wreck the first time I went to him. He put me very much at ease."

"Is he the only LC you've engaged?"

"Yes. I liked him, trusted him. I could think of our appointments as going to a therapist."

"Are you willing to give consent for Mr. Monroe to speak to us about your relationship?"

"Oh God." Ava pressed a hand to her face. "I suppose there's no place for pride or privacy any longer. Yes, I'll consent to that. In return, I need your word you'll keep this private business out of the media."

"You can have my word on that."

"I'll have to tell Bridge," Ava murmured. "I'm going to disappoint her."

"Mrs. Plowder strikes me as a woman who sticks," Peabody said, and Ava smiled a little.

"Yes, you're right. She is. She does. Am I to blame for this? Am I responsible? If I'd been more open, more flexible about what he wanted, Tommy would still be alive, wouldn't he? I keep asking myself that."

"The killer's responsible, Mrs. Anders. That's your answer." Eve rose. "Thank you for your time and cooperation."

When they stood inside the hammered steel of the elevator, Peabody shook her head. "Tough spot for her, the guilt on top of the grief. She can't help but ask herself is this because she has sexual hang-ups, or because he went over-the-top. Since he's the one who's dead, she's probably going to settle on door number one."

Eve only said, "Hmm." When they hit the lobby, she dug out a card. "Thanks again, Detective." She offered her hand, then the card to Frank. "You can reach me at any of those contacts, should something strike you."

"Can do." He tucked it into a pocket. "Luck, Lieutenant. Detective."

"Yeah," Eve muttered, striding to the car, "we're going to need it." She got behind the wheel. "Sounds like the vic took a hell of a turn after, what, more than a dozen years of marriage."

"Happens, doesn't it? Divorce litters the land, so does adultery. And LCs do good business for a reason."

"All true." Eve danced her fingers along the steering wheel. "Marriage is mostly a sucker bet."

"Spoken by the woman with Dream Husband."

"You just said Dream Husband might take a turn down the road and decide he wants to do threesomes or—"

"Me! Me!" Peabody shot up a hand. "Pick me!"

"Yeah, I'm dying to get you between the sheets, Peabody. Keeps me up at night. The point is, you've got a dozen years in, and one night the guy comes home and says: 'Look, honey, I picked up this ball gag and anal probe on the way home. Let's go try them out.'"

"That would be a shocker, but I bet it was more subtle than that. Maybe he tries out a few new moves, testing the waters, and she's not receptive, and it goes from there. It's like, okay, here's a man who's got it pretty damn good. He's healthy, he doesn't have a face that scares small children.

He's running a successful business, he's rich, got the good-looking, spiffed-up wife who loves him. Big house, friends, a nephew who stands in as son and heir. Then he has this mid-life deal—a lot of people do—and he starts thinking yeah, he's got all this, all this is good, but what's he missing? And he's not as young or as potent as he used to be so he compensates. Instead of buying a flashy phallic-symbol vehicle, he wants to get some wild on in bed. But the wife's like: 'You want to put your what *where?*' "

"And she's more in the habit of him putting his this there." Eve nodded. "I get that. So she's just, well, okay then, you put your what where into whoever, I'll have somebody else put his this there, and we're jake?"

"There's a whole separate schism of the Free-Agers who believe in open relationships. Everybody puts their what and their this where and there. But looking at it from your POV—which I have to admit I am, too, as I'm of the opinion if he puts his what anywhere but here?" Peabody jerked a thumb at the car window. "There's the door, asshole. It didn't work for them, either. He went over the line. He couldn't keep the deal they'd made when they got married, and he couldn't keep this deal either."

"That's the pivot point," Eve agreed. "Contact Charles. Tell him we've got client consent, and we're on our way."

Louise answered the door, and put a little hitch in Eve's stride. Her blond hair was tousled, her gray eyes sleepy. She wore winter white lounging pants with a long-sleeved tee.

"Come on in. Charles is putting some breakfast together. I slept in—long night."

"How was it out there?" Eve asked her.

"Cold. Have a seat. I'll see if I can hunt up the coffee."

"It's okay. We just had some."

"Like that would stop you. Charles told me this is about the Anders murder."

"That's right."

"And that Anders's wife is one of Charles's clients."

"Yeah."

"Which, of course, neither of you nor Charles can discuss with me." Louise cocked up her eyebrows. "Why don't I make myself scarce?"

"We can take this somewhere else."

"That's okay, no problem. I'll have myself some breakfast in bed. That's a treat."

She walked off to the kitchen, and Peabody sent Eve a worried look. "Oh-oh."

"Yeah, something's off with them. I caught the buzz from Charles last night."

Louise came back with a pretty place setting on a pretty silver tray. "Hi to Roarke and McNab," she said, then disappeared into the bedroom.

Charles stepped out of the kitchen looking as tired and stressed as his lover. "Dallas. Peabody." He crossed over to buss cheeks. "You got consent."

"On record." Eve took out her recorder, played back the statement.

"That'll work. So." He gestured to seats, took one of his own. "What do you want to know?"

"How did Ava Anders contact you?"

"By 'link. I have a business-only line."

"How did she strike you?"

"Nervous, and trying hard not to show it. Which is how she struck me on our first appointment."

"Where was the first appointment?"

"I looked that up after you left last night. The Blackmore Hotel, downtown. It's a busy place, which is what she wanted. She checked in, contacted me to give me the room number. This way, I could go straight up, but no one would see us together."

"Okay, this is weird, but what did she want?"

"Initially, to talk. She'd ordered lunch, and wine, which we had in the parlor of the suite. We talked—if I remember—about literature, plays, art. For some, this first interlude with a professional is very much like a first date, where you do the surface getting-to-know-you routine."

He glanced toward the bedroom where Louise, presumably, ate her breakfast in bed. "As we got to know each other over the course of time, I understood that her husband wasn't as interested in literature and so forth as he was in sports. So I could offer her that."

"Did she talk about her husband?"

"Not a great deal. It...spoils the mood. She might mention, usually afterward, when we were talking over a drink or coffee, that they were going on a trip, or having a dinner party, that sort of thing."

"How did she feel about him, Charles? You'd know."

"When she spoke of him, she spoke warmly, or casually, the way you do when someone's an intricate part of your life. I remember she'd been shopping once before an appointment and showed me a shirt she'd picked up for him. She said how handsome he'd look in it."

"Sexually, what was she after?"

"She liked to be tended to. She liked the lights off—a few candles were fine, but if we met during the day, which was most usual, the drapes had to be closed."

"You'd classify her as inhibited?"

"Traditional. Very. And maybe a bit self-involved. As I said, she wanted to be tended to. She wasn't as interested in touching as much as being touched. I can say that I noticed in the last few appointments something was off. She was distracted, edgy. She asked me if I ever went to clients' homes—married clients. And if I knew other LCs who did, was it unusual to pay in cash. And she asked if I had a name and address of a client, if I could find the LC hired to go there."

"What did you tell her?"

"That I only accepted home appointments from married clients if both spouses agreed, but that others have different policies in that area. Cash always works," he added with a smile. "And that it would be difficult with only a name and address to locate the LC booked. Considering the number of agencies, freelancers, levels, it wouldn't be an easy task."

"Had she tried to contact you since her husband's death?"

"No."

"When's your next appointment?"

"A week from Wednesday. She canceled our last appointment as she was getting ready for her trip. Two o'clock, at the Blackmore again."

"Okay. If she doesn't contact to cancel, I'd like you to keep it."

He let out a sigh that had Eve's brows drawing together.

"All right."

"Problem with that?"

"No. No, no problem. I'm sorry, but if there's more, can we do it later? I actually have an appointment shortly."

"That's fine. That's it for now anyway."

"Charles," Peabody said as they got to their feet. "Is something wrong?"

"No, nothing. Just a lot on my mind. We should all have dinner soon. The six of us."

"That'd be great. You know you could tag me anytime, if you need to talk about anything."

This time when he smiled, it hit his eyes, too. "I know." He cupped Peabody's chin, lowered his lips to hers. "You tell McNab I said he's a lucky man."

Rather than climb right into the car, Peabody paced the sidewalk outside Charles's building. "Why does he seem so worried? Like something's balled up in his belly?"

"I don't know, but that's a good description."

"It can't be about the case, Dallas. It's not about Anders. If Charles knew something—"

"No, it's not about the case. I caught it from him last night before I brought up Anders."

"Maybe he's sick." Worry and distress hitched through the words. "I know how carefully LCs are screened, especially top-levels like Charles, but what if—"

"Peabody, there's nothing we can do about this. And if he was sick, Louise would know."

"You're right. You're right. It's just...I love him, you know? Not like *love*—McNab love, but—"

"I get it. I've got a soft spot, too. You can't know everything there is to know about a friend, or fix every problem. It's tough knowing they've got one, but..."

She trailed off, narrowed eyes staring at a middle distance.

"What?"

"Just thinking of friends. We've got time to drop in on the last of the mimosas-for-breakfast trio before I meet with Mira. Let's see what Sasha has to say."

Sasha Bride-West wasn't inclined to say much. She was too busy groaning through crunches under the command of the hunk of beefcake she introduced as Sven, her personal trainer.

"Ava and Tommy were going through a patch. Have you ever seen a marriage that didn't? Sven, you're killing me."

"Ten more, my warrior. You'll have abs to slay."

"I can *buy* frigging abs." When he made tsking sounds, she gritted her teeth and kept going. "Anyway, I've had three marriages. Not much smooth sailing, plenty of rough road. Seemed to work the opposite for Ava. But when she asked me to recommend a love machine, and to keep it to myself, I gave her a name—guy's a genius in bed, and damn good company out of it—and kept it to myself."

She collapsed, panting. "Water, Sven, I'm begging you."

He offered her a towel first, to mop her face. She dabbed sweat off skin the color of rich caramel cream.

"Did you follow up?"

"You mean did I ask her for the deets after?" Sasha gulped down water, paused, gulped again. "Of course I did. She wouldn't spill. And I wheedled pretty good."

Sven took the nearly empty water bottle. "It's time for your cardio."

"I hate cardio. Let's skip it and go straight to the massage."

"Sasha," said Sven, severely, and tsked again.

"All right, you sexy sadist." She pulled herself up off the floor of her home gym to climb on the cross trainer. "Give me Paris, Sven. If I'm going to hike and sprint and step, it might as well be Paris. I was going to go over and see her this afternoon," Sasha continued as the Arc de Triomphe flashed on her view screen. "But Bridge has it under control, and she's better with this kind of thing than I am. When Ava's ready for a distraction—for a trip or good drunk or retail therapy—I'm her girl. Brigit's the soft shoulder."

"How was Ava, on this last trip?"

"Good. Fine. Maybe a little tense and moody when we started out, but she chilled. Listen, I can't talk and do this torment at the same time, so is that it?"

"Yeah, that's it. Thanks. We'll see ourselves out."

As Eve turned away, she heard Sasha curse. "Sven, you bastard! There's no hills like these on the frigging Champs-Elysées."

Chapter 7

The morning interviews gave Eve a lot to chew on. If there'd been time, she'd have done just that, in her office, with her boots on her desk and her eyes on her murder board. But sessions with Mira were gold, and not something she could afford to fluff off.

With Peabody writing up the statements and reports, Eve strode into Mira's outer office.

"Dr. Mira is running a bit behind today," the palace guard in the guise of admin informed her.

"How behind is a bit?"

"Only a few minutes." The woman smiled. "You're a minute late yourself, so it won't be long."

"Fine." Turning away, Eve screwed up her face and mouthed, *You're a minute late yourself*. Then pulling out her 'link called her oldest friend, Mavis Freestone. Seconds later, Mavis's happy face, surrounded by an explosion of lavender hair, popped on screen.

"Dallas! Guess where we're going? Me and Belly Button?"

"To hell in a handbasket?"

"To the baby doctor. Yes, we are!" Mavis said in an excited coo. "We're all clean and shiny and we're going to the baby doctor so he can look at our little dumpling butt, our magalicious baby girl ears, and our yummy tum-tummy. Isn't that right, Bellamia? Say hi to Auntie Dallas, sugarcheeks. Say hi."

Mavis's face was replaced by the round-cheeked (maybe it did have something to do with sugar), bright-eyed, curly-haired infant Mavis had popped out a couple months before. There were candy-striped ribbons tied in bows in the curls, drool dripping down the pudgy chin, and a huge, gummy grin. "Say hi to Bellaloca, Auntie Dallas."

"How's it going, Belle. Mavis."

"Wave bye-bye, my itsy-bitsy baby-boo. Bye-bye to Auntie Dallas. Give her a cooey-dooey—"

"Mavis!"

"What?"

"Mavis, I'm saying this for your own good. You have to stop the insanity. You sound like a moron."

"I *know*." Mavis's eyes, currently purple, rolled. "I can *hear* myself, but I can't stop. It's like a drug. So totally S. Hang on." She set down the 'link, and the screen filled with the rainbow hues of the nursery. Eve heard Mavis cooing and gooing, and assumed she was putting the kid down somewhere.

"Back. She's so beautiful. And she's *so* good. Just this morning—"

"Mavis."

"Sorry. Back." Mavis blew out a breath that fluttered the lavender bangs spiking over her eyes. "I'm kicking out to the studio later, working on a new disc. I'll be around grown-up people, lots of crazy artistic types. That'll help."

"Yeah, crazy artistic types. That's the ticket. I just have a question."

"Lay it down."

"If you and Leonardo were having problems in bed—"

"Bite your tongue in three sections and swallow it!"

"Just hear me out. If you were, and it got sticky."

"It wouldn't get sticky in bed if we were having problems there."

"Ha. Serious. If it got serious, would you tell me?"

"Affirmative." The purple eyes registered quick worry. "You and Roarke aren't—"

"No. Second part of the question. If you started going to an LC—"

"Can it be a really frosty one? Can it be two frosty ones, with really big wanks?"

"Solid ice, mongo wanks. If you did that, you'd tell me about it."

"Dallas, if I was doing it with a pro, you couldn't shut me up. Which you'd want to because you wouldn't want to hear how they licked warm, melted chocolate off my—"

"No, I wouldn't."

"But since my big, cuddly bear already does that, and his wank is mucho mongo, I wouldn't need the LC."

"Okay." Eve turned when she heard Mira's door open. And staring, quickly ended the call. "Thanks. Later. Hey, Charles, small world."

She might have bashed him with a brick. His expression jumped from shock to disbelief and ended on flustered. "I've heard people call New York a small town," he managed. "I guess this is what they mean. I was just . . . Well."

"Eve." With a warm and welcoming smile on her pretty face, Mira stepped beside Charles. "I'm sorry I kept you waiting. Come right in. Charles, always a pleasure."

"Thank you. I'll . . ." He gestured without any of his usual style. "Let you get to work."

Over her shoulder, Eve watched him stride rapidly away as she moved into Mira's office. "What's all that about?"

"Have a seat. We'll have some tea."

While Eve frowned, Mira moved with her usual graceful efficiency between the two scoop chairs to the Auto-Chef to order the flowery tea she seemed to live on. Her hair, a cannily highlighted sable, swung smoothly around her patient face, setting off her calm blue eyes. Her suit, a warm and dull gold today, showed off good legs.

"Since you don't have a hair out of place, I'm guessing he didn't drop by to bang you."

Mira set delicate cups on the table between the chairs, and laughed with delight. "Wouldn't that have been interesting? Because it is, I have no intention of confirming or denying." She sat, crossed her legs smoothly, studied Eve's face. "You're annoyed because two of your friends have some private business they're not inclined to share with you."

"I'm not annoyed." Irked, Eve decided, maybe she was a little irked. "The vic's wife is one of Charles's clients, and I interviewed him regarding that this morning, so—"

"I'll tell you that what Charles and I discussed has nothing whatsoever to do with your investigation. Now, about your investigation—"

"Is he in trouble?"

Mira's eyes softened. "No, Charles isn't in trouble. He has a lot on his mind at the moment."

"So he keeps saying," Eve replied, and dropped into a chair. "People are too much damn work."

"They certainly can be."

"I could find out. It's my damn job to find things out."

"But you won't, because I've just told you he isn't in trouble, and you won't intrude."

"If these people wouldn't crisscross all the time in front of where I need to go, I wouldn't have to think about them."

Mira sipped her tea, but hiding her smile didn't hide the open amusement in her eyes. "Your life's more crowded than it used to be. And you're more contented."

"Yeah, I'm feeling real cozy right now. Forget it." She shrugged it off. Charles was a big boy. "You read the file?"

"Yes." Mira took another sip of tea as—Eve knew—she aligned her thoughts. "In my opinion, Anders knew his killer. The method used, the staging surrounding it, wasn't just personal, but intimate. Sexual, of course, but sex isn't always intimate. And there is no physical or forensic evidence that the victim engaged in sexual relations with the killer, or anyone on the night of the murder."

"Nope, he was still holding a full load. No fluids on the sheets or on the body itself. No hair, but for a few strays from the vic, skin."

"Yet it was staged to appear otherwise, and the staging's important. It took time, and planning and preparation. The killer thought about how this could and would be done for some time. There's no impulse here, no passion. A sense of the dramatic, even the theatric, but that underlying sense of order. It feels female. That may be sexist, but it doesn't feel like a same sex crime."

"If it was, he'd've staged the body differently. Given the logistics of man-on-man scx, I think a male killer would have positioned the body differently."

Mira nodded. "That's a good point."

"And even though I told Peabody not to jump to female off the get, it strikes me that if we were dealing with a man—again, if sex was part of it—there'd have been more anger. If Anders was gay, he was deep in the closet. Added to it, in my interviews with the wife, she admits they'd had discussions about his sexual preferences, and she always speaks of women."

"A female killer, then, one who is able to resist impulse, at least long enough to plan, and to execute that plan. One who enjoys the elaborate, the symbolic. Who had or believed she had an intimate relationship with the victim, who certainly at some point had a sexual one with him. Someone who finds sex both powerful and compelling, and demeaning."

"There are LCs like that," Eve speculated. "Who get wrapped up in it—like an addict—then burn out."

"Yes, which is why they're screened so thoroughly before licensing and thereafter to keep the license."

"Are you leaning toward pro?"

"It certainly could be—there are factors that indicate

that sort of intimacy again, and distance. A professional companion must subjugate his or her own needs in order to tailor the relationship to the client's demands. The nature and the length of the relationship is completely in the client's hands."

"That's what they're paid for," Eve commented.

"Yes, and the most successful are able to consider it *as* a profession. They enjoy their work, or consider it a public service. Here, the victim was bound, was naked. He was the supplicant, the submissive. The scarfing, another symbol of who is in control, who is dominant.

"And speaking of S-and-M, bondage, and other fringe areas of sex." Mira sipped her flowery tea. "This was a sex crime, certainly, but not one of sexual rage, or revenge. The genitals aren't destroyed or mutilated, but spotlighted."

"There's the word for it."

Mira smiled a little. "Your crime-scene notes indicate he insisted the bedroom door remain closed, had black drapes, and so on. This was a private man, one who had strong feelings about bedroom privacy. So by spotlighting his most private area, his most private business, the killer demeans him. Humiliates him even after death. And yet—"

"She—since we're going with she—tranqs him halfway to a coma first. She didn't want him to feel the pain or the fear. Didn't want him to suffer the pain." And that was a particular element that stuck in Eve's craw. "It doesn't fit."

"It's a contradiction, I agree. But people can be contradictory. It may have been an accident, may have been she miscalculated the dose. And before you say it, I will: No, I don't think it was a miscalculation. Too much prep work to make such a big mistake."

Eve sat a moment, then picked up the tea and drank before she remembered it wasn't coffee. "Ah." She set it down again. "I like the wife for it."

Intrigued, Mira cocked her head. "I thought it was confirmed the wife wasn't in New York during the time of the murder."

"She wasn't."

"You suspect she hired the killer?"

"I've got nothing to support that. Nothing. Plus, I work back to why does a hire tranq him so heavily. What does a hire care if the target suffers? I'm going to have Roarke go over her financials, dig for other accounts, but it doesn't feel like a hit. At least not a pro."

"Why do you like the wife?"

"She's smart. She's a planner. She's got an answer for everything. Her responses, reactions, her demeanor, all perfect, all just right. Like she fucking studied on it. And maybe it's pushing me toward her, but I can't get my head around this *arrangement* she said she and the vic had."

Pushing up to pace, Eve ran it by Mira, condensing it down to the basics.

"You don't believe her," Mira concluded. "More, you don't believe a couple inside a marriage could, or would, come to an agreement like this arrangement on sexual relationships."

"Objectively, I know people could, and would, because objectively I know people are completely screwed up. But it doesn't fit for me, it doesn't. . . . It's like this one false note playing over and over in a song, and it throws me out every time. I don't know if I don't like the damn song, or if the song's bullshit."

"Objectivity is key to what you do, but so is instinct. If the note strikes you false, again and again, then you'd need to decide which note you'd play instead."

"Huh. How does it strike you?"

"I haven't heard it played from the source, and that can make a difference. But I will say that marriage partners often make arrangements and bargains that seem odd, or even wrong, to someone looking—or listening—in."

"Yeah, I keep coming back to that, too. People do the whacked all the time."

Time to let it stew, Eve decided as she hopped on a glide to start the trip back to Homicide. Time to take another look at the facts and evidence, and let the personalities and speculations simmer. With that in mind, she switched glides to detour to the Electronic Detectives Division. A face-to-face with its captain, and her old partner, might give her another angle on the security breach. She skirted by a couple of cops leaning back on the glide and jawing about basketball, wound her way around a grim-faced woman with her arms folded and piss in her eye before she ran into a logjam of bodies.

She smelled bad cologne, worse coffee, and fresh-baked goods as she snaked and elbowed her way through. Because the elevators were always worse, she stuck with the glides. As she neared EDD, the tone changed. The cops got younger, the clothes more trendy, the visible body piercings more plentiful. The smells edged toward candy and fizzy drinks. Every mother's son or daughter was hooked up—pocket 'links, ear 'links, headsets so the chatter jittered out, the noise of it rising through the corridor and reaching critical mass inside the squad room.

She'd never known an e-detective to be still for more than five minutes. They bopped, danced, tapped, jiggled. Eve figured it would take her less than that five minutes to go stark-raving mad if she rode a desk in EDD. But it suited Feeney. He might have been old enough to have fathered most of his detectives, and his idea of fashion ran to making sure his socks matched, but the color and buzz of EDD fit him like one of his wrinkled suits.

Naturally.

She turned toward his office and his open door. An explosion of sound had her pausing, then approaching with more caution. Feeney sat at his desk. His ginger hair with its generous dashes of gray sat on his head like an electrified cat. Beneath it, his comfortably droopy face was clammy and pale, if you overlooked the bright red nose that sat in the middle like a stoplight.

The explosion of sound came again in the form of three blasting sneezes, followed by a rattling wheeze, and a barking curse.

"Man, you look bad."

His puffy eyes lifted. The shadows under them seemed to droop right down to his clammy cheeks. "Got a freaking son of a bitching cold."

"Yeah, I heard that. Maybe you should be in bed."

"I'm in bed, the wife's on me like white on tofu, how she told me I shoulda worn the muffler, and how didn't she give me those nice earmuffs for Christmas. Damn things make me look like I got a couple of red rats coming out of my ears. She'll want to be pouring Christ knows what into me."

He hacked, sneezed, cursed. And Eve eased back another few inches.

"Plus, she's been taking some godforsaken class on alternative medicine, and has it in her head colonics are the cure for every damn thing. You think I want a colonic?"

"I really don't."

He blew his nose heroically. "You want a rundown on the Sanders electronics."

"Anders." She could almost see the microscopic germs dancing and mating gleefully in the air around him. "Feeney, you gotta go home."

"I'm going to ride it out. Got inhalers, and decongestants. Don't work for shit, but I got them. I get a brain tumor, they can fix it, no problem. I get a lousy germ, and they got nothing."

"Blows, but—"

"Come on in, I'll bring up the file."

She studied him, her trainer, her mentor, her longtime partner. He was, in every way that counted, a father. And she thought of the gleeful germs banging each other all over the office. "Ah, actually, I've got to get back down. I forgot something."

"This'll only take a minute."

"Feeney, I'm not coming in there, I'm not taking one step closer without a hazmat suit. You're dog sick, you're contagious, I can actually see your germs flying around in the air having a party. You need to go home."

He lowered his head to the desk. "Stun me, will you, kid? I'm too weak to pull my own weapon and do it myself."

"Shit." She glanced back, saw McNab's cube was empty. Figured. "You." She jabbed a finger at the closest live body, even if it was clad in a banana yellow skin-suit with knee-high purple airboots. "Your captain needs transportation home. Now. Arrange it. Who's next in rank?"

"Ummmm."

"Jesus. Get the transpo. I want a vehicle ready to go, and an officer at the elevator door of the garage, this sector, ground level, by the time I get there. If it's not—who are you?"

"Um, Detective Letterman."

"If it's not, Detective Letterman, I'm coming back up here and peeling you like the banana you resemble. Clear?"

"Yes, sir."

"Then do it!" Eve took several deep breaths, like a diver preparing to go under, then holding it, went into the red zone. She grabbed Feeney's coat, his hat, his scarf. "Come on, get these on."

"Wanna die at my desk," he whimpered, "not in bed like an old man."

"Jesus, stop being a baby. You're not going to die. Get your coat on. Don't breathe on me. Wear the hat. What the hell's wrong with you coming in today?"

His glassy eyes rolled up to hers. "You're turning into a woman on me, fussing and nagging."

Insulted, she yanked the hat down over his ears herself. "Watch it, pal, or I'll deck you and have a couple of your fruit baskets out there cart you out."

"That's better." He braced a hand on the desk. "You know, Dallas, I think I'm pretty fucking sick."

"That's the smartest thing you've said since I got here. Let's go." She put an arm around his waist, led him out. In the squad room, one glare cut off any questions or comments. "Call Maintenance," she ordered as she hauled Feeney out. "Have them disinfect that office."

"Sanders," Feeney wheezed.

"Anders," she corrected and called for the elevator.

"Remote was a slick one. Custom."

"Okay." When the elevator doors opened, occupants took one look at Feeney. The protests rang out immediately. "Make room or get the hell off." People scattered, deserted the ship as she pulled Feeney on. "Garage," she ordered, "ground level."

"Shut it down, booted it up the same way," Feeney continued. "No tampering with the locks. Knew the code or had a clone. Can't find any indication of cloning. Have to be slick, too."

"Okay." How *long* did it take to get to the damn garage? How soon after breeding did germs give birth to new ones?

"Nothing on the house 'links looks hinky. Got a list of 'em in the report."

"Yeah."

"Pocket 'link, either. Office 'links. Going back another week on the lot, but nothing popping."

"I got it, Feeney."

"Nothing popping on his comps, either." He slumped against Eve like a drunk. "Guy had a million of 'em, so it's taking a while. Personals don't show anything off."

"You get to the wife's yet?"

"Whose wife?"

"Never mind." When the doors opened, a burly, hard-eyed uniform stepped forward. Letterman, she thought, could live.

"Captain Feeney?"

"Right here. Where's your ride?"

He gestured to a black-and-white. "Let me give you a hand. Poor bastard looks pretty sick."

"What's the closest health center?" she asked as between them they maneuvered Feeney into the backseat where he simply sprawled out facedown.

"Got a walk-in clinic on Broadway and Eighteen."

"Take him there."

"Aw, Dallas," Feeney mumbled.

"Stay with him," Eve continued. "I'll contact his wife. When she gets there, if she wants you to stay, you stay."

"Yes, sir."

"Name?"

"Klink."

"Take care of him, Officer Klink."

She slammed the door, stepped back. And watching Klink drive Feeney away wondered if she had time for a detox session.

She settled for scrubbing her hands as if her next task were to perform surgery. And tagging Feeney's wife on the move, made her way back to her own division to track down McNab. She had visions of EDD throwing an orgy of biblical proportions without Feeney in command. Just as she was about to try for McNab, she swung into her own bullpen and saw him.

His back was to her, but there was no mistaking Ian McNab. Who else had that skinny build, the long tail of blond hair flopping down the back of a shirt that resembled the view through a kaleidoscope? And who else would have his flat ass on her partner's desk?

"McNab, get your pitiful excuse for an ass off Peabody's desk and into my office."

She didn't bother to wait to see if he obeyed. She didn't doubt he would, or that he'd slip Peabody a little pinch or tickle before he did. Some things she didn't need to witness.

By the time she got coffee, he was bouncing into her office. "Hey, Dallas, I just came down to—"

"Who's the ranking officer under Feeney?"

"Ah, that would be . . . yeah, that would probably be DS Reedway. Why?"

"I just had Feeney hauled off to the health center. His—"

"Jeez." MacNab's soft green eyes clouded with worry. "Is he that bad? He looked rough this morning."

"Bad enough. Inform your detective sergeant that your

captain's out sick. If he needs any information or assistance, he can contact me."

"She. DS Melodie Reedway."

"A cop named Melodie. It's just not right." She waved that off. "If your ranking officer has no objections, I'd like you as primary e-man on the Anders investigation. You're annoying, but at least I know what to expect from you."

He grinned at her. "I've been working it. I came down to give you an update."

"Feeney just gave me one on the way down to transpo—or partially. Have you started on the wife's electronics?"

"We focused on the vic's first, and he has serious boatloads. Fairly iced. Guy liked UTD—up-to-date," he translated when Eve frowned. "I can shift over to the wife's if you want. Anything special I'd be looking for?"

"Yeah, her having a conversation with the killer would be nice. You know the particulars of the case, you're a detective. You'll know when you see or hear it. Get back up there, McNab."

"Okay. Listen, I'll give Mrs. Feeney a call, let her know."

"Already done. But you could check in with an Officer Klink. He's with Feeney."

"Okay. Hey, it's mag about Peabody doing *Now* tonight. She's freaked. I was giving her a pep talk just now."

"As long as that's all you were giving her. Leave now, and don't touch my partner on the way out."

She shut the door behind him. After topping off her coffee, she sat at her desk, put her boots up on it. And studied her murder board.

Anders, Thomas A., she thought. Age sixty-one, wealthy and successful. Married, no children. Loving uncle to his only nephew, who stands as a major heir and successor. Enjoyed sports and electronic toys—and according to his spouse, kinky sex. Staunch friend. Fair employer. Golf dates, tennis dates, season tickets to every sport known to man. Boxed seats.

Swiveling away from the murder board she brought the file up on her computer, flipped through for the crime-scene photos not on the board, then studied her own record of the victim's closet/dressing room area.

Suits, sure. Looked like maybe a dozen. Two tuxes. Dress shirts, ties. Yeah, yeah. All that took up one wall of the room. The short wall. And filling the two longer walls were the casual clothes, the sports clothes. Golf pants, khakis, sports shirts, shorts, track pants, sweatshirts. And in the drawers, what had she seen when she'd opened the drawers?

Dress socks, she recalled, pulling it into her head. High-end sweaters—the cashmere, the merino wool, the alpaca. Lots of T-shirts—short- and long-sleeved. A lot with sports logos, team emblems. His own brand. Dozens of sports socks. Boxer shorts. Plain white boxers, plain white undershirts. Tailored pajamas.

Interesting.

She added some notes to the file. After a quick knock, Peabody poked her head in. "Dallas, Ben Forrest is here. He'd like to see you."

Eve thought of the murder board, started to tell Peabody to have him wait, then thought better of it. "Send him on back."

She finished her notes, saved to the file. When the next knock sounded, she called out an absent, "Come in."

"Lieutenant, I appreciate you—"

She watched Ben's face. Watched the tired eyes go wide, and the stunned horror turn them glassy. "God, oh, God."

"I'm sorry, Mr. Forrest." She stood, angled so she blocked his view of his uncle's photos. "I wasn't thinking. Let's take this outside."

"I—I...I know what you told me, and what they're saying in the media. How he died. But..."

Eve took her coat off the hook, tossed it over the board.

"Sit down." She gave him a light shove to see that he did, then got him a bottle of water.

"Who would do that to him? Who would humiliate him that way? Killing him wasn't enough?" Rather than drink, Ben slapped the bottle against his palm. "It wasn't enough to take his life?"

"Who would want to humiliate him that way?"

When his gaze lifted to Eve, the fury burned. "I don't know. I swear to God, I don't know. If I did, if I even thought, maybe, maybe him or her, I'd tell you. I loved him, Lieutenant Dallas."

"I believe you. You traveled with him on occasion. On business, or pleasure. Golf trips, sports events."

"Yeah. I guess we averaged at least a trip a month."

"Ben, look at me. I believe you loved him, and I'm telling you if you hold back you're not helping him. So think before you answer me. When you traveled, just the two of you, did he ever seek out women, did he ever arrange for companionship—professional or otherwise."

"No. Wait." He held up a hand, closed his eyes, and took a few breaths. "We nearly always shared a two-bedroom suite. We could hang out together that way. I can't swear that he was always alone in his section of the suite, or that he never went on the prowl after I was down for the night. I can't swear to it. I can only swear to you that I never saw or heard any sign of that kind of thing. I never knew him to seek out companionship. He used to ask me, to razz me sometimes, about finding a woman and settling down. Lieutenant, he was *settled.* If you're digging through the dirt somebody smeared on him, you're never going to find who did this to him. Because it's a goddamn lie."

"Okay, Ben. How about this? The two of you traveled a lot together, just the two of you. Did you ever hit any strip clubs, sex clubs? Just a boys' night out kind of thing?"

"No. That wasn't Uncle Tommy's style, and he'd've been embarrassed to go to a place like that with me. We went to games, sports bars, that kind of thing."

"All right."

He nodded, then twisted off the cap, drank the water. "They contacted Ava and said we could have him now. I'm taking care of the arrangements. I wanted to come here to see if there's anything. Anything you can tell me."

"I can tell you that your uncle is my priority. Are you having a memorial?"

"Tomorrow." He drank again. "We didn't want to wait. Brigit's helping with the details. He'd want simple. He liked simple best."

"Who decorated the house?"

He let out a surprised laugh. "Ava. And yeah, it's not simple. Uncle Tommy liked it though, got a kick out of what he called Ava's Palace."

"I bet. The style's a lot different in his office."

"Yeah. Guy world. That's what he'd say."

"Did he take sleep aids?"

"I . . . I don't think so. I mean, maybe once in a while. I don't remember him mentioning anything like that, but I don't guess it ever came up. I know he liked the door closed, the drapes drawn when he went to bed. He said it was the only way he could get a good night's sleep. So, I guess that sort of thing was his sleep aid."

"Okay."

"Okay. Anyway, thanks." He got to his feet, and his gaze traveled back to the board covered now by Eve's coat. "I'm glad I saw that. Not the images, I'll never be glad of that. I'm glad I saw that you had that in here. That you're looking at it, that you can't turn around in this room without seeing what was done to him. It helps me know you mean it. He's your priority."

Alone, Eve turned back to the board. She lifted off her coat, tossed it over the visitor's chair. And she looked into Ava Anders's eyes.

"You're a liar," Eve stated aloud. "You're a liar, and I'm going to prove it."

Chapter 8

Eve checked the transmission herself, then rechecked it. It was indisputable that Greta Horowitz contacted Ava Anders, the call originating from the house in New York and going to the room registered to Ava on St. Lucia. The transmission ran from 6:14 A.M. to 6:17 A.M.

With her eyes closed, Eve replayed the copy of the transmission provided by EDD. Ava had blocked video, but Eve did the same herself when calls came in while she was in bed. A pity though, a damn shame. It would've been good to see Ava's face, to read her body language. Still, the voice was pitch-perfect—every hill and valley. Sleepy annoyance, to impatience, to shock and through to grief. Every note perfectly played.

Still...

"Computer, send a copy of this transmission, and a copy of the recorded interview with Ava Anders today to the lab. Mark attention Chief Berenski. Memo attached: Require voiceprint analysis and verification ASAP. Require verification recorded voices are the same individual, and that neither sample was prerecorded or transmitted from a remote location. Dallas, Lieutenant Eve."

She added the case file name and number.

Could've worked it that way, Eve mused. Tricky, but not impossible. A voice double, a transmission bounce. She'd have EDD take another look at that possibility. But if that didn't work . . .

She did a search on private transportation, and the fastest shuttle time possible from New York to St. Lucia. The results frustrated her.

Not enough time, she admitted. There just hadn't been enough time to travel from the crime scene back to St. Lucia, back to the hotel room on the island to take the call, not even if Ava had gone off book with the transportation. Physics gave her an unimpeachable alibi.

She went back to the time line, tried to find a hole in it. Her 'link signaled, with an order to report to her commander.

To save time, she squeezed herself on an elevator. She rode up partway with cops, lawyers, and a small, long-eared dog.

"Eye wit," the cop standing beside the dog told her.

"That so?"

"More like nose witness. Owner got himself mugged while he was walking Abe here. Claims Abe'll ID the guy who mugged him by smell." The cop shrugged. "We got three possibles, so, what the hell."

"Yeah, good luck with that."

Eve tried to work out how they expected to convince the PA to bring charges against a suspect on the nose of a dog as she covered the rest of the distance to her commander's office.

"Go right in, Lieutenant." The admin gestured. "They're waiting for you."

Commander Whitney sat at his desk, his back to the view of the city he'd protected and served more than half of his life. His face showed the years, but Eve had always felt it showed them in a way that mattered. Showed in the lines and grooves dug into his dark skin that he'd lived those years, and remembered them.

He wore his hair short, and though she suspected his wife would have preferred it otherwise, he let the salt sprinkle liberally over the pepper. He carried his big, wide build well, and held his command with a strong hand.

"Commander," she began, then paused as the man sitting in the high-backed visitor's chair facing the desk rose. "Chief Tibble."

Not just the commander, she thought, reevaluating, but the Chief of Police.

"Lieutenant." Whitney pointed to the second chair. "Have a seat."

She obeyed, though she preferred standing, preferred giving her oral reports on her feet.

"Lieutenant." Tibble took the jump, and made her wonder why, if this was his meet, she wasn't sitting in The Tower. "I asked the commander to give me a few minutes with you here. Regarding the Anders investigation."

"Yes, sir."

He sat back. A lean man, he favored good suits, and—as she recalled—a good Scotch. Like Whitney, he'd come up through the ranks, and though he was now—essentially—a politician, the office hadn't shoved the cop out of him.

"My reason for asking is somewhat personal."

"Did you know Mr. Anders, sir?"

"No, I didn't. My wife, however, is acquainted with his widow."

Eve thought: *Crap.*

"They've served on several committees together. In any case, when my wife contacted Mrs. Anders to offer her condolences, Mrs. Anders expressed considerable concern over how the current media tone will affect not only her late husband's reputation, the business, but the charitable programs associated with Anders Worldwide. I'm in the position of asking you to assist in damping down the media."

"With all respect, Chief Tibble, how do you propose I

do that? It's not Code Blue, and if it was termed such at this point, if we instigated a media blackout now, it would only feed the beast."

"I agree. Is there any area of your investigation at this point that would give them a different bone to gnaw on?"

"I believe the circumstances under which the victim was found was a setup. But if I toss that bone out, I would jeopardize the investigation, and alert the suspect to the line I'm pursuing."

"You have a suspect?"

"I do. The widow."

Tibble let out a sigh, tipped back his head and looked at the ceiling. "Hell. How—" He cut himself off. "Sorry, Jack, this is your area."

"Lieutenant, explain how a woman who was several thousand miles away at the time of the murder heads the top of your list of suspects?"

"It's not confirmed she was in St. Lucia, Commander. There was no video on the transmission from the house manager. I've sent that transmission and a sample of Mrs. Anders's voice from an interview this morning to the lab for voiceprint comparison. Even if that confirms her alibi, she's involved. She's part of it. She's lying, Commander. She's lying," she repeated, looking back at the chief. "She tells your wife she's concerned about the fallout from the media. The fallout revealing her husband engaged in extramarital sex, which included bondage, scarfing, but the widow is the only person interviewed who confirms those allegations."

"Arguably," Whitney said, "the wife would know her husband's sexual proclivities while others don't."

"Yeah, and that's something she counted on. She's wrong, Commander. I don't have it solid yet, but I know she's wrong. The staging's wrong. It's too elaborate, too . . . fussy," she said for a lack of better. "Whoever did it knew the house, the security, knew Anders's habits. There were little mistakes, but for the most part, it was well planned. Whoever did it wanted to humiliate him, to open him to the very media frenzy that's happening. Mrs. Anders is an expert in PR. Just like she knows that if she plays this right, after the jokes about *her* die down, she'll come out golden. Who gets the sympathy, the support, the understanding? She'll be the victim, and she'll be the one squaring her shoulders and going on."

"Are you saying she did this *for* the publicity?" Whitney demanded.

"No, sir, but it's a side benefit she'd be aware of, and will find a way to exploit.

"It wasn't a stranger, Commander, it wasn't a pro, and it wasn't an accident. That leaves me with Ava Anders."

"Then prove it," Whitney told her.

"Yes, sir. I have Roarke on as expert consultant, analyzing all the financials, looking for any hidden accounts."

"If anyone could find them."

"Yes, sir," she repeated. "I intend to run a deeper background check on Mrs. Anders, and interview her first husband, as well as other friends and associates of hers and the victim's."

She rose. "Regarding the media, Chief Tibble, Detective Peabody will be appearing on *Now* this evening. I can't speak for Nadine Furst, but I do have knowledge she knew the victim and liked him. Respected him."

"Why Peabody," Whitney demanded, "and not you?"

"Because, Commander, she needs a shove into the deep end of the pool. And Nadine is very fond of Peabody. That doesn't mean she won't push or dig, but she won't eat her alive. And, in my opinion, sir, Detective Peabody can and will handle herself."

"If she fucks up, Lieutenant?" Tibble smiled. "You'll be the one dealing with my wife."

"So noted. Actually, it might be helpful for me to speak with her, if you don't object."

"Go right ahead. But fair warning. She's feeling very protective of Mrs. Anders at the moment."

Varying approaches on interviewing the wife of the Chief of Police occupied her mind all the way back to

Homicide. Diplomacy could be key, and that particular key tended to go slippery in her fingers. But she'd hold it steady. Next came the trick of interviewing a cop's wife—the *top* cop's wife—without letting her suspect *you* suspected the woman she was "feeling very protective of."

Just have to pull it off, Eve thought. That's why they paid her the medium bucks.

"Lady! Yo, lady!"

It took her a minute, but she made the voice, and the small package it came from. Coffee-black skin, vivid green eyes, a curly high-top of hair. The boy hauled the same battered suitcase—approximately the size of Staten Island—he'd hauled in December when he'd been hustling the fake cashmere scarves inside it near the splatted body of a jumper on Broadway.

"Didn't I tell you before I'm not a lady."

"You're a cop. I tracked you down, and I've been waiting here, and these other cops tried hassling me about why wasn't I in school and that shit."

"Why aren't you in school and that shit?"

"'Cause I got business." He shot a finger at her. "With you."

"I'm not buying anything."

"I gotta tip."

"Yeah? I've got one, too. Don't bite off more than you can chew."

"Why not? You can't chew it, you just spit it out anyway."

That wasn't stupid, Eve noted. "Okay, what's your tip?"

"I'll tell you, but I'm pretty thirsty." He gave her the same grin he'd flashed the previous December.

"Do I look like a mark, shortie?"

"You look like the top bitch cop in New York City. That's word on the street."

"Yeah." Maybe she could spare a minute, and the price of a Pepsi. "That is the correct word. Give me the tip, and if I like it, I'll pop for a drink."

"I know where there's suspicious activity, *and* suspicious characters. I'm gonna take you."

"Kid, you're hard pressed to find anywhere in the city where there aren't suspicious activities and suspicious characters."

He shook his head in disgust. "You a cop or what?"

"We established that. And I've got cop work to do."

"Same guy, same place, same times. Every day for five weeks. I seen it. Maybe they see me, too, but they don't mind me 'cause I be a kid."

No, Eve thought, not stupid. Most people didn't see kids. "What does this same guy do at the same place at the same times every day for five weeks that makes him a suspicious character involved in suspicious activity?"

"He goes in with a big old shopping bag heavy the way he carries it. And a couple minutes later, *bop!* he comes out again, and he's got a different bag. It ain't heavy, either." The kid adjusted the airboard slung at his back.

"Where is this den of iniquity?"

The kid's brow furrowed like an elderly grandfather's. "Ain't no den. It's a store. I'm gonna take you. It's a good tip. I oughta get an orange fizzy."

"You oughta get a kick in the ass." But she pulled out credits, passed them over, jerked a thumb at Vending. While he plugged in credits, she considered. The kid was sharp enough, and had probably seen just what he said. Meaning the store was a front—or a beard—for passing off wallets, bags, and whatever else the street thief could lift from tourists and New Yorkers foolish enough to get their pockets picked.

The kid sucked on the fizzy. "We gotta get, so you can catch them."

"Give me the location, and I'll send cops over."

"Uh-uh. I gotta show you. That's the deal."

"What deal? I didn't make any damn deal. I don't have time to go driving around, waiting for some pocket man to make his bag drop."

The boy's eyes were like glass, and just as sharp. "I guess you don't be much of a cop."

She could've stared him down, she was pretty sure of it. But he made her shoulder blades itch. "You're a pain in the ass." She checked the time, calculated. Odds were the drop spot was in Times Square where she'd had the misfortune of meeting the kid in the first place. She could swing by there on the way home. Maybe she'd get some damn work done at home without being interrupted every five minutes.

"Wait here," she ordered. "If you're not right here when I get back, I'll hunt you down like a dog and stuff you inside that suitcase. Dig?"

"I gonna show you?"

"Yeah, you're going to show me. Stay." She strode into the bullpen. "Peabody, I have to make a run, semi-personal, then I'm going to work at home."

"But—but—I have to leave for 75 in...in like any minute!"

"Do that, copy any new data, shoot it to my home office."

"But..." On a run, Peabody rushed after Eve. "You're not going with me?"

"Pull yourself together, Peabody." Eve grabbed file discs, tossed them into her bag. "You've done on-air before."

"Not like *this*. Dallas, you've gotta go with me. I can't go there by myself. I'll—"

"Jesus, how can people be *worth* all this? Take McNab. Tell his DS I cleared it." Eve dragged on her coat. "And don't fuck up."

"You're supposed to say break a leg!" Peabody called out as Eve stomped away.

"Fuck it up and I'll break your damn leg myself."

"Dallas."

"What?" She rounded on Baxter with a snarl, then remembered. "Sorry. Any new leads?"

"No. Have you—"

"No, I haven't had a chance to look at the file. Soon as I can, Baxter." A headache brought on, she knew, by sheer irritation, began to pulse behind her eyes. "Let's go, kid, and if you're stringing me you'll find out firsthand why the word is I'm top bitch cop."

In the garage the kid shook his head sorrowfully at her vehicle. He climbed in, steadied the suitcase on his lap, took a long study of the dash, then turned those Venusian green eyes on her. "This ride is crap."

"You got better?"

"I ain't got ride, but I know crap. How come top bitch cop has a crap ride?"

"This is a question I ask myself daily. You got a name?"

"You got one?"

She had the oddest feeling she amused him. "Lieutenant Dallas."

"What kinda name's Loo-tenit?"

"It's rank. It's my rank."

"I don't got no rank, don't got no ride."

"Name, kid, or the adventure stops here."

"Tiko."

"Okay, Tiko, where are we going?"

He put on what Eve supposed was his enigmatic face. "Maybe we cruise over round Times Square."

She drove out of the garage, wedged into traffic. "What's in the case this time?"

"I got me the cashmere scarves *and* matching caps. How come you don't wear no cap? Heat falls out the top of your head you don't wear a cap."

"How come you're not wearing one?"

"Sold it." He grinned at her. "I'm a selling fool."

"As a selling fool, Tiko, why did you haul yourself and that case all the way down to Central to tell me about the drop?"

"I didn't drop nothing."

Not as streetwise as he appeared, she decided. "About the suspicious activities."

"I don't like suspicious activities round my yard. I got business. Somebody steals wallets and shit, then people don't have the money to buy my scarves and caps and pretty soon in good weather my one hundred percent *silk* scarves and ties."

Since it made perfect sense, Eve nodded. "Okay, why not tell one of the uniforms on the beat?"

"Why do that when I gotta line on the top bitch?"

Tough to find a hole in his logic, Eve decided. "You got digs, Tiko?"

"I got digs, don't you worry. Maybe you turn on Forty-fourth, and dump the ride there. Anybody knows anything sees this crap ride, makes it for a cop's."

Once again, he had it nailed. She cut over, shoving her way crosstown. Maybe the kid was lucky, but she scored a second-level street spot between Seventh and Eighth.

"You got your weapon and shit, right?" he asked as they started to hoof it through the throng and east toward Broadway.

"I got my weapon and shit. Is this place on the west or east side of Broadway?"

"East. I got my yard on the west side, work it from Forty-second right on up to Forty-seventh. But I can stay mostly round Forty-fourth. Place is 'tween Forty-third and Forty-fourth, right on Broadway. He gonna be coming along pretty soon now."

"Here's how it's going to work. You're going to go on ahead, set up in your usual spot. I'll come along, take a look at your merchandise. You see this guy, you point him out—without pointing, get me? I'll take it from there."

Excitement danced in his eyes. "Like I'm undercover."

"Yeah, that's it. Scram."

He scrammed, short, sturdy legs pumping, huge suit-case bumping. Eve pulled out her communicator and called for a couple of uniforms. When Eve turned the corner onto Broadway, Tiko had his convertible case un-folded and set on its tripod legs. It didn't surprise her in the least to see he already had a couple of customers.

Broadway's perpetual party rocked with its flashing lights, sky-scraping screens, and billboards. Whole platoons of teenagers filled the sidewalks, zipping on airboards, cruising on skates, or clomping on the current trend of three-inch, gel-soled boots. On their corners, the carts did business zippily, passing out dogs, pretzels, kabobs, scoops of fries or hash, and all manner of liquid refreshment.

Tourists gawked at the colors, the ad blimps, the arcades, and the sex shops, which also did business zippily. Most of those tourists, in Eve's opinion, might have been wearing a neon sign with a blinking arrow pointing at their pockets.

PICK ME.

She sidled up to Tiko's table, and he gave her an exaggerated eyebrow wiggle. "Hundred percent cashmere. Scarves and caps. Got a special price today you buy a set."

"What's so special about it?"

He grinned. "Hundred for the set. Usually it cost you $125. Charge you five times that easy in the store. This here striped one— He's coming now." Tiko dropped his voice to a dramatic whisper, as if his words might carry through the avalanche of noise and across the street. "Red shopping bag. See him—"

"Don't point."

Eve glanced casually over her shoulder. She saw the red bag, and the tall, gangly man in a gray field jacket and black watch cap.

"You gotta go get him. Hundred dollars for the set," Tiko said to a woman who stopped to browse his stock. "Today only. You go on and get him."

Where the hell were her uniforms? "I got cops coming."

"*You* a cop."

"I'll take these," the woman said, digging out her wallet.

Tiko grabbed a clear plastic bag. "He's gonna go in!"

"I'm Homicide. Is there a dead body in there?"

"How do I know?" He managed to bag the cap and scarf, take the money, make change, and stare holes through Eve.

"Crap. You stay here. You stay *exactly* here."

To keep from drawing attention, she crossed at the light, kicked it up to a weaving sprint, ignored the curses from people she bumped aside. She kept the bagman in her crosshairs, and was less than three yards behind him when he turned into a storefront offering New York City souvenirs, including T-shirts at three for $49.95.

She pulled open the door. Short, narrow shop, she noted, evaluating quickly. One male, one female working the side counter, and the bagman heading straight back.

Goddamn uniforms, she thought.

"Help ya?" the woman said, without much interest.

"Yeah, I see something I want." Eve strode up behind the bagman, tapped his shoulder. She angled so his body was between her and the counter, in case the others got frisky, then held up her badge. "You're busted."

The woman at the counter screamed as if an ax cleaved her skull. In the split second that distracted Eve, the bagman's elbow connected with her cheekbone. Stars exploded.

"Goddamn it." Eve rammed her knee up his ass, and backhanded him into the T-shirt display. With the side of her face yipping and her weapon in her hand, she pivoted. "Lady," she warned as the woman scrambled over the counter in a bid for the front door. "One more step and I stun you stupid. On the floor. On the fucking floor, facedown, hands behind your head. You." She jerked her head toward the counterman who stood with his hands high in the air. "You're good. Stay like that. And you."

She gave the bagman an annoyed boot. "Why'd you have to go and do that? It's all worse now, isn't it?"

"I just came in here to buy a T-shirt."

"Yeah? Were you going to pay for it out of one of

these?" She toed the collection of wallets and handbags that spilled out of the shopping bag.

She stared blandly at the two uniforms who rushed in from the street. "Gee, sorry, guys. Did I interrupt your coffee break? Check the back. I believe I detect suspicious activity in this establishment." She pressed her fingers lightly to her throbbing cheek. "Fucking A. And call for a wagon to haul these fuckheads in. Robbery, trafficking in stolen goods—"

"Hey, Lieutenant! There's a couple hundred wallets and bags back here. And credit/debit card and ID card dupes."

"Yeah?" Eve smiled winningly at the now very sad-eyed man with his hands in the air. "Fraud, identity theft. The gift that keeps on giving."

It took another twenty minutes, but when Eve crossed the street again, Tiko stood exactly where she'd told him.

"I told them, the cops when I saw them coming." He bounced on the toes of his black skids. "I told them where."

"You did good."

"You gotta mouse coming on. You get in a fight with the suspicious character?"

"I kicked his ass. Break it down, Tiko. You're done for today."

"I can get another hour in, make up for going downtown and all."

"Not today."

"You taking those people to jail?"

"The uniforms are taking them. They don't need the top bitch cop to turn the key," she said, anticipating him. "Where are your digs, Tiko?"

He narrowed his eyes. "You don't think I got digs?"

"If you've got them, tell me where so I can take you."

"Round the corner. Apartment on the third floor, above the Greek place. Told you this was my yard."

"Yeah, you did. Break it down. Let's go."

He wasn't happy about it, she could see, but he did it. "Cost me five easy, quitting this early when I took off to go down and get you."

"I bought you a fizzy."

Because his stony stare appealed to her, she dug out some credits. Counted fifty. "That's ten percent of the five you say you lost. I figure it covers your time and your transportation."

"Solid." The credits disappeared into one of several pockets. "You stun any of those people in there?"

"No." What the hell, Eve thought. She could add some juice to the fifty. "But the woman screamed like a girl and tried to run. I told her to drop, or I'd stun her."

"Would ya?"

"Damn right. They'd stolen from a lot of people, and they were making dupe cards in the back. Looks like they were lifting IDs, too."

He shook his head in disgust. "Stealing's lazy."

Intrigued, she looked down at him. "Is it?"

"Shit, yeah. Any lazy dumbass can steal. Takes brains and some juice to *make* money. We up here." He opened a door next to a tiny gyro place. The closet-sized lobby held an elevator. On it the Out of Order sign looked about a decade old. Eve climbed the stairs with the boy. The place smelled like onions and garlic, not entirely unpleasant. The walls were dingy, the steps stained and steep.

She imagined him climbing up and down them every day, hauling his case. Yeah, it took some juice.

On the third floor, he dug out a set of keys from one of his pockets, unlatched three locks. "You can come in if you want to meet my granny."

Something was cooking. Eve caught the tomatoey scent when she stepped into the tiny room, which was sparse and lace-curtain tidy.

"That my boy?" someone called through a narrow doorway.

"Yes, ma'am, Granny. I got somebody with me."

"Who you got?" The woman who stepped out of the

doorway held a short-handled wooden spoon. Her hair was a white ball of fluff over a face mapped with wrinkles. But her eyes beamed that same vivid green as the boy's. She wore a baggy brown sweater and pants over her thin frame.

Fear came into those eyes, and knowledge with it. She might as well have shouted *Cop!* and thrown her hands in the air like the counterman.

"There's no trouble here," Eve said.

"This is my granny. Granny, this is Loo-tenit Dallas. She's the top . . . She's a police."

"He's a good boy." The woman held out a hand so Tiko hurried to her, and she held him tight against her side.

"He's not in trouble."

"We got them, Granny, that's what we did. We got them good."

"Who? What's this about?"

Tiko tugged at her hand. "'Member how I told you I seen those suspicious characters? You said how they was likely stealing hand over fist. And they were. I went down and told Dallas, and I took her where they were, and she went on over there and arrested them good. Ain't that the way?"

"Isn't that the way," his grandmother corrected absently.

"Tiko alerted me to suspicious activity, and assisted the NYPSD in identifying a front for street theft and identity fraud."

"Oh, my sweet Lord."

"Mrs. . . ."

"I'm so sorry. I'm so flustered, I can't hardly feel my head on my shoulders. I'm Abigail Johnson."

"Mrs. Johnson, you have a very interesting grandson, and one who went above and beyond what most people would. A lot of people owe him for it." She took out a card, searched her pockets until she came up with a pencil stub. "This is my contact information. There's a reward."

"I get a reward? Over my time and transpo?"

"A good deed is its own reward," Abigail told him.

"Yes, ma'am, that's true. However, the NYPSD would like to express its appreciation for good citizenship, and it has a program for just that. If you'll contact the person I've listed on the back of my card, they'll arrange it." She handed the card to Abigail, held out a hand to Tiko. "Nice job, kid."

"Back at cha. Sorry about the mouse."

"Not the first, won't be the last."

"Tiko, go ahead and wash up for supper now. Say good-bye to Lieutenant Dallas."

"See you around. You come on back to my yard, I'll make you a good deal." When he dashed off, Abigail drew a slow breath.

"I homeschool him two hours every evening, seven days a week. We go to church every Sunday. I make sure he's got clothes and good food. I—"

"There's no trouble here, Mrs. Johnson. If you have any, you contact me."

Eve jogged down the stairs, and back out into the cold. A good deed might be its own reward, she thought as she pressed a hand to her aching cheek. But she could sure as hell use an icebag with hers.

Chapter 9

Eve walked into the house prepared for her daily snarkfest with Summerset, who would no doubt have something withering to say about the black eye she was brewing.

And he wasn't there.

She stood for a moment in the empty foyer almost expecting him to materialize like smoke. Puzzled, she poked her head in the front parlor. Fresh flowers, nicely simmering fire—but no Bony Ass. Mild concern jabbed its way through the puzzlement. Maybe he'd caught something like what Feeney had—and there was no possible way she was playing nurse for the resident ghoul.

Still, if he was lying unconscious somewhere in a pool of fever sweat . . . Roarke would just have to get his ass home and deal with it.

She started to turn to the house comp to run a search for him, then the top cop bitch jumped like a rabbit when Summerset's disembodied voice floated into the room.

"As I assume you might have some interest in your partner, you should be aware that Detective Peabody's appearance on *Now* begins in approximately four minutes."

"Fuck." Eve breathed out the word, scowled at the intercom. "I know what time it is." Or she did now. Annoyed, she started up the stairs, and his voice followed her.

"You'll find cold bags in the top, far right drawer of your office kitchen."

She hunched her shoulders—oh, she heard the smug satisfaction—and kept going. In her office she dumped the file bag on her desk, ordered the proper channel on screen. And because her cheek throbbed like a bitch in heat, retrieved and activated the stupid cold bag. With the blessed chill pressed against her face, she booted up her computer. Might as well deal with the next irritation on her list, she thought, and write up her report on the Times Square bust.

She'd barely begun when *Now*'s theme music boomed on. With half an ear, she listened to Nadine's intro, spared a glance at the screen where the reporter's cat's eyes stared soberly back at her. Polished and powerful was the image, Eve supposed, with the streaky blond hair, subtle jewelry, the good legs highlighted in a sleek copper suit. Of course, most of the viewing audience hadn't seen Nadine dance half naked at a sex club after a pitcher of zombies.

She introduced Peabody as a dedicated, decorated police officer, and cited some of the more media-worthy cases she'd helped close. When the camera panned over to her partner, Eve pursed her lips.

Trina hadn't gone freaky on her hair and face, Eve noted. She looked young, but not soft, so that was good. The suit, with its military cut, probably worked. And if you didn't know her, you wouldn't notice the utter terror in Peabody's eyes.

"Don't screw up," Eve muttered.

Nadine led her in, softballing a few, and Eve could see Peabody begin to relax. Not *too* relaxed, Eve thought. She's not your friend when you're on air. Nobody's your friend when you're on air.

"Damn it, now *I'm* nervous." And because of it, Eve rose and paced in front of the screen as she watched.

Handling it, handling it. Pursuing all leads, blah, blah, blah. Unable to comment on specifics, yada, yada. Peabody confirmed there had been no sign of forced entry—that was okay—and better, dropped in there were indications the security system had been compromised.

They circled around each other on the sexual nature of the murder. It was Nadine's job to dig for details and Peabody's duty to avoid giving them. Standing in front of the screen, Eve felt a quick little twist of pride. They both did nice work.

Enough got in, just enough to confirm the murder had sexual elements. But the tone, the message, transmitted clearly that Thomas A. Anders was the victim. A life had been taken.

Wrapping it up now, Eve realized. Thank Christ.

"Detective," Nadine began, "Thomas Anders was a wealthy man, a strong, visible presence in social and business circles. His prominence must bring a certain pressure onto the investigation. How does that influence your work?"

"I . . . I guess I'd say murder equalizes. When a life's taken, when one individual takes the life of another, there's no class system, no prominence. Wealth, social standing, business, those might all go to motive. But they don't change what was done, or what we as investigators do about it. We work the case the same way for Thomas Anders as we do for John Doe."

"Still, some departmental pressure would be expected when the victim has prominence."

"Actually, it's the media that plays that kind of thing up. I don't get it from my superiors. I wasn't raised to judge a person's worth by what he owns. And I was trained as a cop, as a detective, that our job is to stand for the dead—whoever they were in life."

Eve nodded, dipped her hands into her pockets as Nadine cut away to end the segment and preview the next.

"Okay, Peabody, you can live."

Ordering the screen off, Eve sat at her desk and got back to work.

There she was. Roarke stood in the office doorway, took a few enjoyable minutes to just watch her. She had such a sense of purpose, such a sense of focus on that purpose. It had appealed to him from the first instant he'd seen her, across a sea of people at a memorial for the dead. He found it compelling, the way those whiskey-colored eyes could go flat and cold as they were now. Cop's eyes. His cop's eyes.

She'd taken off her jacket, tossed it over a chair, and still wore her weapon harness. Which meant she'd come in the door and straight up. Armed and dangerous, he thought. It was a look, a fact of her, that continually aroused him. And her tireless and unwavering dedication to the dead—to the truth, to what was right—had, and always would, amaze him.

She'd set up her murder board, he noted, filling it with grisly photos, with reports, notes, names. And somewhere along the line in her day, she'd earned herself a black eye.

He'd long since resigned himself to finding the woman he loved bruised and bloody at any given time. Since she didn't look exhausted or ill, a shiner was a relatively minor event.

She sensed him. He saw the moment she did, that slight change of body language. And when her eyes shifted from her comp screen to his, the cold focus became an easy, even casual warmth.

That, he thought, just that was worth coming home for.

"Lieutenant." He crossed over, lifted her chin with his hand to study the bruising under her eye. "And so, who'd you piss off today then?"

"More like who pissed me off. He's got more than one bruise."

"Naturally. Who might that be?"

"Some mope named Clipper. I busted a snatch, switch, and drop."

"Ah." He cocked his head. "Why?"

"Good question. This kid named Tiko dragged me into it."

"This sounds like a story. Do you want some wine to go with it?"

"Maybe."

"Before you tell me the story, did you catch Peabody's appearance?"

"Yeah. Did you?"

Across the room he contemplated the wine selection, made his choice for both of them. "I wouldn't have missed it. I thought she did brilliantly."

"She didn't screw up."

He laughed, opened the bottle. "High praise, Lieutenant. It's you who trained her. The last thing she said. It's you who trained her to stand for the dead, no matter who they were in life."

"I trained her to work a case. She was already a cop."

"As you were, when Feeney trained you. So it trickles down." He walked back to hand her a glass of wine. "It's a kind of inheritance, isn't it?" With his own wine, he sat on the corner of her desk. "Now, about that eye."

He listened, by turns amused and fascinated. "How old is this Tiko?"

"I don't know. Seven, maybe eight. Short."

"He must be very persuasive as well as short and seven."

"He digs in, that's for sure. It wasn't much of a detour anyway." She shrugged. "And you had to admire his logic, pretty much down the line. They're stealing from potential customers, which cuts into his business. I'm a cop."

"Top bitch cop."

"Bet your ass. So as such I'm supposed to fix it."

"As you did." He brushed a finger over her cheek. "With minimal damage, I suppose."

"Guy had skinny arms, but they were as long as a gorilla's. Anyway, I figure the kid's got a flop—he's too clean and warmly dressed for street—probably with his gray market supplier. Couldn't've been further off there. Little apartment off Times Square with a granny cooking his supper. Great-grandmother," she added. "I ran them on the way home."

"Of course you did."

"Neither's been in any trouble. The same can't be said of Tiko's mother. Illegals busts, solicitation without a license, shoplifting that upped to petty theft that upped to grand larceny. Last couple busts were down in Florida. The granny's been guardian since he was about a year old."

"The father?"

"Unknown. She was afraid I was going to call Child Services. Afraid I was going to call them in, and she could lose the kid."

"Another cop might have."

"Then another cop would've been wrong. Kid's got a decent roof over his head, warm clothes on his back, food in his belly, and somebody who loves him. It's . . ."

"More than we had," Roarke finished.

"Yeah. I thought about that. There's no fear in this kid, and that's about all that was in me at his age. No meanness either, and you had plenty of that running your Dublin alleys. Had to have plenty of it. He's got the chance of a good life ahead of him because someone cares enough."

"From what you've said, he sounds like the kind who'll make the most of that chance."

"That's my take. And I thought about Anders. He wasn't afraid, and from everything I find, he wasn't big on the mean. But his chance at life was taken. Because someone cared enough to end him."

"Cared enough. Interesting choice of words."

"Yeah." She looked over at her murder board, looked at Ava Anders's ID photo. "I think it fits. Listen, I couldn't get by the lab to browbeat Dickhead into running a voiceprint. I've got a couple samples here. It probably wouldn't take you long."

"It probably wouldn't." He considered it over a sip of wine. "I might do that for you, if you fixed my supper."

It seemed a fair trade. And if she went for one of her own personal faves—spaghetti and meatballs—he hadn't specified a choice. She continued her run on Ava Anders first, left another message on Dirk Bronson's—the first husband—voice mail. Then she wandered into the kitchen to program the meal.

She'd only set the plates on her desk when Roarke came back in. She wondered why she even bothered with the lab.

"Good news is, it didn't take long. Bad news, from your standpoint anyway, they're a match."

"Shit. Could the St. Lucia transmission have been by remote?"

"It's not reading that way. I ran it through several types of filters. As your expert consultant, civilian, I have to tell you Ava Anders received that transmission while in the room registered to her in St. Lucia."

"She couldn't have made it back there from New York in the time frame."

"No. It's a bit too tight for that."

"Maybe the time frame's off. Anders was still alive—unconscious, dying, but still alive when the security was booted back, the doors locked again. Maybe it didn't take her as long as I calculated for the setup, and if she reactivated it all by remote, she might have been on her way back to St. Lucia earlier. It'd be tight, but maybe not too tight."

"Ground time from the crime scene to a shuttle hangar, and the same from shuttle to hotel on the island have to be added in. You're reaching, Eve."

"Damn right I'm reaching." Irritated, she scooped up some spaghetti. "I know she's in it. Okay, the vic liked electronics. Could he have a security setup that could be turned off and on by long-distance remote?"

"Not impossible. What do your e-men say?"

"Cloning remote—good shit—short-range. But they weren't looking for long. And Feeney's dog sick with a cold."

"Sorry to hear that."

"I had to practically carry him down to transpo, send him off to a health center, call his wife."

Roarke didn't bother to hide his grin. "Haven't you been the busy little scout today."

"Bite me."

"I rarely think of anything else but. I can take a look at the system. As for financials, I haven't found anything off there. No suspicious withdrawals or transfers, no accounts tucked away. Not yet."

Clean, covered, Eve thought. But her gut kept adding "calculated" to that. "If she didn't do it herself and had it done, maybe she didn't use money. There are other incentives. Sex, position, blackmail. Friendship. Isn't there some saying about a real friend's the one who helps you hide the body? She's got a couple of women who strike me as real friends."

"What is it about her, Eve?"

"Things." She stabbed at a meatball. "Her clothes."

"You don't care for her fashion sense?"

"How would I know if she has any? You do." She jabbed the fork with its bite of meatball at him. "Fashion king."

"We do our best."

"So, you're dead asleep, and you get a call. Something terrible's happened, and I'm dead. What do you do?"

It took him a moment to quell the terror, to ignore the small, dark place inside him that feared getting that call every day. "Before or after I fall prostrate with grief?"

"Before, during, and after. Do you peruse your wardrobe and select a coordinating outfit—down to the footwear? Do you deal with your hair so it's perfectly groomed?"

"With my considerable skills and innate instincts that would take no time at all."

"Keep it up and I'll dump red sauce all over your fashionable smarty-pants."

"That statement is one of the countless reasons why, under the circumstances you described, I'd be lucky to remember to dress at all. But then not everyone loves the same way, Eve, or to the same levels. Or reacts the same way to hard news."

"The call for transpo went out from her hotel room six minutes after she ended the transmission with Greta. But, there's nearly a fifty-minute lag between then and her leaving the hotel. She ordered coffee, juice, fresh berries, and a croissant from her in-room AutoChef—I had the hotel look up her record. She ordered her little continental breakfast *before* she called for transpo arrangements."

"Ah. There's cold blood."

"Yeah. A little thing maybe—not evidence, but it's a thing. A lawyer would argue it's nothing. She was in shock. But it's bullshit. She was wearing perfume when she got to the house, and earrings, and a bracelet that matched her wrist unit. She didn't contact Forrest, not for hours after getting the news.

"Little things," Eve repeated. "I believe she planned it out, studied every detail, covered every track. But she can't cover who she is. She can't quite cover up her self-interest, her vanity, or the calculation I see in her eyes every time I look at her."

"She didn't plan out everything. She didn't plan on you."

"I'm going to the memorial tomorrow. I'm going to talk to her again, to her friends again, to Forrest, track down this ex-husband of hers. To the housekeeper, to Charles, back to her. I'm going to annoy the living hell out of her, even if she is a friend of the chief's wife."

Idly, Roarke wound pasta on his fork. "She knows Tibble's wife? Sticky."

"Yeah." Eve blew out a breath. "It wouldn't surprise me if she'd sought out that connection as part of her outline. Get chummy with a high police official's wife. Check."

At Eve's questioning glance, Roarke nodded. "I'd agree, yes. It would be very good planning on her part. How did she make the connection?"

"Committees, charities, the usual. Next financials in

line are the charitable trusts and scholarships. Maybe she siphoned off some of the money, the vic found out. She comes out better a widow than in a divorce, especially if she had any part of siphoning funds meant for the less fortunate kiddies."

"Ben would know. I should say I'd be very surprised if Ben wouldn't know about any mishandling of funds. Possibly they could have been misappropriated and replaced quickly, books cooked in a way he would miss it. But, with his uncle dead, he's majority stockholder, and acting chairman of the board. I'd imagine he's having an internal audit done to make certain the house is in order, on every level."

"She's got him snowed. That's how it looks to me. And she smears the victim with this sex dirt, automatically makes people look sideways. Could be if she played with funds, she's thought of a way to twist it so it looks like the victim did the playing."

"I can take a look."

She twirled more spaghetti onto her fork, smirked. "Aren't you going to be the busy little scout?"

"Cute. Should we go for a drive after dinner? Back to the scene of the crime?"

She studied him over a mouthful of pasta. "Here's what I like about you. Almost everything."

"So," Eve said as they stood in Anders's bedroom, "the guy's lying there, dead as Judas, and his wake-up system goes off. Good morning, Mr. Anders. Gives him the time, turns on the fireplace, starts the coffee, the shower, reminds him what he ordered for breakfast, and details his first appointment of the day."

"Who needs a wife?"

Her response was a bland stare. "Anyway, it was kind of creepy. How come you don't have a system like that, ace?"

"We do. I just don't use it. It's kind of creepy. Plus I rarely need an alarm, and why would I want to order breakfast the night before or have the shower going before I was ready to take one?"

"You have habits and routines, but you're not a creature of habit and routine. He was. That was part of the weapon used against him. He was predictable. You could count on him being in bed at three in the morning, count on him programming his wake-up system, putting on his sensible pajamas. Door closed, drapes drawn. Night-night. He'd have been sleeping facing toward the door. From the angle and position of the pressure syringe mark, he'd have been sleeping on his side, facing the door. I bet he always did. She'd have known that. Checklist. Just another checklist."

She shook her head. "Go ahead and take a look at the system. We're going to have to clear the scene. I can't keep her out of the house much longer. I want another look around while I'm here."

She went through the room, this time focusing more narrowly on Ava's things. The clothes, the shoes, the lingerie. Expensive, fashionable, but on the sedate side, Eve supposed. As fit the proper woman, of a conservative bent, of her social and financial level. Nothing too flashy, everything high-end.

Eve circled the bedroom with its surplus of gilt and shine. Maybe not exactly flashy, she mused, but certainly ornate. Ava's Palace. Which was the truer reflection of the woman?

The dressing area held a salon's worth of cosmetic enhancers. Creams, lotions, rejuvenators, skin boosters lived behind shining silver doors in the bath area. Bath salts and oils filled tall clear jars arranged like art on various shelves.

Liked to pamper herself, liked to sink into the deep jet tub or stand under the sprays of the silver-walled shower and luxuriate—in an area separate from her husband's.

This is yours, this is mine.

Yet they shared a bed. Still, with a bed that size, if sex or companionship wasn't on the menu, they might as well have been sleeping in separate counties. Walking back, Eve touched one of the gold rungs on the footboard.

"This was her room," she said aloud. "Hers. He just happened to be in it. She tolerated that. Tolerated his presence, his fussy morning routine because it was hers. She *allowed* him here as long as he was useful."

Stepping out, she sealed the door again, then went down to find Roarke.

He'd pulled his hair back with a twist of leather and sat at the controls in the security area. Besides the extensive equipment built in, Roarke had one of his own handheld devices on the counter.

"It's an excellent system. One of mine," he said with a casual glance over his shoulder. "So I know it quite well. It's been extensively customized for this site. Every available option's in here. I won't say it's absolutely impossible to breach or operate by long-distance remote, but I will say if the client had ordered such a thing, he would've been advised it could compromise his system. And, if he still wanted that ability, it would've been custom-made. We'd have a paper trail. I'll check on that, but I sincerely doubt he authorized something like that."

"And the short range?"

"Every security system can be breached, and I've breached most of them myself. In my misspent youth."

"You were still misspending a couple of years ago, pal."

"Only for . . . entertainment purposes. In any case, this system's alarms and cameras were shut down by short range. But the code was keyed in before the backup went on. That was quick work, either by someone with an excellent clone or in possession of the code. Whoever it was needed only to stand out of camera range, shut them down, along with the alarms, then walk up to the keypad and do the rest. With the right equipment, a child could have done it."

"But Ava Anders didn't. Disappointing," she admitted.

"Now I have to find out who did her dirty work. Let's close up here. I want to pay a call on the way home."

"It seems to be our week for it."

They found Sasha Bride-West at home—barely. She answered the door herself, wrapped in luxurious layers of white mink. But the interruption didn't appear to trouble her in the least. Not when she leveled her gaze at Roarke and purred, "Well, hello."

"Sorry to disturb you," Eve said. "Can I have a minute?"

"You can have a minute." She aimed a sultry smile at Roarke. "How long do *you* want?"

"He's with me. Sasha Bride-West. Roarke."

"Yes, I know." She offered her hand, back up, as a woman does who hopes it'll be kissed. "We met once, briefly. I'm devastated you don't remember."

"I'll remember now."

She laughed, stepped back. "Come in. I'm on my way out to meet some friends. I'm always late anyway."

"On your way to see Mrs. Anders?" Eve asked.

"Dressed like this?" Sasha tossed the white coat aside. Under it she wore riotous red, thin and snug as a layer of skin. Sven did good work. "Hardly. Ava's in seclusion until the memorial tomorrow. I do have other friends." She sent Roarke that smile again. "I always have room for more."

"For the moment, maybe we can stick to Ava."

"All right." She gestured, glided on silvery heels into a living area as bold and brash as she was. She slid into a chair. Eve wasn't sure how she managed to sit in a dress that tight and cross her legs. "What about Ava?"

"I'm just confirming some time lines, for the report. Routine stuff."

"Do you always drop by unannounced at night—and with such a gorgeous companion—for routine stuff?"

"We were out." Roarke took a seat beside Sasha, kept his tone casual. "My wife rarely leaves the cop behind."

"Poor you."

"On the morning of Mr. Anders's murder," Eve continued, "what time did Mrs. Anders wake you to tell you what had happened?"

"She didn't."

"She didn't wake you when she learned her husband was dead?"

"I don't know if she believed he was, honestly. She left a message cube. It was Bridge who woke me. About eight-thirty. A bit before nine in any case. In a state. I remember being annoyed at first as I didn't have my facial scheduled until eleven. She said Ava was gone, something had happened to Tommy. I . . ."

She let out a breath, and the brashness ebbed away. "I made some careless, callous remark, which I very much regret. Something like, 'For Christ's sake, unless he's dropped dead on the sixth green, let me sleep.' Then Bridge played the message, and it was awful. You could hear the panic and tears in Ava's voice."

"What did she say in the message?"

"I remember exactly. 'Greta called. Something's happened to Tommy. Something terrible's happened. I have to go home.' She left the message on the table in the parlor. We shared a three-bedroom suite, so she left it on the table."

"What did you do?"

"Well, we called her right away, called her 'link. She was very shaken, as you can imagine. She told us Greta had said Tommy was dead. That he was dead in his bed, but she was sure that was a mistake. That he must be ill, so she needed to get right home. She'd call us as soon as she got there, and took care of things."

"Thank you. That's very helpful." Eve waited until Sasha rose to lead them back to the door. "It's a shame she didn't wake you and Mrs. Plowder. She wouldn't have had to make that difficult trip alone."

"Brigit was furious about that, the kind of mad you get when you're incredibly worried. I don't know how many times that morning I said to her not to worry about that, how Ava must've been panicked. How she must not have been able to think of anything but getting home. It was an awful morning for all of us, Lieutenant. When Ava called to tell us Tommy was gone, we were already packed. I guess we knew she wasn't coming back. That trip, it's always the three of us, and...how do you mistake death? We knew she wouldn't be able to come back."

Outside Eve walked with Roarke through the crystal cold. "Panicked," she repeated, "can't think of anything but getting home. But you can think to leave a message cube. Not to wake your friends, sleeping right in the next rooms. But you can think of ordering a croissant and matching your wrist unit with a bracelet."

"She didn't want them to see her." Roarke opened the passenger door, then stood looking at Eve over it. "She didn't want them with her, didn't want to have to put on the façade on the trip back."

"No, she didn't. She wanted a little alone time, so she could sit and wallow in how fucking clever she'd been." Her eyes were flat again, cold again. "I'm going to nail her ass, Roarke. Then we'll see how clever she is."

Chapter 10

Under the pulsing jets of the shower the next morning, Eve considered her options. She could bring Ava in, try to sweat a confession—fat chance—out of her, or just shake her confidence by letting her know she was being watched.

And she'd lawyer up in a quick, fast minute, sob to the media, and possibly Tibble's wife. Which would, most likely, alienate possible sources of information such as Forrest, Plowder, and Bride-West.

Sweating her might be satisfying, but likely unproductive at this stage.

She could continue to scrape at layers, cutting through the dirt and the bull until she found enough inconsistencies, enough probable cause to make a solid case.

But it had to be faced, she admitted, ordering the jets off to step into the drying tube. The woman was good. She'd covered her undoubtedly surgically sculpted ass in every direction. Where was the loose end? Eve asked herself as the warm air blew around her. Where was the person whose hands had secured the ropes? Where was the person who'd walked into that bedroom and done the deed Eve was flat-out sure Ava had designed?

A lover was a hard sell. The woman had a husband and a twice-monthly LC, and only so many hours in a day. Could Ava have squeezed in an affair, have juggled that many balls without anyone who knew her suspecting? Not impossible, not for someone that organized and calculating, but . . . a hard sell.

A friend? Could Plowder or Bride-West—or both—have conspired to kill Thomas Anders? What incentive could Ava have offered them to commit murder? She rolled that around while she pulled on a robe and walked into the bedroom to hunt up clothes.

Roarke sat drinking coffee and scratching Galahad between the ears. Sometime during her shower, she noted, he'd switched from stock reports to the morning news. "They've just run a brief interview with Ben on today's memorial. More of a quick statement, really, as he wouldn't answer any questions on the nature of his uncle's death or the investigation. He looked shattered."

Eve went with black because it was easiest and made it simpler to blend in during a memorial. "Let me ask you this, taking away the fact you like this guy personally. Could he have been having an affair with Ava?"

Roarke muted the screen, watching Eve as she dressed. "I can't imagine him betraying his uncle in that way—in any way, really—but particularly in that way. Even if his love for Anders was a sham, Ava isn't his type."

"Why not?"

"He tends toward younger, career-oriented, athletic types who'd be happy kicking back with a beer." He paused as she strapped on her weapon. "Good thing I snatched you up before he saw you."

"Well, now I know where to go when I'm done with you. Try this one on. The three women go off to St. Lucia. They go off somewhere together every year, so nobody thinks anything of it. But this year they have more to do than get wrapped in papaya leaves and suck down mimosas."

She shrugged into her jacket, and as Roarke observed, didn't so much as glance in the mirror as she crossed over to get coffee.

"One of them comes back to New York clandestinely, kills Tommy as per Ava's plan while Ava's ass is covered on St. Lucia. Ava's there when Greta calls, and she takes her time leaving. Giving her partner time to get back. Then she takes the shuttle home while the other two wait a reasonable amount of time, then call her to cement the story."

"Involving all three of them? Risky."

"Maybe Bride-West was still asleep, just as she said in her statement. They slip something in her martini, whatever, and . . . I'm not buying this myself, so why am I trying to sell it to you?"

He rose, placed his hands on her shoulders, kissed her brow. Then knowing she'd never think to do it herself, walked over to program some breakfast.

"It had to be someone she could trust. Absolutely. Without question. Someone who would kill for her. Her parents are divorced. One lives in Portland, one lives in Chicago. Both remarried. Nothing jumped up and bit me on the runs I did on them, and I can't find any record of either of them traveling anywhere, much less New York on the night in question. She has no siblings. As far as I can determine she hasn't seen her ex-husband in about two decades. Who does she know, who does she trust to kill for her and to kill in a very specific way?"

Roarke carried back plates of bacon and eggs. Galahad feigned disinterest. "You'll have to get the coffee if you're after more. If I take my eyes off these plates for two seconds, this food will be in the cat's belly."

Eve frowned at the plates. "I was going to grab—"

"Now you're not. Get the coffee, I'm after more."

She could've argued. Thinking about the case made her want to argue, blow off the steam of it. But she wanted another hit of coffee. She got two mugs, came back, and plopped down.

"I got nothing. I got nothing on her. No connection that works. And I'm talking myself into circles."

"Maybe you'll come up with something more linear when we see her at the memorial today."

The eggs were there, so she stabbed a forkful. "You're going?"

"Ben and I are friendly. Anders Worldwide is in my building. I'll pay my respects. And maybe I'll catch something you've missed. Fresh eyes."

"Fresh eyes." She picked up a piece of bacon, then swore. "Fresh eyes, damn it. I forgot. I promised Baxter I'd take a look at a case file for him. Going cold. I've been putting him off. Damn it." She bit into the bacon. "I'll have to do it this morning."

"That might be a good thing. Put your mind on that for a bit, let it rest on the other."

"Maybe. I told him some of them get by us. We can't close them all. It burns my ass to think this one could get away from me."

Galahad bellied over an inch, two inches, his bicolored eyes fixed on Roarke's plate. Roarke simply shifted his gaze, stared, and Galahad rolled onto his back to paw lazily at the air. "No one believes you're innocent," he said to the cat.

"Everyone believes she is," Eve murmured. "Hmm. What happens if somebody doesn't?" Turning that over in her mind she ate her breakfast before Galahad made his next move.

Before her shift began, Eve sat in her office at Central with Baxter's murder book on the Custer case. She studied the crime-scene photos first, as if coming to it fresh, without the input of the ME, the sweepers, the investigator's notes, the interviews.

Somebody, she thought, had done a quick, hard number on one Ned Custer. The room itself looked like a typical sex flop. Cheap bed, sagging mattress where Christ knew what microscopic vermin partied in a variety of body fluids. Particleboard dresser, fly-spotted mirror, dull, yellowing floor, crappy paper drapes at the crappy little window. A bad joke of a bath with a rust-stained, wall-hung sink and a toilet where more vermin partied.

The cliché of sex flops, she thought.

What kind of man was Ned Custer, who needed to get his rocks off in an ugly little dump while the wife and kiddies waited at home?

A pretty damn dead one. The slash across the throat went deep, went long. Sharp blade with some muscle behind it. And some height, she mused, checking the angle. Vic topped off at five-nine. The killer...Eve closed her eyes, put herself in the nasty room, put herself behind Custer. Had to be at least the same height, probably an inch or two taller.

Tall for a woman then, but a lot of street whores went for high platforms and heels. Still, not a shortie.

And no one who owned a delicate stomach. It took steel-lined to hack off a guy's dick.

The blood spatters and pools told the story clearly enough. The killer stepped out of the excuse for a bathroom, attacked the victim from behind. One fast slash. No hesitation. Had to get some backsplash from that kind of blood jet. More blood from the homemade castration. With no blood in the drains, the killer either exited carting the blood—no trail, so unlikely—or came out of the bathroom sealed and protected.

Not a street whore. Not even one pumped up on illegals. Too prepared, too vicious. A whore wants to roll a mark, maybe she sticks him, but more likely she gets herself a zapper off the black market, immobilizes and cops his money and jewelry. Walks away.

Custer was dead before he walked in that room, he just didn't know it. Would anyone have done? she wondered. Or was it target specific?

She dug deeper, shooting out a message for Baxter and Trueheart to report to her when they came on shift. And she made her own notes.

She grunted at the tap on her doorjamb, then glanced up at Trueheart in his spotless uniform. "You wanted to see me, Lieutenant."

"Yeah. Where's Baxter?"

"He's not in yet. I, um, try to get in a little before shift when I can, to look over yesterday's work."

"Uh-huh." Eager beaver, she mused. Young but steady, with a good eye. And he'd lost a lot of the green he'd had on him when she'd first seen him on scooper detail. "I've been looking over the Custer murder book. You and Baxter were thorough. How many cases have you caught since?"

"Nine," he said immediately. "Two open. Plus Custer, so that's three open."

"What's your take on this one?"

"The vic led a dangerous kind of life, Lieutenant. He cruised the bars and the red lights, picked up his dates from low-level LCs. We talked to a lot of working girls and found a couple who remembered him. They, ah, said he liked it fast and rough—and ah, cheap."

"I see that. You covered the area of the crime scene, did the door to doors, hit the bars, the working girls."

"Nobody remembers who he went off with that night, other than a couple saying he might've been hooked up with a redhead. Short, straight hair—or short curly hair, depending on the wit. You know how it is."

"Yeah."

"It's not the kind of area where people remember. The guy working the desk on the flop said maybe he'd seen her before, maybe not, but he's pretty sure about the hair that night. He's on the red, short, straight side."

She'd read all this in the book, but let Trueheart wind it out.

"One thing he swears on is she didn't come back down. If he didn't check them off when they came down, how could he turn the room? He gets paid on the turn. So he swears she didn't come back by the desk, and you can't get out the front without going by the desk. The fire escape was engaged. She had to go out through the window and down. And the scene, it was full of prints and DNA, fiber, hair. It's not the kind of place where housekeeping's a priority. We ran everything, interviewed everyone when we could find a match and locate the individual. Nobody stands out."

She started to speak, held off as Baxter hurried up to join his aide. "This about Custer?"

"I've reviewed the book. It's a thorough investigation so far."

"Without a single suspect."

"You're not looking at the wife."

"She's alibied up, Dallas, literally on her house 'link trying to reach the vic when he was being sliced. Trueheart and I were the ones to notify. She wasn't faking her reaction."

"No like crimes before or after, not following this pattern. It smells target specific."

"Yeah, it does."

"So who benefits?"

Baxter raked his fingers through his hair. "Okay, the wife gets rid of a guy who cheats and may be bringing home an all-you-can-eat buffet of STDs, and who tunes her up when the whim strikes. She comes into a pension and life insurance policy through his employment. Not princely, but solid. But she wasn't there, that's a fact. The vic wasn't going to go into that flop with his wife when he hunted strange. And he'd've recognized her. She's three inches over five feet so she's not tall enough or strong enough to have made the cut."

"Maybe she knew somebody who was. A relative, a friend, somebody who thought she was better off with the cheating, heavy-handed husband dead. And she is."

"She's got a sister down in Arkansas, a father doing a dime on assault with intent down there, and who used to knock *his* wife around. Her mother's in New Jersey, but believe me, she couldn't have pulled this off either. As for friends, she doesn't have anybody she's tight with.

Sure as hell not tight enough to slit her husband's throat for her."

"A boyfriend. The killer skews tall and strong for a female."

"Working a team." Baxter's eyes changed as he considered. "Guy's already in the bathroom, she brings the mark in . . . Then why doesn't she just go out the front? Why—"

"Lots of whys," Eve interrupted. "Who says he went up there with a woman?"

Trueheart cleared his throat. "Um, everybody, sir."

"And did everybody see the killer's plumbing? You've seen enough trannies, Baxter, to know how pretty they are when they're on the stroll. If you're not looking close enough, if you've had a few brews under your belt, a guy could find a big surprise when he reaches into the box. Everybody sees a woman, so you're looking for a woman."

"And don't I feel stupid," Baxter mumbled. "I never made the lateral move to male possibility."

"Wife's got a secret admirer, he might be man enough to dress like a woman."

"Sir? Lieutenant?" Trueheart nearly raised his hand. "It's hard to see how Mrs. Custer could've had a relationship, a boyfriend. She's got those kids, and none of her neighbors reported seeing anyone visiting her apartment regularly. We looked at that, because you have to, but we didn't find anything that indicated she had a boyfriend."

"A woman with a husband who likes to use his fists learns to be a careful woman." Eve glanced back at her own murder board. "And maybe I'm letting some of my own investigation bleed over into my thoughts on yours." She swiveled back, held out the murder book. "You've got two fresher cases open, but find time to poke at the boyfriend angle, and the doing her a favor."

"Since we'd run out of angles, I appreciate it. Come on, faithful sidekick." Baxter dropped a hand on Trueheart's shoulder. "Let's go think about men in dresses."

She toggled her mind back to her own case, checked her incomings and her messages. The lab in its better-late-than-even-more-late mode verified what Roarke had already told her. Voiceprint match. Rising, she added that report to her board.

"Good morning!" Bright, bouncing, and beaming, Peabody sang out the greeting and shook a pink bakery box. "I've got crullers."

"And you got through the bullpen alive?"

"I bought two boxes, tossed one at the rioting horde as I came through."

"That's not stupid."

"I would've come back before, but you were with Baxter and Trueheart, and I was collecting my kudos."

"I thought they were crullers."

With a laugh, Peabody set the box on Eve's desk. "I'm celebrating with pastries because I looked really good last night. I know how the camera's supposed to add pounds, but I didn't look tubbo. I think it was the jacket. It's slimming, and the way the buttons run and all, they trick the eye. And I was sitting on my ass, so that wasn't a problem. Jesus, I was so nervous. Completely freaked."

She dug in the box, pulled out a cruller and bit in. "Trina was great, sort of talking me down. She says you're due for a treatment, by the way."

"She's due for an ass-kicking."

"And McNab was mag, seriously mag." Peabody licked sugar off her thumb. "But you have all those people and the cameras and if you think about how many *other* people are sitting home watching, you'll throw up. Nadine was the ult, she really eased me in. But she didn't baby me, so I didn't come off like a moron. When we got home, McNab and I watched the segment like twelve times, and had lots and lots of celebration sex. Boy, I feel *great!* So what did you think when you watched it?"

"I was busy."

The bright, beaming bounce dropped hard through the

trapdoor of shock. "You didn't . . . But I thought you'd—oh."

Eve let it sit for another five seconds, but even she couldn't be that mean. And there were crullers. "Jesus, Peabody, you're easy. Of course I watched. I had to know if you screwed up and I needed to kick your ass, didn't I? You didn't screw up."

The beam bounced back. "I really didn't. McNab said I sounded smart and completely on top. And I looked sexy. Did you think so?"

"I dreamed of you all night. Can we move on now?"

"One more thing. Thanks for pushing me into this. I won't be so freaky about it next time. Oh, oh, and just another thing. Mavis and Leonardo tagged us when we were on our way home from the studio, and Mavis said Belle smiled and cooed when she saw me on screen. Okay, done." She took another bite of her cruller.

"If you're ready to set your kudos aside, we're in the field. Anders Worldwide."

"The memorial's this afternoon," Peabody reminded her. "I don't think Forrest will be in. Do you want me to check?"

"No. He may not be in, but I bet his admin is. And I like the drop-in. Let's move."

Eve grabbed her coat, considered the crullers. If she left them there, out in the open, even the box would be devoured when she got back. She could hide it, but the vultures would sniff it out, which could lead them to the candy she'd stashed where—so far—the Candy Thief hadn't discovered it.

She snatched up the box on the way out. Better safe than crullerless.

Leopold Walsh had struck Eve as a man who manned his station, and guarded his prince whatever the crisis. She was right. He met them in his office—sober eyes, dark suit, and a black armband.

"I don't expect Mr. Forrest today," Leopold began. "Mr. Anders's memorial is scheduled for two this afternoon."

"We're aware of that." No offer of coffee, Eve noted, no invitation to sit. Don't like us much, do you, Leo? "Mr. Forrest and his uncle were very close, personally and professionally. Would you agree with that assessment?"

"I would."

"As you work closely with Mr. Forrest, you'd be privy to their dealings together."

"Of course."

Eve smiled. She had to admire a man who knew how to answer without saying anything. "I imagine you formed opinions regarding Thomas Anders—professionally and personally."

"I hardly see how my opinion is relevant."

"Humor me."

"In my opinion, Mr. Thomas Anders was a fair and honest man who brought that fairness and honesty into business. He trusted, correctly, that his nephew would do the same."

"The manner of Mr. Anders's death must have caused some speculation and gossip within the organization, and its accounts."

Leopold's jaw tightened. "People will talk, Lieutenant. It's human nature."

But you don't, she thought. No juicy office gossip for you. But you hear it, file it.

"What's the buzz about Mrs. Anders?"

"I don't understand what you mean."

Tighten that jaw another notch, Leo, something's going to snap. "Yes, you do."

"Mrs. Anders devoted—devotes—much of her considerable energy into the charitable and humanitarian programs sponsored by Anders Worldwide. She's very well respected."

"She puts in time around here?"

"Of course, though she most often works from home, or by attending or hostessing functions."

"You'd have been privy to her dealings with her husband, and with his nephew."

"Somewhat certainly, as Ben—as Mr. Forrest was gradually taking over his uncle's duties. Some of those duties involved the programs. I'm sorry, Lieutenant, I have a very crowded day, and a very difficult one. If that's all—"

"It's not. How would you describe the relationship between Mr. Forrest and—shit, let's simplify. How did Ben and Ava get along?"

"They were very cordial, of course. Ben admired her talent and her energy, and was certainly impressed with many of her ideas."

"Cordial. Not affectionate. He strikes me as an easy and affectionate sort, but you choose the cooler, more formal, 'cordial' to describe their relationship."

"Mrs. Anders was his uncle's wife." Leopold's tone was equally cool and formal. "Their relationship was perfectly proper."

"'Proper,' there's another cool term. Ben doesn't like her much, does he? Neither do you."

"I've said or implied nothing of the kind. I don't—"

"Relax. I don't like her either. So, you can keep standing there with that rod up your ass or . . ." She dropped into a chair without invitation. "Tell me why. Record off, Peabody," Eve said as she switched off her own. "Just the three of us, Leo. Off record. What about Ava sticks in your craw?"

Eve watched him debate. Propriety or the opportunity to speak his mind. Opportunity won. "She's studied, she's deliberate, and she's cold. Those aren't crimes, but personality traits. And . . ."

"Don't stop now." Eve lifted her hands, palms up in invitation.

"There's a pettiness about her. She would often circumvent Ben by making plans or decisions without consulting him or seeking his input. Her plans and decisions were always well thought out and researched. She had—has—excellent ideas. But it's been her habit to brush over Ben, a very deliberate habit. In my opinion."

"How'd Ben take that?"

"It frustrated him from time to time, though I admit, it frustrated me more."

"Did he ever complain to his uncle?"

"Not to my knowledge, and I believe I would know. He might complain to me, or use me as a sounding board. Invariably, after he had he'd say the same thing. 'Well, it's the end result that matters.' Mrs. Anders gets excellent results."

"I believe that."

"I think . . ."

"We're off record, Leo. What do you think?"

"I think she often did the same regarding Mr. Anders. That is, failed to keep him in the loop until whatever she planned was essentially a *fait accompli*. There was some office gossip, and I don't like office gossip."

"Me, I love it. How about you, Peabody?"

"Revs up the day. What kind of gossip?" Peabody asked Leo.

"There was talk that she charged certain personal expenses to program budget. Household purchases, wardrobe, salons, that sort of thing. Nothing major, you understand. That pettiness again, from my point of view. I heard Mr. Anders, I mean Mr. Reginald Anders, called her on it."

"Her father-in-law? When would this be?"

"I couldn't say, exactly. He's been gone nearly two years now. I only remember the talk because they got along very well, so the reprimand—if there was one— wouldn't be expected."

Leopold shifted his stance. "I don't understand why this matters to you."

"Oh, every little thing matters to me. This reprimand, that may or may not have happened? How did they get along afterward?"

"Back to status quo. I believe she sent Mr. Reginald a box of his favorite caramel creams as an apology."

"Hmm. Mrs. Anders's position here rises with the death of her husband. The late Mr. Anders held fifty-five percent of the shares in the company, Ben came in with fifteen, and Ava held a token two percent. Is that correct?"

"I believe so."

She had his attention now, Eve noted. Big-time.

"At his death, those fifty-five shares are divided between Ben and Ava. Forty to Ben, giving him controlling interest. But fifteen added to Ava's original two brings her well up in the world. And there are twenty-eight more shares out there. A smart, resourceful woman should be able to get her fingers on a few of those, particularly when her two closest friends hold small percentages. She could bump that share up to thirty, thirty-five without breaking too much of a sweat. That's a powerful chunk of a company like this. And you know what, Leo, now that we're just pals chatting, you don't seem shocked and surprised by what I'm implying here."

"If you're asking if I believe Mrs. Anders killed her husband, no, I don't. She was out of the country, and the nature . . . the circumstances of his death are a personal humiliation to her. She's not a woman who enjoys humiliation. If you're asking if I'm surprised you'd find her capable of killing, again, no, I'm not."

"I'm a cop. Nobody's surprised that I think anyone's capable of killing. Why do you believe she's capable?"

Leopold was either relaxed enough now, or interested enough to take a seat. "I don't like her, on a personal level. I find her ruthless, under a veneer of sophistication, under a guise of good works. The good works—this is my opinion—they didn't matter to her as much as the attention she gained from them, the media and the accolades. She resents Ben because his uncle doted on him, and I think, because people enjoy and admire Ben. She didn't love her husband."

"At last!" Eve slapped a hand on her leg. "Somebody says it. Why did you?"

Leopold's eyes widened at Eve's reaction. "I—I honestly don't know. She was invariably affectionate, even attentive. Patient. But every now and then there was a tone, or a look. I can only tell you that I don't believe she loved him, but she loved being Ava Anders. Everything I've said here is off the record. Everything I've said here I'll deny on the record."

"We're just talking here. Anything to add, Peabody?"

"You covered a lot. I was just thinking that one of the quickest and surest ways to gain sympathy and support is to be humiliated by the actions of another. A little red-face might be a reasonable trade-off for all the shoulders, all the 'isn't she brave's.' It's a thought."

Leopold stared. "She was in St. Lucia."

"Yeah, she was." Eve nodded, pushed to her feet. "Still, it's interesting. You might want to mention to Ben that my partner and I came by and were asking you these interesting questions about Ava. Meanwhile, I'd like to have copies of all the files on all the projects she worked on. With Ben, or otherwise."

"All? For the last sixteen years?"

"No, all the way back to when she started at the company." She grinned at the way that previously tight jaw dropped. "Might as well be thorough."

"There will be hundreds. Hundreds of hundreds."

"Then you'd better get started."

"This will take a little time. You may want to wait in the client lounge."

"We'll come back. An hour enough time?"

"Yes, that should do."

In the elevator, Peabody turned to Eve. "How did you know he'd be the go-to guy on this?"

"He's in love with Ben. Knows it's hopeless, but he can't help what he feels. First, anything that has to do with Ben, he's going to pick up on his emotional radar. Second, I figure somebody who's got all those repressed feelings recognizes when someone else's feelings are a sham. Third? We got really lucky, pushed the right button at the right time. Contact Edmond Luce. I'm betting he and his wife are still in New York. I want another talk with him."

Chapter 11

Luce and his wife remained in New York, in residence in one of the ritzy suites at Roarke's Palace Hotel. Linny Luce—Eve wondered how she felt about ending up with that name—opened the door and introduced herself.

She was what Eve thought of as a solid woman, well-built and compact like an efficient car designed for low maintenance and long usage. Thick brown hair with white wings framed a face more handsome than pretty. She wore a long-skirted black suit with sensible low-heeled boots and exquisite pearls. Her handshake was firm and businesslike.

"Edmond is on the 'link with London. He shouldn't be long. Please sit. I ordered up tea. It's quite good here. But I expect you know that, it being your husband's establishment."

She sat on the fat cream and white cushions of the sofa, poured out. "Milk or lemon?"

Neither was going to make Eve like tea any more than she did. "Just black, thanks."

"Detective?"

"Milk, one sugar, thanks."

"This is a difficult day for us. I hope you'll understand how I mean it when I say your call was a welcome distraction. Edmond and I . . . we can't quite fathom what to do with ourselves. After the memorial . . . Maybe it will be easier after the memorial, after we go back home."

She sighed, looking toward the wide windows that opened to the towers of New York. "Life goes on, doesn't it? It has to."

"You knew Mr. Anders a long time."

"Yes. Edmond and Tommy were friends longer, of course. But I knew Tommy over forty years. We can't think what to do with ourselves. I'm sorry, I said that, didn't I?"

"Can I ask you, Mrs. Luce, since you knew him well before his marriage, if you could tell us if he had any serious relationships before his wife?"

"Serious? I wouldn't say. He enjoyed the company of women, but he simply enjoyed the company of people. We used to tease him quite a bit about settling down. I admit I tried matchmaking a few times."

"I wonder if you could give me some names and contact information, of women you remember Mr. Anders . . . enjoying."

"Yes, I could do that." Linny looked straight into Eve's eyes. "You're asking this because of the way he was killed. That was not Tommy. I will never believe otherwise."

"When did you first meet Ava Anders?"

"Oh, she was still working for Anders—a public relations exec. I can't recall her title, if I ever knew. I first met her at a charity event here in New York. Ava had done the PR. A fund-raiser for one of the sports camps Tommy built. Black-tie, with dinner and dancing, a silent auction, an orchestra. Very elaborate, as I recall. She was very bright and clever. I remember watching them dancing at some point during the evening, and telling Edmond Tommy better watch out with that one."

"Watch out?"

"I suppose what I meant was, she very much had her eye on him, and seemed a woman who knew how to get what she wanted. Which proved to be true. It wasn't long after that they began to see each other socially, and whenever the four of us got together, it was obvious he was besotted by her, and she so . . . tickled by him."

"Did you like her?"

Linny's eyes widened. "Yes, of course, I did. Do. The four of us had some very lovely times together."

"Would you say he remained besotted and she tickled?"

"It's very difficult even for good friends to judge the inside of another's marriage. And marriages evolve and adjust. They remained devoted to each other, certainly."

"Friends, women friends," Peabody put in, "often discuss aspects of their marriage with each other. Dish a little on their husbands, vent their frustrations, have some laughs over the little quirks and habits."

"They do," Linny said with a smile. "Yes, they do. Ava and I aren't intimate in that way. We get along quite well, but we don't have as warm or close a relationship, you might say, as Tommy and I did. Frankly, Tommy was the glue there. I enjoy an afternoon at the football pitch, and Ava preferred the shops and galleries. I have grandchildren, and she doesn't. I'm fifteen years her senior, after all."

She glanced over as her husband strode in. "There you are, Edmond."

"Sorry for the delay. Lieutenant, Detective." He sat like a man weary to the bone. "There's to be a memorial in London, in fact, in every city around the world with an Anders base. There were details I needed to address quickly."

Linny put a hand on his knee, patted it briskly in a gesture that translated absolute unity to Eve. "You'll have some tea now."

"Mr. Luce, with Mr. Anders's death, how much influence in the company will Mrs. Anders gain?"

"Considerable, if she wants it, I suppose, but Ava's never been interested in the business per se. In the charities, the programs, the publicity, but not the mechanics of running things. That will be for Ben." He let out a long sigh. "In fact, he called just as I was finishing with London. He plans to arrange a meeting of the board and executive officers early next week. He's asked me to consider coming on as his second in command."

"Oh, Edmond."

"I know." It was his turn to pat his wife's knee. "I planned to ease back a bit. More than a bit," he admitted. "With the goal of retiring within the next two years. I hadn't told Tommy yet. In fact, I planned to broach the subject when we golfed, the day . . . the day he died. He'd want me to help Ben during the transition, Linny. I may still make that two-year goal."

"Mr. Luce, did Ben indicate he'd discussed this with Mrs. Anders?"

"No, why would he?"

"She has a seventeen percent share of the company now."

"Yes, yes, of course. I'm sorry, I'm not thinking very clearly today. In any case, as I said, Ava's never been interested in the company."

"But as the next majority shareholder, as the widow of the company's president, she would be within her rights to expect a more hands-on position, a seat on the board maybe—and all that goes along with that."

"Technically, yes, I suppose so. But realistically, I can't imagine it."

"You knew Reginald Anders?"

"Oh yes." Edmond's face lightened with a smile. "In fact, it was Reggie who first hired me, more than half a century ago."

"At his death, Thomas Anders inherited the majority share of the company, correct?"

"Yes. As Ben will now. Tommy considered Ben his son, and followed his own father's lead on that."

"Just so I have all the details straight. I understand Ava Anders has a small percentage of the company—well, a larger one now. But the initial share, did she come into that at her father-in-law's death?"

"I believe that's correct. Reggie was very fond of Ava."

"All right, we appreciate you seeing us at a difficult time." Her 'link signaled, and checking the display, she ordered it to answer, identify, and hold. "I need to take this. Is it possible I could use another room?"

"Of course." Linny got quickly to her feet. "Let me show you to the office. Would you like to take your tea?"

"No, that's fine." She followed her hostess into a top-flight office done with plush leather and glossy wood.

"I'll write down those names you asked for while you're taking your call. Be comfortable," Linny told her, and backing out, closed the double doors behind her.

Eve engaged her 'link. "This is Lieutenant Dallas, Mr. Bronson, thank you for holding."

"Well, well. If I'd known you were this attractive, I'd have gotten back to you sooner. What can I do for you, Lieutenant Brown Eyes?"

"First, you can cut the crap."

"Mmm. I love 'em sassy." He grinned at her, the same shit-eating grin from his official ID photo. Eve figured he'd practiced and perfected that one in the mirror. "So tell me what a sassy, brown-eyed police lieutenant from New York wants with Dirk."

Dirk, she thought, was a complete asshole who had smooth, tanned cheeks that told her he'd had considerable and skilled work. Golden brows arched over eyes of Mediterranean blue like the sea she caught glimpses of behind him. His golden hair waved in the undoubtedly balmy breeze.

"You were married to an Ava Montgomery."

"Wasn't I just? A brief yet memorable episode in my past. Don't tell me Ava's in trouble." He laughed as though little could amuse him more. "What did she do? Hire the wrong caterer?"

"Her current husband was murdered a few days ago."

"Really?" His eyebrows quirked, and for a moment his face seemed to hold an expression other than smug conceit. "That's . . . inconvenient. He's a, what is it, a sporting goods king or something? I believe I own one of his tennis rackets." Then he laughed, all brassy amusement. "Do you think I killed him? After all these years, to win back the fair Ava? This is exciting."

"Why don't you tell me where you were on March eighteenth, and we'll get that little joke out of the way."

"Cruising the Aegean, as I am now—with a bevy of beauties, a number of friends, and a full crew. Would you like to come interrogate me?"

"I'll keep that in reserve. When's the last time you saw your ex-wife?"

"Which ex-wife?"

"Don't waste my time, Dirk."

"So serious. Let's see, when did Dirk last lay eyes on the lovely Ava? Ten years ago? No, longer. How time does fly. Closer to fifteen, I think. I bumped elbows with her in New York, if memory serves, at some party or premiere. Whatever. I believe she'd been recently married to the sports king."

"Why did you and Ava divorce?"

"Who remembers? I'm sure I strayed, as I do enjoy variety. Dirk is no damn good and has a selection of ex wives and women who would be delighted to verify that."

"She didn't satisfy you sexually?"

Avid amusement shone in his eyes. "Well, aren't we nosy?"

She saw him shift, heard the rattle of ice in a glass, then watched him sip something tall and rosy. "She was—and my memory is clear on this—delightful in bed, and other interesting places. We wouldn't have gotten as far as marriage otherwise. But I have a weak will and a roving eye. In any case, I wasn't ambitious enough for her as I was—and am—content to coast and cruise. She wanted something— someone—who would provide her with opportunities for money and fame, respect. Like, I imagine, the dead sports king. I enjoy my sloth. We weren't suited."

"So she left you."

"With a tidy sum and not a backward glance. Her cold heart and steely resolve were part of her appeal to me. As I recall, she introduced me to the woman I strayed with, and gave me far too many opportunities to take advantage. But somehow, she didn't see it as her fault when I took advantage. Imagine that!"

"Imagine that. Thanks for your time."

"It's been entertaining. If you ever want to coast or cruise, be sure to look me up."

"Yeah, I'll jump right on that." She clicked off, stood for a moment absorbing. Then she went out to take leave of the Luces.

"Sounds like a big, oily ball of smile," Peabody commented after Eve filled her in.

"Yeah, he does. Polar opposite of Anders."

"Devil's advocate. A woman gets burned like that, it's reasonable she'd look for a completely different type."

"Yeah, absolutely logical, absolutely reasonable. Good plan."

"You really think plan? Like, okay, sleazy ex-husband dispatched. Check. Now hook nice guy with deep pockets?"

"She introduced the ex to the woman he cheated with. Read between the lines, Peabody. If you know a kid's addicted to ice cream, do you put a big chocolate sundae in front of him and walk away? If you want out of a marriage with a tidy sum, sympathy, and no fault on you, what better way than to set up your weak-willed, roving-eyed husband? It's something she'd do. It's exactly something she'd do.

"I want to talk to Greta again. You go back, pick up the files. If you need help transporting, order it up. When you get back to Central, do a search for repeating names. Any that show multiple times in any program. Run those first."

She pulled over, spoke over the ensuing storm of horns. "Take the wheel. I'll catch a cab, then tap Roarke for a ride to the memorial."

She checked the address in her book, then decided to walk a few blocks to clear her head before engaging in the war for a cab. Since she was on foot, she pulled out her 'link to check on Feeney.

He answered, honking like a dying goose. "Man, you sound sick."

"I *am* sick. Goddamn it. You think I'm lying here in bed drinking this disgusting boiled tree bark they gave me for my health?"

She waited a beat. "Well. Yeah."

"I'm burning up. I've got hot shards of glass in my throat and ten pounds of snot in my head. And what do they do? What do they do?" His eyes bugged out like glass marbles. "They give me fucking liquid tree bark and the wife's poured so much chicken soup down me, I'm starting to cluck. I don't want to die here in this damn bed. If this is the end, I want to buy it at my desk, like a man. You gotta get me out of here, Dallas. You gotta bust me out. You can take Sheila."

His face was wildly flushed, but Eve thought that was as much from sick panic as sickness. And she wasn't altogether sure she could take Feeney's wife. "Ah, what? I can't hear you. It must be a bad 'link."

"Don't you pull that crap on me."

"Okay, okay. How about this? I've got Peabody picking up files, hundreds of them from Anders Worldwide. It's the wife, Feeney, I know it in my guts. But I've got nothing to take to the commander, much less the PA. The search and runs on these files are going to take hours. Maybe days. Peabody could fill you in, toss some to you. You could work from there."

"Best you can do is throw me a bone?" He honked again. "I'll take it."

"It's a big bone, Feeney, and I need somebody to dig out the meat."

"All right. You tell the wife."

"What? Wait!"

"You convince her you need me on this. Make it life and death."

"No! Feeney, don't—"

"Sheila!" He honked the name out, and in the lingering chill of March, Eve's hands went damp with sweat.

What people did for friendship, Eve thought, as she paid off the cab. Now *she* was responsible, according to Mrs. Feeney, if the work set back his recovery. Should've left him hacking up a lung at his desk in the first place, she told herself as she buzzed Greta Horowitz's apartment from street level.

She angled toward the view screen.

"Lieutenant Dallas?"

"Yes. Can I come up?"

"I'll open the locks."

The doors beeped clear, opened smoothly. Inside, the entryway was small, and absolutely pristine. Eve imagined Greta would tolerate no less. The elevator hummed cooperatively to the fourth floor where Greta stood in the doorway of her unit.

"Has something happened?"

"Just some follow-up questions."

"Oh. I was hoping you'd found who killed Mr. Anders. Please come in."

The apartment was as unpretentious and efficient as its occupant. Sturdy furniture, no frills, a scent of . . . clean, was the only way Eve could describe it.

"Can I get you something hot to drink?"

"No, thanks. If we could sit down for a few minutes."

"Please." Greta sat, planted her shoes on the floor and her knees together. Smoothed down the skirt of her dignified black suit.

"You're attending the memorial," Eve began.

"Yes. It's a very sad day. After, I'll go to Mrs. Plowder's, to help with the bereavement supper. Tomorrow . . ."

She let out a little sigh. "Tomorrow, I am back to work. I will prepare the house so Mrs. Anders can return home."

"Prepare it?"

"It must be freshened, of course, and some marketing must be done. The bed linens . . . you understand."

"Yes."

"I'll supervise having Mr. Anders's clothes packed."

Don't waste time, do you, Ava? "Packed?"

"Mrs. Anders feels it will distress her to see them. She prefers they be removed before her return, and donated, of course, to charity."

"Of course. Mrs. Horowitz, how long did it take you to put away, give away, your husband's clothes?"

"I still have his dress uniform." She glanced over, and following, Eve saw the framed photo of the soldier Greta had loved. "People grieve in their own way."

"Mrs. Horowitz, you strike me as the sort of woman who not only knows her job, but does it very well. Who not only meets her employers' needs, but would anticipate them. To anticipate, you'd have to understand them."

"I take pride in my work. I will be glad to get back to it. I dislike being idle."

"Did you anticipate Mrs. Anders instructing you to pack away her husband's clothes?"

"No. No," she said again, more carefully. "But I was not surprised by the instructions. Mrs. Anders isn't sentimental."

"I doubt anyone would describe either of us that way, either. As sentimental. If I lost my husband . . . I'd need his things around me. I'd need to touch them, to smell them, to have them. I'd need those tangible pieces of him to get me through the pain, the shock, the sadness. You understand me?"

Gaze level on Eve's, Greta nodded. "Yes, I do."

"Would you have been surprised, if the situation were reversed, and Mr. Anders instructed you to pack up his wife's clothing?"

"Very. I would have been very surprised."

"Mrs. Horowitz, I haven't turned on my recorder. I'm just asking you for your opinions. Your opinions are very helpful to me. Did she love him?"

"I managed their house, Lieutenant, not their marriage."

"Greta," Eve said in a tone that had Greta sighing again.

"It's a difficult position. I believe honesty and cooperation with the police is an essential matter. And I believe loyalty to and discretion about an employer is not a choice, it's duty. You would understand duty, Lieutenant."

"Mr. Anders was your employer, too. Yes, I understand duty. We both have a duty to Thomas Anders."

"Yes." Greta looked at her husband's photograph again. "Yes, we do. You asked me before about their relationship, and I told you the truth. Perhaps not all shades of the truth, perhaps not my feelings on that truth."

"Will you tell me now?"

"Will you tell me first if you believe Mrs. Anders had anything to do with her husband's murder?"

"I do believe it."

Greta closed her eyes. "I had that terrible thought, not when I found him that morning, you understand. Not then. Not even that night, or the next morning. But . . . with so much time on my hands, so much time to think instead of work, I began to have those thoughts. Those terrible thoughts. To wonder."

"Why?"

"There was affection, gestures—on both sides. An indulgence on both sides. You would see this and think they are nicely married. Comfortably married, you understand?"

"Yes, I do."

"If she encouraged him to go out, play his golf, or attend his games, how could you fault her? If she encouraged him to take his trips, even to extend them, it would be natural enough. Women come to prize their solitude, especially when they're long married. A little time without the man underfoot."

"The reasonable, loving, indulgent wife."

"Yes. Yes, exactly what it would seem. But, in fact, she was happier when he was gone than she was when he was home, and the longer he was gone, the happier she would be. This is my opinion," Greta hastened to add. "My sense only."

"That's what I'm after."

"I would sense an annoyance in her on the day he was scheduled to return. I could sense it even as she fussed about what meal to serve him to welcome him home. When he was gone, she would have dinner parties or cocktails with her friends. Friends of hers, you understand, that were not so much friends of his. And never with Mr. Benedict."

Greta paused, pressed her fingers to her lips for a moment, then folded her hands neatly in her lap again. "I might not be saying this to you if she hadn't instructed me to clear his clothes out of his dressing room, as she might instruct me to see that the floors were polished. Just another household task. I might not be telling you this if I didn't know she saw the disapproval I didn't hide quickly enough. And seeing it, Lieutenant, her manner changed. Her voice thickened with the tears that came into her eyes. But it was too late. I'd seen the other, heard the other, so it was too late. It was then she asked me to help at Mrs. Plowder's, and told me what she would pay for my time, which is more than it should be. It was then she told me I would have a raise in salary when I returned to work tomorrow, and that she depended on me to help her through this difficult time."

Greta looked down at the hands folded in her lap, nodded. "It was then, Lieutenant, I decided I would begin to look for other employment. Only this morning, I contacted an agency for this purpose."

"She miscalculated with you, Greta. Will you be able to go to the memorial, to the Plowders, to go back to work, for the time being, without letting her see what you think or feel?"

The faintest smile touched Greta's mouth. "I'm a domestic, Lieutenant. I'm very skilled at keeping my thoughts and feelings to myself."

"I appreciate you sharing them with me." Eve rose, held out a hand.

Getting to her feet, Greta took it, then held it. And held Eve's eyes. "We may be unfair to Mrs. Anders. But if we aren't, I trust you, Lieutenant, to make justice for Mr. Anders."

"I'm good at my job, too."

"Yes, I believe you are."

Rather than cab it all the way back to Roarke's office, Eve flipped out her 'link as she hit the street again. The transmission bounced straight to his admin. "Hey, Caro, could—"

"Hello, Lieutenant."

"Yeah." Was she supposed to make small talk? Hadn't she done that enough already? "Well . . . sorry to interrupt. Maybe you could tell Roarke I'll meet him at the memorial."

"If you'd hold a moment, I'll put you right through to him."

"But—" Too late, she thought with a roll of her eyes as the calming blue wait screen came on her screen.

And, as advertised, a moment later Roarke's vivid blue eyes replaced the calm. "Just called to chat?"

"Yeah, it's just talk, talk, talk with me. Listen, I just wanted to leave a message that I'll meet you at the memorial. It's still too early, so I'm going to duck into a cyber-café or something, get a little work done, then cab it over."

"Where are you?"

"I'm over on Third, heading down to Fifty-fourth. So—"

"Wait there."

"Listen—" Too late, she thought again, as this time her screen went blank. "Wait there," she mumbled and jammed the 'link back in her pocket. Wait so he could drive across town to pick her up when she was perfectly capable of getting herself where she needed to go.

She could hardly call any of the women on the list Linny Luce had given her while she stood on the damn street. Those conversations would involve considerable delicacy, she imagined. And privacy.

At loose ends, she strode to the corner, swung wide of the throng waiting for the light, and studied them for a while.

Briefcases, shopping bags, baby carts—strollers, she corrected. Three people at the curb tried to out-jockey each other for position while they held up their arms to signal a cab. And the fleet of yellow streamed by, already hauling fares. Up the block a maxibus farted as it lumbered to a stop to disgorge passengers, take on more.

Some guy bopped by eating a slice, and as the scent reached out and beckoned like a lover, Eve remembered she'd not only given her ride to Peabody, but left the crullers in it.

Damn it.

She leaned back against the corner of the building while sky trams cruised overhead, traffic clogged the street, and the subway rumbled under it. Everybody going somewhere, or coming back from somewhere else.

While she waited, a couple of women already loaded like pack mules with shopping bags stopped by the display window beside her. And cooed, Eve thought, with the same over-the-top, slightly lame-brained adoration as Mavis cooing over Belle.

"Those *shoes!* They're absolutely beyond."

"Oh God! And the bag. Do you *see* the bag, Nellie? It looks positively gooshy!"

Eve tracked her gaze over. They looked like a couple of perfectly normal, perfectly sane women, she noted. And they were about to drool on the display glass over a pair of shoes and a purse. They continued to rhapsodize as they pulled the shop door open. Where, Eve assumed, they would shortly drop many hundreds of dollars for something to cart their junk around in, and many hundreds more for something that made their feet cry like babies.

She glanced away in time to spot some guy in a green army coat come flying across the street, dodging vehicles, clambering over others with a wild, happy grin plastered on his face. Happy, she assumed, because the beat cops in pursuit huffed half a block back, losing ground.

People scattered as people tended to do. Eve continued to lean back against the building, but she rolled to her toes and back as she gauged the timing. Green Coat bugled a hooting call of triumph when his combat-booted feet smacked the pavement. And flicking a glance—and his middle finger—behind him, kicked in for the dash down Fifty-fourth.

Eve simply shot out her foot.

He flew, the green coat rising like wings, and landed with what had to be a skin-scraping slide over the sidewalk. He groaned, grunted, managed a half roll. She helped him the rest of the way to his back with a shove of her boot, which she then planted on his sternum.

"Nice takeoff, bad landing." She pulled out her badge as much for the people rubbernecking as the guy under her boot.

"Shit, shit! I had it cooked and in the pan."

"Yeah? Well, now it's burnt, and so are you."

He held his hands out to show his cooperation, then used the back of one to swipe blood off his face. "What the hell're you doing standing around the damn corner?"

"Just waiting for my ride." She saw it cruise up, the mile-long black limo that actually made her stomach hurt with embarrassment. When Roarke lowered the back window, cocked his head, grinned, all she could do was scowl.

The beat cops huffed and puffed their way up to her. "We appreciate the assistance, ma'am. If you'd just— Lieutenant," the cop panted when she badged him in turn. "Lieutenant. Sir. We were in pursuit of this individual as—"

"This individual made your pursuit look like a couple of old ladies hobbling back to their rocking chairs."

"Fucking-A right," said the individual.

"Shut up. You're winded, sweating," she continued. "And this guy was fresh as a daisy until his face met the sidewalk. This embarrasses me. Now if you've got your breath back, wrap him up."

"Yes, sir. For the report, Lieutenant, the individual—"

"I don't care. He's all yours." She strode toward the limo. "Lay off the crullers," she called back, then climbed inside the shining black car.

Chapter 12

"I wonder," Roarke said conversationally, "how the city of New York and its population manage without you personally patrolling its streets."

She'd have come up with a smart remark, but he distracted her by handing her a cup of coffee. She reminded herself as she settled back that the windows were tinted. Nobody could actually see her stretched out in a limo with white rosebuds in crystal tubes while she drank coffee out of a porcelain cup.

So she did. "Why?" she asked. "Why did you pick me up in this ostentatious street yacht?"

"First, I don't find it ostentatious, but convenient. And very comfortable. Second, I had a bit of work to polish off on the way over and didn't want to drive myself. Third, *you* mentioned work, so if you need to do any, this is more comfortable than a cyber-café."

"Maybe that's logical." She drank more coffee, closed her eyes a moment. And Roarke's fingers brushed her cheek.

"Did the man sprawled on the sidewalk and under your boot get any licks in?"

"No. He never saw it coming. I've just got a lot in my head."

Now he brought her hand to his lips. "Why don't you let some of it out."

She eyed him. "Was there a fourth reason we're in this boat, and was that so you could put moves on me?"

"Darling, that would be the underlying reason for all my decisions."

Because she could, she grabbed his lapel, yanked him over, and took his mouth in a kiss full of heat and promise. Then pushed him away again. "That's all you get."

"I'd prove differently, but it seems a little crass as we're biding some time before attending a memorial."

He could prove differently, she knew. And the hell of it was, she enjoyed when he did. She sat a moment, trying to put her thoughts back in order. "You got any crullers on tap?"

"You want a cruller?"

"No. Damn that Peabody. Anyway—"

Roarke held up a finger, pressed the intercom. "Russ, swing by a bakery, will you, and pick up a half a dozen crullers."

"Yes, sir."

No wonder her head was screwed up, Eve thought. A couple of minutes before she'd had her boot on some idiot's chest while she dressed down a couple of lead-footed uniforms. Now she was gliding around New York drinking outrageously good coffee and getting crullers.

"You were saying?" Roarke prompted.

Might as well go with the flow. She crossed her booted ankles. "I spent the morning conducting interviews. So yeah, it's been a chatty day."

She ran it through for him, which never failed to organize her thoughts for herself. She paused only when the driver passed Roarke a bakery box, shiny white this time. She wrapped it up snacking on sugar and fat.

"It appears," Roarke said, offering her a napkin, "that when people scrape the veneer away, as you've prompted them to do, Ava Anders doesn't appear quite so smooth and glossy."

"They don't like her. What they liked, with the exception of Leopold who liked nothing about her, ever, was filtered through Anders. Tommy. With him not there as filter, the smudges are coming through. She doesn't care about being liked. Or cares only because being liked is a stepping-stone to being admired. Being admired, now that's important, and it's a stepping-stone to being influential."

"And Tommy. Another stepping-stone."

"Yeah. People have been sleeping and/or marrying their way to the top since the first cavewoman said: 'Ugh, that one's the strongest and has the biggest club. I'll shake my mastodon-skin-covered ass at him.' "

"Ugh?"

"Or whatever cave people said. And it's not just women who do it. Cave guy goes: 'Ugh, that one catches the most fish, I'll be dragging her off to my cave now.' Ava sees Tommy and—"

"Says ugh."

"Or today's equivalent thereof. There's a rich guy, a guy people like, who has good press. A nice, easygoing sort. You can bet your ass she researched him inside out before she settled on him. Worked the transfer to New York, made sure to put herself in front of him as often as possible. Four-walls him, too. But subtly. Too aggressive, you could scare him off; too delicate, he might not pick up on it. You put on the suit, the 'what Tommy likes and how Tommy likes it' suit, and you wear it like skin. And after you reel him in, you keep the suit on. Maybe a few adjustments here and there, but you keep it on. You get some power, you get the big houses, fancy life. You get some prominence, some *position*. And nudge him out of the house every chance you get so you can take the suit off and fucking breathe."

"For nearly sixteen years?"

"She could've done it for twice that. But you know

what happened? His father died. I gotta look at that." She tucked it into a handy corner of her mind. "And I need to check with Charles, but I'll lay you odds her first session with Charles was only weeks after the old man went under and Tommy inherited. Boy, the stakes just went way up. 'Look at all this, and it could all be mine. How can I have it, and get out of this frigging suit.' It's gotta be itching some, and he's only got a decade on her. He could live another fifty, sixty years. It's just too much. Anyway, she's earned it. God knows, she's earned it. Divorce won't do. She could work it, sure she could work it so it was all his fault, like she did the first husband."

"But as that's already been done, it wouldn't do to repeat herself."

"You got it," she said, pleased. "And the payoff wouldn't be enough in a divorce. Not anymore, not with all the years she's put in. If he'd just die, she could be the shattered widow, the widow who picks up the pieces of her life and goes on. Why can't he just die, why can't he have a fatal accident, why . . . What if?"

"She wouldn't be the first to hook herself to wealthy then grow weary of the price," Roarke commented. "Or the first to kill over it. But the method in this case seems particularly vindictive."

"Had to be. Terrible accident, but more, one brought on by his own weakness, his own disloyalty to her. The worse he looks, the brighter her halo. And, I think, once she saw a way out, that suit got tighter and tighter until it was cutting off her blood supply. Whose fault is *that*?"

"Why his, of course."

"Oh yeah. He had to pay for that, for all the years she wore it, all the years she played the game." As she sat in the fragrant air of the limo, Eve could all but feel Ava's rage. "She hated him at the end. Whatever she felt at the start, or during, at the end she hated him."

"And the killing itself was so intimate, and so ugly," Roarke said, "because of the hate behind it."

"Bull's-eye."

"If it played out the way you think, she still has an obstacle. There's Ben."

"I bet she's got plans for Ben. She can bide her time. Unless he gets in a serious relationship, starts thinking marriage. She'd have to move faster then. Or she might consider setting it up soon. An overdose would be best. Pills, too many pills. He couldn't take the grief, couldn't take the pressure of stepping into his uncle's shoes. Opts out. There's a risk there, but if I close this case with her in the clear, as she expects, she might take it."

"Do you intend to warn him?"

"He's clear for now. Case is open, and she needs more time." Calculating it, Eve tapped her fingers on her thighs. "She needs time to lean on him, to turn to him. To present the image that he's her support now, all she has left of Tommy now. She plans, and she considers contingencies. She needs public displays of their mutual grief and dependence to establish the foundation."

"I can't say I knew Thomas Anders well, but I would have said he was a good judge of character."

"Love clouds things."

"It does, yes." Roarke danced his fingers over the ends of her hair.

She shifted to face him. "You never asked yourself, not even once, if I made a play for you because of the money?"

"You didn't make a play for me. I made the play."

"*That* could've been my play." She smiled at him. "And you fell heedlessly into my wiles."

"Where I landed very comfortably. The only suits you wear, darling Eve, are the ones in your closet. And then they're worn reluctantly." He laid his hand, palm down, between her breasts. "I know your heart, *a ghrá*." And drew the chain she wore under her shirt. On it winked a diamond and the metal of a saint, gifts from him. "Do you remember when I gave you this?"

He swung the chain lightly so the diamond flashed and burned.

"Sure."

"You weren't just horrified and confused, you were terrified. Fearless Lieutenant Eve Dallas, terrified by a piece of compressed carbon and what it represented."

"Love wasn't supposed to happen. Not in my what-if. Not then."

"Yet, when you finally came to me, you wore it." The diamond sparked between them. "And you wear it still. Hidden most of the time to preserve your odd cop sensibilities, but worn just there, against your heart." He slid it under her shirt again. "It was you, Lieutenant, who fell into my guile, after I gave you a bloody good shove."

"I guess we both took a fall." She glanced out the window as the limo drew to a curb behind other limos—the somber glamour of death. "Too bad Anders didn't have a better landing with his."

Photographs of Anders stood throughout the elegant double parlor. He swung a golf club or a bat, hiked a football or returned a tennis volley among the meadow of flowers on display. Sunflowers, with their deep velvet brown eyes, dominated.

"His favorite," Ben told them. "Uncle Tommy used to say if he ever retired he'd buy a little farm somewhere and grow nothing but sunflowers."

"Did he have plans for that?" Eve asked. "For retiring?"

"Not really. But he did make some noises about finding a place outside the city, taking long weekends. As long as there was a golf course handy. He was sort of toying with the idea of building a farmhouse by the sports camp upstate. A real country home, where he and Ava would eventually retire. He'd have his sunflowers, get out of the city a little more until then, and have full use of the camp facilities. Said he'd have to put in a spa for Ava, to get her to go along with it."

He smiled with grief raw in his eyes. "Anyway, he loved sunflowers. He was loved, too. We're having simultaneous memorials, all over the world. Right now, all over the world people are . . . Sorry, excuse me a minute."

He turned toward the door. Eve wondered if he'd make it out before breaking down. And she saw Leopold cross the room quickly, and laying a hand on Ben's shoulder, walk out with him.

Love, Eve thought, in sorrow and selflessness.

Then she turned to study the widow who sat pale of cheek, damp of eye in a blue velvet chair surrounded by flowers and people eager to console her. Once again, her hair was coiled at the back of her neck to show off fine bones, sharply defined features. Her widow's weeds were unrelieved black, perfectly cut to showcase her statuesque build. She wore diamonds, exquisitely, at her ears, her wrists.

"Careful," Roarke murmured, "the way you're aimed at her, the hair on the back of her neck will stand up in a minute."

Not such a bad idea, Eve thought. "Let's go offer our condolences."

Tommy had drawn a crowd, Eve thought as she moved through it. That would please the widow, that good PR the media would run with. As she approached, Ava lifted her gaze, glimmering with suppressed tears, and bracing a hand on the arm of her chair as if she needed the support, rose.

"Lieutenant. How kind of you to come. And Roarke. Tommy would be so pleased you took this time."

"He was a good man." Roarke took Ava's offered hand. "He'll be missed."

"Yes, he was, and he will be. Have you . . . have you met my friend, my dear friend Brigit Plowder?"

"I believe we have. It's nice to meet you again, Mrs. Plowder, even under such difficult circumstances."

"Sasha will be devastated you remembered me and not her." Brigit smiled at Roarke, a warm hostess to a guest. "Would you sign the mourner's book? It's an old-fashioned custom we thought Tommy would appreciate." She gestured to the narrow podium beside her, and the gilt-edged white book open on it.

"Of course." Roarke took up the gold pen to sign.

"You should have some wine." As if confused or mildly ill, Ava touched her fingers to her temple. "We're serving wine. Tommy so enjoyed a party. He wouldn't want all these tears. You should have some wine."

"I'm on duty." And for a moment, for just an instant, Eve stared into Ava's eyes and let her see. *I know you. I know what you are.*

In Ava's, behind that sheen of tears, flashed surprise. And for only a moment, for just an instant, heat flared with it. Then she swayed against her friend. "I'm sorry. I'm so sorry. I feel..."

"Sit now." Brigit eased Ava into the chair, stroked her cheek. "Sit back, Ava. You're taking on too much."

"How can it ever be enough? How can I...Where's Ben? Where's Ben?" A single tear spilled out of each brilliant eye. "I need Ben."

"I'll fetch him for you." Roarke glanced at Eve, then made his way through the crowd of mourners.

"He'll be right along," Brigit soothed. "Ben will be right along. We'll take you upstairs, sweetheart. You need some quiet. It's too warm in here, too close, with so many people. It's all too much."

"I'll give you a hand with that." Eve stepped closer. "Why don't I help you upstairs, Mrs. Anders?"

"I want Ben." Ava turned her face away to press it against Brigit. "I'll be stronger if I have Ben. He's all I have left of Tommy."

"He's coming now. He's coming, Ava."

Ben rushed through the room, the grief coated over with concern. He bent over Ava like a shield. "I'm here. I just went out for some air. I'm right here."

"Stay with me, Ben. Please, stay with me, just until we get through this."

"Let's take her upstairs."

"No, Brigit, I shouldn't leave. I need—"

"Just for a few minutes. Just a few minutes upstairs until you feel better."

"Yes, you're right. A few minutes. Ben."

"Here we are. Take my arm. You'll have to excuse us, Lieutenant."

"Sure."

So the widow, overcome, was led away to her private grief. Pitch-perfect, Eve thought. She could use some air herself, she decided, then spotted Nadine Furst across the room with Roarke.

"Personal or professional?" Eve asked when she joined them.

"Like cops, it's always both for journalists. But personal leads the way here. I liked him, very much. And Ben." She glanced toward the doorway, brushing back the sleek sweep of hair as she watched them go. "I was outside with him, having a word, when Roarke came out for him. Poor Ava, she looks so lost."

"Oh, she knows where she's going."

Nadine's eyes lit and narrowed. "What's that I hear? You don't seriously think—" She cut herself off, took a sip of the wine in her hand. "Too many ears in here. Why don't we step outside?"

"Not ready for a one-on-one."

"Peabody's better than I thought," Nadine said after a moment. "If what's going on is what I think is going on. She never dropped a crumb. Some pals you are."

"You be a pal first. Dig up those old interviews you told me about, send them to me."

"I can do that. What's in it for me?"

"That's going to depend."

"Look, Dallas—"

"Did I mention," Roarke interrupted, "how strong I found your interview with Peabody last night? You drew the best out of her, effortlessly."

"Teamwork." Nadine sulked at both of them. "I hate that."

"Get me the interviews, Nadine, then I'll give you what

I can when I can. But for now, I've had enough of this place. So—shit. It's Tibble's wife. Damn it."

Not ready yet, was all Eve could think as the tall, whip-thin woman aimed toward her. Brutally short, honey brown hair crowned a strong, stunner of a face the shade of the well-steeped Irish tea Roarke occasionally enjoyed. Eve had heard the stories that once upon a time Karla Blaze Tibble made her living—and considerable sensation—as a fashion model. If she'd stalked the runways with the same purpose and panache as she crossed a mourning room, Eve decided, she would've been hard to beat.

"Lieutenant." Her voice was smoky music, her eyes tiger gold.

"Ma'am."

"Ms. Furst, Roarke, I wonder if you'll excuse us a moment? I need to speak to the lieutenant in private."

It might've been posed as a request, but there was command in the posture. Karla simply turned, and people parted for her as the Red Sea parted for Moses as she strode to the door.

"Courage." Though there was amusement in his tone, Roarke gave Eve's shoulder a supportive squeeze.

"Why do they have to have wives? Why do cops have to have wives? I'll be back in a minute." With little choice, Eve followed in Karla's wake, and joined her on the narrow, third-floor terrace.

With the traffic snarling below, Karla stood with her back to the rail. "As the primary on an open homicide, can you possibly think it's appropriate for you to speak with a reporter at the victim's memorial?"

"Excuse me, ma'am, Nadine Furst is also a personal friend."

"Friendship doesn't apply. You have a position to uphold."

Screw this, Eve thought. "Yes, I do—as do you. As the wife of the chief of police, can you possibly think it's appropriate for you to attend the memorial of the victim of an open homicide case, and speak with individuals who may be on the investigator's suspect list?"

The fury flashed, a beautiful blaze that kindled in those tiger eyes, on that amazing face. Then it banked down to an irritated simmer. "You have a point. It's very annoying that you have a point."

"I can assure you that I haven't discussed the details of the investigation with Nadine, or any other media contact."

"Yet."

"She's a useful source, and—at my discretion as primary—I may elect to use that source. As she's no pushover, I may elect to trade information for information."

"Dirt for dirt."

"If it's useful dirt, yes, ma'am."

"Oh, stop calling me 'ma'am' as if I were your third-grade teacher." She spun around to lean on the rail, facing the street this time. "I'm upset, and it set me off to see you huddled with Nadine Furst."

"I'd huddle with Jack the Ripper if it aided the investigation. I have a job to do. I understand this is upsetting to you. Your friend's husband has been murdered. You should understand that finding his murderer and building a case against that individual are my priorities."

"And I've already poked my nose in twice." Karla lifted her hands off the rail in a gesture Eve interpreted as truce. "I don't make a habit of that."

"No, you don't."

"Ava and I are friendly. We've worked closely together on several projects, and I admire her energy, her creative thinking. I liked Tommy Anders very much. He was a generous, unpretentious man, so yes, it's very difficult to accept he was murdered. And the circumstances of it, the media coverage of it. As the wife of a prominent man, I sympathize with Ava on many levels right now."

Karla turned around. "As the wife of a prominent man, so should you."

"As the primary investigator, my sympathies are with the victim."

"You're a hardcase, Lieutenant." Karla shook her head, but the fire had gone out. "Your commander considers you the best of his best. My husband believes you to be brilliant. While I generally stay out of my husband's business, I pay attention. So I know you have a reputation for getting it done. I suppose it takes a hardcase to get it done. So I'm told you wanted to speak to me about Ava and Tommy."

"Most specifically about your work with them."

"You suspect that something within the charity work precipitated Tommy's murder."

"I need to cover all areas to conduct a thorough investigation."

"Which is cop-speak for none of your business." Karla waved a hand. "I'm not offended. Ava and I worked on a number of projects over the last couple of years. She contacted me initially to ask me to cochair and help coordinate a fashion show. Logical, given my background."

"A sports fashion show?"

"No, actually, this was geared toward the mothers of children qualified for the sports camps and associated programs. Affordable daywear, work wear, sportswear, with several of the mothers as models. Participating merchants offered generous discounts, and Anders provided each woman with a thousand-dollar wardrobe allowance. Something fun for them, as most of the emphasis is on the children. We followed up a few months later with a children's show—school clothes, athletic gear. Both were very successful. Ava was tireless."

"So I've learned."

"We've also implemented other activities. We—or Ava and some of the staff and volunteers—took the mothers to a spa resort while their children were at camp. A kind of retreat where for five days they could relax, be pampered, attend seminars, workshops, have discussion groups. It's a lovely time."

"You've attended."

"Yes, once or twice. As a den mother, so to speak. It was very rewarding to see these women who rarely have any time for themselves have an opportunity to focus on their own minds, bodies, spirits."

"They must have been incredibly grateful for that, and to Ava for providing them with a sample of a lifestyle outside of their own."

"A break from work, children, responsibilities, yes. Fun was a priority, but also education, networking, a support system. Just as in the one- or two-day retreats held in New York, or other locations throughout the year for the Moms, Too, program. A number of these women are single parents, and as such have little time to socialize, to *be* anything but a mother."

Enthusiasm for the program infused Karla's voice. Her hands moved, energetically conducting her words. "Often when a parent loses herself—or himself—in the day-to-day responsibilities and demands of raising children, they become a less effective, and less loving parent than they might be. Than they want to be. So Ava conceived of Moms, Too."

"Being together like that, at that kind of retreat or organizing a fashion show, it would be natural, wouldn't it, for you and Ava to become involved with the participants? Develop relationships."

"Yes, it's something else I've found rewarding. Tommy went beyond providing children with equipment, or even a place to use it. His idea of bringing them together, in training, in competitions, encouraging them to work and play together does so much more than put a ball glove in a child's hand. It gives them pride, friendships, an understanding of teamwork and sportsmanship. Ava's vision for the adjunct program is to give exactly that to the mothers. And to put a personal face on it, as Tommy does—did—with his active participation in the camps, in the fathers' programs, the parent-child competitions.

"And I'm going to start campaigning for funds any minute," Karla said with a laugh. "But yes, involvement is key, I think. Charity can be difficult, Lieutenant, to give or receive. These programs are designed to instill pride and self-worth."

"Outlining and executing the programs you've done with Ava must take incredible planning, an eye for details, a skill for delegation."

"Absolutely. Ava's a master at all of that."

Eve smiled. "I believe it. I appreciate you taking the time to speak to me."

"And I'm dismissed. I should get back in, say my good-byes. I hope there are no hard feelings between us."

"None on my side."

"Then I'll wish you luck with the investigation." She offered her hand again. "Oh, and, Lieutenant, a little concealer would cover up that bruise under your eye."

"Why would I want to do that?"

In the limo, Eve stretched out her legs and said, "Huh."

"As neither of you limped back inside bloody, I assume you and your chief's wife came to terms."

"Yeah, you could say. And it's funny what people say and how they say it. She's *friendly* with Ava. She liked Tommy very much. She admires Ava's energy and creative thinking. Tommy was generous and unpretentious. Mrs. Tibble's a smart woman, but she doesn't get what she just told me. That, and more," Eve shifted to Roarke.

"The other day, you gave a few bucks to a sidewalk sleeper."

He lifted his eyebrows. "Very possibly."

"No, I saw it. Outside the morgue."

"All right. And?"

"A lot of people probably tossed that guy a few that day, and a lot of other days. They don't remember him after, he doesn't remember them. But you crouched down and spoke to him eye-to-eye. Made it personal, made the connection. He'll remember you."

"He's likely to remember the twenty more."

"No, don't get cynical on me. Back when you were

running the streets in Dublin, when your father beat down on you until you were half dead. Summerset took you in, fixed you up. He offered you something—a chance, a sanctuary, an opportunity. What would you have done to pay him back? Cut out the years between then and now, and what developed between you," she added. "Then, right then, what would you have done to pay him back?"

"Whatever he'd asked."

"Yeah. Because then, he was the one with the power, with the control, with the . . . largesse. However much of a badass you were, you were vulnerable. Smaller, weaker. And he'd given you something you'd never had."

"He never asked," Roarke said.

"Because despite being a tight-assed fuckface, taking advantage of the vulnerable isn't his style. But it's Ava's."

"Where are you going with this?"

"To work. I need to see what Peabody's got so far, see if I can wheedle a quick meet with Mira. I have to get some of this organized in my head, get it down. I'll fill you in at home, then take advantage of your vulnerability of being crazy about me and curious about the case so I can put you to work."

"I'll accept that, particularly if you take advantage of me otherwise afterward."

"I'll schedule that in. I want—whoa, whoa. Wait!" She fumbled for the intercom. "Pull over. Pull over here."

"Why?" Roarke demanded as the limo swept to the curb. "We're two blocks from Central yet."

"Exactly. Do you think I want to pull up in front of my house in this thing? Jeez. I'll walk from here."

"Want the crullers?"

"Keep 'em." She grabbed the door handle with one hand, his hair with the other. One hard kiss and she was out the door. "See you."

And he watched as her long stride ate up the sidewalk, her coat billowing. Watched until she was swallowed up by distance and people.

Chapter 13

With her mind tapping out details, Eve headed toward Homicide with the same ground-eating stride Roarke had admired outside. Not a break in the case, she thought, not yet, but damn if she didn't think she had a crack. And she was going to chisel and hammer away at that crack until it busted wide open.

Another part of her brain registered a need for caffeine, debated between supplying it hot or cold. When cold won, she stopped in front of Vending and eyed the machine with suspicion and dislike.

"Don't fuck with me," she mumbled, and plugged in credits. "Tube of Pepsi."

The machine seemed to consider, to ponder—she all but heard it whistling a taunting tune. And just as she reared back to give it a good kick, it spat out the tube along with its tedious content data. Eve snatched the tube out before it changed its mind, and turning, saw Abigail Johnson sitting on the same bench Tiko had used the day before.

Tension tightened at the back of Eve's neck as she approached the woman. "Mrs. Johnson."

"Oh, Lieutenant Dallas. I was daydreaming, didn't see you there." Shifting the box on her lap, Abigail got to her feet.

"Is there a problem?"

"No. No, indeed. The fact is, Tiko's about nagged the skin off my bones about that reward. I felt like he should understand doing what's right is enough, then, well, I started thinking it's good for a boy to get something back for doing right. And don't I punish him for doing wrong, and maybe give him some extra screen time or bake his favorite cookies when he does something especially good?"

"Works for me."

"So I contacted that number you gave me, to see about it. It was all taken care of already, they said how you'd seen to that." The bright green eyes stared into Eve's. "Why it was a *thousand* dollars, Lieutenant."

"Early estimates hit about ten thousand a day that ring was pulling in. Tiko was key in shutting it down."

"I can't get over it, that's God's truth. Fact is, I had to sit down fanning myself for a good ten minutes after that Sergeant Whittles told me how much." Abigail tipped back her head and laughed, and the sound was bright as birdsong. "Then, well, I baked you a pie." She thrust the box at a puzzled Eve.

"You baked me a pie?"

"A lemon meringue pie. I hope you like lemon meringue."

"I'd be a fool not to. Thanks."

"When they told me you weren't here, I was going to leave it for you. But I got the strong feeling there wouldn't have been anything left of it time you got back."

"You'd be right about that."

"They said how you'd be back shortly, so I just sat down to wait. They put that right through security downstairs, so they could see I wasn't bringing in anything dan-

gerous. Course, I've been told my baking's dangerous to
the waistline, but you don't have to fret about that."

Because it seemed to be expected, Eve opened the lid,
peeked inside. The meringue looked frothy as a snow-
cap, with golden beads scattered over its peaks and
planes. "Wow. It looks like edible art."

"Isn't that a thing to say. I know it's not much, but I
wanted to give you something for what you did for my boy,
for my Tiko. He told me all about it, well, about a half a
dozen times he told me all about it. I wanted to say to you
how it seems to me somebody like you could've brushed
him off, or could've called Child Services, or a lot of other
things but what you did. I've taught him to have respect for
the law, and for right over wrong. But you showed him
why, and you put a face on the law and on what's right that
he won't forget. He won't be forgetting the reward either,
but it's you he'll remember first. And so will I."

"And it seems to me, Mrs. Johnson, that a lot of boys in
Tiko's position could've looked the other way—or more,
tried to angle their way into a piece of what was going on.
But I'll take the pie."

"I hope you enjoy it."

"I may have to knock a few of my men unconscious to
get it into my office, but believe me, I will."

Eve got a good grip on the box, and put blood in her
eye as she walked into the bullpen. She swore a dozen
noses lifted up, at the very same instant, to scent the air.
"Not a chance in hell. Peabody, my office."

After shooting a smug and evil smile at her sorrowful
colleagues, Peabody breezed in behind Eve. "What kind
of pie is it?"

"It's my kind of pie."

"You can't eat a whole pie by yourself. You'll get sick."

"We'll find out."

"But . . . I brought you crullers."

"Where are they?"

Peabody's mouth opened, closed on a pout as she
shifted her eyes away. "Um . . ."

"Exactly." Eve set the pie box out of reach on top of her AutoChef. "What have you got besides cruller breath?"

"It's not like I ate them all personally, and you left them behind so— Okay." She deflated under Eve's icy stare. "I've got the duplicate names, and I've started running them. FYI, Mrs. Tibble's on there. She's worked on multiple projects with Ava Anders."

"I think we can take her off the list."

"Yeah. Also the mayor's wife and a number of other prominents."

"We won't discount them. Staff and volunteers go into the mix, but we're going to focus on the participants. The women Ava played Lady Bountiful with."

"I've got some with criminal, got some who were or are LCs."

"Keep them at the top. Trying to figure her. Would she go for somebody with experience, with tendencies, or somebody blank, somebody who'd run below the radar?"

She paced to the window, stared out. "She wouldn't expect us to get here, to look where we're going to look. But somebody who plans as meticulously as she does would have to consider all the possibilities. How did she weigh it?"

"Another question would be how do you convince somebody to kill for you."

"Some people bake pies. Copy all the files, shoot them here and to my home unit. And keep working it, Peabody. If somebody in there was her trigger, I bet she has plans for them, too. I just bet she has plans."

She worked it as well, formulating notes from her conversations that day, pushing through the repeated names Peabody had culled out. And she considered the logistics and man hours of interviewing literally hundreds of potential suspects.

Needle in the haystack. But sooner or later.

She pushed back, circled her head around her shoulders to loosen knots. Her incoming beeped, and it pleased her to see Nadine had sent her a file. "Copy to my home unit," she ordered.

She rubbed her tired eyes. Time to go home herself, she admitted. Take it home, pick it up again, bounce it off Roarke.

She shut down, loaded her bag, shrugged into her coat. She picked up the pie box as Mira stepped into the doorway.

"On your way out?"

"Yeah, but I've got time. They told me you were booked solid today."

"I was. And I'm late heading home. If you're leaving, why don't we walk out together, and you can tell me what's on your mind."

"That'd be good. I've got this theory," Eve began.

She briefed Mira as they took glides down to the main level, then switched to the elevator for the garage.

"The dominant personality, the benefactor, or employer, convinces, pressures, or cajoles the subordinate or submissive to execute her will."

"Execute being the operative term," Eve commented. "But I think *cajole* is a passive term for getting someone to do murder."

"Passivity can be a weapon if used correctly. And such methods have certainly been used for gain. Anything from lying to protect the superior's mistake or misconduct, to providing sexual favors and yes, all the way up to murder. To insure continued cooperation *after* the fact, the dominant would need to continue the relationship, offer and supply reward, or threaten with exposure or harm."

To finish, Eve got off on Mira's garage level. "We're running the ones with jackets, and any LCs—currently or previously—first."

"The most logical place to start."

"The nature of the crime. You'd have to have that in you, or be so completely under Ava's thumb you couldn't so much as wiggle to see that through."

"Or utterly enthralled," Mira added. "Love comes in a lot of forms."

"Yeah, so does gratitude. And fear. I need to figure out which one of those levels she pulled. I let her see today. I let her see I know. Maybe that was a mistake, but I wanted her to sweat a little."

"It's good strategy. It gives the opponent something to worry about, and worried people make more mistakes."

"If I had a little more, just enough to bring her in, to get her in the box, I think I could trip her up. But I need to push her out of her comfort zone, isolate her from..." Realizing they were standing beside Mira's car, and she was down to talking out loud, Eve shrugged. "Anyway."

"If and when, I'd like to observe. I think it would be fascinating."

"I'll let you know. So... say hi to Mr. Mira."

"I will. Eve, don't go straight to work when you get home. Take an hour. Recharge." In a gesture that never failed to fluster Eve, Mira leaned over, kissed her cheek.

"Well. Good night."

She'd planned to go straight back to work, Mira had her there. More, she'd planned to drag Roarke into it with her. How was she supposed to hammer that crack open if she sat around for an hour doing nothing? She walked into the house with the notion of recharging later.

Summerset loomed; the cat sat and stared.

"I haven't got time for you, Flat Ass."

"Or little else, apparently, as you arrive late. Again. And have used your face as a punching bag. Again."

"That was yesterday. I offered yours, but they judged it too high on the ugly scale."

"Roarke is in the pool house, if you have any interest in your husband's whereabouts."

"I got interest." She tossed her coat over the newel post, dropped her file case at the foot of the stairs, then shoved the box she held into Summerset's hands. "I brought dessert."

That, she thought as she strolled to the elevator, confused him speechless, and was almost as satisfying as her best insult. As she rode down, she rubbed at the back of her neck. Maybe she could take time for a quick swim, stretch out some of these damn kinks she'd earned from too many hours at the comp.

Fifteen minutes, that would set her, then a big, fat burger while she played some of the data and speculations off Roarke. The man sure as hell knew about being the dominant personality.

She stepped out into the moist, fragrant warmth, into the lush green foliage and bright blooms of the tropical gardens of the pool house. Music came from the sparkling waterfall flowing down the wall—and the smooth, rhythmic strokes of the man cutting through the bold blue water of the pool.

He swam like a seal, she thought, sleek and fast, and looked like—well, if she couldn't think it, who could? He looked like a damn Irish god, with that rangy body, the ripple of muscle, the streaming black hair. When he changed up strokes, executed a surface dive, she grinned. With an ass like that, who wouldn't want to sink their teeth into it?

Maybe she could take more than fifteen minutes.

She stripped where she was, took position on the edge, and dove in. When she surfaced, he was treading water, and watching her with eyes that made the bold blue of the pool seem pale.

"It seems I've caught a mermaid."

"You haven't caught anything yet, pal. How many laps have you got in?"

"Twenty-two. I'm after thirty."

"Then I'll catch up."

She pushed off the side. He paced her awhile, which made her kick in to up the speed. Still, they hit the wall together, rolled into the turn and push. She lost him after eight, but moments later heard the rumble that told her he'd settled into the grotto corner, and its jets.

So she lost herself in the rhythm, in the water, in the effort, and somewhere in the twelfth lap, her crowded mind cleared. When she hit thirty, her muscles were loose to the point of limp, her breathing shallow, and her mind utterly relaxed.

She skimmed under the water, surfaced in the grotto beside him.

"God! *That* was a good idea."

"I have any number of them."

She let her head fall back, her eyes close. Under the water her fingers linked with his until she had her breath back. "I've got one of those coming on. Oh yeah, there it is."

She ducked under, rolled, then skimmed her way up to take him into her mouth. The water churned around her as she gripped his hips, as she felt the muscles she'd admired quiver for her. She surfaced, letting her lips run up his belly, his chest, his throat to where his mouth waited to mate with hers.

"I like your idea better than mine."

"Thought you might." She scraped her teeth over his throat. "Mira said I should recharge." Tossing her head back, she shot him a look of pure challenge. "So, recharge me."

He pulled her under with him, into that breathless, beating blue.

He'd thought himself prepared. Relaxed, comfortably aroused watching his wife burn off the day as he had. He'd imagined persuading her into wet, lazy love once she had. Instead the need for her had simply leaped into him, torn through him as a hungry animal who wanted feast and conquest.

It burned through him, a fever in the blood as he devoured her mouth, as his hands sought and took. Her gasp for air when they surfaced ended on a cry of shocked pleasure that only stoked the flames.

Her hands dug into his shoulders when he took her breast. Greedy mouth, demanding teeth. Wet and warm from the water, she trembled from the assault.

And still she said, "Yes."

"Yes," as the water closed over them again.

Her ears roared from the pound of the water, from the pound of her own blood. How could anyone survive wanting, being wanted, like this? How could anyone live without it? He set a storm inside her of feelings, sensations, of desires that throbbed toward pain. A storm that raged and blew and thundered until there was nothing left of her but a drowning, helpless love.

Rough hands pushed her back to the wall where hers gripped the edge, where her moans echoed in the heavy air as his mouth streaked up her thighs, as his tongue arrowed inside her. He tugged, shifting her so the gush of hot jets pulsed over her, inside her—hot, relentless—as his mouth worked her toward frenzy.

"I can't. I can't. God!"

The orgasm was brutal and fierce, a ripping of self from sanity.

He felt it break through her, felt the force and wonder of release. And saw when he looked into her eyes again the complete surrender to it. To him.

"Take. Take me." He drove into her, into that surrender. And lifting her hips, plunged deeper yet. As the madness pummeled him, whipped him, he heard his own voice, thick and breathless, murmuring demands and pleas in Irish she couldn't possibly understand.

And still once more, as his body battered hers, she said, "Yes."

On that single, whispered word, he surrendered.

Sprawled in the pulsing water, limbs like melted wax, Eve wasn't sure who was holding up whom. She thought, vaguely, that a double drowning was a distinct possibility. But couldn't seem to care.

"Maybe it's something in the water, some sort of sex drug. You could bottle it, sell it, and make another fortune."

"Hell with that. I'm keeping it all for us. Did I hurt you at all? I'm a bit bleary."

"I can take care of myself, pal." She let her head fall like a rock onto his shoulder. "Besides. My idea."

"And a bloody good one it was."

"I was going straight up to work. Got big, fat, sticky piles of it, so I was going straight up to work. Then the gargoyle said you were down here. I thought maybe I'd take fifteen minutes for a swim, loosen up."

"Well, we sure as Christ loosened up."

"Then I saw you knifing through the water. All wet and ripply and . . . you." She tilted her head back to look at him. "I saw you, and that's all it took. Sometimes I can't breathe, I love you so much."

"Eve." Emotion deepened his eyes as he kissed her, very sweetly, then he just rested his brow against hers.

"I keep thinking, well, this'll settle down. It's bound to level off and settle down. But it doesn't. Even when things are just going smooth and we're just . . . living, I can look at you, and I've got no breath left."

"Every minute with you, I'm alive. I never knew before there were pieces of me unborn, just waiting for you. I'm alive with you, Eve."

She sighed, touched his cheek. "We'd better get out of here. We're getting mush all over the pool."

It was back to murder as she pulled on the comfort of her old NYPSD sweatshirt and a pair of worn-out (just the way she liked them) jeans. While they dressed, she relayed to Roarke the conversation she'd had with Mira.

"You're worried now she'll find a way to dispose of this subordinate—as you're thinking of her, or him."

"Gotta have a plan for it. I think she *thinks* this individual wouldn't dare betray her, but she'll have a plan. She's got Brigit Plowder, who doesn't strike me as a moron, completely wrapped. Pretty much ditto on Tribble's wife. But Plowder . . ."

"Are you looking at her? At Brigit Plowder?"

"I look at everyone, but no, she doesn't strike me as a subordinate or . . . what's the word? What is it? *Supplicant*.

Yeah, that's what our Ava likes. She likes having her supplicants. She bought herself plenty of them with Anders's money."

She caught a glimpse of the two of them in the mirror, paused, took a closer look. He'd put on basically the same thing she had—jeans and in his case a dark blue sweater. But...

"How come you always look better than me?"

He glanced in the mirror as well, and smiling stepped behind her to wrap his arm around her from the back. "I can't agree with that. Eye of the beholder."

"You're still tuning from water games." She shook her head, studying them, he thought, as she might suspects in a lineup. "It's just not right. Anyway, back off, ace, we've got a load of work ahead of us and—crap, I forgot. I need to tag Charles. I need to do a follow-up there."

To amuse himself, and annoy her, he only tightened his hold.

"Hey."

"Hey, back. It'll be a working meal again, and would that make me your subordinate or your supplicant?"

"Ha-ha. You're nobody's subordinate, and you wouldn't know how to supplicate. Is that a word?"

"I'll look it up. Working meal, and you're thinking... burgers."

Her eyes narrowed. "What, have you gone all psychic on me?"

"Logic, and an intimate—as I've recently proven—knowledge of my wife. You missed lunch, discounting a limo cruller, and you've expended a great deal of energy in the pool, with various activities. You're hungry, which leads you to red meat. A steak won't do as you won't want the trouble of cutting anything up. So it's a burger you want."

"What am I having for dessert?"

He cocked a brow at her reflection. "Well, there you have me."

"Yeah, I got you." She turned, bit his lip. "I brought home pie."

"Really? What sort of pie?"

She only smiled, pulled out, and picked up her 'link to tag Charles.

Nervous, distracted, Charles paused outside the brownstone in the West Village and checked the display on his signaling 'link. "It's Dallas," he told Louise.

Worried, uncertain, she watched him frown at the display. "Aren't you going to answer?"

"Ah . . . no. No, I'll get back to her."

"It'll be about the Anders case. Charles, if there's something about it that you haven't told her, something you're holding back because of loyalty or discretion—"

"There isn't." He slid the 'link back in his pocket. "Let's go in."

"Actually, Charles, I'm not really in the mood to socialize, especially with new people." She glanced toward the house. "I really think you and I need to talk."

The nerves already buzzing in his belly kicked up to a dull roar. "We will."

"Things haven't been—"

"Don't." He took both her hands. "Just don't. Let's go inside first. I really need to take you inside."

"All right." Inside her belly, something sank. "All right."

He led her through the iron gate, down the walk cutting through a small and lovely front garden, then up the short flight of stairs to the main level of the three-story home. But when he took out keys, she stared.

"What—"

"One minute. Just one minute." He keyed a code on the security pad, unlocked the door.

Baffled, she stepped inside.

Floors gleamed, old, rich wood providing a lovely base for the foyer, for the sturdy stairs with their glossy rail, and on to a spacious room where a fire simmered in a hearth of lapis blue.

"It's empty."

"Yes, for now."

Her footsteps echoed on the wood as she wandered into what she assumed was the living area, as she turned to look at the trio of tall windows with their carved trim.

"It's a lovely space."

"There's a lot more," he told her. "Let me show you through."

"Why?" She turned back to him. "Why are we in a beautiful and empty house in the West Village with you offering to show me through?"

"I bought it." He hadn't meant to tell her exactly that way, but she was standing there, framed by those windows, looking at him with such serious, such somber gray eyes.

"You . . . you bought this house?"

"Yes. Two weeks ago."

"Two . . . I see." She smiled. "Well, congratulations. I didn't realize you were even thinking of relocating, much less buying a home. No wonder you've been so distracted lately. So, show me the rest. These floors, Charles, they're just gorgeous. Are they all the way through? And all this space!"

She started to hurry by, but he caught her arm. "You're upset."

"No, no, just surprised. It's such a big step. Enormous."

"I've taken a couple more. I didn't tell you."

"No, you didn't tell me." Though her eyes stayed on his face, she eased back from him. "You haven't told me much of anything for weeks. So, let me be grown up and civilized about this, will you? Let me try. Is there a dining room? I bet there's a wonderful dining room, perfect for dinner parties."

"I've retired."

Though she'd pulled away to move on, that stopped her again. "What?"

"I turned in my license, the end of last week."

"Last week? I don't understand this, don't understand you. You've turned in your license, bought a house. What is this, Charles?"

"I wanted—needed to have it, to have everything in place before I told you. I applied for, and have been granted a license in psychology, specializing in sex therapy. Dr. Mira helped me there, and agreed that it was a good lateral move."

Louise stared at him with something like grief in her eyes. "You spoke with Mira, but not with me. Asked for her help, but not for mine."

"I wanted to be sure I could pull it off, Louise. She agreed to help me with the applications, the testing, the screening process. And well, talking to her throughout all this helped me be sure it was something I really wanted to do, really could do."

"As talking to me wouldn't have helped?"

"No. Yes. She's neutral, objective. And while she was helping me through it, I was dealing with buying this place. The lower level here is a good space for the office and therapy rooms. And there's ... I'm not doing this right."

He stopped, pushed at his hair again. For a man who'd made his living, and a damn good one, he thought, on being smooth, he was bumbling this like a first-nighter. "I haven't been able to figure out how to do this. Every time I tried to work it out, I hit a wall. Louise—"

"Then let me make it easy for you. You want to change your life. A new home, a new profession. A new start then." Tears burned, but she'd be damned if she'd end this weeping and sniveling. "New relationships I'm not part of. Fine, show your gorgeous new house to her, you bastard."

"Who? No!" He had to move fast to grab her before she reached the door. "Not part of it. For Christ's sake, Louise, you're the center of it. You're the reason for it."

"How? How am I any part of any of this when you do it all without even *telling* me?"

"What would you have said to me if I told you I was going to retire because of you?"

"That's ridiculous. I've never had a problem with your

work. It's your *work*. And it was your work when I met you, when I fell in love with you, damn it, Charles."

"Exactly. It never bothered you. Never made a difference in how you felt about me. But it began to bother me. It began to bother me when I just couldn't give my clients my . . . best. Because, Louise, I don't want to be with anyone but you. I don't want to touch anyone but you. I needed—for myself—I needed to lay the foundation for the new, to believe I could do this. And offer this, to you."

"Offer . . ." Her eyes widened. *"This?* This house?"

"It's closer to your clinic than either of our apartments. It's a nice neighborhood, and it's . . . it's a home, Louise. Not a place to sleep or hang clothes. It's a place to live, together, to build something together."

"I need a second." She put a hand on his chest, eased him back. "You did all this, changed your life, for me?"

"For us. I hope. If you don't like the house, we'll find another. Mira said it would probably be better to wait on the house, to consult you there. But . . . I didn't." At a loss, he lifted his hands, let them fall. "It was probably a mistake to buy it without you. But I wanted to give you something. Something solid, I guess, symbolic, and a little spectacular."

"I thought you were tired of me, that you didn't love me anymore and didn't know how to tell me." She managed a watery laugh. "You've been breaking my heart, Charles, for weeks."

"Louise." He drew her to him, kissed her damp cheeks, her lips. "It must be loving you so much, and being terrified you wouldn't want all this, that's had me screw up so badly."

"I was going to be so sophisticated and cool when you broke things off. Then I was going to gather up any of your things at my apartment and set them on fire. I'd worked it out."

"I was prepared to beg."

She tipped her head back, laid her hands on his cheeks, and smiled beautifully. "I love you, Charles. You didn't have to do this for me, or for us, but I love that you did. I love that you screwed it up. Oh! Show me the rest!" She spun away and into a circle. "Show me every inch so I can start planning how to drive you crazy with decorating ideas. I'll nag you so relentlessly over window treatments and wall colors you'll wonder why you ever wanted to cohab."

"Cohab?" He shook his head. "For two smart people who're desperately in love, we're certainly having a hard time understanding each other." He slipped a small velvet box out of his pocket, flipped the top. The diamond exploded with light and brilliance. "Marry me."

"Oh." She stared at the ring, stared into his eyes. "Oh my God."

Chapter 14

With the burger devoured, Eve paced in front of her wall screens. "What we have to do is divide these into categories, cross-reference. First, the people we know she had multiple contacts with. The more contact, the easier it is to establish a relationship. We put those into categories. Staff, volunteers, beneficiaries."

"She may have met any number of these people off book," Roarke pointed out. "Private meetings. The nature of that would make the relationship more personal, more intimate."

"Yeah, can't argue. So we divide those up, too. Peabody's got a good start with the multiples, and with those we have individuals with criminals, and we have the LC angle. We need to press that."

She turned back to him. "If you were going to have someone killed—"

"Some chores a man just wants to see to himself."

She blew out a breath, scratched the back of her neck while he smiled serenely. *"If,"* she repeated. "And if you didn't want to get your manicured hands dirty, would you exploit someone with some experience in criminal behavior, someone whose past deed or deeds could also give you a lever, if necessary, or would you go with the blank slate?"

"Interesting, as both have their advantages, and their pitfalls. And it would depend, too, on what the criminal behavior consisted of."

"Yeah, we're going to do a subset there on violent knocks."

"Someone who's killed before—or has a history of violence—would bring that experience or predilection to the table." He continued to enjoy a glass of the cabernet he'd selected to go with the burgers. "Might be, one could assume, more open to bribe, pressure, or reward. However, that sort may not be as trustworthy or discreet as the clean slate. Whereas, the clean slate might balk at the idea of murder, or clutch in the execution of it and botch the job."

"Maybe she did."

"The heavy tranqing." Roarke nodded as he was right there with her on that point. "It could indicate a delicacy of feeling, yes."

"Yeah, it takes delicacy to wrap a rope around an unconscious guy's neck so he chokes to death."

"From a distance," Roarke pointed out, "where she didn't have to see it. So it happened after she was gone."

"You're leaning toward clean slate."

"If, in my hypothetical murderous bent, I wanted to have someone eliminated—and didn't go the tried and true route of hiring a hit—I'd certainly explore that clean slate. What could I get on her? Where is the pressure point or the vulnerability? What could I offer in exchange?"

"A business deal?"

He tipped his glass toward her. "Isn't it? Even blackmail is business."

"Okay. Okay. We'll divvy up this first batch. You take clean slates, I'll take the ones with jackets. And we'll divide the licensed companion connects between us."

"Aren't we the fun couple?"

"We'll dig out the party hats later. Look for any significant change in income, or anything that looks like addictions—gambling, illegals, sex, alcohol. Any debts paid off, any major purchases. They've got kids, so look at tuitions to private schools, or medical procedures. Sick kid's a big button to push. *Any* change in buying habits, income, routine in the last six months. She wouldn't want to string this out too long.

"On the staff—"

"I know what to look for, Eve. It's not my first ride on the hay cart."

"Okay, fine. But this is going to be a long ride on a really big hay cart with a tiny little needle in it somewhere."

"I walked into that one. And now," he said as he strolled toward his office, "I'm walking away."

Eve sat at her desk with coffee, with files. She spent a moment drumming her fingers and staring at her murder board. Then she shifted to begin the first of many detailed runs.

It was the kind of tedious, ass-in-the-chair work that put the knots and kinks back in no matter how thoroughly they'd been smoothed out. She felt them working up between her shoulder blades in hour one, only to lodge gleefully at the base of her neck by hour two.

"How many kids are there who need freaking hockey equipment?" she asked aloud, rubbed her neck. And zeroed in.

"Lookie here. Current data on wall screen," she ordered, then rose, stretching out as she studied the information.

Bebe Petrelli, DOB April 12, 2019. Current address 435 107th Street, Bronx. Parents Lisbeth Carmine, Anthony DeSalvo (deceased). Siblings Francis, Vincente. Married Luca Petrelli (deceased) June 10, 2047. Two children, Dominick Anthony, DOB January 18, 2048, Paul Luca, DOB July 1, 2051.

"Enough, enough, give me the damn criminal."

Working...
Charged with possession of illegals substance 2042. Probation. Charged with possession with intent to distribute illegals substance 2043, probation on first charge rescinded. Sentenced to three to five, suspended. Licensed Companion license revoked. Community service with mandatory rehabilitation therapy ordered, and completed. Charged with solicitation without a license, assault, and resisting arrest 2045. Assault charges and resisting charges dropped. Served one year Rikers, with completion of anger management program.

"Wonder if it worked. Computer, was subject's father Anthony DeSalvo of the purported organized crime family?"

DeSalvo, Anthony, father of subject, alleged captain in DeSalvo family, alleged to be Mafia-based with interests in illegals, weapons running, protection. DeSalvo, Anthony, garroted 2044, rival Santini family suspected of ordering his execution. Brief gang war followed with several deaths and/or disappearances of purported members. No arrests or convictions made. Do you want full case files?

"Not at this time." Eve walked over to Roarke's doorway. "I've got a hot one."

"I've got bleeding nothing. Let's see yours."

He walked in, stood as she did, studying the data with his thumbs hooked in his front pocket. "Ah, yes, the feuding DeSalvo and Santini clans."

"Know any of them?"

"I've made the acquaintance of a few over the years. They've learned to give me a wide berth."

The casual way he said it, the utter disregard in his tone, reminded Eve once more how dangerous Roarke could be. Yeah, she thought, she bet the wiser of the wise guys gave him a wide berth.

"In any case," he continued, "they're fairly small-time. Bullies and posturers and greedy hotheads. Which is why they're small-time. This family tree and the bloody roots of it would make your current subject of interest to Ava Anders, I'd think. She comes from a family that murders as part of their standard business practices. She's had her own bumps with the law, served time. How'd her husband die?"

"Good question. Computer, details on the death of Petrelli, Luca."

Working…Petrelli, Luca, COD fractured skull. Accompanying injuries: broken jaw, broken nose, broken fingers, both hands, broken leg, arm, shoulder. Severe facial injuries, contributory internal injuries. Body was found in the East River near Hunts Point, June 12, 2047.

"Beat the bastard to death," Eve commented. "Computer, was Petrelli known to be or suspected of being connected to organized crime?"

No connection known. Suspected due to relationship with Petrelli, Bebe. None found through surveillance or other investigative methods. Petrelli, Luca, owned and operated, with wife, Bebe's, a restaurant in Hunts Point, Bronx. No criminal record on Petrelli, Luca.

"So she marries clean," Roarke speculated. "Has a couple of kids, opens a restaurant. Not in Queens, where her family claims its contested turf, but in the Bronx. Away from that. Away from them. Then someone beats her man to death."

"And with two kids to raise, money tight, a spotted record, the blood ties, it's hard to make ends meet." Eve eased a hip down on her desk, absently stroking a hand over the cat when he bumped his head against her arm. "Hard to soldier on. You'd be grateful to someone who offered a hand, who didn't hold the past against you. Looks like Peabody and I are heading up to the Bronx in the morning. Computer, list Bebe Petrelli as a person of interest, copy all data to file. Send copy of same to Peabody, Detective Delia, home unit."

"You won't be stopping there."

"No, but that sure gave me a boost. I think it's time we took a break and had ourselves some pie."

"It's always time for pie." He glanced over as the house 'link beeped. "Yes, Summerset?"

"Dr. Dimatto and Mr. Monroe are at the gate."

"Let them in. Oh, and we'll have the pie the lieutenant brought home, with coffee for our guests. In the parlor."

"I'll see to it."

"How come people can drop by out of the blue and get pie?" Eve wondered.

"Because we're such warm and welcoming hosts."

"No, that's you. And it's my pie. Technically." She looked over at the work on her desk with the cat currently sprawled over it all. "Well, hell, I wanted to talk to Charles anyway. Computer, send a notification to Detective Peabody. Report, my home office eight hundred—no, strike, seven hundred thirty hours. Dallas, Lieutenant Eve."

Acknowledged.

"Run next subject, store data." Eve shrugged. "I'll get a little jump on it while we're being warm and welcoming hosts. Anyway, Petrelli was in this fashion show Ava sponsored, attended a number of the one- and two-day mom breaks, one of the five-day retreats just last summer, and both her kids have attended sports camps three years running."

"Solid connection," Roarke agreed as they started out of the office.

"Last year both of the kids were awarded Anders scholarships. They're in private schools now—Anders pays the freight as long as they meet academic standards and stay out of trouble. That's a lot of motive, a lot of reasons for Petrelli to keep Anders happy. A lot of reasons to be grateful."

"Use the children, particularly the children." Such things always burned in his belly. "Here's what I'll give your boys, here's how your boys can be educated, the opportunities they can have if you just do this little thing for me."

"It clicks pretty good."

"It clicks. And she would ask herself, wouldn't she, how or why anyone would connect her to Anders's murder. How would she ever be brought into it?" Roarke ran a hand down Eve's back as they descended the stairs. "Because she couldn't anticipate you. And neither, no matter how well she planned, could Ava."

Eve stopped at the parlor doorway, winced. Charles and Louise stood inside, wrapped together like pigs in a blanket, sharing a big, sloppy one in front of the parlor fire.

She slipped her hands in her pockets. "You guys need a privacy room?"

"And there's the warm welcome," Roarke murmured as the couple eased apart. And his eyebrows rose as they grinned at each other, then at their hosts like a couple of cats with bellies full of cream.

"Sorry to drop by so late," Charles began. "I got your message that you needed to speak to me, and since we were out—"

"And that's not the reason at all." With her cheeks flushed and glowing, Louise laughed and leaned against Charles. "We wanted to share our news, and used the 'link message as an excuse."

"Congratulations." Roarke crossed over to shake Charles's hand, to kiss Louise's cheek.

"We haven't told you the news yet," Louise complained.

"You don't have to, not with that rock you're wearing blinding us." Eve stood where she was, studying them both. "When did all this happen?"

"Tonight, a couple of hours ago." Louise shot out her hand with the diamond sizzling. "Look, look, look."

The woman was a doctor, Eve thought. A tough-minded, strong-spined woman with a solid core of sense. And she was bouncing like a spring over a chunk of rock. But Eve walked over, let Louise hold the ring up to her face. "Shiny," Eve said.

"It's exquisite." Roarke poked a finger into Eve's ribs. "I have all her taste in jewelry. Ah, Summerset, we'll keep the pie," he said as his man wheeled in a cart, "but we'll want to switch out the coffee for champagne. We're celebrating Charles and Louise's engagement."

"Best wishes. I'll see to it right away."

"I feel like I've already had a couple bottles. I'm so giddy!" Louise threw her arms around Eve, squeezed. "We're thinking May, late May or early June. Something small, sweet. But I'm getting ahead of it. Tell them the rest, Charles."

"We'll be moving into a house in the West Village."

"Oh, God, it's *fabulous.* One of those amazing old brownstones, wonderfully rehabbed. It even has a courtyard garden in the back. Working fireplaces, three levels. I've already earmarked a room on the third floor for my home office. And the lower level is perfect for Charles's clients."

Eve opened her mouth, slammed it back shut. But apparently some sound had snuck out before she zipped it.

"Not those clients." Charles shot Eve a look. "Part three of the news is I've retired, and am about to begin a new career in psychology, specializing in sex therapy."

"*That's* what you were doing with Mira." Eve punched his shoulder.

"Yes. Ouch. She's been an enormous help to me in the transition. A lot of LCs are married, or get married, and manage very well. I didn't want to be one of them."

"Well, good, because that's just screwy. I can say that," Eve complained when Roarke poked her again, "because he's not doing the screwy. Jeez, like you weren't thinking it."

"Excellent timing," Roarke announced when Summerset

brought in the champagne. He popped the cork himself, and began to pour while Louise wandered over.

"Wow, look at that gorgeous pie. Look how beautiful the lemon is against the white meringue." She scanned over to Eve. "You'd look good in a lemony yellow."

"I'm more interested in eating the lemony yellow."

"I'm thinking wedding again—matron of honor dress. Charles and I want the two of you to stand up for us. We met through you."

"We'd be absolutely honored." The quick glance Roarke sent Eve was the equivalent of a poke. He passed around champagne, lifted his glass. "To your happiness, and the life you'll make together."

"Thank you." Charles laid a hand on Roarke's arm, then leaned over to kiss Eve, very softly on the lips. "Thank you."

"This is so . . ." Louise blinked at tears. "Everything. I'm so happy, so beyond happy. And now there's champagne and pie."

"Don't drip on it," Eve advised and made Louise laugh.

"I'm so glad you called Charles, so glad you gave us the excuse to come over. I can't think of a better way to cap off the best night of my life."

"About that," Eve began, then wondered why her brain didn't explode from the laser beam Roarke shot out of those wild blue eyes. "It can wait."

"It's all right," Charles told her. "You want to ask me something more about Ava."

Friendship, she thought, was always screwing with procedure. "Tomorrow's fine."

"It's all right," Louise echoed. "If Charles can help, we both want him to. Really," she said to Roarke. "It's another, less giddy reason we stopped in."

"I've thought about it—about Ava," Charles began. "There's been so much going on in my head it's been hard to squeeze it in. But I have thought about it."

"Ah . . . maybe we could go up to my office for a couple minutes."

"Dallas, I know you can't quite get a handle on how I can look at Charles's work—his prior work," Louise added, "as separate from our relationship. But I can. I have. It's not a problem for me. So if you have a question about the LC–client relationship, just ask it."

"I talked to her first husband. Did she ever mention him to you?"

Charles shook his head. "No. I knew she'd been married before. I do a check on any potential client. For safety, and to give myself a sense of them. A fairly early, fairly brief marriage, if I'm remembering right."

"He's an operator. Struck me that way. A womanizer with more money than morals and a really high opinion of himself. Nothing like the type I'd have put her with."

"She was young. Younger," Charles said.

"She walked away from the marriage with a nice financial settlement, after she caught him with another woman. One she'd introduced him to, and according to him, then provided him with ample opportunities to bang. She never brought that up?"

"No, she didn't."

"He also told me that Ava was enthusiastic in bed. Or good in it anyway. I tend to go with that, as his type would be more than happy to say she was a lousy lay. You indicated she was on the shy and cool side. Lights-off type."

"That's right. Sexual levels, preferences, abilities, they all can change. Inhibitions can set in for a lot of reasons."

"And women can fake enthusiasm, or lack thereof. It's tougher for a guy, seeing as you wear your enthusiasm or lack thereof between your legs."

"She has such a way with words," Roarke commented. "And imagery."

"She ever fake it with you, Charles? You've been in the game long enough. You'd know. You're too professional not to."

"No, she didn't, and yes, you're right, I would've known. Clients do, occasionally, and it would be my job to determine whether to let it go, or to explore the reasons why they didn't, or couldn't orgasm." His brow knitted as he sipped champagne. "And now that you bring it up, I expected her to have some trouble there, at least the first time or two. Nerves, shyness. But she responded easily."

"You said you get a nice percentage of clients through recommendations, referrals. Did she ever send anyone to you?"

"As a matter of fact, yes. I think she sent a couple clients. One-timers. I don't remember right off, but I can look it up for you."

"Do that." She brooded a moment, trying to think if there was any angle she'd missed. "Okay. Back to pie." She took a good forkful, sampled. "Holy hell. Speaking of orgasms."

"A subject of which I never tire." Roarke took a bite himself. "Well now, this is miraculous. Where did you get it?"

"This kid's granny baked it. Talk amongst yourselves. The pie and I are busy." She got down to it, bite by tart and frothy bite. Until some bit of conversation intruded on her concentration.

"An option for you," Roarke continued. "As you consider the where and when of it."

"A wedding here? In the gardens? I don't know what to say. Charles?"

He smiled at Louise. "Bride's choice."

"Then I know exactly what to say. Yes. It's my second best yes of the night! Yes, thank you so much."

"That's fine then. Come around whenever you like to have a look around. Summerset would be a help to you there. It's a lovely spot for a wedding." Roarke looked over at Eve. "And, I think, a lucky one."

"Yeah. It's pretty damn lucky."

When the happy couple left, Eve walked back up with Roarke. "One question," she began. "Does having a wedding here mean I have to do stuff?"

"Stuff, as in?"

"Screw around with caterers and florists and decorators."

"I believe Louise will want full control there."

"Thank God."

"Of course, as matron of honor, you'll have certain duties."

"What? Duties? You stand there in a fancy dress, probably holding a bunch of flowers."

He patted her shoulder as they turned into her office. "You keep thinking that, darling, for as long as it comforts you."

She scowled, pulled at her hair. "It's like Mavis having a baby, isn't it? I have to do all this stuff because they're doing all this stuff, which is completely—when you think about it—*their* stuff, but it gets to be my stuff because somehow or other *they* got to be my stuff."

"The fact I followed that clearly from point to point proves you're my stuff."

"I'm not thinking about it. I'm just not. It makes the backsides of my eyes ache. Computer, display last run."

Blowing out a breath, she dropped down at her desk to get back to murder. That was the stuff she understood.

Shortly after one A.M., she roused when Roarke slid an arm under her knees. "Damn it, I dropped out. Just for a minute. You don't have to..." But when he picked her up, she shrugged a shoulder. "Okay, what the hell. I got two more possibles. Not as strong as Petrelli, but possibles.

"Mmm." Her voice was slurry, a sign she'd not only hit the wall but slid bonelessly under it.

"Need interviews, then could run some probabilities. Gotta hammer the crack," Eve continued.

"Absolutely. I'll fetch you a nice big hammer first thing in the morning."

"Got hundreds left to run. Longer it takes, longer she has to patch up the damn hole. Not going to run though, no sir, not going to run."

"No, indeed." He carried her up to the bed, laid her down. As he started to unbutton her jeans, she sat up, patted his hand away.

"I can do it. You get ideas."

"Yet somehow I can resist them when my wife's all but comatose. Heroic of me."

She smiled sleepily as she wiggled out of the jeans. "Better not forget that, 'cause I'm sleeping naked." She tossed aside the sweatshirt, then climbed under the fluffy duvet. "Gonna nail it down," she murmured as she snuggled in. "It's coming around, I can feel it, and I'm going to nail it down."

"There's that hammer again." He slid in beside her, draped an arm around her waist. "Pick it up tomorrow, Lieutenant. Time to lay the tools down for the night."

"Bet she sleeps like a baby. I bet she...Shit!" She flopped over in bed so quickly, Roarke had to shoot down a hand to catch her knee.

"Mind the jewels, then."

"He had traces of over-the-counter sleep aid in him."

"A lot of people take sleep aids routinely. In fact, on nights such as this it's a wonder I don't."

"Didn't think about them overmuch as the trace matched with what he had in his bathroom. Just a standard. But I asked Ben and the house manager, and neither of them can confirm he was a routine user. So what if she planted them there? What if she found a way to get some into him that night."

"When she was in St. Lucia."

"He took vitamins—a whole buncha vitamins regularly. He had this, ah...crap, my brain—"

"Is begging you to turn it off."

"It has to wait. He had this weekly dispenser deal. You fill up each day's dose, so you don't have to open a bunch of bottles or try to remember if you took the E and not the C—whatever. She could've pulled a switch."

"So he fell asleep at his desk that morning, or while putting on the third green."

"He took them at night." She smiled in the dark. "He took them at night because he thought that helped them absorb better. That's in my notes somewhere."

"All right, then, she switched pills. How would you prove it, and what would you do with it should you?"

"Just another piece to poke at. I don't remember seeing any sleep aids in her bathroom, in her night table. But she said she might take a soother, or take an aid now and then."

"She was traveling," he reminded her. "She might have taken them with her."

"Yeah, I'm going to check on that. And what if—"

"Eve?"

"Yeah?"

"Remember that hammer I said I'd fetch you in the morning?"

She frowned in the dark. "Sort of."

"Don't make me get it now and knock you out with it." He kissed the tip of her nose. "Go to sleep."

She frowned in the dark for another minute, but her eyes began to droop. She felt his arm go around her again, drawing her in, then the muffled thud as Galahad pounced onto the foot of the bed.

As the cat arranged himself over her feet, she dropped into sleep.

Chapter 15

In sleep, she arranged them. Thomas Anders at the center with the others fanning out like rays. Ava, Ben, Edmond and Linny Luce, Greta Horowitz, Leopold Walsh, Brigit Plowder, Sasha Bride-West.

But no. She shifted restlessly in sleep. No, that wasn't right. He wasn't the sun, he wasn't the center. Not to her. He was only the vehicle, he was only the means.

Expendable, when the time was right. Steady, reliable, not very spectacular, predictable Tommy.

Left with a nice chunk of change. Dirk Bronson lounged in a deck chair behind Ava, sipping a frothy drink. *Not a backward glance.*

Seed money. The kickoff. The flashy lead-off batter.

Change the lineup.

In the dream, the ball field was summer green and rich brown, the white bases gleaming like marble plates. The players took that field in uniforms black as death. Brigit crouching behind the plate—catcher to Ava's pitcher—Sasha fussing with her hair at short, Edmond at first, Linny at second, Ben playing the hot corner at third with

Leopold and Greta patrolling right and left fields, respectively.

Short a man, Eve thought. They're short a man at center field.

I'm always the center. Ava smiled, wound up, and winged a high, fast curve. At the plate, Tommy checked his swing.

Ball one.

The crowd, in their black mourning clothes, applauded politely. *Nice call, ump.* Eve glanced back, scanned the dugout. Even in the dream it seemed strange to see Mira in a ball cap drinking tea out of a china cup. Feeney sat on the bench in his pajamas, sneezing. He's on the disabled list, she thought, but the rest of the team's here. Peabody, McNab, Whitney, even Tibble. And Roarke, of course, watching as she watched.

Ava, set, glanced over her shoulder toward third. The pitch missed, low and outside. *Ball two.*

Ava took a bow, for the crowd, for the field. *I can keep this up for years. Slow ball, fast ball, curve ball, slider. It's not a strike until I'm ready to throw one.*

She threw again, high and inside, brushing Tommy back from the plate.

Ball three.

There were mutters from the dugout, restrained hoots from the crowd. As Brigit jogged up to the mound, Ben called over to Eve, *We're playing on the wrong team. Can't you call the game? Can't you call it before it's too late?*

Not without more evidence, Whitney said from the dugout. *No cause. You need probable cause. There are rules.*

Roarke shook his head. *Far too many rules, don't you think? After all, murder doesn't play by the rules.*

Brigit jogged back, gave Tommy a pat on the cheek, then turned to Eve. *She's going to the bullpen. She needs some relief. You have to admit, it's all a little boring this way, and she'd put in a great deal of time.*

I can't stop it, Eve thought. I can only call them as I see them.

A shadow crossed the field, an indistinct form gliding over the summer grass. No, I can't stop it, Eve thought again. It had to play out. I can only make the call after the pitch.

I'm sorry, she said to Tommy, *there's nothing I can do.*
Oh well. He smiled kindly at her. *It's just a game, isn't it?*

Not anymore, Eve thought as the shadow merged with Ava, as they set, checked, wound up together. Fast ball, dead over the plate.

He lay on the rich brown dirt, the marblelike plate his headstone, and his eyes staring up at the clear blue of the sky.

On the mound, Ava laughed gaily, and took another bow for the now weeping crowd. *And he's out! Want to see the instant replay?*

It might've been a weird dream, maybe a stupid dream, Eve thought, but she rearranged her murder board in her home office the next morning.

Take a new look, she told herself. Look with fresh eyes.

Roarke came in behind her, studied the board with his hand on her shoulder. "Making patterns?"

"It's that damn dream." She'd told him about it when she'd dressed. "See, she's got her infield—the people she trusts most because she's seen to it they trust her, or have that connection to her through Anders. She's aiming to take him out. She's aimed for him from the first pitch of the first inning, but they don't see it. *He* doesn't see it, even though the batter and pitcher are in an intimate, one-on-one relationship."

"And she doesn't throw strikes."

"Exactly. No, no, not the first inning," Eve corrected. "The first was Bronson—warmed up on him, got some rhythm going on him. Maybe there were others, before Bronson, between him and Anders."

"But she struck them out, or let them get on base, then picked them off. No score, no memorable stats."

"Yeah." She glanced back at him. "For an Irish guy you get baseball pretty well."

"And still you benched me in the dugout. No batter on deck, either."

"No, no potential next batter. This ends the game. When she goes for Ben, and she will, it'll be another game, after a nice, relaxing hiatus. She pitches, she coaches, she manages. And she's the center." Eve put her fingertip on Ava's photo. "She's always the center. She didn't call in relief, she called in a shadow. Nobody sees, nobody knows. And the shadow just follows the steps. One strike, in this case, and he's out."

"And the shadow fades off, so that she—once more—remains the center. If it follows your metaphor, the late inning relief pitcher only has one job, doesn't she? Throw the strike."

"Exactly right. This pitcher doesn't have to do anything but follow orders. Doesn't have to strategize, or worry about base runners because there aren't any. Doesn't have to depend on the field, or even know them. Follow orders, throw the strike, fade away. No postgame interviews, no locker-room chat. One pitch, and out of the game. It's smart," Eve had to admit. "It's pretty damn smart."

"You're smarter, slugger." Roarke gave Eve's hair a quick tug. "It's going to piss her off when you step up to the plate and hit a grand slam."

"Right now, I'd settle for a base hit. With Bebe Petrelli."

"Ava would never have considered you'd look that deep in her lineup. And that is the end of the baseball analogies." He turned her, kissed her. "Good luck with the former Mafia princess."

Bebe Petrelli lived in a narrow row house on a quiet and neglected street in the South Bronx. Paint peeled and cracked like old dry skin over the brittle bones of the houses. Even the trees, the few left that used their ancient roots to heave up pieces of the sidewalk, slumped over the street. Along the block, some windows were boarded like blind eyes while others hid behind the rusted cages of riot bars.

Parking wasn't a problem. There couldn't have been more than a half dozen vehicles on the entire block. Most here, Eve thought, couldn't afford the cost and ensuing maintenance of a personal ride.

"Revitalization hasn't hit here yet," Peabody commented.

"Or it took a detour."

Eve studied the Petrelli house. It looked as if it might've been painted sometime in the last decade—a leg up on most of the others—and all the windows were intact. And clean, she noted, behind their bars. Empty window boxes sat like hope at the base of the two windows flanking the front door.

"You said both her kids go to private school on Anders's nickel?"

Why the empty window boxes stirred pity inside her, Eve couldn't say. "Yeah."

"And she lives here."

"Smart," Eve replied. "It's smart. What better way to keep someone under your thumb? Give them this, hold back that. Let's go see what Anthony DeSalvo's girl, Bebe, has to say about Ava."

As they walked toward the front door, Eve saw shadows move at the windows on the houses on either side. Nosy neighbors, she thought. She loved nosy neighbors in an investigation. Rich mines to plumb.

No perimeter security, she noted. Decent locks, but no cams or electronic peeps. Locks and riot bars had to serve.

She knocked.

Bebe answered herself, through the inch-wide gap afforded by the security chain. Eve saw both the wariness and the knowledge of cop in the single brown eye.

"Ms. Petrelli, Lieutenant Dallas and Detective Peabody, NYPSD." Eve held her badge to the crack. "We'd like to come in and speak to you."

"About what?"

"Once we're in, we'll talk about it. Or you can close the door and I'll call in for a warrant that would compel you to come into Manhattan to Cop Central. Then we'll talk about it there."

"I have to be at work in another hour."

"Then you probably don't want to waste any more time."

Bebe shut the door. Eve heard the rattle of the chain through it. When it opened, Bebe stood, tired and resentful, in a red shirt, black pants, and serviceable black skids. "You're going to have to make this fast, and you're going to have to talk while I work."

With that, Bebe turned and stalked toward the back of the house.

Neat and tidy, Eve thought as she glanced at the living area. The furniture was cheap, and as serviceable as the black skids, but like the windows, clean. The air smelled fresh, with just a hint of coffee and toasted bread as they approached the kitchen.

On a small metal table sat a white plastic laundry basket. From it, Bebe took a shirt, then folded it with quick, efficient moves.

"You don't need to sit," she snapped out. "Say what you have to say."

"Ava Anders."

The hands hesitated only a second, then pulled out another shirt. "What about her?"

"You're acquainted."

"My boys are in the Anders sports programs."

"You've attended Mrs. Anders's seminars and mothers' breaks. Retreats?"

"That's right."

"And both your boys are recipients of scholarships through the Anders program."

"That's right." Bebe's eyes flashed up at that, and some of the fear, some of the anger leaked through. "They earned it. I got smart boys, good boys. They work hard."

"You must be very proud of them, Ms. Petrelli." Peabody offered a hint of a smile.

"Of course I am."

"Their school's a clip from here," Eve commented.

"They take the bus. Have to change and take another."

"Makes a long day, for them and you, I imagine."

"They're getting a good education. They're going to be somebody."

"You had some rough times in the past."

Bebe tightened her lips, looked away from Eve and back to her laundry. "Past is past."

"The DeSalvos still have some money, some influence in certain circles." Eve glanced around the tiny kitchen. "Your brothers could help you out, you and your boys."

This time Bebe showed her teeth. "My brothers aren't getting near my boys. I haven't said word one to Frank or Vinny in years, or them to me."

"Why is that?"

"That's my business. They're my brothers, aren't they? It's not a crime if I don't want anything to do with my own brothers."

"Why does Anthony DeSalvo's only daughter hook up as an LC?"

"As a way to stick it to him, you want to know so bad. Ended up sticking it to myself, didn't I?"

A lock of graying hair fell over her brow as Bebe yanked out a boy's sports jersey to fold. "He wanted me to marry who he wanted me to marry, live the way he wanted me to live. Like my mother, looking the other way. Always looking the other way, no matter what was right in her face. So I did what I did, and he didn't have a daughter anymore." She shrugged, but the jerkiness of the movement transmitted lingering pain to Eve. "Then they killed him. And I didn't have a father."

"You did some time, lost your license."

"You think I got shit around here, with my boys in the house? You think I'm on the shit?" Bebe shoved at the laundry basket, threw her arms wide. "Go ahead, look around. You don't need a warrant. Look the hell around."

Eve studied the flushed face, the bitter eyes. "You know how you strike me, Bebe? You strike me as nervous as you are pissed off. And I don't think it's because you're on anything."

"You cops, always looking to screw with somebody. Except when it matters. What good did you do when they killed my Luca? Where were you when they killed my Luca?"

"Not in the Bronx," Eve said evenly. "Who killed him?"

"The fucking Santinis. Who else? Fucking DeSalvos mess with them, they mess with us. Even if Luca and me, we weren't the *us*." She gripped the basket now, as if to steady herself. And her knuckles went as white as the plastic. "We had a decent place, a decent life. He was a decent man. We had kids, we had a business. A nice family restaurant, nothing fancy, nothing important. Except to us. We worked so damn hard."

Bebe's fingers tightened on, twisted a pint-sized pair of jockies before she tossed them back in the basket. "Luca, he knew where I came from, what I'd done. It didn't matter. The past's past, that's what he always said. You've got to make the now and think about tomorrow. So that's what we did. And we built a decent life and worked hard at it. Then they killed him. They killed a good man for no good reason. Killed him and torched our place because he wouldn't pay them *protection*. Beat him to death."

She stopped to press her fingers against her eyes. "What did you cops do about that? Nothing. The past isn't the past with your kind. Luca got killed because he married a DeSalvo, and that's that."

She began to fold clothes again, but her movements were no longer efficient, and the folds no longer neat. "Now my boys don't have their father, don't have the decent place to grow up. This is the best I could do, the best of the worst. I don't own a restaurant, I work in one. I rent out a room and a bath upstairs so I can pay the goddamn rent, and so somebody's here to watch over my kids when I have to work nights. This is the life I've got now. My boys are going to have better."

"Ava Anders offered you a way to give your boys a better life."

"They earned their scholarships."

"There was a lot of competition for those scholarships," Eve said. "A lot of kids qualified, just like yours. But yours got them. Full freight, too."

"Don't you say they didn't earn what they got." She lashed toward Eve like a whip. "If you say that to me, you're going to get out of this house. You get your damn warrant, but you'll get out of my house."

"She offered a lot," Eve continued. "Little vacations, drinks by the pool. Did she single you out, Bebe?"

"I don't know what you're talking about."

"Compliment you on your boys, commiserate with you on your losses. She knew where you came from, too, and what you'd done. One little favor, just one little favor, and she'd set your boys up."

"She never asked me for a damn thing. Get the hell out of my house."

"Where were you on March eighteenth from one to five A.M.?"

"What? What? Where I am every blessed night. Here. Do I look like a party girl? Do I look like I spend my nights out on the town?"

"Just one night, Bebe. The night Thomas Anders was murdered."

She went very white, and her hand lowered to the table to brace her body. "Are you out of your *mind*? Some crazy, hyped up LC killed him. It's all over the screen. Some..." Now she lowered to the chair. "God, God, you're looking at me? At me because I used to be in the life? Because I did some time? Because I got DeSalvo blood?"

"I think that's why Ava looked at you, Bebe. I think that's why she took a good, hard look. Me, I'd've asked for some of the ready, too. Get myself a nicer place, closer to the school. But you were smart not to be too greedy."

"You think I . . . How was I supposed to get to their swank place in New York? How was I supposed to get inside?"

"Ava could help you with that."

"You saying, you're standing here in my kitchen saying that Ava—Mrs. Anders—*hired* me to do her husband? I'm a goddamn hit man now? Mother of God, I cook for a restaurant, to put food in my boys' mouths and clothes on their backs. I'm going to do hits for a living, why in hell am I folding laundry?"

"Doing Ava a favor would be a way to get your kids a good education," Peabody put in. "A way to give them a chance for better."

"They *earned* it. Do you know what I had to swallow to sign my boys up for the program? To take charity, to let them know they had to take handouts? Dom wanted to play ball so bad, and Paulie wants what Dom wants. I couldn't afford the fees, the equipment, so I swallowed it and signed them up. They earned the rest. They earned the rest," she repeated as she got to her feet. "Now I got nothing more to say. You get your warrant to take me in if that's the way it is. I'm going to call Legal Aid. You get out, 'cause I've got nothing more to say."

"Shook her," Peabody said when they were back on the sidewalk.

"Yeah, it did. She relaxed some when we veered off into her family. Stayed bitchy, but relaxed. That's interesting."

"She didn't like seeing us at the door either. Most don't," Peabody admitted. "But she got the jumps the minute she made us. Guilty conscience, maybe."

"Maybe. The boys are good levers, excellent buttons to push. Takes half a minute to see she'd do most anything for her sons. Ava would've seen that, factored that. Used that."

"She'd have to get from here to there and back again," Peabody considered. "I know you said Ava could've helped her with that, but I don't see Ava putting down bread crumbs by hiring personal transpo for her."

"No, neither do I. Have to be subway or bus. Take the neighbor on the right, I'll take the one on the left. Let's see what they say about the comings and goings. Then we'll go have a talk with her boarder."

"I mind my own," Cecil Blink stated the minute Eve stepped inside the musty, overheated row house. "What's she done?"

There was an avid look in his eye, and the smell of fried meat substitute in the air. "We're just making inquiries in the neighborhood. Why would you assume Ms. Petrelli had done anything?"

"Keeps to herself. That's what they say about serial killers, ain't it?" He nodded knowledgeably, and a thin storm of dandruff trickled from his scalp to the shoulders of his red-checked bathrobe. "And she don't say three words to nobody if one will get her by. Don't trust a closed-mouthed female. Used to own a restaurant, before they beat the horseshit and guts out of her husband and tossed him in the river. Mafia, that's what. She's connected."

He said it as if he were giving her hot news, so Eve pasted a look of interest on her face. "You don't say?"

"I do say, and right out loud. Probably was running illegals outta that restaurant, and they killed him—rival Mafia types. That's how it's done."

"I'm going to look into that, thanks. Meanwhile, did you notice anyone in the neighborhood out very early in the morning on March eighteenth? This past Tuesday. Say four A.M.?"

"I mind my own."

Like hell. "Maybe you were restless that night, or got

up for a drink of water. Maybe you noticed activity out on the street. Someone walking, or getting out of a car or cab?"

"Can't say I did." Which seemed to disappoint him. "Her next door, she comes home late—midnight maybe— three nights a week. They *say* she cooks for Fortuna's restaurant. Me, I don't go to restaurants. They charge an arm and a leg."

"Any visitors next door?"

"Boys have boys over. Probably up to no good. Woman who lives there with her—Nina Cohen—has some other biddies over every Wednesday night. *Say* they're playing bridge. Couple of the other neighborhood women got boys her boys fool with, go over now and then. *Her* boys don't go to school around here. Not good enough for her. They go to *private* school. They *say* on scholarships or some such thing. More likely Mafia money, if you ask me."

"Okay. Thanks for your time."

"I'm going to be locking my doors double quick. A closed-mouth woman's a dangerous woman."

Unable to resist, Eve gave him a closed-mouthed smile, and left.

"The boys are well-behaved," Peabody reported. "She keeps a clean house. Both the neighbor and her husband were sound asleep—bedroom's at the back—on the night in question during the time line. She gives Petrelli big mother points." When Eve only nodded, and continued to sit in the car, Peabody looked around. "What are we doing now?"

"Giving Bebe a little more to think about. Unless she's going to blow off work, she should be coming out soon." Eve settled back. "You know what would be an even bigger incentive for somebody who earns mother points? You give the kids this big juicy carrot, then you threaten to yank it away. Unless."

"Get the boys in school, into the camps, give them a good taste of how it can be. Then, it's the old 'If you want them to keep this, you have to do this one little thing for me. Nobody'll ever know.' "

"It could play. There's something about her though." Eve studied those hopeful window boxes and tapped her fingers on the wheel. "But there's also something under the something. So we give her a little more to think about."

It didn't take long. Bebe came out of the house wearing a dull brown coat. Don't notice me, it said to Eve. Just getting through here, just getting by.

Her gaze flashed to the car, to Eve, and her mouth folded into a sharp, thin line. The neighbor might've given her points for motherhood, but Eve gave her points for shooting up her middle finger. It took spine to flip off a couple of cops who were dogging you for murder.

Bebe stomped up the block. Giving her a few yards, Eve eased from the curb and slowly followed. Two and a half blocks to the bus stop, Eve thought. Had to be a bitch in the worst of the winter, in the rain, in the wind. Eve slid back to the curb as Bebe stood at the stop, arms folded, eyes straight ahead.

When the bus lumbered up, Bebe stomped on. And Eve pulled out to follow. It chugged to the next stop, then the next, belching its way out of the tattered neighborhood into the next. The houses grew brighter, the sidewalks smoother, the vehicles more plentiful and newer.

"Has to be hard," Peabody said, "to come out of where you landed to work for somebody else in what you used to have."

"Slap you in the face every day." She watched Bebe get out at the next stop, shoot her a furious glare, then hurry down the block to a white-washed restaurant with a bright yellow awning.

"Peabody, see what precinct covers this area. And let's see if we can impose on a couple of our brothers from the Bronx to have Italian for lunch."

"Going to keep the pressure on."

"Yeah. She's tough, but she'll pop."

"I don't know. I think making another pair of cops is just going to piss her off, dig her in. Legal Aid lawyer's going to call us whining about harassment."

"She didn't call Legal Aid. She'll pop," Eve repeated. "Twenty says she pops before end of shift today."

"Today? With those DeSalvo genes?" Peabody snorted at the idea. "I can use twenty. You're on."

Chapter 16

At central, Eve signed Anders's vitamin dispenser out of evidence. She set it on her desk, sat, studied it. A solid gold pill dispenser, she mused. Even Roarke didn't have one of those to her knowledge. Of course, he wasn't one for popping a bunch of pills every night of his life either.

If and when that day came, he'd probably have a platinum one, with diamond accents. Okay, no, he wouldn't. That was entirely too fussy and girly.

Which, she thought, Anders certainly wasn't.

More sports clothes than stylish ones. A man cave for an office.

"Bought this for him, didn't you, Ava? Planting those seeds. The poor schmuck had to use it if it was a gift from you."

Program it, she mused, turning the heavy gold box over in her hands, lift the cannily hidden tube, dump pills in. Pills tumble into proper slot. Load it up, and it tells you how many pills in each slot. Request number of any type, or any combination of types, and it dispenses, IDing by slot.

"Well, you liked your gadgets, Tommy, and she knew it."

She put in a call to EDD expecting to get the acting captain, and was surprised to hit Feeney.

"So. You're alive."

"Back in the saddle." He grinned at her. "Feel like a couple billion, tax-free. Whatever they gave me knocked the bastard out of me. Or the wife's chicken soup did."

"Glad to hear it. I've got this thing. Electronic pill dispenser."

"Why in hell would anybody need that?"

"Your guess is as good as mine. It was Thomas Anders's, and I'm working on the idea that his wife slipped a couple sleepers in here. All right if I bring it up?"

"Sure. I can send somebody down for it."

"No, I'll bring it. I want to run it by you anyway. Give me five."

She clicked off, resealed the box, initialed it, then tucked it under her arm as she headed out and up. In EDD, she veered straight away from the color and sound, and into Feeney's office.

With healthy color back in his basset hound face, Feeney sat at his desk. "I got work up the wazoo," he told her, "and already had to kick a couple asses this morning. It's good to be home."

"I spent a couple hours this morning intimidating a widowed mother of two. I love this job."

He laughed, then lifted his wiry eyebrows at the box she put on his desk. "Jesus, a *gold* pill spitter, with engraved initials?"

"For the man you want to kill who has everything."

"You said a couple of sleepers. They wouldn't do that much."

"He had traces of over-the-counter in him, but nobody can confirm he took same routinely. Ingesting one would put him out good enough to let somebody get into the bedroom, shoot him up with barbs and cock hardener. Or groggy enough so he could be bound up before he came around enough to know what was going on, because I think the barbs weren't on the order sheet. They threw the scene off from the jump. Our girl Ava isn't going to make a wrong turn like that."

"Wanted him awake for it."

"Yeah. Killer was meant to come up, truss him up, noose him—throat starts to constrict, what do you do?"

"Open your mouth and try to suck air in."

"And when he does, killer shoves the dick trick into him. The asphyxiation would get him going, then you ring the cock. Let him gasp and flop while you set the scene. If you do it right—and it wasn't done right—it's going to look like the vic was playing around on the side, dipping into the kink. Kink got out of hand. I bet part of the instructions were to loosen the scarfing after he was cooked, at least loosen it so it would appear some attempt was made to revive. Then you have your kinky cheater, a tragic, embarrassing, but fairly routine accident, and the panicked partner fleeing the scene."

"Voi-fucking-là."

"We'd look for her, sure, but we'd get nowhere. Because Anders didn't cheat, wasn't into the kink. But the scene and the evidence would read that way."

That, Eve realized—taking his decent reputation as well as his life—gripped her guts. "But see, the killer shot him up with the dick hardener. It wasn't taken orally. Shot him up with that, I'm betting, after she shot him up with the tranq."

"You want me to see if the wife diddled with the box?"

"Yeah. If you can open it up, see if anything was taken out or added before his death. Couple of days before, probably. The wife left New York on March fifteen."

"Let me play with it." Feeney initialed the bag, unsealed it to draw the box out. "Bitch is heavy. It's got voice or manual settings. She did it manually, it's going to be tougher to pin. Even if she did it by voice, a lawyer's going to argue she was his wife. She filled it or added to it at his request, even the sleeper. He's not here to say different."

"One step at a time."

She left him to it, started back down. She needed to see if Peabody had contacted Petrelli's tenant, then they needed to start working on the other possibles she'd culled from the files. Run some probabilities.

She had a feeling the computer would look favorably on Petrelli, given the data, but . . .

She paused when she spotted Benedict Forrest outside her bullpen. It was getting so she couldn't scratch her ass without coming back and finding some civilian waiting for her.

He sprang to his feet. "Lieutenant Dallas, I need to talk to you."

Since she wouldn't mind having another round with him, she gestured. "Let's take it in my office." She led the way, caught Peabody's eye as she moved through the bullpen. The gleam in it had her pointing Ben toward her office. "Go ahead in. I'll be a minute."

She skirted around desks to Peabody's. "What do you have?"

"Charles and Louise are getting *married*."

"I know. Did you—"

"I know you know because Charles just told me he told you, but you didn't tell *me*. All morning you didn't tell me."

"It wasn't the first thing on my mind."

"But this is huge." She bounced in her chair, and made Eve wonder what it was about weddings that made grown women bounce. "It's mega-mag! And he said he's turned in as LC and he's opening a practice as a therapist, and they're going to have the wedding at your house in a couple months, and—"

"Gee, Peabody, I have this connection to a murder waiting in my office. Maybe we could not take an hour later to talk about somebody else's life."

"Aw, but it's so *sweet*. And romantic."

Eve leaned down. "You do not sit here getting shiny-eyed at your desk, Detective. Not in my bullpen. Not unless you've gotten tagged by Ava Anders who gave you a full confession. Also, the words 'sweet' and 'romantic' don't come out of your mouth in my bullpen unless they are coated and dripping with sarcasm. Now suck it up."

"Spoilsport."

"Lieutenant Spoilsport to you. Nina Cohen."

"As far as she knows, Petrelli didn't leave the house on the night of the murder. But she also says Petrelli never leaves the house after midnight, so she'd assume she didn't leave." Peabody checked her watch. "Getting closer to the time you owe me twenty."

"Don't count your twenty before it crosses the road," Eve warned, and walked to her office.

Ben paced. Eve could hear the slap of his feet on her worn floor. Back and forth, back and forth. She tended to do the same herself if something was screwing with her mind.

"Sorry about that," she said as she went in. "Have a seat."

"You're looking at Ava as a suspect."

Eve closed the door behind her. It turned her office into a smaller box, but it was private. "It's a habit of mine to look at people as suspects."

"But if you're wasting time looking at someone who couldn't possibly have hurt my uncle, then you're *not* looking for the person who did." He pushed at his hair with both hands. "Leopold told me you were in asking questions about her. He's half inclined to think you're right and felt he had to warn me. As if she'd strangle me with my own belt or something. It's crazy."

"Your uncle was a wealthy man. Now she's a wealthier woman than she was when he was alive."

"So am I. Man, I mean. I'm wealthier if you want to look at the damn dollars and cents of it."

"Dollars and cents are a tried and true motive for murder."

"She wasn't even in the country. Now you're asking for

files on staff and volunteers, on women with kids in the programs. Good God."

Eve eased down on the corner of her desk. "You're pretty passionate in her defense."

"I'm the only family, the only *close* family she has left." He rubbed the back of his neck as if pain lived there. "Uncle Tommy would expect me to take care of her, to support her, and damn right to defend her."

"I got the impression you and Ava weren't particularly close. Before."

"As I said—" Both his voice and his handsome hazel eyes chilled. "I'm the family she has left."

"And between you, you own all but a fistful of Anders Worldwide. I guess something like that brings people closer."

Coldness flipped so quickly, so completely into shock, it surprised Eve the man didn't physically revolve with it. "That—that's a despicable thing to say."

"You're a healthy single man. She's an attractive woman."

"She's my uncle's *wife*. His widow. God, is this how you have to think? Do you make everything ugly and obscene?"

"Murder does, Mr. Forrest. Both you and Ava have tight, solid alibis. That's interesting, that both of you should be so solidly alibied."

"Interesting that she was away on a long-planned trip and that I got lucky? What's wrong with you? If you want to take shots at me, fine. But I can't have you taking them at her. Not with what she's going through."

"Does she know you're here?"

"No. As if I'd tell her what you're doing, add to her stress."

"Good. Now, take a step back. Take one back and describe your relationship with Ava before your uncle was killed." She lifted a hand before he could speak. "Don't bullshit me, Ben. Every lie I have to unknot wastes time. You want your uncle's killer caught and justice served?"

"Of course I do. Jesus, Jesus, I can hardly think of anything else. Of course I do."

"Tell me how you and Ava got along before Tuesday morning."

"All right, all right." He pressed his hand to his temple, then dropped into her visitor's chair. "We weren't particularly close. Not at odds or anything, not exactly."

"What, exactly?"

"We just . . . I guess we didn't have anything in common. Except for Uncle Tommy, and maybe we didn't always see eye-to-eye on how the programs were run or handled. But—"

"Don't but, don't qualify. Give me a picture."

He blew out a breath. "Maybe it felt, in a weird way, as if we were in competition for him. That sounds so stupid. You could say I felt the longer they were married, the less she wanted me around. Maybe the less I wanted to be around her. We just . . . But she loved him, and that's what matters. She loved Uncle Tommy. She was always buying him little gifts, or arranging for him to take a golf trip or a ski weekend, whatever."

"Uh-huh."

"Okay, maybe it would gripe me, a little, that she wouldn't always tell me until the last minute if she was planning something, then she'd blame it on Leo. Say she told Leo to tell me. That just didn't wash. Leo forgets nothing. So we'd get together, Uncle Tommy and I, at the club or the course or the game. I didn't go around the house that much. It didn't feel like his house much in the last couple years anyway."

"Why is that?"

"All that redecorating. God, you saw the place. Nowhere for a guy to put his feet up and watch some screen. He didn't mind it," Ben continued. "He said she put up with his foolishness, and he put up with hers."

He sat silent a moment, brooded. "It doesn't matter now. It's different now."

"Yeah, it is. Now tell me this. If your uncle had died of

natural causes, or say in a skiing accident, would you feel this strongly, this protective of Ava?"

"How can I know something like that?"

"All she's been through, you said. You weren't just talking about his death, but about the circumstances of it. And the scandal, the embarrassment to her. So think a minute, factor that out."

"I don't know what difference it makes to—"

"Humor me," Eve interrupted.

"Well, I guess, maybe I wouldn't feel as if she needed me the way she does. What I mean to say is Ava's not generally the kind of woman who needs care." His handsome face set itself into stubborn lines. "But the circumstances are what the circumstances are."

"The circumstances are that you're sitting there feeling disloyal and crappy because you made a few minor complaints about her." A nice guy, Roarke had termed him. Eve knew some couldn't help being a nice guy, even after being kicked repeatedly in the teeth. "How'd she get along with her father-in-law?"

"With . . . fine. Great, in fact. My uncle used to joke that it was a good thing he saw her first, or she'd have hooked up with Granddad. I don't see what that—"

"Just wondering. Didn't I hear they had a little trouble shortly before his death?"

"I don't remember . . . Oh, that. Yeah, there was something, probably my fault. As I said I don't—and didn't—always like how she handles the programs. I complained to Granddad about Ava hitting the program budget for what I felt were personal expenses. He got a little hot over it, but he and Ava worked it out. Lieutenant, I understand you're doing your job, and I understand you're good at your job. But it feels wrong, just wrong, for you to look at, to think about, Ava this way. I don't want whoever killed Uncle Tommy to get away with it."

"Neither do I. I have a lot of looking at and thinking about to do, about a lot of people. Right now I'm going to ask you to put your uncle first. Don't say anything to anyone else about this conversation." She pushed off her desk. Understanding the signal, Ben rose.

"All right. I'll let you get back to work. Lieutenant, no one who knew him, really knew him, could have hurt him. It had to be a stranger. It's the only thing that makes sense."

She didn't disagree.

A couple of years, she thought as she sat back down. A couple of years ago, Anders's father died. A couple of years ago, Ava redecorated. A couple of years ago she launched her mommy programs. Short pause, and she hired Charles. Laying the groundwork, Eve mused. She thinks ahead. But, Eve wondered, just how far ahead. She called up all data on Reginald Thomas Anders.

She read official data, bios, society page squibs, interviews. He struck Eve as a tough-minded businessman who'd enjoyed his retirement, his pursuit of leisure activities. He'd suffered from and was being treated for hypertension. Slipped in the shower of his son's weekend home in the Hamptons. Reaches for something, maybe he's dizzy or just off-balance, then *whoops*, fractured skull when his head slams into the Italian marble.

Son, daughter-in-law, grandson, and several houseguests in residence at the time.

What if? Eve considered, then printed out Reginald Anders's ID photo and data to add to her murder board. Back at her desk, she made a call to the Hampton investigator.

An hour later, her boots planted on her desk, she continued to study the board when Peabody came in.

"I think she did the old man," Eve said.

"Yeah, I know."

"No, the older old man. Reginald T. Anders. Maybe it was just a happy accident, one that inspired her, kicked off the rest, but she's a schemer. Petty, too, as Leo said. The older old man slapped her back for padding her expense account. She wouldn't like that one bit. And you know, I bet she already had the decorator lined up before he took his header in the shower, bumping her up to the wife of the head guy."

"What?"

Eve shook her head. "The old man had essentially retired, turning the reins over, but he still held controlling interest. That seems to be a pattern with the Anders men. Shift the controls, but hold on to the power. He dies, Tommy inherits controlling interest, at which time he transfers a little bit to his devoted wife. I bet she asked for it, too. 'Tommy, I hope it's not too much to ask, but you know how I loved Reggie. If I could have just a few shares of the company, just a reminder of him, it would mean so much to me.' Yeah, she could work that. Little sliver of the pie, just a taste while she waits for the bigger slice."

"If she wanted a big slice, why didn't she go after the old man? I mean, if she'd been able to work marrying him, she'd have cut out the middle man."

"Bet she considered it," Eve replied. "But he went for younger. About a decade younger than Ava would've been when she hooked Tommy."

"Eeuuw."

"And the *eeuuw* would be reason two. A man in his eighties marries a much younger woman, then croaks, who does everybody give the fish-eye to first?"

"The younger woman."

"Which is exactly what the investigator did, though it looked accidental. He still took a hard look at the twenty-six-year-old aspiring actress who'd been sharing the old man's bed for a few months. He did a skim over Tommy and Ben, the main beneficiaries. He never took more than a cursory glance at Ava."

Peabody rolled it over. "If it's playing accidental anyway, she wouldn't pop out."

"I bet the party, the house party, was her idea. Yeah, I bet it was. Perfect cover. Who's going to notice if the busy hostess slips away for ten minutes? Less if she prepped it, and you can bet your ass she did."

Simple, Eve thought. Quick and easy. "All she has to

do is go in, strip down. Needs to strip down so she doesn't get her clothes wet. Dad-in-law's singing in the shower. Step in, give him a shove. Step out, towel off, get dressed. Take the towel with you to your own bath. Freshen your hair and makeup, join your guests. It wouldn't take more than ten."

She dropped her feet, swiveled, sent Peabody a hard smile. "And guess who noticed first that the old man was missing. Gee, where in the world is Reggie? He's missing all the fun. Tommy, be a darling and go up and tell your father I'm making him the perfect martini."

"Cold."

"And smart. Can't do the husband the same way, not even close to the same way. People might turn that fish-eye on you. Just might. Not a household or routine accident this time, too many accidents in the Anders family. And unfortunately, I can't turn the eaten-by-a-shark incident on her."

"Switch to murder," Peabody said. "Juicy sensational murder that shines a big spotlight on it. Who's going to try to connect a bathroom accident two years ago with a sex crime now? Except you."

"It was supposed to look like kink gone wrong. An accident, technically, but yeah, a big, juicy, sensational accident. Or failing that, a sex crime. Partner gets pissed, doesn't stop at the safe word. Either way, it works for her. It makes Anders responsible for his own death. Empty house this time, with her tucked in with pals thousands of miles away. She's damn good at this. I need to . . . why are you in here?"

"Oh, I forgot with all the singing in the shower. Bronx checked in. They enjoyed spaghetti Bolognese and manicotti, respectively, while sending intimidating looks toward Petrelli in the open kitchen. She left midway through her shift. Their waitress told them she screwed up two orders, then told the owner she was feeling ill. They'd be happy to go back tomorrow, try the stuffed eggplant and lasagna."

"The sacrifices cops make. I don't think it's going to take that long. We'll keep them on tap, but meanwhile I have to review the rest of this data on the old man, write up a report, the notes, get them to Mira for her take. I've still got the Nadine interviews to watch, and I want to dig up the old man's girl toy, the rest of the houseguests, and re-interview. Then . . . you know, it was a lot easier when you were the aide and I could just dump the grunt work on you."

"Aw. Besides, you still dump grunt work on me."

"It's not the same. Wait a minute. Wait." Eve bolted up in her chair. "Every-fucking-body's got aides and admins and personal assistants."

"Except you."

"And Ava. Where's Ava's? Study and review the reports and data on the Reginald Anders death, write up notes on the new theory we just discussed. Run the list of names of houseguests, start setting up interviews."

"Not that I do any grunt work."

"Out." Eve reached for her 'link, contacted Leopold. "Who does Ava use as an aide or PA?" she asked. "I don't have a name."

"Because there isn't one, officially. If she had a PA, his or her salary and benefits would come out of her pocket."

Not the Ava Eve knew. "Are you telling me she did all the drone and grunt work personally, made all the contacts, read all the files and so on?"

"No, I'm going to tell you she tapped volunteers, other staff routinely. For just quick, little favors. She used several of the mothers over the life of the program, claiming it gave them pride and training for job opportunities. She never paid any of them. Gifts, now and then." He offered a sour smile. "She likes giving gifts."

"Do you have names, specific names for people she tapped?"

"There's no list. It's unofficial, as I said. But I can probably put something together for you. I'll need to ask around, as I wasn't privy to all of who did what for her."

"I'd appreciate that."

"Lieutenant, I know Ben came to see you. I apologize. I shouldn't have said anything to him, even though you said—"

"It's no problem."

"It got in my craw, that's all I can say. It got in, and it stuck, the way she's slathering it on. Grunt and drone work? That would be his job now. She—" He cut himself off. "Obviously, it's still in my craw. I'll start putting a list together for you."

"Thanks."

She bet Petrelli was on the list. She just bet—"What!" she demanded when her in-office 'link signaled.

"Dallas, guess who's here?"

"Guess how long it's going to take me to tie your tongue into a square knot?"

"Jeez." Peabody folded said tongue safely inside her mouth. "Bebe Petrelli. And she is pissed!"

"Excellent, book an interview room, put her there."

Eve kicked back in her chair—the better to let the pissed Bebe stew a bit—and looked at the murder board. "It's starting to break, Ava. Can you feel it? Do you feel it cracking under your stylish and tasteful shoes? I'm looking forward to watching you drop through the hole. I can't quite figure out why I'm looking forward to it quite so much. But hey, I've got to get my kicks somewhere."

Eve gave it another ten minutes, then strolled out to take on Bebe in Interview.

"This is crap. This is harassment." Eve shrugged, dropped into the chair across the little table from the very pissed-off Bebe. "Call a lawyer, file a complaint. But you don't want to do that, Bebe, so let's not waste time pretending you do. You have the right to remain silent," Eve began, and recited the Revised Miranda while Bebe gaped at her.

"You're *charging* me?"

"I didn't say anything about charges—yet. I asked if you understood your rights and obligations in this matter. Do you understand them?"

"Yes, I understand them, goddamn it. I don't understand why I have any obligations. I didn't *do* anything."

"Did Ava Anders ask you to?"

"No." Bebe folded her arms tight at her waist.

"Really? She never asked you to make 'link calls for her, or maybe whip up some cannolis for a party? Run errands, take care of a little office work?"

"I thought you meant about..." Her arms relaxed. "Sure I helped out some. Volunteered. Anders was giving my boys a lot, and giving me a lot. So I was happy to pay Mrs. Anders back. It made it feel less like charity."

"Gave you some pride. So first, let's say, she asks you to do some little thing, then next time it's a little bit bigger thing, then bigger yet. Would you say that's the way it was, Bebe?"

"I said I helped out. I was happy to."

"Did you confide in her? Open up? You got to be tight, right? With you doing these little jobs for her. With her trusting you to do them. And you hanging out with her some at these retreats she took you on. Did you tell her how you missed your husband, how hard it was sometimes to raise your boys on your own? What your hopes and dreams for them were?"

Bebe's lips quivered before she clamped them tight. "Why shouldn't I? Part of the reason for the retreats was to share, to network and support. Why shouldn't I? There's no shame in it."

"And she was sympathetic, even intimate." To close off some of Bebe's space, Eve leaned in. "Did she open up to you, Bebe? Did she share, so you'd know even a woman in her position, with her resources had it tough?"

"It's personal. It's none of your damn business."

"It's my damn business when her husband's dead!" The rapid change of Eve's tone, from mild, even cajoling to hard and mean had Bebe jolting. "It's all my business now, so don't fuck with me. It was tit for tat, was that how she made it seem? I'll do this for you, if you do me this little favor? I can play that."

Leaning back, Eve took a casual sip from the bottle of water she'd brought in with her, and throttled down again. "You tell me what I need to know, and I'll see to it that your husband's case is reopened, reopened, Bebe, and assigned to the best available in the Bronx Homicide Division."

"They don't care about me, they don't care about Luca."

"I'll make sure they do. Peabody, can and will I make sure the Bronx cares about Luca Petrelli, and bringing his killers to justice?"

"Yes, sir, you can and will if you choose to. Bebe," Peabody added, "the lieutenant doesn't bullshit about murder. You should've figured that out by now. And after your lunch visit, you should figure she's got some pull in the Bronx."

"I'm telling you, Bebe—look at me! I'll make sure they reopen Luca's case. I'll make sure they care. I'm telling you that on record. Now. Do you want the case reopened?"

Tears shimmered and swam. Then spilled. "Yes."

"Did Ava Anders ask you to kill Thomas Anders?"

"No. No. No. She didn't. I swear on my boys, she didn't. But . . ."

"*But.* That's the sticker. The *but*'s why you didn't attend the retreat six weeks ago. The *but*'s why you haven't attended or served at any of the seminars or outreach programs for the last five months. Tell me about that."

Bebe swiped at tears with fingers that trembled. "I couldn't get off work. I couldn't take the time. My boys . . . She was good to me, do you *get* that? She gave us a chance, and you want me to rat her out."

"She used you, and in your gut you know it. Your father used you, your brothers used you, your dealers and your johns used you. You *know* when you're being used. What did she ask you to do?"

"She didn't ask. She . . . she told me how he abused her sexually, how he was bringing women into the house, and wanted her to . . . to participate in . . . in the kind of sex that disgusted her."

When Peabody offered her a cup of water, Bebe drank it down in one go.

"She shared that with you?" Peabody spoke gently. "Those intimate details of her marriage?"

"She said she knew I'd understand, and I did. I did understand. She said he was going to toss her out, stop the programs, cancel the scholarships, destroy everything she'd put in motion unless she gave in. It was making her sick."

"You had to feel awfully sorry for her," Peabody prompted. "And upset at the idea he'd take all that away from her. And your boys, too."

"I did. God. I didn't know what to think. I could hardly believe it. He seemed like such a nice man. But she broke down, just broke down, went to pieces. She said she'd found out he was abusing some of the kids, the girls, and she couldn't do anything about it. No one would believe her, and how he had to be stopped."

"When was this?" Eve demanded.

"Last summer. Like July. Kids were in camp, and I was doing a little work for her on a Sunday at her house."

"Just the two of you, right? Nobody else there."

"Yeah, yeah. And what set her off was she was talking to one of the women's shelters about one of the mothers who had kids in the program, about getting her job training and stuff, and when she finished, she just fell to pieces."

"Convenient."

Bebe's head snapped up at Eve's comment. "It wasn't like that. It's just, she was so upset, and it all came pouring out. He was away, her husband. He went away a lot. There was so much on her, you know? And now he's saying if she doesn't fall in line, she's out on her ass, and all those kids . . . my kids. I said something about there had to be a way to stop him, to protect herself, to protect the kids. She said, the only way to stop him, a man with his kind of power, his kind of sickness, was if he was dead. How it was horrible to say, but she wished he was dead, and sometimes after he went at her, she'd lie there and think of how it could be done. How he could have an accident, if she had someone she could trust and depend on to help her. How if he had an accident, the kids would all be safe. My kids would be safe."

"What kind of accident did she suggest?"

"She didn't. She didn't because I cut her off. I cut her off because there was something in her eyes that made me think she wasn't just imagining it. I know something about that, something about that look."

As if exhausted, Bebe covered her face with her hands. "She wanted it. God, she wanted him dead, and she wanted me to help her. So I cut her off and started on about how she should talk to someone, like they were always telling us in the seminars. How she should make the break, and move on. He wouldn't really cut the programs because it would make him look bad. Stuff like that, and I got out. I got out as soon as I could, even though she backed off, told me I was right. She'd just had a bad moment, and she made me promise I wouldn't talk about what she'd said with anyone. It wouldn't be good for the programs."

Bebe heaved out a long breath. "She didn't get in touch after that to ask me to volunteer. I figured she was embarrassed. And when I went to the retreat, the last one I went to at the end of August, she avoided me. When I pinned her about it, because, I guess, I thought we were friends—sort of friends—she was really cold. Ice cold. Told me she was a very busy woman, with a lot of responsibilities, how I should remember all she'd done for my boys, and be grateful for that. How I should take care of them, and myself, concentrate on that so . . . so the scholarships didn't go away."

"Did you notice her being friendly with anyone in particular at that retreat?"

"I stayed away from her. Like you said, my father used me. My brothers. Then I put myself in the position so the johns could use me, and the dealers. I stopped letting myself be used and I met Luca."

Resentment, and some of the spit came back in her eyes. "I got it, okay? I got it. After that, she was using me. I didn't blame her so much, considering, but I wasn't going to put myself in that spot again. So I stayed away."

"Smart move."

"Is that enough? Is that want you wanted?"

"It ain't bad."

"You're going to push for them to open Luca's case? You're going to do that?"

"I did it this morning," Eve told her. "The two cops you made who had lunch in the place you work are supposed to be good, and they're picking it up. They'll be in touch with you after they review the file."

"You . . . why did you do that when I didn't give you anything for it?"

"Because your husband deserved better than he got. Because it seems to me you and your kids deserved better. And because I don't like it when a good man is killed for no good reason."

Bebe stared for another moment. Then she simply laid her head down on the table and wept.

"Record off." Rising, Eve signaled Peabody. As she left the room, she heard Peabody's voice comforting the sobbing woman.

Chapter 17

Eve tagged Feeney on the way from Interview to her office. "Give me something."

"Christ, kid, do you know how much I got piled up here from being out? I got the backlog down from my armpits to my asshole. I'll get to your box."

"Can't you just open it and see if she reprogrammed or reloaded it before..." She trailed off at his stony stare. He had a good one, she thought. She'd modeled hers after it. "Okay, all right. Just as soon as you can."

"If you don't interrupt me to nag, it'll be sooner."

She clicked off.

Circumstantial, she reminded herself. Even if Feeney proved that the dispenser had been reprogrammed and/or reloaded, it was circumstantial. She hated building a case on circumstantial. And that's all she had. Impressions, comments, Bebe's statement, personalities. And not a single solid piece of evidence.

Yet.

She strode back into Homicide, where Baxter turned from the AutoChef. "Dallas. The boyfriend/trannie/cross-dressing angle's not panning out. Custer case," he said when she looked blank.

"Right. Sorry, my mind's elsewhere. What's your sense, Baxter?"

"That the case is as cold as the victim. The kid and I can keep taking pokes at it when we squeeze out some time. I don't want to put it in Inactive yet. We're going to have to slap it down to the bottom of the pile, maybe give it a shake every now and then."

"Not all of them close."

"Yeah. I know. Pisser when they don't. We closed six others since we caught this one, and it's still a pisser."

She sympathized, but she had her own case to close, and needed to shuffle some of the pieces, try to see a different angle. In her office, she pulled up a couple of the possibles who'd come in below Petrelli on her list. After zeroing in on the next, gauging the time, she detailed a report on the interview with Petrelli, added notes and speculations.

"Computer, run probability. Given the data, the statements, what is the probability Ava Anders is a big, fat liar?"

Your question is not properly structured and cannot be answered on a probability scale. Please rephrase.

"Seemed straightforward to me. Try this. Run probability given the data and statements included in the Anders, Thomas A., homicide that Anders, Ava, has lied to the primary and/or to other individuals who gave an account of conversations with subject."

Working…

Eve rose, programmed coffee. Stared out the window.

Task complete. Conflicting statements given regarding conversations with subject indicate a 97.3 percent probability Anders, Ava, has given false statements. Probability cannot determine which statements are false and which are factual.

"I think I can figure that out. Run second probability. Given the data, and assuming the statement just logged by Petrelli, Bebe, is factual, what is the probability that Anders, Ava, arranged, devised, or is involved in the murder of Anders, Thomas A."

Working...

"Yeah, chew on that. Circumstantial, more circumstantial. But probabilities have some weight. Enough weight, somebody sinks. Who else did you set up the way you set up Bebe, Ava? Who else did you have on the line?"

Task complete. Factoring Petrelli statement as a factual account, the probability is 50.2 percent that Anders, Ava, arranged, devised, or is involved in the murder of Anders, Thomas A.

"Bollocks to that," Eve stated, pulling out one of Roarke's phrases. "Fifty doesn't add weight. It's a wash. I need another. I need one of the other fish on the line to flip."

"Dallas." Peabody gave the doorjamb a quick rap. "I arranged transpo for Petrelli. Didn't want her having to deal with the bus or the subway. She was pretty wrecked."

"Fine." Eve turned, held out a hand, rubbed her fingers and thumb together.

Peabody shoved her hands in her pockets. "I don't have twenty on me. Isn't it enough reward that you got her to spill it on Ava?"

In answer, Eve simply wiggled the fingers of her outstretched hand.

"Okay, okay, man." She snatched up a memo cube from Eve's desk. "This is going to have to come out of my Roarke fund."

"You have a fund for Roarke? To donate to him, or to try to buy him?"

"I wish—on the buying part. It'd be a skim for McNab. We have a deal where we both got to pick one person, and if we ever got the chance to..." She closed her fist, pumped it while she wiggled her eyebrows. "With said person, the other of us would understand. A one-shot deal. I picked Roarke."

"Well, he's a superior lay, so you'd have that before I peeled the skin off your still quivering body, roasted it on an open fire, then force-fed it to you."

"Okay then. So..." Clearing her throat, Peabody turned the cube on record. "I owe Dallas, Lieutenant Meaniepants Eve, twenty dollars to be paid out of my hard-earned, under-appreciated detective's salary next payday. Peabody, Detective Churchmouse Delia."

She tossed the memo cube. Eve caught it one-handed, slid it into her pocket. "What's the Roarke fund?"

"Oh, I'm earmarking a little every payday and socking it away. When I get a decent amount I'm going to have him invest it for me. He said he would. It's not a superior lay, but hey, could be a nice bang."

"Never known him to misfire. Start on the interviews on old man Anders. Plowder and Bride-West are on there. Don't hit them. Start with out-of-towners. Start with the ones Ava isn't tight with. The girl toy, any of the staff who were there, particularly any temps or staff who've been fired or have resigned. Low-key it, just following up on additional information that's come to light. Just reconfirming, blah blah. I'm heading into the field shortly, then I'm working from home."

"You're going solo?"

"Actually, I'm going to call in a superior lay, who also looks like a superior lay. He could be handy in my next interview."

"Okay, but if you get laid in the field, I expect to read the details thereof in your report. All the details."

"Keep that up and you'll usurp Jenkinson's Sick Bastard title."

"That's a personal goal of mine. Dallas, are we getting anywhere? I mean, we know what we know. But are we getting anywhere toward bringing her down for it?"

"She won't think so. And that's why we're getting somewhere. Get started on the interviews, full reports on all of them."

"How many houseguests?"

"Sixteen houseguests, eight staff."

"Twenty-four interviews? It'll take hours."

"Then I'd get started. Out."

Eve picked up her 'link, and considered it a good omen when Roarke answered personally. "Lieutenant. What can I do for you?"

"I was wondering how you'd feel about meeting me at a sex club."

"How odd. I was just thinking what we might do this evening, and that was top of my list."

"Bang She Bang, downtown on Spring. Does an hour from now work for you?"

"I can make it work considering the incentive."

A stray thought brought on a scowl. "You don't own it, do you?"

He cocked a brow. "I don't believe I own any establishment with that name. I could probably pick it up within the hour if that would help."

She'd bet more than Peabody's twenty he could do just that. "No, thanks. I'll just use the Power of Roarke to my advantage on this one."

"I thought it was the Fear of Roarke."

"Depends on the situation. I'm thinking power will squeeze more juice out of this one than fear."

"Either are at your disposal. In an hour, Lieutenant."

After he clicked off she made a few calls, scribbled a few notes, imagined sitting on her hands to keep herself from nagging Feeney.

Peabody hailed her as Eve started out. "I talked to the girl toy—Angel Scarlett. She got all choked up when I mentioned the old man. I don't think she's going to be winning any awards as an actress. Her rundown was consistent with her earlier statement, but not so exact it felt practiced."

Peabody did a left-to-right swivel in her chair. "She and the old man had taken a nap—which she made sure I knew was a euphemism for boinking, then she went down to take a swim. She was in the pool with some of the other guests—and that's consistent with their original statements—when the old man went down in the shower."

Peabody glanced down at her notes. "Cocktails and canapes were being served out there. I asked casually about her hostess, and she was offhand about that. Ava was flitting around somewhere, like always. You were off on the martini. It was a gin and tonic, which was the old man's summer drink of choice. Ava was mixing gin and tonics herself, and commented that the old man wasn't down. Wouldn't Tommy go up and tell his father they were all having cocktails. A few minutes later, he ran out on the terrace, up outside the old man's room, yelled for help. He'd already called nine-one-one, already moved the body in an attempt to revive. That's all in the reports. But I did get something new."

"Stun me."

"It probably won't stun you that Angel wasn't, and isn't, Ava's biggest fan. Cold, snobbish, self-righteous—and those were the compliments. And she said she thought things were a little chilly between Ava and the old man that weekend."

"Why?"

"Didn't know. Her 'big white bear' as she called him never talked business with her, and never gossiped about family. He didn't care for it when she complained about Ava's attitude toward her, so she kept it to herself. But she noticed they weren't all chummy, as usual. Didn't have coffee together by the pool that morning, and that was a habit of theirs. She suspected they'd had a little spat, but since she didn't know, kept that to herself, too."

"Write it up, log it in. I may have a line to tug on that. Later."

The trip down to Spring, an exercise in tedium on the best days, became a pitched battle due to an overturned glide-cart and the stalled Rapid Cab that had crashed into its grill. Even from ten cars back, Eve could see it would only get worse as the cab driver and the cart operator were currently beating the snot out of each other.

Eve called it in, snapping out an order for a black-and-white or patrol droids. Pissed, she slammed out of her vehicle, whipping out her badge as she strode forward. Mostly, she noted, the two men were just rolling around on raw soy fries and dogs, bapping each other on the back.

"Break it up! NYPSD, and I said break it up." She gave both of their shins a sharp rap with her boot. "Break it up or I'm hauling you both in. And as God is my witness, if any piece of either one of you makes contact with any piece of me, you're serving the full pop on assaulting an officer."

Both men lifted bloodied faces to hers, and began to shout complaints and accusations.

"Zip it! And you people! Go and find something else to do. Show's over here. You, cab guy, what's your story?"

"I'm cruising for a fare." His voice was musical, a tropical island song that contrasted sharply with the bleeding mouth and swollen eye. "Guy's hailing half a block down, and I gonna pick him up. And this one, this one, he *shoves* the cart out in the street. In front of me!"

"Fuck I did! Why'd I wanna do that? Wreck my cart thataway?"

"'Cause you crazy, man!"

Eve pointed at Cab Guy to shut him down.

"Your cart's in the street, pal." A scrapper, Eve noted, about half the size of Cab Guy, with New York as pugnacious in his tone and attitude as his bloody nose.

"Yeah, it's in the ever-fucking street, but I didn't shove it there. Goddamn kids did. Damn kids, they come along, and one's ordering a dog and fries so I'm on him, you know? And another one of 'em musta flipped off my brakes. Next I know the bunch of 'em are shoving my cart off the corner. Laughing like hyenas. Look what they done to my cart." He spread his arms wide as blood dribbled out of his nose. "What they want to do that for? I'm just trying to make a living here."

"Can you ID them?"

"I don't know. Maybe. Look at my cart, wouldja? Look at my stuff."

"I see these boys!" Cab Guy waved a hand in the air. "I see them go flying across the street. Airboards."

"Yeah, yeah." Cart Guy bobbed his head. "They had airboards. Couple of them riding tandem. I didn't see which way they went. I was trying to grab the cart, get to the brake, but the cab..." He shoved back his hair. "Man. Sorry about your cab."

"Not your fault. I see the kids. I can help identify." Cab Guy offered a unifying smile with bloodied teeth. "Sorry about your cart, man."

Eve turned the situation over to a black-and-white and a couple of beat droids. Cab and Cart Guy were now enjoying solidarity. They'd be neighborhood kids, she assumed. And they'd likely roll another cart or two before the day was done. But damned if she was going to help track them down.

She was ten minutes over the hour already.

It came to a total of twenty minutes behind before she could park, flip her On Duty, and hit the sidewalk. She'd already seen him—her expert consultant, her superior lay. He leaned against the wall of the graffiti-scrawled, post–Urban War rattrap that held Bang She Bang, wearing a dark suit with the thinnest of pinstripes with a spring-weight overcoat billowing a bit as he worked on his hand-held.

His wrist unit was likely worth more than the building

against which he braced. In this neighborhood with its funky junkies, chemi-heads, grifters, shifters, and spine crackers, a man's life was at risk for his shoes. From her vantage point, she saw what Tiko would've called a suspicious character swagger in Roarke's direction, his hand in his pocket and his fingers very likely closed over a sticker.

Roarke simply flicked his gaze up, over, locked them on. And suspicious character kept on swaggering by.

"You." Eve jabbed a finger at one of the grunts loitering in a doorway.

"Fuck you," he called back, and added his middle finger in case English wasn't her first language.

Eve flipped out her badge as she crossed the sidewalk. The badge itself didn't mean much here. It was all about what she put behind it. "That's Lieutenant, as in: Fuck you, Lieutenant."

Beside the grunt, his gap-toothed companion sniggered.

"Here's what I could do," Eve supposed. "I could slap your head against that wall, while I'm kicking your balls into your belly," she added to the companion. "And after that, I can have you in restraints while I turn out your pockets. You're carrying illegals."

"Fuck you know. You can't rouse without probable."

"I see the illegals. I've got X-ray vision."

"No shit?" The companion grinned at her, wide-eyed. "That is frosty, complete."

"Ain't it? But I'm not going to do that. I'm not going to do runs on both of you, then come around to your flops and turn them upside down and inside out. I'm not going to personally see to it that you spend the next several days in a cage. I'm not going to do that because you're both going to stand right here until I come back, and you're going to watch my ride there as if it were your own beloved child. I come out, and my official police vehicle's exactly where I left it, in exactly the condition I left it, we part friends. Otherwise, I'm going to be paying you a visit later. Got it?"

The first guy shrugged. "I got nothing better to do."

"That's handy, because I do. You got ten now," she said and pulled out the bribe. "You get another when I come back. I bet your name's John Smith," she said to the companion.

"Hell, no. Clipper Plink."

"That's what I said. You're Clipper Plink."

"How do you *know* this stuff?" He eyed her as if she were the Second Coming. "You got superpowers, bitch?"

"Damn right."

"Jesus, Clip," she heard the grunt say as she strode toward Roarke, "can you be any fucking dumber?"

He loved to watch her work, Roarke thought. It never failed to fascinate and entertain him. So he'd done just that, relaxed against the wall while she'd taken aim at the pair of street toughs. Well, one and a half toughs, he supposed was more accurate. They hadn't stood a chance against her when she'd tossed on the badass cop as she did her coat.

Now she strode to him, the faintest hint of a smile on her face. "How many street thieves, muggers, and spine crackers did you flick off with one 'Try it, boy-o, and you'll be pissing blood for some time to come' stare?"

"I didn't count. I don't believe this is a very safe neighborhood. I'm relieved I have a cop nearby."

"Yeah, like you need one."

"Only you, darling. Night and day. Boy-o?"

"That particular stare has the boy-o in it. Don't tell me you came down here in a ride as fancy as the suit?"

"Then I won't. Why don't you tell me why we're heading into this sex dive on an evening that makes me almost believe spring may come again?"

"One of the strippers, LC for club work, also happens to be one of Ava's mommies. I'll fill you in on the rest later, figure you can follow along as we go. But I want to take her now. She's only on about another hour."

"Let's not waste time, then." He pulled open the door.

They walked out of the almost spring evening and into the sharp, bright world of sex for sale.

It smelled of sweat, cum, smoke from a variety of illegal substances, and the cheapest of alcoholic liquids. A great many of those unattractive substances splattered the floor. Men and women with hard eyes, glassy eyes, crazed eyes, bored eyes hunched at tables or squatted at a short, stained bar on backless stools while two servers—one male, one female—carted drinks or empties on trays. Both were naked, unless you counted tats and piercings, their skin pulsing faintly red in the ugly light.

On a small, raised stage, two women—it would be absurd to term them dancers—humped long silver poles while what only the deaf could mistake for music blasted. Each wore a sparkling band at the waist, with a few bills tucked in. Neither, Roarke noted, had pulled in much for this particular number.

He walked to the bar with Eve. The man running the stick had skin so white it nearly glowed. The faint pink around his eyes usually indicated funky-junkie, but Roarke noted the eyes were the palest of blues—water blue—and just as clear.

The albino slapped a short glass of something the color and consistency of coal oil on the bar in front of a customer before moving down to them. "Stand at the bar, you order one drink minimum. Table runs two."

"Cassie Gordon?"

"Stand at the bar, one drink minimum."

Even those pale eyes should've made her for a cop, Roarke thought. Roarke pulled out a ten, covering them both, even as she pulled her badge. "Keep the drinks," Roarke told him. "I've a fondness for my stomach lining."

Eve slapped the badge down. "Cassie Gordon."

"We got a license." The albino gestured behind him where it was displayed, as per city ordinance. "Up to date."

"I didn't ask for your license. Cassie Gordon."

The bartender plucked up Roarke's bill, slid it into his own pocket. "She's up with a private. Got another five minutes on his roll. Then she's on in twenty, you can catch her between, wait till she's done. No matter to me. You take a table, cost another ten."

"Pal, I wouldn't sit at one of those tables if I was decked out in a hazmat suit. What you're going to do is show us a clean private room—not one of the sex rooms—and you're going to send Cassie there. You're going to signal her to cut it short, and come down. If you don't, my partner and I are going to make your life really unhappy."

"This isn't a cop." The bartender jerked his head at Roarke. "Cops don't dress like that."

"I'm not, no," Roarke said in what seemed like the most pleasant of tones, if you were deaf and didn't hear the jagged threat under it. "And that's why I'll hurt you more, and enjoy it more. Where's the owner's peep?"

"Got no reason to cause trouble." The bartender reached under the bar. Even as Eve braced, she heard a faint buzz. A door behind the bar slid open.

"That'll do nicely, then. I'll be matching that first ten when we're done." Roarke's terrifyingly pleasant tone never altered. "Unless you do something to annoy me or my partner here. That happens, I'll be having the first ten back along with a chunk of you."

Eve said nothing until they were inside the peep—a small, relatively clean room holding a couple of chairs, a little desk, and boasting a wall of screens that surveyed the club.

"I've got the badge. I get to do the intimidating and make the threats."

"Why'd you ask me for this romantic date if you weren't aiming to let me play, too?"

"I wanted to scare the albino bartender in the sex club."

He laughed, tapped his finger on the dent in her chin. "Aw, darling, I promise you can scare the next one."

"Yeah, because the city's loaded with them. We've probably got a couple minutes. So lightning-round version."

She zipped through the salients on Bebe Petrelli, skimmed over her theory about the senior Anders to give

Roarke a taste, and ended with her supposition Ava might have approached Cassie Gordon.

"She made a mistake with Petrelli," Roarke pointed out. "Do you think she made another?"

"Won't know until I ask. Gordon's done strip and sex work for eight years. A woman makes it through eight years doing that, she probably knows how to read people. She's got a daughter. Ten-year-old daughter, in the program. Ice skater. No father in the picture. Kid didn't cop a scholarship, but Anders is paying for her rink time. She's got a private coach. On paper, Gordon's paying her." Eve nodded to the screen. "Do you figure she makes enough in a dive like this to pay for a private coach?"

"Not in a thousand rides on the pole, not here."

"She's going to tell us where she's getting the money for the coach, how many favors she's done for Ava. And I'm going to know if one of those favors was killing him."

"There she is."

Roarke looked away from Eve's fierce eyes to the screen where a tall blonde in a short green robe swayed through the tables on glossy, high-platform heels. As she passed, one of the men at a table for three reached out, stuck his hand under her robe.

The blonde backhanded him, knocking him out of the chair without breaking stride.

"Well now, there's another woman who can take care of herself." He smiled at Eve. "That sort never fails to appeal to me."

Chapter 18

It was certainly interesting, to Roarke's mind, sharing a small room with the outsized personalities of two women. Cassie Gordon shoved herself into the room, a provocatively dressed Amazon with annoyed eyes the same hard brown as her roots. The eyes latched on Eve, and the wide, mobile mouth curled.

"You got ten minutes. I'm on in twenty. I don't dance, I don't get paid, so unless the freaking NYPSD plans on compensating me for my . . ."

Her gaze tracked over to Roarke, zeroed in. Annoyance one-eightied to pleasure; the lips rearranged themselves from curl to curve. "Well, hello, Officer Incredible. Are you here to search and manhandle me? I hope."

Roarke didn't have time to decide if he felt amusement or insult at being mistaken for a cop before Eve stepped into Cassie's face. "You're going to want to talk to me."

"I'd rather talk, and lots and lots of other things, with him." But she shrugged, dropped into a chair, crossed her long, bare legs. "What's the beef?"

"Let's start off with your whereabouts between one and five A.M. on the morning of March eighteenth. Tuesday morning."

"Home." She skimmed back her hair, gave Roarke what he considered a rather masterful eye-fuck. "In my big, lonely bed."

"Cut the crap, Cassie, or we'll be having this conversation at Central."

"What's your twist? That time of night I'm home. I work days."

"A lot of people in your profession put in overtime. You were acquainted with Thomas Anders?"

"Not especially. I know who he is—was," she corrected. "My little girl's in the Anders sports program. She's a figure skater. She's a champion. But I didn't hob with the nob."

"Ever been to the Anders home?"

"Are you fucking kidding me?" Cassie reared back her head and laughed. "Is she fucking kidding me?" she said to Roarke.

"She's not, no. Why is the question so amusing?"

"I take my clothes off and turn tricks for a living. Not the kind of dinner party guest I expect the Anderses entertain regular."

"But Mrs. Anders did indeed entertain you," Roarke continued. "At retreats, spas, hotels."

"That's different. Those things were for mothers of kids in the programs. I'm a goddamn good mother," she snapped, pointing at her own partially concealed breasts. "Nobody can say different."

"No one is," Roarke said smoothly as Eve appeared to be giving him the line. "But you did socialize with Ava Anders."

The sound she made combined snort with Bronx cheer. "If you can call it that."

"What would you call it?"

"Same kind of arrangement I just concluded upstairs."

"She fuck you, Cassie?" Eve asked.

"Not literally. I got no problem doing the girl-on-girl if the fee's right, but I don't think she's into that." A shrug shifted the robe so her right breast peeked out coyly. "She wanted something, I gave it, and I got paid. That's how I look at it."

"What did she want?"

"I figure I got the invite so she could show how—what's the word—democratic she is. And I figure that's bull. But my kid? She's a freaking jewel, so I can take the bull or anything else gets thrown at me if it's for her."

"What did Ava throw at you?"

"Look, I gotta get in costume. It's my last round this shift, and I can't afford—"

"You'll be compensated." Roarke remained relaxed, answered his wife's stony stare with the mildest of glances while Cassie studied them both.

"I can earn five hundred on the last round."

"Talk about bull," Eve began.

"You'll be compensated," Roarke repeated. "Answer the lieutenant, stop playing it out, and you'll get the five."

Those hard eyes narrowed. "You ain't no cop."

"A fact for which I give thanks daily. You can answer the question the cop asks and get the five, or well, you'll be answering them anyway in less comfortable surroundings and get nothing. And since you'll be squeezing in the round after we leave in any case, you've a chance at five clear in your pocket."

"Not a cop, but not stupid." Another shrug, but Cassie followed this one with an absent tug that closed the front of her robe again. Or nearly. "Okay, it's like this. I take Gracie, my kid, to the ice rink in the park. Been doing that since she was about three. Even I can see she's got a knack for it, and she freaking loves it. I can't afford rink time, or not much of it, so she only got to skate in the winter. And good skates, good lessons, they're out of orbit. I applied for the Anders program, and she got in. Man, it was like I'd given her the world. I'd do anything to make sure she keeps it."

"Anything Ava asked?"

"Look, bitch wants to know how I handle tricks, I'm not going to get razzed about it. She wants to get a peek into the dirty, no skin off mine. She figures I owe her volunteer time, I work it in. My kid gets good skates, nice skating clothes, solid rink time. She wants to pretend her old man's interested in the dirty, what's it to me?"

"Pretend?"

Smiling, Cassie ran a fingertip up and down the front of her robe. "I know when I'm being played. These little *chats* were for her benefit. Maybe she wanted to try some shit out with her old man. Couldn't hurt, right? Except he's dead, right? Died doing the dirty. She do him?"

"She was out of the country at the time."

"Lucky for her, I guess."

"You don't like her one bit," Roarke commented.

"Not one small bit." Cassie held up her thumb and forefinger a fraction apart, then slapped them closed. "She lords it over—or ladies it over—you. Covers it up with the 'we're all part of the big happy Anders family,' but she expects you to do plenty of bowing and scraping. I can give a fat asshole a bj upstairs, I can bow and scrape. I get compensated."

"Did she share information about her sex life with you?"

"She said her old man was into the dirty and the strange and she wasn't, but more subtle than that. Feeling me out was my sense. I half-expected her to hire me to do him so she could watch and get pointers. Thing is, I don't think she liked me any more than I liked her and we both knew it. Both knew we were shoveling the shit."

"What did you have to do for her to earn the private coach?"

"I pay for the coach." Cassie tapped her thumb between her breasts. "I pay."

"You don't earn enough juice working here to cover private coaching."

"I get a lot of tips."

"What's that I hear?" Eve cocked her head. "Oh yeah, that's the sound of five hundred sucking down the drain."

"Goddamn it." Cassie pushed to her feet, stared hard at Eve. "This is about the murder, right? That's big-time. You're big-time. Christ knows you are," she said to Roarke. "I need some assurance you're not going to shake me down over small-time."

"If you're working off book, I'm not interested in rousting you for it."

Cassie took a moment to stare, to study, then apparently satisfied by what she read on Eve's face, nodded. "I do some private. I'm not licensed for private. And I do the coach's father for free, every week. It's like a barter, cuts down on the fee. He's a nice guy, actually. Can't get out much 'cause he busted himself up bad about thirty years ago. He's gimpy, got scars. Even if Anders offered coaching, I'd keep it how it is, because it's working. And I gotta have a part in providing for my kid. If you've got some cop idea that I was doing Anders, and screwed up the deal so he kicked, that's off, way off. I'm home nights. I don't leave my kid home alone. Not ever. You ask anybody. You want to look at somebody, you ought to take another look at the wife. Make damn double sure *she* wasn't there."

"Why is that?"

"Bitch got stones. She's got cold, hard stones."

They were done. Roarke knew Eve's rhythm well enough to know she'd written Cassie off. But he was curious. "Why are you working here? You could make more in a classier place."

"I can't dance worth shit." She said it cheerfully. "Classier places expect classier strippers. I got this." She opened her robe, revealing a curvy body that showed some wear. "It's good, but it ain't great. I go more upscale," she continued, absently tying the robe again, "they'd want me to get the shifting parts put back in place. Here, they don't care about that, long as you put in your rounds and pull in your quota of bj's and handjobs upstairs.

"I can work days, and be home at night with my girl. Not a lot of places going to let me call that shot. And I don't work weekends, because I'm with my kid. It's a trade-off. It's worth it. She's worth it. You're going to see her take gold in the Olympics one day. She's a freaking champion."

"Gracie Gordon. I'll remember. Appreciate the time." Eve took a step toward the door, and Roarke slipped a money clip out of his pocket, peeled off bills.

"Shit a brick, you carry like that?" Sheer shock covered Cassie's face. "In this neighborhood?"

"I carry as I please. There's the five, and one extra. For the champion."

Cassie stared at the six hundreds in her hand. "You're all right, Blue Eyes." She lifted her head to look into them. "You're all right, down the line. You ever want a free bang, you got one coming."

"It would, no doubt, be a memorable bang. But my wife is fiercely jealous and territorial." He grinned over at a very cold-eyed Eve.

"Her? You? That's a kick in the ass."

"Every damn day," Eve muttered, and strode out.

She kept striding, out of the club, back into the comparatively fresh air of the city street. And fisted her hands on her hips as she spun to him. "Did you *have* to do the 'my wife' crap?"

His grin remained, and only widened. "I did, yes. I felt a desperate need for your protection. I believe that woman had designs on me."

"I'll put a design on you that won't come off in the shower."

"See, now I'm excited." Reaching out, he toyed with the lapel of her coat. "What have you got in mind?"

"And you gave her six fucking hundred dollars."

"Looks like you'll be buying dinner tonight."

She made a sound, a kind of grinding grunt as she fisted her hands in her hair and yanked. No wonder she got headaches, he mused.

"Look, King of the World, you've got no business giving some stripper who's also a suspect six bills."

"Isn't that the Power of Roarke?" he countered. "And I didn't give her the six for the very intriguing flash. *And*," he continued, giving her a quick poke, "she stopped being a suspect, a serious one, the minute you saw her backhand that drunk degenerate in the club."

Before she could argue, the grunt in the doorway yelled out, "Hey, cop. You gonna move this crap ride or leave it here all damn night?"

She only turned her head, burned him to silence with one stare. "If she makes six bills in six rounds in that dump *I'll* go up and dance on a pole."

"As much as I'd enjoy seeing that—in fact, am in my head at this moment—I'm forced to agree. But it's neither here nor there. She named the five, I agreed to it. The sixth was for the child, and she'll see the child gets it. I admire and respect a woman who does the necessary, whatever it might be, for her child."

She let out a breath, and it was the wind coming out of her sails. He'd thought of his mother, of course, Eve realized. Of what she'd suffered and sacrificed. Of what she'd died for. "Still," she said because she couldn't think of anything else. "And why did I take her off the list when she knocked that jerk out of his chair?"

"Because you saw, as I did, a direct woman who handles business in a straightforward manner. She might have killed Anders if her reasons were strong enough, but she'd never have left him to choke to death."

"You should've been a cop."

"You're just saying that to get back at me for the 'my wife' comment. We'll consider ourselves even."

She considered. "I'm not buying dinner because I'm tapped, and we can get it free at home. Give Sulky and his friend Stupid another ten, will you?"

When he joined her in the car, she gave him a smirk. "Bet you didn't give them a tip."

"Actually, I did. It was that if they ever saw this particular crap ride in the neighborhood again, they should remember the pair of tenners, and your considerable wrath. Now why should you be tapped?"

"What? Oh. I don't know. Because people keep wanting money for stuff. Buy a damn Pepsi, they expect some coin. Bastards."

"How much shagging Pepsi do you drink?"

"I don't know. Plus there's, you know, stuff that comes up. Weasels to pay off."

"Weaseling is departmentally covered in your budget."

Her lips curled. "Yeah, and by the time I get the kick-back from that I'll be retired and taking hula lessons in Maui. What is this, an inquisition?"

"I don't understand why—and yes, I'm saying it, so suck it up—my wife is walking around tapped. Make a bloody withdrawal from your account, or ask me for a bit of the ready."

"Ask you for . . ." Fortunately, the light turned red, forcing her to stop. It was marginally safer to swing around and glare at him while stopped. "I'll be damned if I'll ask you for money."

"You just asked me for ten to pay your street thug."

"That's different."

"How?"

"Because . . . It wasn't for me, it was for him. I'll put in a chit for it, pay you back."

"While we're taking those hula lessons, possibly eating poi. Don't be an idiot."

"Call me an idiot again, all you'll be able to eat is poi, seeing as you'll be missing most of your teeth."

"I didn't call you an idiot, I told you not to be one," he snapped back. "And if you don't drive this bleeding car we'll have a riot on our hands."

She supposed the explosions going on in her head had blocked out the blaring horns. She zipped through the light, steamed up the next few blocks, then swung back when she hit the next red. "I've been handling my own ready all my life and I don't need a freaking allowance from my daddy. I do just fine."

"Obviously, since you're walking about with empty pockets."

"I got the plastic, don't I?"

The look he gave her would have withered stone. "How things must've changed since I was running the streets. I never accepted the plastic."

He had her there. "So I didn't get around to pulling out a little cash the last few days. So what? I don't know why you're so pissed about it."

"You don't, no. Quite obviously, you don't."

The fact that he didn't add to that, said nothing at all as she fought and maneuvered her way uptown, told her he wasn't just pissed, he was over the line into furious.

She didn't get it, didn't get it, didn't get it. How had they gone from perfectly fine to taking a few acceptable pokes at each other to furious?

So now he sat there, ignoring her, working with his PPC again. Probably prying into her bank account to see what an idiot she was in his gazillionaire opinion. Snapping and slapping at her because she'd run a little short between paydays.

So the fuck what?

She picked at it, gnawed at it, brooded over it the rest of the way. When she stopped in front of the house, when they got out of opposite sides of the car, she stood with the car between them. "Look—"

"No, you're going to need to look, Eve. We'll go inside so that you do."

Since he strode away, she had little choice but to follow. *Don't need this now,* she thought. *Don't need some marital knot to unravel when I've got work.* She always had work, a little voice reminded her, and did nothing but make her feel guilty.

When he stepped inside, Roarke simply held up a finger. Eve watched, with surprise and envy, as Summerset slipped back out of the foyer without a word. With the path effortlessly cleared, she trudged up the steps after Roarke.

She expected him to head to one of their offices or their bedroom. Instead he walked into one of the quiet and beautiful sitting rooms. A banquet of blooming plants charmed a trio of windows. A pair of curved settees in muted stripes faced each other across a slim, glossy table. After shrugging out of his coat, Roarke tossed it over one of the pretty fabric chairs.

"I'll have a drink with this."

It didn't surprise her to see the wine fridge when he crossed over, opened a panel. When he'd drawn the cork, he took two glasses from another panel, poured.

"Why don't you sit?"

"I feel like I'm about to get dressed down by an annoyed parent because I blew my spending money on candy. I don't like it, Roarke."

"I'm not your father, and I don't give a damn what you spend your money on. There, better?"

"No."

"Well then, that's a pity. Myself, I'm going to sit down, drink this wine, and continue to resist the urge to rap your head against the handiest solid surface."

When he sat, when he sipped, she continued to stand. "You can't be this mad because I ran short before payday."

"You'd be wrong about that."

She'd have preferred the heat, a good fiery blast of it. And she knew he understood that, *knew* it, as he gave her rigid ice. "Jesus, what's the big deal? I had some unforeseens. I had to flip a couple to a weasel last week, and I don't know, other stuff. There was that kid, and—"

"I've just said I don't care how you spend your money. I care that you'd rather walk around without any in your pocket than ask me for a bit of cash. Or get it for yourself as you know the combination of the damn safes around here."

"I'm not going into one of your safes for—"

"And there it is." He set the wineglass down in a gesture

so careful, so deliberate, she understood he'd barely resisted heaving it. "You won't go into *my* safes. And you can't see how insulting that is to me? To us?"

To give herself a moment, she took off her coat, tossed it over with his. Then she sat, picked up the wine. Studied it. "You think it should be easy, that because we're married it should be smooth for me to hit you up—"

"There it is again. How the hell is it hitting me up?"

"Christ." Despite the fact that her head throbbed, she took a good slug of wine. "Because that's how it would feel. Do you know how long it's taken me to get used to living here—well, almost used to it—to feel, really feel that it is my home? Not yours, not even ours, those were easier. But mine? Your money came down in the minus column for me. I fell for you in spite of it. If that makes me an idiot, too damn bad."

"I came from nothing, and built this. I've pride in that, and so I understand yours. Your pride. I also know the money means little to nothing to you. So why then, can't you take a bit of what means so little rather than running on empty when it's so ridiculously unnecessary?"

Not so pissed now, she noted with some relief. Baffled, maybe even a little hurt, but no longer furious. "I didn't think about it. I didn't notice I was so light until I pulled out the ten. I've had other things on my mind besides... And all that's true, but all that's an evasion."

She drank again to ease the tightness in her throat. "I can't. I'm sorry, really, that it hurts or upsets you. I can't hold out my hand to you, not for money. I just can't. So it's going to have to piss you off or insult you or whatever it does. I just can't do it, Roarke."

He picked up his glass again, said nothing for several moments as he sat, as he sipped. "You could if we were on more even ground, as you see it?"

"No. It's not how much, it's at all."

He searched her face. "That's hardheaded, shortsighted, and tight-assed. But, all right then."

"All right then?" Flabbergasted, she gaped at him. "All right? That's it?"

"Those may be three of your qualities that land in the minus column for me," he said with a hint of a smile. "I fell for you despite them." He pulled out his money clip, and that finger came up, silencing her as effectively as it had Summerset. He set fifty on the table between them. "You'll do me a favor and take that as a loan so you don't walk out of here with nothing but your hard head and tight ass in the morning. That'll make sixty you owe me come payday, counting the previous ten."

"Okay." She took the fifty, stuffed it in her pocket. "Did we just compromise?"

"I believe we did."

"Good." She took another sip of wine, looked around. "So. This is a nice room."

"It is, yes. It's just been redecorated. Came out well, I think."

"Get out. Really? When?"

"Just after the holidays." He smiled fully now. "I believe I mentioned something to you about it, in case you wanted any input on the colors and fabrics and so on."

"Oh. Yeah. I guess I remember something about that. You probably did better without me."

"I never have, never will."

She sighed, sunk into love with him. "Maybe we could have dinner in here tonight."

"Is that another compromise?"

"I was thinking of it more like interest on the sixty."

He laughed. "Well then, I charge high rates. You'll have to get the meal to work that off."

"No problem." She stood up. "And in the spirit of compromise, it's going to be pizza." She looked around again. "Where the hell's the AutoChef in here?"

They sat together on one of the curved settees, the mood mellow as they shared pizza and wine. And if the conversation turned to murder, it suited both of them.

"So Feeney's got the pill dispenser thing. If I'd known

he was going to dick around with it, I'd've brought it home and shoved it on you."

"If it was played with, he'll find out soon enough. In any case, even if it was, it wouldn't prove she'd done it. He could have reprogrammed it himself. That wouldn't work for you in court."

"It's another weight. Even small weights add up. It goes to opportunity. Conversely, she can't prove he routinely took sleep aids, or ever took them, for that matter. There's only her word he had sidepieces, brought them home. I spoke with three of his former romantic interests. Every one of them describes him as a shy sort of lover— sweet, not very adventurous. Gentle. Every one of them."

"More weight, certainly, but Ava planted seeds that this was a relatively recent change."

"A guy goes from sweet, shy, and gentle in bed to a raging perv who molests minors? She's going to have a hard time convincing a jury there. And, her diddling with Charles is documented, while there isn't any documentation Anders diddled. That'll work against her instead of covering her ass like she planned. I've got Petrelli's statement. It would've fit in nicely for me if Cassie Gordon's had run parallel. I have to figure Ava saw she wasn't going to be able to use Gordon, not that way. So there's at least one more. The one she worked well enough to kill for her."

"You have another candidate there?"

"Yeah, we'll go into those possibilities tomorrow. But I need to spread it out. Maybe it's not a repeater on the mommy breaks. Or somebody with some smears and smudges. She goes for clean, say—the way you liked it— and keeps her away from the group. Makes her more a personal pet.

"So many damn names," she complained. "It'll take weeks to get through them. Chasing my tail. Pisses me off."

"I'll give you a hand with it. You'd eliminate anyone with a husband or cohab, I'd assume. As she wouldn't have wanted to risk her surrogate telling her mate. Single parents would be highest probability. Ones without any close family—but for the children—or friends, for that matter. Someone smart enough to follow directions, and also weak enough or frightened enough to follow them."

"See, you should've been a cop."

He only sighed. "Why would you want to start another fight when we've just made up?"

"We have to have sex to really make up."

"Well then."

"Not now, ace." She gave him a light shove back. "Work first, makeup sex later." Rising, she wondered if she'd regret scarfing down that last slice of pizza. "I need to take another hard look at the case file on the old man's death. Her father-in-law. Pick it apart, find the chinks. People don't commit perfect murders, and she sure as hell didn't pull off every last detail twice. If I can find the cracks there, they could lead to the cracks here. Or vice versa."

"I guess you'll be wanting that hammer again."

She grinned at him. "Sex, sex, sex. That's all it is with you."

"That's my one-track mind." He stood, pulled her close and took her in a kiss that had her eyes rolling to the back of her head. "Just collecting my down payment," he told her.

She glanced back at the room as they walked out together. "Redecorating, redecorating. How much lead time did you need to get somebody in to do the room?"

"Essentially none, but I do own the firm who did the job."

"Yeah, you being you. How much for normal people?"

"It would depend on the size of the job, the demands of the client, and how much money the client was willing to throw at the decorating team."

"I bet your people could find out easy who Ava used, and when she had her first consult."

"I bet they could. I'll make a call." He gave her ass a friendly pat. "I'll be in shortly. I want to change out of this suit."

She kept going, then turned, walked backward. "Roarke?"

He glanced back. "Hmm?"

"I'd have fallen for you even if you had twice as much money, which is virtually impossible. But still."

"I'd have fallen for you even if your head was twice as hard, again virtually impossible. And still."

"We're good," she said, then continued on to her office.

Chapter 19

When he came in, she sat at her desk, her jacket tossed on the back of her sleep chair. The jacket, he knew, would bother her while she worked. The weapon she still wore? Its weight wouldn't register any more than the weight of her own arms.

Steam rose out of the mug on her desk. Coffee, he thought, nearly equaled the weapon as part of her essential makeup.

She hadn't yet worked herself into exhaustion on this one. He'd seen her work, worry, wrangle with a case until her system simply collapsed from neglect. But this one, he realized, was different. She was juiced.

"It's a competition."

She glanced over, brows knit. "What?"

"You're as involved and determined as you are, always. You've made the victim yours, as you always do. But you're not suffering this time around."

"Suffering? I don't suffer."

"Oh, but you do, darling Eve. Murder infuriates you, insults you, and the victims haunt you. Every one. But for this, for this particular one, it's challenged you above all else. She challenges you—and your attitude toward her, which strikes me as a personal level of dislike, kicks that up a notch. You're damned if you aren't going to beat her."

"Maybe. Whatever works. Whatever gets the job done. So, the efficient Leopold came through. I've got his incoming here, the list of parents Ava tapped for grunt work. The ones he had some record of or remembered, anyway. We'll split those if you're up for it."

"Shoot my share to my unit."

"Okay. We'll divide by alpha. We should . . . I don't like her," Eve said suddenly. "Didn't like her pretty much from the jump. Didn't like her when I stood watching her on the security screen as she walked into the house the morning of."

"With her well-groomed hair and coordinating wardrobe," Roarke remembered.

"Yeah. It was . . ." Eve snapped her fingers. "But that screws objectivity, so I pushed it back. Thing is, it kept pushing back in again. It took me a while—well, not that much of a while, but some—to figure out why."

Since he sensed something there, he sat on the corner of her desk. "All right. Tell me why."

"Don't get bent over it."

He angled his head. "Why would I?"

"She reminds me of Magdelana."

He said nothing for a moment, just watched her face, then rising, he walked over to the murder board to study Ava's.

"Not just the high-class blonde thing," Eve began.

"No," he said quietly, "not just." He thought of Magdelana, the woman he'd once cared for. The woman who'd betrayed him, and on the return trip had done everything in her power to hurt Eve and chip away at their marriage.

"Not just," he repeated. "They're both users, aren't they? Manipulators with a wholly selfish core polished over with sophistication and style. Very much the same type. You're right about that."

"Okay."

Hearing the relief in her voice, he looked over at her. "Did you think I'd be annoyed or upset by the comparison?"

"Maybe some, maybe more if I'd finished it out and said that because she reminds me of Magdabitch, I'm going to experience a tingly, even orgasmic satisfaction by bringing her down."

"I see. Revenge by proxy."

"She deserves the cage on her own merits or lack thereof. But yeah, maybe some element of revenge by proxy."

Walking back, he leaned down, kissed the top of Eve's head. "Whatever works. And now that you've pointed it out, I'll enjoy some of that tingly satisfaction as well. Thanks for that."

"It's small, petty, and probably inappropriate of us."

"Which will make it all the more orgasmic. Send over the file. I'll just cop some of your coffee, then get started."

Whatever works, Eve thought again as he strolled into the kitchen. What really worked, was them.

She ordered her unit to copy and send Roarke's unit the names on file beginning with N surnames. Then she opened the first half of the file, took a quick scan.

Plenty of little slaves and servants to pick from, she thought. A nice wide field of the vulnerable, the needy, the grateful. The bitch just had to keep circling until . . .

"Wait. Whoa. Wait."

With coffee in hand, Roarke stepped back in. "That was fast."

"Wait, wait, wait." Scooping back her hair, Eve launched to her feet. "Computer, display on screen, data for Custer, Suzanne."

"Who might that be?" Roarke wondered.

"Wait, wait. Computer, display on second screen, data on Custer, Ned."

Roarke did wait, studied both photos, the basic identification data. "Husband and wife, and he's deceased. Recently."

"He's Baxter's." She dropped back down into the chair. "I didn't keep the damn file. I need the damn case file on this guy."

"Move," Roarke ordered. "Get up. Give me a moment."

"Don't hack into Baxter's police unit. I'll tag him and—"

"And I'll have it for you a great deal quicker. It's hardly hacking, as it's ridiculously easy. And you're authorized in any case." He gave her shoulder a light, but purposeful shove. "Give me the chair a minute."

"All right, all right." In any case, it gave her time to pace and think. She stared at the woman on screen—pretty in a toned-down, tired-eyed kind of way. Couple of kids, professional mother's stipend, philandering, heavy-handed husband.

"Coincidence, my ass."

"Quiet," Roarke muttered. "Half a minute more here. Ah, and there we are. What do you need from this?"

"Take down the data on screen, put that up. We'll scroll through." She felt it, felt it in her bones. But . . . "I want your take here without any of my input first."

He read, as she did, of the quick and nasty death of one Ned Custer by person or persons unknown. Cheap sex flop, slit throat—attack from behind—castration, no trace or DNA, no witnesses. No trail.

"So the wife was well-alibied, I see."

"Solid. They ran the 'link calls, confirmed the source. She was in her apartment when he got sliced. No boyfriends, no close relatives or friends. Baxter and Trueheart are thorough, and they didn't pop anything on this."

"She's one of Ava's mothers."

"Yep."

"Strangers on a Train."

"Huh?" Her head swiveled back toward him. "What train? Nobody was on a train."

"I haven't run that vid for you, have I?" Coolly, he continued to study the screen, continued to read data. "It's a good one. Mid-twentieth-century, Hitchcock film. You've enjoyed Hitchcock."

"Yeah, yeah, so?"

"Briefly, two men—strangers—meet on a train, and the conversations turn to how each wishes to be rid of a certain individual in his life. And how it could be done without the police suspecting them if each did in the other's. Very clever, as there's no real connection between the two men. It was a book first, come to think of it."

"Strangers," Eve repeated.

"In this case, the one who wanted his wife done didn't take the other—an unstable sort, who wanted his father done—seriously. But, the wife was dispatched, and the unstable sort pressured the sudden widower to complete the bargain. It's twisty and complex. You'll have to watch it."

"The exchange is what clicked for me," Eve told him. "The possibility of that. You do mine, I do yours. We're both alibied, and who'd look at either of us for the other's? Why would Baxter look at Ava Anders in the murder of this guy? She doesn't know him, and even if you note that Suzanne Custer's in the Anders program, it doesn't pop. It doesn't mean a thing."

"Until you look at Anders's murder, won't let it slide as an accident, and dig deep enough to see this. And wonder."

"Probability scan's going to bottom out." Already annoyed by that, Eve hissed out a breath. "It'll bottom out until I can plug in more. What about you? Do you buy it?"

"The stronger personality, the more powerful one, hatches the plan, draws the weaker one in. And does the job first, to add pressure and obligation. Even threat. When the weaker follows through, it's not quite as clean and tidy. Yes, I'd buy it."

"It's easier to pry open the weaker one. We pull Suzanne Custer in, we work her." Pacing, Eve circled the murder board. "Work her right, work her hard enough, she'll flip on Ava. Need more first. You move."

He pushed back from the desk. "Do you still want runs on the other names?"

"I'll put a drone on that. This is the money shot here, this is the one. I've got a tingly."

"Save it for me, will you?"

"Ha. I need everything I can get on her. Baxter's got a solid murder book. We just have to look at the data from a different angle now. Suzanne didn't kill her husband. She killed Ava's."

"There had to be contact between the two murderers," Roarke pointed out. "Confirming the first, setting up the second."

"Where did Custer get the murder weapon, the drug, the enhancer? That's a place to pick at. Ava had to give her the security code, the layout." As she spoke, Eve scrawled down names, connections, questions. "They changed the code every ten days, so there had to be a way to pass that on. We pick at Ava at the same time. She's not going to be alibied so damn tight for the night of Ned Custer's murder. She fits," Eve added. "She's the right height for the angle of the killing strike. The right personality to have planned it without leaving a trace behind, the right personality to use someone else to get what she wanted."

"Baxter would have had EDD check all Custer's 'links, her comp for communication and activity before her husband's murder, and—I assume—for a week or so after it."

"Yeah, but not for before Anders." Eve planted a finger on Thomas Anders's name on her notes. "No point. She wasn't a suspect, not with her alibi, in her husband's. You look, you check, but Baxter didn't feel it. Because it wasn't there to feel. We'll pull them now, all of them. Anders's, too. We'll go back to before the Custer murder on them."

She drummed her fingers. "Asshole like Custer, I bet he kept cock enhancers around. The barbs, now... where's a nice mom of two like Suzanne going to get her hand on them? They came from her. That part wasn't in Ava's plan."

"A terrible thing when your husband's murdered that way," Roarke commented. "I'll bet a kindly doctor would prescribe tranquilizers for the widow. Put them all together instead of doling them out for yourself . . ."

"Good. That's good. A medical won't want to give us that information, not without a warrant, but we start with her financials, see if she paid a doctor, paid a pharmacy between the murders. Close to the second murder, yeah, close, I bet. Got cold feet as it got toward the sticking point."

She engaged her 'link, put through to Baxter's home. When she hit voice mail, she ordered a transfer to his mobile.

She heard music first, something low and bluesy that said sexual foreplay to her. Baxter's face came on with dim lighting in the background.

"This better be damn good."

"My home office, tomorrow, eight hundred hours."

"I'm not on the roll till Monday. I've got—"

"You are now. Tag your boy, too."

"Give me a break, Dallas. I've got a clear field and a hot brunette on tap."

"Then you'd better turn her on full tonight, because you're here at eight. How much do you want to close the Custer case, Baxter?"

The irritated scowl vanished. "You got something there?"

"Hotter than any brunette who'd give you a clear field. Eight hundred. If you've got any personal notes not in the murder book, bring them."

"Give me a goddamn hint, will you?"

"*Strangers on a Train*. Look it up." She clicked off, contacted Peabody, then Feeney.

"Sounds like we'll need the standard cop breakfast buffet," Roarke decided. "And a Saturday one at that."

"You don't have to feed them. I want Mira, too," she considered. "I'd like her take on the suspect profiles." She glanced at her wrist unit. "It's not really all that late."

"While you're interrupting the Miras' evening, send me the file. I'll poke into the financials."

She frowned at him. "It's still open and active. Yeah, you could do that. And I can order the full search on the electronics. When you do the financials, see if anything pops back a ways that points toward Suzanne Custer buying the sex aids."

After copying and sending the file, Eve stared at her 'link. It wasn't really that late, she reminded herself. But she had sex aids on the brain, and that nudged her into thinking how the Miras might be spending their night together. "Jesus, way to wig myself out."

She hedged, and ordered the transmission to go straight to voice mail. "Dr. Mira, I didn't want to disturb your evening. I've got something on the Anders case, a strong possibility of a connection with a previous homicide that's still open and active. I realize tomorrow's Saturday—" Or she did now that Roarke had mentioned it. "But I have a team meeting at my home office tomorrow at eight—"

"Eve?"

"Oh, hey." There was music again. It wasn't porn vid music, thank God, but it spoke of an intimate evening at home to Eve. "Sorry to bother you when you're . . . whatever. I have something I'd like to pull you in on. I've set a meeting at my home office in the morning, if your schedule—"

"What time?"

"Eight hundred."

"I can make that. I'll be there. Do you want me to study anything in the meantime?"

"I'd actually like you to come into this fresh."

"Fine." Mira glanced away, laughed as she sent a warm look off screen. "Dennis sends his best. I'll see you in the morning."

"Thanks."

Eve swiveled away from the 'link, pressed her fingers to her eyes. "They're going to do it," she mumbled. "If not now, soon. I wish I didn't have to know that."

To clear the image, and the thought, out of her head, she turned back to Baxter's file, and started digging.

At some point the cat wandered in to leap on her desk. When he got nothing but, "Don't sit on my stuff," he leaped back down to stalk into Roarke's domain.

She started a new file listing the correlations, the connections—actual and possible—the time lines. Using the backside of her murder board, she arranged photos, notes, reports. Stood back, studied it.

She could see it, actually see it. The steps, the stages, the moves, the mistakes. Not enough, she admitted, not for an arrest, not for a conviction. But there would be.

Lock and key, that's how she saw it. The Anders case the lock, the Custer case the key. Once she fit them together, turned it just right, it would open. Then she'd reach in and grab Ava by the throat.

She turned to Roarke's office. He sat at his desk, the cat draped over his lap. "Find anything?"

"Custer's financials don't allow her much wiggle room. From what I can see, the husband ran the show there previously. Most of the withdrawals, debits are in his name. There are several in one particular sex shop—Just Sex—in the six months before his untimely. As it wouldn't have surprised me to find certain items you had interest in—"

"Hopefully you mean professional interest."

He only smiled. "As, and so forth, I entertained myself and did a bit of searching at the vendor's . . ."

"You hacked."

"You say that in such a disapproving tone. I explored. You'll certainly do so yourself, legally and tediously, but I like having my curiosity satisfied."

He said nothing more, only picked up the bottle of water on his desk and drank. And his eyes laughed at her over the bottle.

"Crap. Yes, I'll get the data by fully legal means, but what did you find?"

"Multiple purchases of what's delightfully marketed as Hard-on. It comes in a phallic-shaped bottle."

"Check one."

"Purchases of various sexual aids and toys. Cock rings, probes, textured condoms, vibrators."

"Check two."

"Nothing on the ropes, I'm afraid."

"But they carry them. We checked venues for that type of rope, and they carry them. Did Suzanne pay a visit there?"

"No record of that, no. They do take cash. She did, however, visit a clinic two weeks before Anders's death. She saw a Dr. Yin there according to the records—"

"Which you hacked into?"

"Which I explored," he said mildly. "And she incurred a debit at the attached pharmacy, filling a prescription for a box of home pressure syringes, and a liquid form of lotrominaphine—a barbiturate used to aid sleep and nervous conditions."

"Big, fat, red check. I have to get all this data through channels, get it all lined up. Then I'm going to knock her down with it."

"Where are you going?"

"It's never too late to call an APA," she said as she hurried back to her desk. "I'm going to contact Reo, do the fast talk, and get the paperwork started on warrants for the data you just gave me."

"And after we dropped it all nicely tied in a bow into her lap," Roarke said to the cat. "That's a cop for you."

He heard her giving her pitch to Cher Reo, then arguing with the soft-voiced, tough-minded APA. He busied himself for the next few minutes studying and analyzing the last weeks of Suzanne Custer's financials.

"Find another spot," Roarke told Galahad, and hauled the limp mass of cat up, dropped him lightly on the floor. When he walked into Eve's office, she sat at her desk, keying in more notes.

"She's getting them. Whined about it, but she's getting them."

"Whined, perhaps, because you contacted her at very close to midnight."

"Mostly. You can put them together like that." Eve lifted her hands, fingers open and pointed toward each other, then slid them together. "Like teeth. Like gears. You just have to see the big picture. It's a nearly perfect, well, machine, to stick with the teeth and gears. Clean and efficient. The problem is the operators. She made her mistake selecting this operator."

He eased back down on her desk. "Why was this particular operator a mistake?"

"Look at her." Eve gestured toward the screen. "Look at her background data, look at her face. Ava looks and she sees somebody weak, easily manipulated, easily cowed because she stayed with a cheating, abusing husband. She sees ordinary, a woman nobody's going to look at twice. A woman who *owes* her."

"What do you see?"

"That, all that. But I also see a woman who takes the time and trouble to find something better for her kids, something that makes them happy. One who, according to the statements in Baxter's knock-on-doors, kept those kids and herself clean and out of trouble. She never crossed the line before this. When you push somebody like that across the line, or seduce them over it, sooner or later they look back and regret it. I'm going to make her regret sooner."

"You can get started on that in just under eight hours."

"Why . . . Oh."

"There's nothing more you can do tonight."

"Not really." She saved, copied, shut down. "Probably better to let it cook anyway."

He took her hand, tugged her along when she looked back at the murder board. "You should be interested that Suzanne Custer's better off financially with a dead husband than she was with a live one."

"Little life insurance, decent pension."

"More than that. On a quick analysis of their financials for the past twelve months, he spent approximately forty-six percent of their combined incomes on his personal needs, wants, and pursuits. Leaving the fifty-four to cover housing, food, medical, clothing, transportation, educational supplies for the children, and so on. She has his life insurance payment now, and—as a widowed professional mother, with the pension from his employment—nearly the same income as before. About eight percent less."

"With forty-six percent less outlay. So she's actually— why do I have to do math at midnight?"

"Thirty-eight percent to the good—using that table, and one year as an example."

"Good enough for me. It's not the megabucks Ava reaps, but it's solid. It's . . . proportionate, if you think about it. And it's another button to push when we get Custer into Interview. Thanks."

She mulled it over as she undressed. "Some of the seminars Anders offered are on budgeting, financial planning. What do you bet Ava talked to Suzanne about her money situation and how it could get a lot brighter?"

"A basic strategy would be to list all advantages. And push home all the disadvantages of the status quo. I imagine some of those seminars dealt with being proactive, with empowerment, making tough choices to improve your family situation. Any and all could be twisted by a clever woman to seduce, as you said, a vulnerable one."

"So many mind games," Eve mused, "so little hard evidence."

"It's cooking until morning," he reminded her. "And speaking of seductions." He gripped her hips. "I believe we have to finish making up."

"Oh yeah. I guess I could work that in now." Bracing her hands on his shoulders, she pushed off the balls of her feet, rising up with his helpful boost to wrap her legs around his waist. "How mad were we?"

"Furious."

"It didn't seem that bad, looking back."

"It was a pitched battle that nearly shook the foundation of our marriage."

"My ass."

"Yes, it is." He gave it a squeeze before tumbling to the

bed with her. He laughed down at her, then kissed her lightly. "It's a good day when it ends like this."

She laid a hand on his cheek. "They're pretty much all good days for me now, even the bad ones."

All good, she thought, *with him.* When her mouth lifted to his, they both sank in.

So it was to be slow and easy, quiet and sweet. And so married, Eve thought, with one anticipating the other. A rise, a fall, a turn, a glide. A thrill, yes, it would always and ever be a thrill—the feel of him, the taste of him. But comfort twined with it, a velvet ribbon through the silver blade.

Her pulse quickened, and muscles, tight from a long, long day, relaxed.

He felt her give, that slow, fluid yielding to him. To herself. She warmed his blood, steadied his heart even as its beat went fast and thick. He drank her in, there, just there under the line of her jaw where the skin was so amazingly sweet. Pleasure slid through him as her hands stroked, gripped, whispered over him.

It was she who took him in, opened and asked and took, guiding him into the heat. Surrounding him with it so that each long, slow thrust pulsed and pumped through them both.

Slow, beautifully slow, drawing out and out and out every drop of pleasure. She stared into his eyes, her fingers locked with his now, clamped together as they held each other to that lazy, that torturous pace. She held, even when her breath came short, her head arched back.

He pressed his lips to the curve of her throat. Skimmed up the scrambling pulse, once again along that sweet spot under her jaw. His mouth found hers, and with that final link, let himself go.

Chapter 20

Eve set up early the next morning, lining up the data she'd already accumulated and organized. For now, she set aside the results of Roarke's *explorations*. The warrants would pull that information in soon enough.

She decided to say nothing about the buffet table, the extra seating, that had found their way into her office. What would be the point? She skimmed over her notes, took a last round with her murder boards.

Baxter surprised her by walking in just before eight.

"Guess the brunette wasn't so hot after all."

"She was smoking. I left her warm and cozy in... that's food. Hot damn!"

Eve watched him bullet over to the buffet, lift the lid of the first warmer. "Yo, that is pig meat." He plucked out a slice of bacon, bit in.

"Just help yourself," Eve said dryly.

"Gonna." Bearing no shame, Baxter grabbed a plate. "While I do you can tell me what you've got that has me here eating meat of pig—and hey!—egg of actual chicken at eight hundred on a Saturday."

"You'll get it when the team gets here."

"We've got a team now?" He surfed the warmers, began to pile the plate with food while he studied Eve and the buffet offerings. It seemed to her it was a tough toss-up which interested him more.

"We've got a team now. Where's Trueheart?"

"On the way. Peabody?"

"The same. I've called in Feeney and Mira and . . . the civilian," she said as Roarke walked in.

"Baxter."

"Primo pig. Thanks."

"My pleasure." Roarke poured himself a cup of coffee, lifted his eyebrows at Eve. "Lieutenant?"

"Yeah, yeah, why not? We'll see if we can work in the briefing between courses."

"Woohoo, breakfast!" Peabody all but skipped into the room, just ahead of McNab.

"I told you not to feed the puppies," Eve scolded.

"But they're so cute." Roarke handed her the coffee.

"Sorry, am I late?" Trueheart hurried in. "I missed the . . . Wow." His young hero face went bright as a birthday candle at the sight of the buffet.

"Grab some pig, kid," Baxter told him. "Team feed. Hey, Feeney, Dr. Mira."

"Good morning. Isn't that lovely!" Mira shot a smile at Eve, beamed at Roarke. "And so considerate."

"Don't eat all the damn bacon, McNab." Feeney muscled him aside to claim his own.

"There's ham, too," McNab told him with his mouth full of it.

"When you all finish stuffing food in your faces, maybe you could listen up."

"I got no problem listening while I'm stuffing." Feeney glanced around. "You?"

"Well, damn it, everybody just fill it up and sit down with it somewhere." Cops and food, she thought. Put them in the same room, invite chaos. "This is a goddamn official briefing not an all-you-can-eat."

"Here you are, then." Roarke handed her a plate of bacon and eggs. "You won't be so cross if you have a bit of breakfast."

"This is your fault."

"It is, isn't it?" He grinned without an ounce of remorse. "Go on, then, shovel some in."

She did, as everyone else was. "Some of you vultures... sorry," Eve said to Mira, "no offense."

Mira took a neat bite of creamy eggs. "None taken."

"Some of you may be aware that Detective Pig-Eater there and his aide, Officer Danish, caught a homicide a couple months back. Baxter, quick overview."

"Custer, Ned," he began, and reeled off the basic facts.

When he'd finished, Eve flipped Suzanne Custer's ID and data on screen. "The widow's alibi holds," she said. "The 'link to 'link transmissions she made originated in her apartment, and EDD analysis verifies they were live trans, not recorded. Suzanne Custer didn't slit her husband's throat. She not only wasn't there, but lacked the physicality for the killing blow."

"Too short, too slight," Baxter confirmed between shovels.

"The extensive and thorough investigation by the gluttonous primary and his aide unearthed no sidepiece, no relative, no friend who might have killed Custer on the wife's behalf," Eve continued. "Said investigation found no financial payment, or other bartering tool that may have been used by the wife to hire the hit. The widow does, however, benefit financially from Custer's death, and as the vic had a documented history of spousal abuse, adultery, and kept his fist closed over the purse strings, the widow also benefits on emotional, physical, and practical levels from his death."

"Dallas, we can't pin her." Baxter lifted his hands, one of them holding a chunk of grilled ham speared on a fork. "We dead-ended on every angle we played with her connected to the murder."

"She went white." Trueheart shifted in his seat as Eve

turned her gaze on him. "When Detective Baxter and I went to inform her, she didn't seem all that surprised to find cops at the door. More tired, resigned. She said how she didn't have money for bail. And when we told her he was dead, she went white. It didn't feel faked, I guess I want to say. It rang true."

"It probably was true. Let's switch over to the Anders case. Peabody and I caught this one."

Baxter rose to get more coffee as Eve laid out the salients. "Are you looking for a connect?" he asked. "Because both vics appear to have been killed by an LC, or a sex partner?"

"That's an interesting connection, isn't it? And one of the mistakes made. Ava Anders." Eve ordered Ava's ID photo and data split screen with Suzanne's. "Also solidly alibied at the time of her husband's murder. While she apparently has more friends, certainly more influence and resources than Suzanne, no evidence leads to murder for hire. Her circle of friends don't play in. She also gains financially, and when you scrape away at the surface of her claims of a happy marriage to the lies and manipulations underneath, she gains on several other levels."

She turned to study the screen. "These women have a great deal in common, under the surface. And they're connected. Another mistake. Suzanne Custer's two kids are part of the Anders sports programs. She's attended several of Ava's seminars and mommy retreats. She's done some volunteering, too."

"Huh." It was all Feeney said, but Eve glanced at him, and saw it had clicked.

"You think the Anders woman got the idea to off her husband from what happened to Custer?" Baxter's brows drew together as he stared hard at the screen. "Little Suzanne caught a lucky break, why can't I? Maybe she talks an LC into doing her the favor, pays her off through the program or the company, then . . ."

"Simpler than that," Feeney commented and enjoyed another scoop of hash browns. "Simpler's best."

Baxter frowned, then . . . "Well, Christ."

It hit, Eve noted, hard enough for Baxter to forget his coffee and pig meat. "Give me a hand, will you," she said to Roarke.

Together they turned Eve's murder board so the second side faced the room. "Ava Anders to Bebe Petrelli and Cassie Gordon. They didn't pan out for her, but she tested waters there. Ava Anders to Charles Monroe. Professional LC, clean record, sterling rep. Use him to build her claim that her husband liked the kink, and she didn't. That she loved him regardless. Ava to Brigit Plowder and Sasha Bride-West. Alibis. Girlfriends, tight circle."

As she outlined, Eve tapped each photo, each connection.

"Ava to Edmond and Linny Luce—friends of vic who would, in turn, testify as to the comfortable and happy marriage. Except they don't like her—under the surface, they don't like her a bit. She didn't count on that. She didn't count on any real connection being made between her—lady of the manor, lady bountiful—with the less fortunate women in the program she oversees."

Now she pinned her finger to Ned Custer's photo. "She sure as hell didn't count on any connection between the murder of a philandering, blue-collar asshole and the murder of her renowned philanthropist husband. Murders committed months apart, with different MOs, in different parts of the city."

"It could work," Peabody said under her breath. "It could really work."

"It did work," Eve corrected. "Two men are dead."

"You think they *traded* murders. Fuck me," Baxter added.

"I know they did. Ava's been planning this a long time. At least two years, since I believe she killed her father-in-law. But probably longer than that. Once the father-in-law was out of the picture—" Eve tapped Reginald Anders's photo on the board. "Lots more at stake. More money, more power, more control. That skin she was wearing, boy, that really had to start to tighten up on her. Every single day, to have to look at this guy she'd married, play the contented wife, listen to him drone on and on about his sports, his business, his programs. Planning the murders, that would help her get through it. That light at the end of the tunnel."

"Yes," Mira agreed when Eve turned to her. "For a goal-oriented personality, one who sees the big picture, the planning is part of the reward. For one who's skilled in long-term role-playing, there would be considerable satisfaction in the success of that role. But you're talking years, Eve. Any actor, even one so amoral and self-serving, would require breaks."

"The vic traveled a lot, she encouraged it. And she would often entertain during those trips, leaving out the vic's nephew and closer friends. Her parties, her way. And Charles. He added to her cover, to the picture, but let's not discount the release of good sex—especially when you're in the driver's seat. The client holds the power with an LC."

"If she did Custer, she must've stalked him," McNab put in. "The wife couldn't know what bar he'd troll in the night of. And Anders couldn't have pulled it off on impulse. She had to be set."

"Exactly right. We'll canvass his haunts again, and show Ava's photo, and the photo of her with red hair I'm having Yancy generate. She picked the flop, had to. Her type wouldn't leave that to chance."

"Agreed," Mira said.

"We find a connection between her and the flop. Show her photo there. She's not going to be alibied for the night of Custer's murder, but we're going to get that solid. She bought the wig, she bought the clothes. We're going to find out where. We're going to go over the case file from the father-in-law's death and find her mistakes. And we're going to bring her in. We're going to sew her up, and we're going to take her down for two counts of murder, and one count of conspiracy to commit."

"Suzanne Custer," Baxter murmured.

"Yeah, she's the needle in the haystack *and* the needle for the thread. She trusts you."

"Yeah." Baxter sighed it. "Yeah, she does."

"We'll use that. We're going to break her down, Baxter, you and me. We'll break her because she's not built like Ava."

"She got nervous." Trueheart shifted his attention to Baxter. "When we went back to talk to her, a few days after the murder, she was jumpy and nervous. She didn't want to talk to us. You smoothed her down."

"Yeah, yeah. It set off a little buzz, but there was nothing to tie her. Nothing. So I put it down to regular nerves and the situation. She had me, goddamn it."

"Now we've got her," Eve reminded him. "Dr. Mira, can you give us a personality profile on Suzanne Custer?"

"From Detective Baxter's overview, I'd say she's a woman who accepts or perhaps expects her own victimization. She accepted, or certainly lived with, her husband's behavior. While it appears she sought more for her children, she failed to take advantage of programs offered for abused women. It's possible she didn't see herself as such. She doesn't control, or seek control. At this point, until further study, my opinion would be she fears and seeks those with authority over her."

"A woman who does what she's told."

"So it would seem," Mira said, "from the data I have at this point. I'd like to look at her background, her childhood."

"I'd appreciate if you could do that ASAP. Feeney, Mc-Nab, I need a search on electronic purchases. Look for the wig, costumes re Ava. Dig in. She may have picked them up a year ago, two years. Hell, she might've had them for a decade. Look for all communications between her and Suzanne Custer and her personal 'links, and any at Anders's. I've got warrants to check all communication devices owned by Plowder and Bride-West."

"On it," Feeney told her, and kept eating.

"Trueheart, you're with Peabody. Check for Suzanne's purchases at a smut shop called Just Sex. Her husband shopped there, so odds are if she needed anything for the job, that's where she'd go. Get the medicals on her from her health clinic—a Dr. Yin—and prescriptions from its pharmacy. Tap the Transit Authority. She had to get from her apartment to the Anders house and back. Mother of two, I bet she uses the subway routinely, and a fare card."

"Lieutenant." Trueheart raised his hand and lowered it again as Baxter elbowed him. "I don't think she'd leave the kids alone. I don't think she'd have gone out and left her kids unattended. She's just not the type for it."

"Okay. Then let's find out if she got a sitter, or where her kids were on the night of. If the civilian has time . . ."

"The civilian can probably carve out a few minutes here and there," Roarke commented.

"A remote was used to shut down the security at the Anders house. A high-end and illegal remote. Where did it come from and which one of our killers obtained it? I haven't picked up a hot one there. You find out."

"Not as entertaining as a visit to a smut shop," Roarke considered, "but the black market has some appeal."

"Good luck." Feeney saluted him. "Coulda been any of a couple dozen types—or versions of types—picked up any time within the last couple years. Coulda been homemade, for that matter, you had any snap for it."

Roarke smiled at him. "Adds to the fun, doesn't it?"

"Let's all go out and have fun. Baxter," Eve said, "with me."

"I wouldn't have pegged her." Baxter brooded out the side window as Eve drove. "She snowed me right from the get."

"You didn't peg her because she didn't do it."

"Same thing as doing it, and I didn't get a whiff. The boy did. When we went back and she was nervy, he caught the whiff. And I blew it off, explained it away. I didn't see it, didn't smell it, didn't hear it."

"Guess you'd better turn in your papers, then. I hear private security's a good gig for washed-out cops."

"To borrow a phrase, bite me." But it didn't seem he could work up any steam. "She's soft, Dallas. Mira'll come up with her psycho-whatever, but it comes down to her being a soft sort, a little wounded, a lot tired. Mousy, if you get me. Right now, with all you worked out, I'm trying to see her going into that house, pumping Anders full of tranqs and setting him up like a kink kill, and I can't see it."

"You like her. You feel sorry for her."

Irritation tightened his face. "I like lots of people, and feel sorry for some. That doesn't stop me from seeing a stone killer when she's in my damn face."

"You're taking it personal, Baxter."

"Damn right I am." There was steam now as he jerked toward Eve. "And don't give me any of that objectivity crap. You wouldn't be so fucking good at the job if you didn't take it personal."

Eve gave him a minute to stew. "You want me to tell you you screwed up? You missed it? You didn't see what you should've seen? Nothing I'd like better because it makes my day to ream out a smart-ass pig-eater like you. But I can't do it. You didn't screw up. You can't miss what's not in play, and can't see what isn't there."

"You saw Ava Anders."

"I didn't like her goddamn face—and yeah, some of it was personal. I wouldn't have seen the how if you hadn't nagged my *ass* off about Custer. So reschedule your pity party, Baxter. We don't have time for it now."

"Assuming we're playing to our strengths, you'll be taking bad cop."

"And you'd be the cop with the soft spot for the tragic, little widow."

"Yeah." He hissed out a breath. "Fucking A. I feel played, so I'll be picking up the hats and balloons for the pity party later."

"Don't forget the cake." She scouted out a parking spot as she neared Suzanne's address. "It's going to spook her, seeing me instead of Trueheart. Having to go into Central. If she's thought about any of this happening, she may have thought about lawyers. You need to reassure her. Routine, tying things up."

"I know how to play good cop." He got out, waited for Eve on the sidewalk. "I need to take the lead with her, initially, keep her steady, make her think I'm a little ticked that you're insisting on the official routine."

"I know how to play bad cop," Eve countered.

It was a miserable post–Urban War building. One of the structures tossed up from the rubble and never intended to last. Its concrete gray walls were blackened with age and weather, scored with graceless graffiti and misspelled obscenities.

They walked into a narrow, frigid entryway and took the rusted metal stairs up to the third floor. Everything echoed, Eve noted. Their feet on the treads, the sounds leaking out of doors and walls as they passed by, the noises from the street outside.

But none of the early spring warmth pushed in to boost the chilly air.

Baxter positioned himself at the door, knocked. The over-bright sound of kids and Saturday morning screen whooped on the other side. One of those odd and somehow creepy morning cartoon deals that had the kids yammering and squealing, Eve imagined.

Who made those things?

A high-pitched girly voice called out for mommy so clearly, the door itself might've been made of paper.

The locks thunked, and the door scraped and groaned as it opened.

She'd been pretty once, Eve thought at her first in-person study of Suzanne Custer. She might be pretty again, given decent nutrition, reasonable sleep, a break from stress. As Eve didn't see those elements in her future, she thought Suzanne's pretty days were long over.

She looked exhausted, pale, too thin, as if the meat under

her skin had been gnawed away. Her dull, listless hair had been pulled back, leaving her tired face defenseless. A small, round-eyed kid of the male variety (probably) stood at her side.

"Detective Baxter."

"Mrs. Custer. Hey there, Todd!" Baxter flashed a grin, shot the boy with his finger.

"We're watching 'toons."

"So I hear. Hi, Maizie."

The little girl had a year or two on her brother, and the soft prettiness that had once been her mother's. She sent Baxter a big, beaming smile.

"I'm sorry." Suzanne shoved at her hair, then reached down to wrap her arm around her son's shoulders. "We're a little disorganized this morning. I was . . . just cleaning up after breakfast, before I take the kids to practice. Is this . . . Do you have any . . . Can this wait until later?"

"I'm afraid it can't, Mrs. Custer." Eve edged Baxter aside, and all but felt his annoyed frown. "We have a number of things to clear up, and we'll need to handle this at Central."

"At Central? But—"

"I'm sorry, Mrs. Custer." Baxter's voice poured warm cream over quiet apology. "This is my lieutenant. As we've been unable to close your husband's case in a timely manner, Lieutenant Dallas needs to see to some procedural matters."

"At Central," Eve said, clipping the words.

"But, my kids."

"I don't—"

"Lieutenant, please." Baxter interrupted Eve, then eased forward toward Suzanne. "I can arrange to have them taken to practice, or you can bring them with you and we'll see they're supervised while we finish this up. Whichever you want."

"I don't know. I—"

"I can't miss practice." Cartoons forgotten, Maizie jumped up. "I just *can't*. Mom, please!"

"Why don't I take care of their transportation?" Baxter suggested. "And have a couple of officers stay with them. Then when we're done, we'll make sure you get to the field. Okay, LT?"

Eve only shrugged, as if she didn't give a damn. "Make it fast. You've put enough time and department resources into this. I'll wait outside."

"Sorry about that," Eve heard Baxter say as she walked away. "The lieutenant's a stickler for procedure. I'll try to fast-walk all this through."

On the street, Eve checked in with Peabody. "Status?"

"Wallowing in smut. I had no idea there were so many devices designed to be inserted in orifices. Many are sold in variety and party packs. You can select one of forty-dollar value with any body piercing."

"That's a deal."

"Well, it's kind of tempting. McNab would wig in a completely excellent way. But seeing as I'm on duty . . ."

"Seeing as. But keep jabbering, Peabody, and I'll give you a completely free piercing back at Central."

"We have a clerk who recognized Suzanne Custer," Peabody said quickly. "Made her right off. Said she remembered because she—Suzanne—looked so off the rails. She bought several of the items that match those on the Anders scene. The clerk didn't want to bother checking on it, but she's flirting with Trueheart."

"Trueheart's flirting with a smut shop clerk? What has Baxter done to that kid?"

"No, no, *she's* doing the flirt thing. He's turned all shades of red, but that's worked for us." Peabody grinned. "It is pretty damn cute. So she checked, and we're getting the paperwork. Suzanne didn't buy the rope here. But, she asked about it. They were out of the velvet bondage set. It's a popular item, as we learned when we did the initial search."

"Check the shops closest to your current location. And if you come back with any piercings, they better not be visible."

"Ouch," Peabody said as Eve clicked off.

Once she had Suzanne at Central, Eve left her in Interview to sweat for fifteen minutes and watched through the observation window.

"She's terrified," Baxter said.

"Good. It probably won't take very long to break her down. You go in first, make your apologies for the mean old LT." She glanced over as Mira stepped in.

"She looks worn down. Eaten up." Her face impassive, Mira stepped closer to the glass. "Guilt would be a viable weapon on her. And her children, they'd be a vulnerable area. She'll fear you the most," she said to Eve. "The capable, powerful female—everything she's not. The authority figure. As, I suspect, Ava Anders is to her. She's accustomed to violence. It won't frighten her overmuch. Nor will threats to her person, as she's accustomed to those as well. She's also used to being isolated, cut off from any support. So offers of friendship, understanding, support draw her in. Her children are her one accomplishment. She would sacrifice a great deal for them."

"I need to make her flip on Ava."

"She'll need to believe you're more powerful, and more dangerous than Ava."

"I am, so she will. Go," Eve told Baxter.

"The friendship offered by Ava," Mira continued as Baxter stepped out, "the support, the bargain struck—if indeed one was—weigh heavily on Ava's side. The power Ava has over her now is tremendous."

"I know how to play her." When Mira said nothing, Eve watched Baxter enter Interview, listened to him speak reassuringly to Suzanne. "I know what it's like to be knocked around regular, isolated, held down so you believe it's the only way. And I know how far you'll go to make it stop."

"She's nothing like you, and neither are her circumstances."

"No. But I know how to play her. Baxter, he feels for her. Decent men tend to feel for women like her."

"But you don't."

"No, I don't. She could've walked. Any time. Packed up, grabbed the kids and walked." Studying Suzanne through the glass, Eve felt not a single twinge of sympathy. "You said she'd sacrifice for her kids, but what has she given them? What kind of life has she opened them to by letting them see, every day, that she's so weak she'll let their father slap her around, come and go as he pleases, spend his money on tricks instead of food. You don't offset that with sports programs, Dr. Mira. That woman took the life of a stranger, the life of a good man, the man who offered her children hope. She did that rather than walk away.

"So yeah, I guess I do feel for her. I feel disgust. I've got no qualms about putting her away. I just want to make damn sure I put Ava Anders away with her."

"Eve." Mira put a hand on Eve's arm as Eve started to step out. "There's a difference between weak and evil."

"Yeah, but there's sure a lot of overlap."

Eve entered Interview. "Record on. Dallas, Lieutenant Eve, and Baxter, Detective David, in Interview with Custer, Suzanne, in the matter of the murder of Custer, Ned, case number HC-20913, and any and all related events or crimes. Detective, have you read Mrs. Custer her rights?"

"No, Lieutenant."

"Do so. For the record."

He sighed. "Yes, sir. It's a formality, Mrs. Custer. You have the right to remain silent."

Fear widened Suzanne's eyes, quickened her breath as Baxter recited the Revised Miranda. Eve took a seat at the table, slumped back. "Do you understand your rights and obligations in this matter?" she demanded.

"Yes, but—"

"Here's something that strikes me, Suzanne. It just seems so damn handy that you'd be sitting at home trying to tag your cheating shitbag of a husband on his 'link while some unidentified hooker's slitting his throat. What, were you going to ask him to bring home a jug of soy milk?"

"No. He was late. I just wanted to—"

"He was late a lot, wasn't he? Did you whine on his voice mail every time he was late?"

"No, but—he promised. He promised he wouldn't be. I said I'd leave him if he didn't stop."

"You were never going to leave him." Eve allowed some of the disgust to eke into her voice. "You didn't have the guts for that. And now you don't have to. Instead he's gone, and you've got that nice life insurance policy, the pension."

"Come on, Lieutenant, ease off a little."

She scorched Baxter with a look. "You've eased off plenty for both of us. Did you find some sap like the detective here to do it for you, Suzanne? Cozy yourself up to some guy who doesn't slap you around, feels sorry for you. So he does this—" Eve pulled out a crime scene photo, tossed it onto the table. "So you can be free."

"No." Suzanne closed her eyes rather than look at the photo. "I didn't want another man. I just wanted my husband to be a good man, a good father. My kids deserve a good home, a good father."

"The money you've got coming in now, you can get them out of that rattrap. Where are you taking them, Suzanne?"

"I don't know. I thought, I think, maybe south, maybe down to Arkansas with my sister. Out of the city. Away. I can't think about it yet. Somewhere else, for a fresh start. There's nothing wrong with that." She looked imploringly at Baxter. "Nothing wrong with wanting a fresh start with my kids."

"Of course not. It's been rough on you here. Rough for a long time. It'd be good for the kids to get out of the city, somewhere with a lot of green. Anders has sports programs all over the country."

She winced at the Anders name, looked away. "If I could get them in a good school, down south somewhere, the schools have teams. They have sports."

"Are you going to give up the freebies?" Eve demanded. "The free equipment, camps, programs, the mom retreats. It's been a pretty good deal for you, hasn't it?" Eve flipped open a file. "You had a few nice vacations here, on the Anderses' dime, didn't you?"

"Seminars, and—and support groups."

"Yeah, Thomas Anders gave you and your kids plenty. Too bad about him, huh?" Eve tossed another photo down, one of Thomas Anders dead in his bed.

Suzanne jerked away, dropped her head between her knees and gagged.

"Jesus, Lieutenant! Hey, hey." Baxter laid a hand on Suzanne's back. "Take it easy. Take it slow. Let me get you some water."

"Let her puke." Eve shoved out of her chair, then dropped down, pushing Suzanne's head back until their eyes met. "Did it make you sick to do it? Did it curdle your guts to strip off his nice, neat pajamas, tie his hands and feet? Did your hands shake like they are now when you wrapped the rope around his neck? He didn't give you any trouble, you saw to that. Put him under so you wouldn't have to see the look in his eyes when he choked."

"No." Her eyes wheeled like an animal's with its leg snapped in a trap. "I don't want to be here. I don't know what you're talking about."

"You still screwed it up. You didn't tie the rope tight enough, so it took him a long time to die. You didn't do it the way she told you. She was so specific, but you couldn't pull it off. Not like she did with Ned. Quick, clean, done. You got messy, you got weak. It looks like she'll walk, and you'll spend the rest of your life in a cage. An off-planet cage. You'll never see your kids again."

"I don't know what you're talking about. Detective Baxter, please make her stop."

"For God's sake, Dallas, let her breathe. Suzanne.

Suzanne." He eased down to sit on the edge of the table, took Suzanne's trembling hand, looked into her eyes. "We know it was Ava's idea. All of it. We know she planned it. If you tell us everything, all of it, maybe we can help you."

"No, no. You're trying to trick me. You're trying to make me say things. She said you'd—"

"She said we'd try to block you in?" Eve finished. "She was right about that. But she told you we'd try to block you in on Ned's murder and you were clear there. Nothing to worry about there. She didn't figure this, did she? Neither of you figured this. I know what you did."

Eve shoved Baxter aside, shoved her face into Suzanne's. "I know you killed Thomas A. Anders. The man who paid for the equipment your kids are wearing right now. You selfish, heartless bitch."

"That's crazy. I didn't even know him. A person doesn't kill someone she doesn't even know."

"That's what she told you? They'll never suspect. She was wrong again, wasn't she? Her mistakes, all her mistakes, and I'm going to make you pay for every one of them. I'm going to put you in a cage, Suzanne. Look at me!"

With one violent yank, she dragged Suzanne's chair around. "I'm going to put you in, and she can't stop me. She won't try because you're useless to her now. She'll cry for the cameras and laugh behind closed doors because you're too stupid to help yourself. And your kids? It'll be strangers raising them now."

"No. Please. God."

"Lieutenant, come on. Give her a second. Suzanne. You need to tell us everything. If you cooperate, I can help you. I'll talk to the PA." Baxter reached down, squeezed her hand. "Maybe she pressured you or threatened you. Blackmailed you. Maybe you felt you didn't have a choice."

"I'm compiling evidence against her right now," Eve broke in. "When I have enough, she'll be in here. She'll be the one turning on you. If she flips first, she'll get the deal.

Personally, I want both of you to live the rest of your miserable lives in an off-planet cage. You've got one minute. One to change my mind. After that, I'm done. You're booked, murder in the first, and your kids are gone."

"Please don't, please! You don't understand."

"No, you don't understand, you weak, pathetic excuse for a human being. I know what you did. I know how you did it. I know why you did it. And you've got one shot to put it out your way or I'll personally toss you in that cage and lock it."

"Lieutenant, Lieutenant, give her a chance. Give her a minute. Help us understand," Baxter said to Suzanne. "I want to understand, so I can help you."

"I didn't think it was going to be real!" Suzanne burst out. "I didn't think it was real. And then it was. I didn't know what else to do. She said I had to."

"Spit it out," Eve snapped. "Who said you had to what?"

Suzanne closed her eyes again. "Ava said I had to kill her husband because she'd killed mine. Just like we agreed." Suzanne laid her head down on the table. "I'm so tired. I'm so tired now."

Chapter 21

Eve stepped out to call Cher Reo, and to give Baxter a few moments to help Suzanne compose herself. She flicked a glance over as Mira slipped out of Observation. Mira walked by, stopped at Vending, and ordered three waters, and a Pepsi for Eve.

After finishing her conversation, Eve tucked her 'link back in her pocket, took the tube. "Thanks. PA's willing to deal for the bigger fish. Ava's a much bigger fish. A big, splashy one."

"And Suzanne is nothing and no one, comparatively. She killed, Eve, there's no disputing it. But she was used."

"The choice was there; she made it." Eve drank. "But I'm willing to deal, too."

"I'll be watching the rest. When she gets a lawyer, there will be a demand for a psychiatric evaluation."

"She can have her head shrunk by a platoon of doctors, after I get my confession. And yeah, I'm perfectly aware I'm using her, too. I've got no problem with that."

"You shouldn't have, but—"

"She's soft," Eve interrupted. "That's what you're seeing,

and you've got some sympathy for her. Go ahead. But I see Thomas Aurelious Anders."

With a nod, Mira went back into Observation.

Eve stepped back into Interview. "Lieutenant Dallas re-entering Interview," she said for the record. "Here's the deal, Suzanne. Are you listening?"

"Yes, I'm listening."

"The PA will drop the charges down from one count of Murder One, one count of Conspiracy to Murder to one count of Murder Two. That keeps you on-planet, with visitation access to your kids."

Tears dripped, as if Suzanne's eyes were leaking faucets. "How long?"

"Fifteen to twenty."

"Fifteen. Oh God. God. They'll be grown."

"You'll be eligible for parole in seven," Baxter told her.

"If you don't cooperate, if this goes to trial, the charges bounce back. You're looking at the probability of two life sentences, running consecutively. Off-planet." Eve sat. "Your choice."

"My kids. I... I have a sister. Can my kids go to my sister?"

"I'll look into that. Personally." Baxter nodded. "I'll talk to your sister, to Child Services."

"They'll be better off with her. I should've taken them and gone to my sister years ago." She swiped at the tears with the tissues Baxter gave her. "Everything would be different if I'd done that. But I didn't. I thought, Ned's their father and they should be with their father. I thought, I'm his wife, and I'm supposed to make the home. If I did better, everything would work out. But I didn't do better, and it just got worse and worse. And then . . ."

"You met Ava Anders," Eve prompted.

"Yes." Suzanne closed her eyes for a moment, took several breaths. "She was so good to us, to everyone. She made me feel like I could do better. Be better. Ned didn't care about the program, but he didn't mind. Got the kids out from underfoot, he said. But sometimes, just sometimes, he'd go to a practice or a game. And that was good. He'd even take us out for pizza after sometimes. It was better when he did. And the last time, after the last time he hit me, he promised he wouldn't do it again. And he didn't this time. He didn't hit me for weeks, and he was around more. I thought, this is going to be all right. But then he started coming home late again, and smelling of sex."

"You talked to Ava about that?" Baxter asked.

"What? No... Before, we talked before. Months ago. Just before the kids went back to school. When they were at camp and I went to the retreat, the end of August. God, Ned was so angry that I went, but it was good to be there. To have that time away. We'd talked before—Ava, I mean."

Taking the cup of water, she sipped, paused, sipped again. "She was so nice to me. She'd sit with me late at night and talk and talk. She understood how hard it was with Ned that way because her husband hurt her, too. She never told anyone but me. He hurt her, and he made her do things. And he did things with girls—girls who were too young to be hurt that way.

"Everyone thinks he was so good." Tears streamed out of Suzanne's eyes, soaking the tissues as she mopped. "But he was a monster."

"That's what she told you?"

"She was afraid of him. I know what that's like. We cried together. She couldn't stand what he was doing to her, and more, to the children. She said he and Ned were alike. One day, Ned would hurt my babies. One day he could... with Maizie."

She closed her eyes, shuddered. "He'd never—he'd never touched Maizie like that, but he hit the kids sometimes. When they were bad, or when he'd had too much to drink. I thought, what would I do if he tried to do to Maizie what Mr. Anders did with young girls? I said, I think I said, I'd kill him if he touched her that way."

Her voice cracked, and began to waver and jump as she continued. "It would be too late then, Ava said, like she was afraid it was too late for her. She said she'd help me. We could help each other. We didn't have to live like this anymore, or risk the children."

Suzanne reached for the water, then simply rubbed the cup over her forehead. "She said it was just like in the seminars and groups, where we talked about being proactive, about being strong. Taking action to make a difference. She'd stop Ned and I'd stop Mr. Anders. No one would ever know."

"Stop?" Eve qualified.

Her shoulders hunched, Suzanne stared at the table. "Kill. We would kill them. No one would know—how could they—because each of us would be innocent of the crime that connected to us. She'd go first, to show good faith. We'd wait a few months and we'd be careful about contacting each other between. Then she'd stop Ned."

She heaved a breath, looked up at Eve again. "She said stop, not kill. I knew what she meant, I did, but it seemed right when she said it. She'd stop Ned before he hurt my children, stop him from hurting me. And then, we'd wait again, two or three months, and I'd stop Mr. Anders."

"Did she tell you how you'd stop him?"

Suzanne shook her head. Her eyes continued to flood, but they were empty behind the tears. Beaten, Eve thought. Broken.

"She said she thought she knew a way, so it would look like an accident. And so when they found him they'd know the kind of man he was. She knew I was strong, deep down, and good, a good mother, a good friend. She knew I'd save her, and she'd save me and my kids. We gave each other our word. We recorded it."

"Recorded?"

"She had a recorder, and we each recorded our intention, our promise. I said my name and that I promised on the lives of my children to kill the monster Thomas A. Anders. That I would kill him with my own hands, and in a way that was symbolic and just. She said the same, except Ned's name, and she swore on the lives of all the children of the world."

"Dramatic."

Little spots of color bloomed on Suzanne's white cheeks. "It *meant* something. It was important. I felt important. I never felt like that before."

"What did she do with the recording?"

"She said she was going to put it in a bank box. For safety. After we stopped Ned and Mr. Anders, we'd destroy it together. We didn't talk much after that. Not for a while. She's very busy. And when I got home, and everything was the way it is at home, I thought, none of that was real. It was just like a session. Or maybe I wanted to think that."

She bowed her head, then shoved at the hair that fell over her face. "I don't know anymore. But I put it away. I forgot about it. Almost all the time. Then things got a little better for a while with Ned. I saw Ava at the offices one day, and I told her how things were better. She smiled at me, and she said they'd get better yet." On a choked sob, Suzanne pressed a hand to her mouth. "I swear, I didn't think, didn't really think about what we'd said that night. I didn't think of any of that, and Ned started staying out again, and we started fighting again. I told myself I was going to leave him this time, that I was stronger now. Because of Ava."

Her breath came in two quick hitches. "I felt stronger, because of Ava, and what she'd given me. How she'd made me feel about myself. And then Detective Baxter came with Officer Trueheart, and they said Ned was dead. They said he'd gone into a hotel room with an LC, and he was dead. I never thought about Ava and what we'd said that night, way back in August. I thought it was just as they'd told me. He'd picked up the wrong kind of woman."

"When did she contact you after that?"

"A few days later." Suzanne pressed her fingers to her eyes. "That's when everything fell apart. The kids were in school. I was going to do the marketing. I always do the marketing on Monday morning, so I was walking to the market, and she came up beside me. She said: 'Keep walking, Suzanne. Keep walking and don't say anything yet.' We walked another three blocks, I think, then we crossed and walked another two or three. She had a car, and we got in. When I asked where we were going, she said somewhere we could talk. I told her I had to do the marketing, and she started to drive. And she started to tell me."

As Suzanne's breath began to wheeze, Baxter nudged the water toward her. "What did she tell you, Suzanne?"

"She said she'd fulfilled the part of the bargain we'd made, and asked how I felt now that I was free. I couldn't even talk for a minute. She was different—um, I don't know how to explain. She laughed, but it was different from before. It scared me. She scared me. I started to cry."

What else is new, Eve thought, you weak, whiny, *worthless* excuse for a human being.

"I started to say I hadn't meant any of it. Not really. But it was too late—that's what she said. It was too late for any second thoughts, any regrets. It was done. Now it was my turn. She kept driving, not even looking at me. She told me how she'd killed Ned."

Eve waited while Suzanne drank, and mopped more useless tears. "I need the details."

"Oh, God." Blubbering, Suzanne covered her face. "Oh, God. I can't."

Brutally cold in face, voice, manner, Eve shoved Suzanne's hands down. "You will. Here's one thing Ava's right about. It's too late. Give me the details."

Staring at Eve, trembling, Suzanne began. "She—she watched him for a few nights. Followed him into bars, watched him drink, watched him pick up women. Studied him is what she said, learned his habits and routines—his territory. She said his territory. And—and she rented rooms in a couple of the places he used for sex, and mapped them out. Preparation, she said. Preparation was key. She said she made herself look like a whore because that's what he liked. That's what most men liked. Please, can I have some more water?"

Baxter rose to fill the cup.

"She stalked him," Eve prompted.

"I guess. I guess. She said she went up to him while he was drinking, told him he looked like he knew how to party. She sat with him awhile—not too long, she said because she didn't want anyone to pay attention to her. She put her hand between his legs, rubbed. She said he came along with her like an idiot dog. That's what she called him."

The water in the cup Baxter gave her sloshed, dripped over the rim as Suzanne lifted it to drink. "They went to one of the places she'd mapped out. And when they were upstairs, he grabbed at her breasts, and she let him, let him touch her. But she told him she needed the bathroom first. And in the bathroom she put on a suit like doctors wear, and she sealed her hands, too, then got the knife. She called out for Ned to turn around. Turn around and close your eyes, she said to him. She had a big surprise for him."

"I'm sorry, I—I spilled water on the table."

"Finish it," Eve ordered.

"God." As if to hold herself in place, Suzanne crossed her arms tight over her own torso. "She said he did what she told him, like a good boy, and she came out, came out and she used the knife. She said he made the funniest noises, and grabbed at his throat like he had an itch there. How his eyes got so big, how he tried to talk. How he fell, and the way the blood just gushed out. How he just lay there and she...God. She cut it off, cut his penis off. A sym—a symbol. She put everything back in the bag she had, and when she knew he was good and dead, she went out by the fire escape. She walked for blocks and blocks. She said she felt like she could've flown, but she walked to where she'd left her car."

"What did she do with the bag, Suzanne?" Eve asked. "Did she tell you?"

"The bag?"

"With the knife in it."

"I feel sick."

"What did she do with the bag?"

Suzanne cringed. "In a recycler."

"Where?"

"I don't know. While she was walking to her car."

"Where was her car?"

"I don't know. Blocks away. Uptown, I think she said. Blocks away from where she killed Ned because the cops weren't going to look for a street whore so far away. She drove home, and she took a long bath with a glass of cognac, and she slept like a baby."

Her face gray now, Suzanne looked back at Eve. "I haven't slept. I don't think I've had an hour's real sleep since that day. She'd stopped the car. A rest stop off the Turnpike. We were in New Jersey now. I don't remember how we got there. I wasn't crying anymore. I got sick. It made her mad, but I couldn't help it. She let me open the door, and I threw up in the parking lot.

"I'm so tired now."

"Dallas," Baxter began, "maybe we should—"

Eve only shook her head to cut him off. "What did Ava do after you were sick?"

"After, she drove away from there, around the back where the big trucks are, and she told me what had to happen next. What I had to do. I said I couldn't, but she said if I didn't, she'd do to me what she'd done to Ned, and then she'd do it to my kids. My kids. No one would believe me if I told them. Who did I think I was? I was nobody, and she was an important and respected woman. They'd lock me up if I tried to tell them, unless she killed me first. She knew where my kids went to school, where they played, where they slept. I'd better remember that."

There was a dreamy quality in Suzanne's voice now, as if the reliving of it had put her into a trance.

"And I was better off, she said. Couldn't I see how much better off I was now? What she'd done for me? She said I had to wait. A couple of months would be best. She would get me a remote, and the passcode. She would explain exactly what I had to do and how I had to do it. She gave me a 'link. I wasn't to use it for anything. She would contact me on it when it was time. And she'd be watching me. And my kids. She told me what I was going to do, how easy it would be. If I messed it up, she had the recording, and she'd send it to the police. Or maybe I'd just have a tragic accident one day, me and the kids. She told me I should be grateful. She'd given me a fresh start. Now I had to pay for it. I had to stick to my part of the deal."

"Take us through it."

"It had to be late at night. After midnight, but before one. I'd use the remote to shut down the security, then I'd use the passcode and go inside. I—I had to seal up first. Straight up the stairs, to the bedroom. The door would be closed, and he'd be sleeping facing the door. He'd have taken a sleeping pill because she'd replaced his nightly vitamins with them. I had to . . . I had to take off his pajamas, use the rope—the rope she told me to buy—on his wrists and his ankles. I was supposed to give him a dose of male sex enhancer, and . . . God, put the rings on him, and some of the lotion. Set out the toys. He'd wake up some, and that was good. I'd see what it was like. It would make it better for all of us. Then I was to put the rope around his neck, tighten it. Watch, watch until I knew he was dead."

She drank again, three small sips. "I was supposed to take it off after, the rope, but leave it there. Then go down, through the house, through the kitchen, and take the security tapes. That would make it look like I'd been there before, that it was all an accident—like it was his own fault. I was supposed to walk out, turn everything back on—the security, then walk all the way to the subway on Fifth."

"What about the 'link, the discs?"

"She was to contact me on it at two. It was supposed to be done by two, but it wasn't. I couldn't . . . Then she called, and she was so angry. So I did it. I did what she said, except I couldn't stand the idea of him knowing, and I used the medication I'd gotten from the doctor to help me sleep, and I couldn't watch him die, so I ran out."

"Where's the 'link, the discs, the remote?"

"I was supposed to put them in a recycler on Fifth. But I forgot. I can't even remember getting on the subway, but I must have because I was home. I didn't remember about them until the next day, after my kids came home from school. They stayed at a friend's the night before, because I couldn't leave them alone. And I guess I always knew I'd do what she told me. I was afraid to put them in a recycler near the house. I was afraid to keep them in the house. I didn't know what to do. I shoved the bag in the closet because I couldn't *think*."

"Do you still have them?"

"I was going to take them to the park today, where the kids practice. I was going to put them in the recycler there. But you came."

Eve signaled Baxter, who rose and strode out of the room. "Detective Baxter has left Interview. Has she contacted you again, Suzanne?"

"No, not since that night—that morning. It's like a dream. I was walking, walking—after—and she called on the 'link. She said: 'Well?' And I said I'd done it. And she said, 'Good girl.' That's all. 'Good girl,' like I'd finished my chores. I killed him. I know he was a monster, but I think she's one, too."

"You think?"

"What's going to happen now? Can you tell me what's going to happen now?"

"We're going to go back over the details. What kind of vehicle did she drive?"

"A black one."

"Do better."

"It was black and shiny. Expensive. I don't know about cars. I've never had a car."

"When you were walking with her, the day you were going to the market, did you see anyone you know?"

"I don't know many people. Ned didn't like—"

"Stop it," Eve said sharply, and Suzanne jerked straight. "You know your neighbors, at least by sight, the people who run the market, your children's friends, their parents."

"I guess I do. I don't remember. I was so surprised to see her, and Ned had just . . ."

"No one spoke to you?"

"Just Ava. It was really cold, and I was looking down—the way you do."

The way *you* do, Eve thought. "Was the car on the street or in a lot?"

"A lot. An auto lot."

"Which way did you walk?"

"Ah, um . . . West because we went right by the market, and then we crossed after a few blocks, and walked north. I think maybe on Seventh. Maybe. I'm not sure."

"Which rest stop did she use?"

"I don't know, I don't know. They all look the same, don't they? I was sick."

"How long were you gone? No, don't give me that 'I don't know shit,' Suzanne. What time did you leave for the market?"

"About nine-thirty."

"What time did you get home?"

"It was almost noon. I had to take the bus. She dropped me at the transpo center across from the tunnel, and gave me bus fare. I had to take the bus back."

"How long did you wait for the bus?"

"Only a few minutes. I got lucky. I got off and walked back to the market. Mr. Isaacs said how he thought I wasn't coming in that day."

"Mr. Isaacs?"

"He runs the market, and I always go on Mondays, before ten. He said how I looked tired, how I should try to get some rest, and he gave me pop treats for the kids. I forgot that. He gave me treats for the kids. He's a nice man. He and his wife run the market. I went home, and I put everything away, and I thought, 'None of this is happening. It's not real.' Then I got sick again, because it was. I have to tell my kids. I don't know how."

"When you were at the retreat and made your bargain, where were you?"

"In Ava's suite. She told me to come up after the last seminar, but not to tell anyone. People get jealous. She just wanted to relax with a friend." Tears spurted again. Eve wondered how the woman had any more in her. "She said we were friends."

"You had drinks. Did she order them?"

"There was a bottle of wine and a pretty platter of fruit and cheese. Everything was so pretty."

"Did anyone call or come by while you were there?"

"No. She had the Do Not Disturb on the door and the 'links. So we could relax, she said."

Eve pressed a little more, then judged she'd wrung Suzanne dry. For now. "You're going to be booked, and you're going to be remanded. The court's going to assign an attorney to you. You've got the best deal you're going to get. Don't expect any more."

She rose as Baxter came back in. "Detective Baxter reentering Interview." When she crossed to him, he spoke quietly.

"Got the search warrant. Do you want me to take that?"

"No. Walk her through Booking. She's tapped out for now."

"I contacted the sister while I waited for the warrant to come through. She's confused and shocked, like you'd expect. She's making arrangements to come up for the kids. CS cleared that."

"You pushed some buttons."

"The kids are going to have it hard enough. Not their fault."

"Walk her through," Eve repeated. "I'll have Peabody and Trueheart exercise the warrant. I need a couple hours to sort through all this. We need to keep this arrest off the radar."

With a nod, Baxter walked to Suzanne. "You need to come with me now."

Eve waited until he'd led Suzanne through the door. "Interview end." Then she dragged her hands through her hair. "Christ. Jesus Christ."

When she stepped out, Mira was there. "I don't want to hear about her emotional trauma, her fear of authority figures, or her goddamn remorse. Thomas Anders died by her hand."

"Yes, he did. That doesn't make her less pitiable. A year in prison, twenty years, Suzanne Custer's life is essentially over. It was over the minute Ava Anders targeted her."

"Tell me this: Did Suzanne Custer know what she was doing when she put that rope around Thomas Anders's neck? Was she legally, mentally—and I'll even go one more—morally aware of right and wrong?"

"Yes, she was. She is culpable for her act, and should pay for what she did. Are there extenuating circumstances, would I—or any other psychiatrist—consider diminished capacity? Yes. But she killed Thomas Anders fully aware of her actions."

"That's good enough for me."

"Eve. You're so angry."

"Damn right I am. Sorry, I don't have time to comb through my own psyche. I've got work." She turned, and pulling out her communicator, strode away.

In her office, she hit the AutoChef for coffee before sitting down at her desk to begin the calculations for the most likely lots Ava had used, and the rest stop where she'd taken Suzanne. Little bits, she thought. Little bits and pieces. While the computer worked, she wrote her report on the interview, made notes, added to her time lines.

When the computer spit out its most probables, she studied the map, gauged the distances, the locations, simmered them with her understanding of Ava.

"I think we've got that. Yeah, I think we do," she muttered. And only grunted at the knock on her door.

"Hello, Lieutenant."

She barely glanced at Roarke. "She doesn't go far—just far enough. But she's not as fucking smart as she thinks she is. Doesn't know people as well as she believes."

"I'm sure you're right." He sat on the corner of her desk. "A moment?"

"I don't have much of a moment. Suzanne copped to it all. Jesus, it was like flipping a switch on a dike or a dam, whatever, and having it all gush out. Ava went for the weak, the runt of the litter you could say. Miscalculated. Makes Suzanne easy to manipulate."

"And that was the miscalculation," he said with a nod. "Because you're very good at manipulating."

"She counted on the power of her personality, of the pecking order to push Suzanne into doing the job. But she read her partner wrong. Way wrong. My take? She believed Suzanne would be flattered and happy to hook up with her, believed Suzanne would be grateful to be rid of her lousy husband, and do exactly what she was told. She had contingency plans, sure—she's always got herself a Plan B, C, or D, but she didn't see that under it, Suzanne's a major fuckup."

"That's harsh."

"She deserves harsh." The anger roiled inside her. "At any point, any fucking point, she could've stopped. Back in August when Ava proposed the plan, she could've stopped. When Ava told her how she'd killed her husband, she could've stopped. Any time over the last two months, she could've stopped. In the hour she was in the house with Anders, she could've stopped. And now it's all, gee, I'm sorry? Boo-hoo? I feel sick? Screw that."

"Does she enrage you for what she did, or that she was weak enough to do it?"

"Both. And I'm happy to be a part of making her pay. Making both of them pay. Ava got what she wanted, but she had to push too hard. And she used the wrong sort of manipulation in the end. Smarter, much smarter to have appealed to Suzanne's soft side. 'Please help me. You're the only one I trust, the only one I can depend on. I've done this for you, just as I promised. Please don't turn your back on me now.' Instead, she was so revved from the murder she played hardball, and cracked her tool. All I had to do was give it a few good knocks."

She pushed away from the desk, crossed over to stare out the window.

Roarke gave her a moment of silence for her own thoughts. "What troubles you about it, Eve? Under your anger?"

"It's personal. I can deal with that, but the way it's personal gnaws a little. Mira's already poking at me about it, and that's irritating."

"Because she sees that you look at Suzanne and think of yourself. The child you were. Battered, trapped, helpless. And the choice you made to save yourself."

Eve glanced back. "It shows? That's irritating, too."

"To me, and to Mira. But you wear your armor well, Lieutenant."

"She wasn't a child, Roarke. She wasn't helpless, or didn't have to be. She chose to kill, to obey another's bidding to kill, rather than deal."

That, he knew, would eat at her. The uselessness of it. "And it pisses you off. She lay down and took it, when there were so many options. She took the life of a man she didn't know because someone told her to. Her husband's dead because she stayed with him rather than walk away. And now her children are, essentially, orphaned."

"She said she thought her children should have their father. That it was her responsibility to stay."

"Ah."

Having said it, Eve realized some of the knots in her belly had slackened. "Yeah, I thought of your mother, and how she'd thought the same. How she'd died for that. But goddamn it, Roarke, your mother was so young, and I can't believe she'd have stayed for years. I can't look at you and believe that. Can't think of the family you found and believe that. She'd have taken you and walked, if she'd had another chance."

"I think of that. Aye, sometimes I think of that. And

that's what I believe as well. But in God's truth, I don't know if it's a comfort or a curse to believe it."

"It's a comfort to me," she said, and watched his eyes warm.

"Then it will be to me as well. Thanks."

"Suzanne Custer sat and made a bargain over wine and cheese. Some part of her knew it was real, however much she denies it. However much she can't face it. She agreed to Ava's terms. She didn't try to back out until after her own husband's throat was slit. She didn't go to Ava the next morning, or the next week and tell her, 'Deal's off. No can do.' She let it ride. Ned Custer was a son of a bitch, and he may have deserved to have his balls kicked black and blue, might've deserved some time in a cage for spousal abuse, but he didn't deserve having his throat slit and his dick sawed off. But the wife who claims she wanted her children to have their father set him up for just that. So I don't feel for her. I'm damned if I will."

Roarke rose, and going to her laid his hands on her shoulders, his lips on her brow. "It's useless to be angry with yourself because you do feel something. Just that thin edge of pity around the disgust."

"She doesn't deserve my pity." And Eve sighed. "Or any more of my time slapping at myself for that thin edge of it I do feel. I need to get in the field."

He gave her shoulders a brisk rub. "Here I've come by as I did my job so well and so quickly; now you're tossing me aside."

"You pinned the remote? Already?"

"I did, yes. I'll have some coffee."

"How the hell—"

"Are you going to get me some coffee or not?"

"Crap." She programmed it. "Spill."

"Assuming you don't mean the coffee—as what would be the point—I've just come from a chat with an old . . . acquaintance. He happens to specialize in electronics that aren't legal in the strictest sense of the word."

"He sells illegal jammers and bypasses on the black market."

"To put a fine point on it, yes. He manufactures them, most usually for specific clients at quite a hefty markup. He's very good at it. In fact, perhaps the best in New York." He waited a significant beat. "Now."

"Now that you aren't in the same market."

"Aren't you clever? I started at the top of the chain, as I assume Ava would want someone talented, efficient, and reliable—also with a reputation for being discreet. She went for Charles, after all, who has those qualities in his former profession. I'll admit I didn't expect to hit straight off the mark. But that's precisely what I did."

"This guy, this acquaintance designed and sold the remote to Ava."

"Three months ago, he received a package at his legitimate place of business."

"His front."

"You're so picky. The package contained an order for a very specifically designed device. It contained the specs for the security system the device was to bypass. He tells me he was impressed with the research the potential client had done. And," Roarke added with a smile, "with the considerable amount of cash as down payment. Another payment would be made on delivery, and the final sent if and when the client deemed the device satisfactory."

"Is that how he usually does business?"

"That would be telling." Roarke stroked a finger down the dent in her chin. "But I can say this arrangement was a bit unusual. The offered fee was more than his usual as well. So he took the job."

"He never saw her. Never had direct contact with her."

"No. He made the device, and as instructed left it in a drop box, which contained the second payment."

"A guy could get stung that way," Eve commented.

"Not this guy, or not easily. He's a nose for cops, and the setup. He also believes in knowing who he's dealing with, so he had an underling stake out the box."

Eve's lips spread in a grin. "I might like this guy."

"Actually, I believe you would. In any case, the woman who picked it up didn't match Ava's description, but she delivered it, along with some dry cleaning, to the Anderses' home. The third payment was made, as promised. And my acquaintance thought little of the matter until he heard of Thomas Anders's murder. This put him in a bit of a sticky situation."

"Yeah, accessory before the fact's pretty sticky. Will he testify?"

"That would depend on several issues. Immunity, anonymity—the man does have a business to protect—and a reasonable payment."

"I'll set it up. We may not need him, but I'll put it in play." Eve took his coffee, drank some herself. "You're useful."

"And always eager to be used."

"I've got Peabody out on something else. Why don't you ride over to New Jersey with me?"

"Being used across state lines. How could I resist?"

Chapter 22

"Yeah, we get your illegals drops, your vandals, your vehicle boosters, rapists, muggers." The NJTP security tech, with VINCE embroidered over his shirt pocket, shrugged. "Get plenty of action, mostly between midnight and six. Me, I work the days. I got seniority."

"It's days I'm interested in," Eve reminded him. "A specific day a couple of months ago."

"We got security cams covering all the lots, the grounds, the vending. Can't use 'em in the johns, so that's where we get the most action." He pulled at his nose, swiveled on his high-backed stool. "But we roll 'em over every seventy-two hours. We got nothing goes back two months."

"Do you go back two months, Vince?"

"Sure. I've been here twelve years come June."

"Two women in a high-end black car, with one of them puking out the passenger door."

He shot her a quick and sour grin. "Jesus, New York, you know how many people we got puking in the lots, in the johns? Every-damn-where?"

"I bet you don't have that many booting it between ten and eleven on a weekday, non-holiday morning." She pulled out a photo. "This would be the puker."

He took the photo, scratched his ass, scratched his head. "She don't ring for me. Looks like mostly anyone."

"What about this one?"

There was more scratching as Vince studied Ava's photo. "Looks like somebody. This one's driving, right? Nice, black Mercedes—new model, two-door sedan."

"You remember that?"

"Yeah, now that I'm thinking about it. Blondie here didn't look like the road-trip sort, and they never got out to use the john. Women hardly ever pass up a trip to the john, they pull into a rest area. The other one tosses it out the door, and I think: 'There goes breakfast.' I remember 'cause I expected they'd go into the john, clean up the sick one. But the blonde, she just drives around to the truck lot, parks again. I let maintenance know they had a cleanup, got me some coffee. Can't say I noticed how long they sat there or when they left."

Back in the car, Roarke stretched his legs. "Are you going to pass up a trip to the john?"

"Ha-ha. I can put her here with Suzanne. Right here in the Alexander Hamilton rest area off the Turnpike. Who the hell was Alexander Hamilton, and why is there a rest area off the Turnpike named after him?"

"Ah . . ."

"Never mind. There's a new model Mercedes sedan, black, registered to Ava Anders. This little chat with Vince confirms the day, the time—and I'll back that up because I'll betcha that big, black Mercedes has a pass scanner for the toll. Can't confirm what was said, but it puts Ava with Suzanne here. How's she going to explain that one?"

"She'll have something. Hamilton was one of America's Founding Fathers, and its first Secretary of the Treasury."

"Who? Huh?"

"You asked," Roarke said, pocketing his PPC again. "Where to now?"

Eve frowned at him a moment. "Is that what you're doing, playing with that thing all the time? Looking up trivia?"

"Among other things. Something else you'd like to know?"

"Whole bunches of things. Right now, we're going to go to the market to find out a few." She answered her dash 'link. "Dallas."

"We got it. Bag was in the closet," Peabody said, "as advertised. A disposable 'link, several security discs, and a very rocking bypass remote—along with a pair of light blue men's pajamas, the pressure syringes, and the meds."

"Get them in, log them. I want chain of evidence pristine. Have Feeney and McNab start on the contents. I'm in the field, got a couple more stops to make."

"It's falling apart on her," Roarke commented.

"She's going to hire a big, fat, sneaky lawyer. A fucking fleet of big, fat, sneaky lawyers. The type who get shit suppressed, tossed out, who pump in reasonable doubt. I don't have enough. I can put her with Suzanne in Jersey a few days after Custer's murder. Proves nothing. What Peabody just picked up only proves Suzanne was in the Anderses' house, and pretty much sews up she killed him. We've got her confession already. She's locked. Your acquaintance can state that the device was taken to the Anders residence. He can't put it in Ava's hands. I've got her lies, her association with an LC, I've got her father-in-law's death, which I wheedled the local cops into opening again. Disposable 'link. Batt's going to be dead, and when the battery dies on those, it wipes the transmissions. I need more."

The chubby and cheerful Mr. Isaacs gave her a bit more. "Right after her husband was killed, yes? I remember very well. Terrible thing. She comes in on Mondays, about nine-thirty on Monday mornings, poor Mrs. Custer. But this day, a few days after I hear her husband's dead, I see her go right by carrying her market bag."

"Was she alone?"

"No. I started to go outside, call out to her, thinking she'd forgotten where she was going. Being upset about her husband. But then I saw she was with someone. She was with a very fancy lady. Beautiful coat with fur on the collar," Isaacs added, brushing his fingers down the front of his apron to demonstrate. "Long black coat, brown fur trim. Very nice. I think I've seen the fancy lady once or twice before, but not that coat."

"You saw the woman before that day?"

"Once or twice. I know my neighborhood, I know my people."

"Is this the woman?" Eve offered Ava's photo.

"Yes, yes, this is the woman poor Mrs. Custer was with that morning. Such pretty hair she has. I remember, it was a very sunny day, and the sunshine seemed to bounce off her pretty hair. She wore shades. As I said, it was a very bright day, but she's very striking. I'm sure this is the same woman. They walked right by. Mrs. Custer looked so sad and tired. She came back, by herself, a couple hours later. Maybe more, we were busy. I thought, 'Poor little thing—Mrs. Custer—she's been crying.' I gave her some pop treats for the children."

She hit the lot next, a small, overpriced two-decker.

"This sort of lot won't have security discs for two months ago," Roarke reminded her. "And their records won't include license number, make, or model. It's just the time in and out, the fee, the slot."

"They'd have tag number, make, and model for reserved parking. No way Ava would cruise around looking for a parking spot. Not someone who plans, who researches. She'd book one. Scanner reads reservation number, and to reserve you need to verify tag number."

"Well now, you're right about that."

"She'd've done the same thing for the Custer stalking and hit. She'd be thinking of her own convenience, and never seriously consider we'd get here. I put her vehicle here, I put it there, it adds weight. You've got a new assignment."

"I'm going to be talking to auto lot owners. With her vehicle number I could find it quicker myself."

"Channels. Pristine chain. We take the long way. I'll drive. You get started."

She closed herself off for twenty minutes back at Central. She shut her door, closed everyone out while she sat, feet up, eyes closed to walk herself through the steps, the stages, the routes.

With a glance at the time, she made another call. "Mrs. Horowitz, Lieutenant Dallas. I have a couple of questions."

"Of course."

"Mrs. Anders attends a lot of functions—balls, parties, and so on. Does she ever attend costume types—masked balls, fancy dress, that sort of thing?"

"There's a fancy-dress gala in October every year."

"Where does she keep her wigs?"

"All the costume pieces she has made or purchased are kept in storage on the third floor."

"Does she own a red wig?"

"I believe she owns a few, in different shades and styles. I haven't been in the storage area for some time."

"Thanks."

Eve ended transmission, and placed another to APA Reo.

Then she called in the team.

In the conference room, Eve paced while Baxter brooded into his coffee and Roarke passed the time on his PPC. Peabody, with no new visible piercings, huddled together with Trueheart. EDD had yet to arrive. Cher Reo entered next, the pretty blonde with the Southern drawl and the raptor claws in court.

"Hello, gang." She nodded at Eve. "Let's hear the pitch."

"We're not all here. Feeney—" Eve narrowed a stare at him as he strolled in with McNab. "You're late."

"You want it fast or you want it right?"

"I just want it. Status, EDD first."

Feeney took out his notebook. "Pill dispenser, vic's, opened and reprogrammed the morning Ava Anders left for St. Lucia. None of her prints inside or out. Office 'links, Anders Worldwide. No transmissions to or from Suzanne Custer during the last six months. Same for the home and personal 'links we were given access to. Security discs recovered from Custer apartment show no unusual activity. Remote recovered from Custer apartment is extreme. Custom job, specific for the system at Anders's residence. We found two uses. One use six weeks ago, and one the morning of the Anders murder."

"Ava test drove it."

"Be my take. Disposable 'link, dead as disco. Those type don't hold transmissions much over twenty-four anyway. If they do that. And this one's cheap shit."

"You're telling me you got zip?"

"I didn't say zip." He stretched out his legs, crossed them at the ankles. "Every electronic byte leaves an imprint. A smudge anyway. You go in right, and you can finesse. We got what you could call echoes. 'Link's a piece of crap, but crap can be manipulated. We need to process the echoes, tune them up, sort them out. Something's there. Give us a day or two, and we'll pull it out."

"Good. Peabody?"

"Adult toy items matching those at the Anders crime scene were purchased by Suzanne Custer, or earlier by Ned Custer. All but the ropes were obtained by her at Just Sex. She purchased the ropes, with cash, at Bondage Baby. Custer also obtained, by doctor's prescription, lotrominaphine, the medication found in Thomas Anders, as well as six pressure syringes. Four syringes were also found in the bag recovered from the Custer apartment, as was the partially used prescription of the tranq. She's wrapped."

"And yet," Reo commented, "Murder Two."

"It'll be worth it," Eve told her. "In Interview, Suzanne Custer stated that at Ava Anders's suggestion the two women entered into a bargain to kill each other's husbands. Reportedly, Anders recorded their promise."

"That's dumbass," McNab put in. "Why incriminate yourself on record?"

"If Ava ever recorded her own statement, she's long since wiped it. But I'll bet she's got Suzanne's tucked away for leverage."

McNab nodded. "Not so dumbass."

"Three days after the Custer murder, Anders waylaid Custer on Custer's way to her usual Monday morning marketing. Custer and Anders were seen together, and today identified by Isaacs, Jerome, the market's owner." Eve pointed a finger at McNab before he could speak.

"Yes, dumbass, but we're dealing with a woman who never believed we'd have any reason to tie her and Suzanne Custer together. And if we asked? She could easily claim she'd dropped by to pay her condolences.

"So moving on. Custer further stated that Anders informed her Anders had killed Ned Custer—and gave all details to same. And it would soon be time to complete the bargain. According to Custer's statement, Anders used threats and duress to obtain her agreement, while Anders drove into New Jersey, to a rest area. A security tech at same has identified Anders and her vehicle, corroborating Custer's statement. At that time, Anders gave Custer the disposable 'link, and described how Thomas Anders was to be killed."

"You're going to get a lot of she said/she said here, Dallas," Reo commented.

"Yeah, so we'll need to make what Custer said stick. We need those echoes cleared, Feeney. Custer did not, as Anders instructed, dispose of the 'link, the remote, the discs. Anders lied about her husband's sexual proclivities."

"Prove it," Reo demanded.

"Your job. But, she told both Custer and one Petrelli,

Bebe, that Thomas Anders was a sexual deviate, and a pedophile. She indicated same to a Gordon, Cassie. There is no evidence this was true. In fact, there is weighty evidence it was not. Ava engaged a licensed companion for several months. There is no evidence Thomas Anders used LCs or engaged in extra-marital affairs, as Ava claims. Let *her* prove it," Eve added.

"After receiving the news that her husband was dead," Eve continued, "Ava ordered a tasty breakfast, ate same, dressed, and groomed meticulously. She didn't wake her friends, but took a shuttle home alone."

"I just don't like her." Reo examined her nails. "I don't like Ava one little bit."

"Get in line. Rewind two months. Custer, Ned, was last seen with a tall woman, a redhead, taken to be a pro. She went from a bar to a flop with the victim, and did not exit by the door. Ava told Suzanne that after slitting Custer's throat, and whacking him off in a permanent manner, she exited via the fire escape. She owns several red wigs."

"Get me something physical," Reo insisted. "It's a good circumstantial case, but—"

"The vehicle registered to Ava Anders was parked eight blocks north and one east of the Custer murder scene," Roarke put in without looking up. "The vehicle had reserved parking for that slot, in that lot, for a period of two weeks. It was used three times, the last on the night of the murder, clocking in at 10:12 P.M., clocking out at 2:08 A.M."

"Okay, that's interesting." Something lit in Reo's eyes. "How do we prove she drove it there?"

"Because she fucking did," Eve snapped. "Because on that night and the ten days prior, Thomas Anders was out of town, and she could come and go as she pleased. Look at the time line. She kills her father-in-law, and that's the turn."

"Reginald Anders's death was deemed accidental." Reo tossed up a hand. "Don't bite my head off, that's the fact. You've got the case re-opened, and I'm inclined to agree she killed him because I don't like her. But at this point, we've got an old man slipping in the shower."

"We won't end with that. She hired a decorator the week before Reginald Anders took the fall. Shortly after it's reported, she and the old man had a private talk in his office about her charging personal expenses to program budgets. She didn't walk out happy. And according to the housekeeper, decorating talk began two weeks after the father-in-law's death, though she'd already contracted with one.

"You're going to say some spouses sneak in something like that—the decorating crap," Eve said, anticipating Reo. "Why would she? Every statement we've taken on their marriage, on Anders, describes him as indulgent. He wouldn't have given a shit about that."

"Then why wait to tell him?" Reo asked. "Picky, I know, but defense attorneys are, as a rule."

"It was her congratulations present to herself. She didn't bring it out until after she'd done the old man. Until that was behind her. Weeks after that, she hires Charles Monroe, telling one of her friends—out of the goddamn blue—that she and her husband are sexually incompatible. She revs up the mommy retreat program, and starts to scope. Here, she approaches Petrelli, whose family has ties to organized crime. She *suggests* Petrelli might find a way to dispose of Anders, who she claims is a pervert. That craps out. She approaches Gordon, an LC who is also in the program, and asks for details about kink. And finally, she finds her mark here, with Custer."

"Suzanne was prime bait," Baxter put in.

"Detective Yancy executed a composite of Ava with the style and color of hair witnesses reported re Ned Custer," Eve added. "We're going to find somebody who'll put her in the bar, in the flop."

"Do it, because I'd love to bring her down." Reo closed her notebook. "Can you get me a confession?"

"That's the plan. I need to get her out of the house so

we can go in and cop the wig without her being aware. Feeney, I need you to mock me up a disposable 'link exactly like that one. We've got her statements on record. I want to hear her voice come out of it. Baxter, talk to Suzanne again, make sure she's clear on exactly what Ava said the morning Anders was murdered. Peabody, put a couple of the men in soft clothes on the sleazy side. Roarke, see if your *acquaintance* will come down. He's not going to have to say a thing. Reo will give him immunity and I'll authorize two bills."

"What am I giving immunity for?"

"We'll get to that. I want Petrelli and Gordon in here, and the night clerk from the flop. Trueheart, I'm going to be sending you to bring Ava in."

He blinked as if something had flown into his eyes. "Sending me?"

"You won't worry her. You're too young and pretty, and you're going to apologize. If she cries lawyer, she cries lawyer, but I don't think she will. Not right off. Take another uniform. A young, green one. I'll tell you when to go, and how to handle her. What are you smiling at?" she asked Roarke.

"It's such an interesting show you're planning."

"Yeah, so let's work out the song and the dance."

It wasn't a stretch for Trueheart to appear apologetic and accommodating. Even with seasoning a la Baxter, he remained a sweet-natured, happy-to-help kind of guy. Young and fresh, and—to the careless or cynical eye—not all that smart. What Ava saw were two young, handsome, somewhat bumbling cops who seemed embarrassed with their current duty.

"I'm awfully sorry, ma'am." Trueheart added a pained smile. "I know it's an inconvenience, especially at such a difficult time, but the lieutenant—"

"Yes, it's very inconvenient, and a very difficult time. I fail to see why I should have to go downtown. Why doesn't the lieutenant come to me?"

"Um, she would, ma'am, but she's in this meeting with the commander and the chief, about the, ah . . . the, ah, media problem in regards to the case."

"Taking some licks for it." The second uniform delivered his first scripted line on cue.

"Come on." Trueheart frowned him down. "And I believe Chief Tibble would like to personally apologize to you about the media stuff. So we were sent to transport you down to Central."

"Young man, I understand you're just following orders, but you can't possibly expect to bundle me in the back of a police car, to add that kind of mortification on top of everything else."

"Ah, well, um . . ." Trueheart glanced at his companion, who only shrugged helplessly. "If you wanted to call a cab, I guess—I don't know. Maybe I could call in and ask—"

"Nonsense, that's just nonsense. I'll take my own car. I'm free to come and go as I please, aren't I? I'm not under arrest, am I?"

"Oh gosh, no, ma'am. I mean, yes, ma'am on the first part. We could follow you in. I'm sure that's okay, and I could arrange a parking permit in the VIP visitor lot. Would that be all right?"

"I'd think it's the least you could do, and thank you. Now, I'll have to ask you to wait outside while I—"

"You didn't do the RM." The second cop delivered his next line, and Trueheart flushed and shifted his feet.

"I don't know that we're supposed to—"

"My sergeant kicked my ass—pardon me, ma'am—for not just yesterday. I don't want to screw up again."

"Okay, okay. I'm awful sorry, Mrs. Anders, but we're just going to read you the Revised Miranda before we go, since you're going to be talking to the lieutenant about the investigation. A formality thing." Trueheart added an earnest, and nervous smile. "Is that all right with you?"

"Fine, fine, fine." Ava waved him on. "Hurry it up. I don't want a police car outside my house all afternoon."

"Yes, ma'am. Well. You have the right to remain silent." To add to the picture, Trueheart pulled out a small card with the warning printed on it, and read it with intense concentration. He hoped it wasn't overplayed. "Um. Do you understand your—"

"Am I an idiot?" Ava snapped. "Of course I understand. Now, shoo, I'll be out in a few minutes."

"Yes, ma'am. Thank you, ma'am." After the door shut in his face, Trueheart walked back to the police car with his companion. "Dallas is a solid genius," he stated, then engaged his communicator. "It's Trueheart, Lieutenant."

At Central, Eve fueled up on coffee. "Trueheart's following her in. I want the sweepers on that car the minute it's parked."

"You, like, read her mind," Peabody said. "You knew she'd drive in."

"She wouldn't turn down an opportunity to have the Chief of Police grovel to her, and lord it over me. And she wouldn't get in a black-and-white unless she was cuffed and carried. Besides, if she left the car at home, the sweepers could process it there. Reo's warrant covers us. I want this to run like clockwork. Everyone in place." Even as she went over the details in her head, Eve turned to her partner. "I need to take her one-on-one, Peabody. You get that?"

"Yeah. And I know my cue. We've got two men in place to swing in, execute the warrant on the house and bring in the wigs. It's like a sting, isn't it, and nearly as juicy as a battering-ram-slamming, blaster-bursting takedown. Without the potential for fatal injuries. It's all: *Psyche!*"

"We twist her, and we twist her. We twist her right, and she snaps." Eve stared at her murder board. The steps and stages, the bits and pieces. Now it was time to put them all together.

"Lieutenant." Roarke studied her from the doorway.

"I'll go check on stuff," Peabody said and eased out.

"She's on her way. Bringing the car in."

"You called that one. Your diverse cast of characters appears to be in place. You know you're risking those big, fat lawyers with this stage you've set."

"Yeah. She's smart enough to lawyer, but I'm betting she's too arrogant to squeal for one right off. At the end she will. At the end she'll be screaming for a lawyer." And for once, Eve admitted, the sound of that would be like music to her ears. "But first she'll be shaken, shaken enough to *have* to put me in my place."

"As Magdelana tried to."

There was no point denying it. "To her eventual disappointment . . . and fat lip. I'm not hanging on to that, if that's worrying you." When he stepped in, those blue eyes level on hers, and traced a fingertip along the shallow dent in her chin, she sighed, then shrugged. "Okay, maybe a little. But I'm not pissed at you about that, about her."

He leaned down, kissed her very softly.

"Much. You didn't see her, at least not until what she was doing was shoved in your face. Must be a guy thing when it comes to a certain kind of female. Thomas Anders didn't see it in Ava, for years and years. He lived with her, and he didn't see her. Not who she really is. I'm not pissed at him about it. He loved her. I'm pissed she used that, and him. Used anyone who came to hand, with absolutely no conscience. For game and profit. She killed him for that. For game and profit."

"And you imagine, if I hadn't had certain things shoved in my face, hadn't seen, if some circumstances had been different, Maggie would have eventually done for me."

"Why share the majority of the known universe if you can have it all for yourself?"

"Right you are. And, yes, she would have tried to end me at some point. Fortunately, I'm married to the top bitch cop in the city, and well-protected."

"Fortunately, you can take care of yourself. Tommy Anders couldn't." She turned back to the board, to the ID photo of Anders's smiling, easygoing face.

"It hits me. Some of them do, and it hits me because he

was a nice man who loved his wife and used his money and position to do good things. He's dead, lives are ruined or at best forever changed, all because she wanted all the marbles. So . . . I'm going to squash her like the ugly spider she is."

"Lieutenant." Peabody poked in. "She's just pulled into the lot."

"Curtain up," Roarke said.

Chapter 23

To Roarke's mind, cop shops tended toward the loud, the confused, and the crowded. One such as Cop Central twisted and twined, rose and fell, in a serpentine labyrinth where cops, suspects, victims, lawyers, techs all bumped and burrowed amid constant clatter and movement.

And still, through all that, the choreography Eve had staged moved seamlessly. Perhaps as so many of the players were unaware of their role, their actions and reactions fell as natural as rainwater.

He watched on screens in an observation room with Feeney and the director herself as Trueheart and his fellow uniform—both looking as wholesome and harmless as apple pie—escorted Ava onto the elevator, then off again.

"It'll be quicker and less crowded," Trueheart explained in his polite tone, "if we take the glides from here, Mrs. Anders."

As they rode up, others rode down. On the down, a man in a stained T-shirt and dingy dreads who Roarke would have made for a cop at six blocks, swiveled, pointed. "Hey, hey! That's the one there. That's the broad left with Cuss. Hey!"

Ava angled away toward Trueheart's agreeable face. "Sorry," he said. "We get all kinds through here."

He led her off the glide, across a short span of floor, just as a female officer walked Bebe Petrelli toward the down. The reaction of both civilians struck Roarke as priceless. Shock on both faces, distress following on Petrelli's, fury darkening Ava's, even as the cop quickly hustled Petrelli to the left and away.

Little fissures in the mask, Roarke noted. And up the next glide they went. This time Baxter brought Cassie Gordon on just below. Cassie's gaze tracked up, latched. "Well, hey. Hey, Ava!" A sharp and deadly amusement colored Cassie's voice. "What're you doing here?"

Ava glanced back, skimmed her cold eyes over Cassie. "I'm sorry. Do I know you?"

"Sure, but then I'm just one of the horde. How's it going?"

"You'll have to excuse me. I'm pressed for time. Can we get this done?" she demanded of Trueheart.

"Yes, ma'am, we're nearly there. This way." Deliberately, he walked her by Homicide where the night clerk from the sex flop sat on a bench outside, flanked by two cops. He stared at her as she approached. The fissures widened as color flooded Ava's face.

"Right in here." Trueheart opened the door of Interview A. "I'll make sure the lieutenant knows you're here. Can I get you something to drink? Coffee maybe."

"I'd prefer something sweet and cold. Ginger ale in a glass."

"Yes, ma'am."

In Observation, Eve hooked her thumbs in her pockets. "Putting her game face on. Knows we're watching. Anybody with a brain, and brains she's got, knows how Interview works."

"Spooked her some."

"Yeah, but pissed her off more. That's what's going to hang her. Well, time to go kick her ass."

"Want me to kiss your head?"

"Want me to mention your sick day pajamas?"

"That's mean. You make me proud. Go skin your fish."

Eve didn't want to keep Ava waiting long. Keep the temper up, those little edges of fear. She walked into Interview carrying plenty of files and attitude. "Mrs. Anders."

"Lieutenant. I've had about enough of your incompetence, and your callousness. I demand to see your chief."

"We'll get to that. Record on. Dallas, Lieutenant Eve, in interview with Anders, Ava, regarding case number HA-32003, Anders, Thomas A., and all related events and crimes." Eve dropped into a chair. "We've got a lot to clear up, Ava."

"Mrs. Anders. I'd like to clear up the way you and this department have handled the media."

Eve only smiled. "It's been an interesting couple of days for me. How about you?" At Ava's stony stare, Eve's smile widened. "I don't catch many like these, and I've got to hand it to you: You damn near pulled it off. I bet you're wondering how I'm going to get you for murder."

"What a hideous thing to say to me! A slanderous thing to say. I didn't kill Tommy. I loved my husband. I was out of the country when he died, and you know that very well."

"Save the shiny eyes and tear-choked voice. I know you." Eve leaned forward. "I knew you the minute I saw you. You're a grasping, greedy, self-important excuse for a human being. But you've got brains, Ava, and you've got patience. So what it comes down to is how you want to play this part of it. Let me give you something to think about. Suzanne Custer."

"Is that name supposed to mean something to me?"

"Think about it. Think about the fact that when we bring her in, we'll give her a chance to slip and slide. She'll have the opportunity to wheel and deal. Personally, I think she's going to grab it like a lifeline."

"Lieutenant Dallas, I have no idea what you're trying to do here, unless it's generate more media frenzy than you've already managed. And that you're somehow blaming me for that, and the fact you've been reprimanded for mishandling it. It's been established, without any doubt, that I was in St. Lucia when my Tommy was killed."

"You weren't in St. Lucia when Ned Custer's throat was slit."

"I don't know anyone by that name. What does that have to do with me?"

"Are you going to deny you know Suzanne Custer?"

"I know a great many people." She paused, offered a considering frown. "Suzanne? Yes, of course. I know her slightly. She's one of our mothers."

"The same Suzanne Custer whose husband was murdered in a sex flop in Alphabet City a couple of months ago."

"How horrible." Ava pressed a hand to her own throat. "Poor Suzanne. I try not to follow media reports on violence. I'm so terribly sorry to hear about this, but I don't know what it has to do with me, or with my Tommy."

"Makes you wonder what Suzanne might say if she gets a chance to address that."

Peabody entered with a red wig inside an evidence bag. She nodded at Eve, slipped out. "Lookie here. Pretty." Eve held up the bag. "Familiar?"

"I assume it's one of mine, as I have one like it. Or did. I attend costume galas from time to time. I'd like to know how it came to be in your possession."

"By duly executed warrant. Let me just mention Ned Custer again, a bar pickup and sex flop. Give you another shot here, Ava. You're a striking woman. Tall and well-turned-out." Opening the file, she withdrew a photo she'd had the police artist compose. It appeared dim, even dingy, just as she'd ordered.

"You even turn out pretty well as a cheap redhead in a crappy security cam still. Maybe not suitable for framing," she added as Ava stared down at it. "But a picture tells a story. Here's a story I like. You pick up Custer in the bar, take him to the flop, slit his throat, carve off his works, and boogie on. Why? You're just going to have to help me out there. Why does a woman like you slum it with a man like Custer, and end up killing him?"

"I can hardly help you as there *is* no why. It's insane."

"Maybe things didn't go the way you figured. He's not a smoothie like Charles Monroe. Maybe you were trying to get your kicks on, seeing as your husband leaned that way. Help me out here. Gotcha, Ava." Eve tapped the photo. "I've got you in the bar, with Custer. In the flop, with Custer. You can help me, and help yourself, or I let Suzanne pick up the story from here."

"It's not what you think. Not at all what you think."

Trueheart came in with a plastic glass filled with ice and ginger ale. "Excuse me. I'm sorry it took so long."

Eve waited while Trueheart stepped out, while Ava sipped. *Yeah, you think,* Eve mused. *Think how to play it. Bet I know how you will.*

"Suzanne . . . I felt sorry for her. I wanted to help her."

"By offing her lousy husband? Man, who couldn't use a pal like you?"

"Good God, no." Ava pressed a hand to her heart. In lieu of the not-currently-in-fashion wedding ring, a blood-red ruby glowed. "I took an interest in her, and it was frustrating that she refused to help herself. I know it was foolish of me, I know that, but to prove a point, I arranged a kind of intervention between her and her husband."

"What kind of intervention would that be? The kind that involves castration?"

"Don't be so horrible and crude! I wanted to *help*. Why would I conceive the mothers' programs unless I wanted to help these women?"

"What did you do? To help?"

"I went to the bar that he frequented and lured him— you could say I lured him—to that horrible hotel room. Suzanne was there. It was a way to catch him in the act, to make him face what he was doing. I left immediately after she came in, to give them privacy."

She pressed her fingers to her eyes. "I haven't spoken to her since. She hasn't contacted me, and didn't take my few attempts to reach her. I assumed things didn't work out as we'd hoped. But I had no idea... If she killed him, Lieutenant, if that's what happened, it had to be in self-defense. It had to be."

"Let me just compact all this. You dressed up like a hooker, went to the bar, to the flop with Ned Custer, as a favor to his wife?"

Ava lifted her chin. "I don't appreciate your implications, or your attitude."

"Gee, pardon the hell right out of me."

"Lieutenant, it's so easy to become involved with the lives of these women, to *feel* for them. Suzanne was desperate to save her marriage, her family. She was so certain that if he was caught that way, he'd agree to counseling. And, well, I admit, it seemed exciting. We're very hands-on at Anders. Tommy and I believed in *involvement.* I made a terrible mistake. And now a man's dead." She covered her face with her hands.

"Okay, let's clarify for the record. You state that you met Ned Custer in the bar on the night of January twenty of this year, that you went with him to the flop."

"Yes, yes, to meet Suzanne. He was angry, of course, but she asked me to go. To leave them alone so they could talk it out. I should never have left. I see that now." As if in a plea for understanding, Ava held out her hands to Eve. "How could I know she'd kill him? She said she wanted to save her marriage, how could I know she'd kill him?"

"That's a tough one. You couldn't know."

"I feel terrible about it. Sick about it. But Suzanne, my God, she must've been—"

This time it was Baxter who stepped in, carrying several evidence bags. He murmured as he leaned down to Eve. "Custer's en route."

"Thanks. And look what we have now. Black market bypass remote. And these security discs taken from your home." Eve lifted the disposable 'link. "Cheap-ass piece of crap. Pressure syringes, cock thickener, tranq. All confiscated from Suzanne Custer's apartment."

"My God, my God, is that . . . is that the device used to circumvent our security?" Ava's voice dropped down to a strained whisper. "When Tommy . . . Suzanne? Oh my God, did Suzanne kill Tommy?"

"Bet she did."

"But, but *why?* Why? Her children were in the program. Tommy and I . . . No. No. No." With her hands pressed to her temples, Ava shook her head from side to side in what Eve considered overacting. "Not because of what happened with her husband. Not because of what I did that night! Please, not because of that."

"Yeah, because of that."

"How can I ever forgive myself?" She wept then, harsh, angry sobs. "It's my fault. It's all my fault. Oh, Tommy. Tommy."

"Do you need a minute, Ava?" Eve reached over, patted her hand. "This is rough. I'm sorry I was so hard on you at the start of the interview. I had to get the motive."

"It doesn't matter, none of it matters. It's my fault. If I hadn't agreed to that foolish business with Suzanne's husband, if I'd never gone to that horrible room with him, Tommy would be alive."

"You're right about that. But here's the thing. You listening, Ava? Can you compose yourself? Okay?"

"Yes. I'm sorry. I'll try, I'll try. This is all such a shock."

"Here's another. Suzanne Custer was never in that flop with you and her husband."

"Of course she was. I saw her. I spoke with her."

"She was in her apartment, blocks away, leaving messages on her husband's 'link while you were slitting his throat. While you came out of the bathroom, sealed up with a six-inch serrated blade and raked it across his throat, she was home, pacing the floor, trying to reach him while you watched him bleed out, while you hacked off his dick, then climbed out the window. While you *practically flew* ten blocks to the auto lot where you had parked your Mercedes, New York plate A AVA, in the slot you'd reserved."

It *was* tingly, Eve realized. It was downright tingly to watch Ava's face.

"I got the time in, I got the time out. Time out comes twenty-one minutes after time of death. Here's something else. You sealed up, but you didn't think about how dirty the windows are in those flops, how nasty the sills are, how that crud might latch on to the bottom of your fuck-me shoes. We'll be processing your shoes, Ava, and I'm betting on them."

Eve shrugged. "Not really important though, since you've admitted—on record—that you were there."

"And I told you why, and that the man was alive when I left. What possible reason would I have to kill him? To-to mutilate him afterward? I didn't even know him."

"You've already said why. If Custer hadn't been killed, Tommy would be alive. See this?" She tapped the 'link. "Piece of crap, as I said. Most people think these crappy disposables can't hold transmission history. But those EDD geeks? They're freaking magicians."

Eve leaned forward, smiled brilliantly. "*Good girl.* Do you remember saying that to Suzanne—from the balmy shores of St. Lucia, when she reported she'd done the job? Wanna hear for yourself?" Eve pressed a button on the link, and Ava's voice buzzed out.

Good girl.

"They'll clean that up some, but I wanted you to hear it as soon as it was ready. Nice of you to give Suzanne that little pat on the head."

"This is ridiculous, and you're pathetic. It's obvious Suzanne killed her husband and mine. She must be horribly sick. As far as that 'link goes, I spoke with her any number of times over the last months."

"From St. Lucia? They triangulate these transmissions really well."

"I don't recall. I might have."

And more tingles, Eve thought, as she saw the pulse in Ava's throat start to pound. "Previous statement: You haven't spoken or had contact with Suzanne Custer since the night her husband was murdered."

"I might have been mistaken about that."

"No, you lied about that. It's the lies that tripped you up. It was a pretty solid plan, I'll give that to you. But you couldn't keep it simple. You had to elaborate, make yourself more of a stoic, loyal, and loving wife by painting your husband as so much less than he was. You had to make him pay for all those years you played the loving wife. He never hired LCs, never had affairs, never demanded kink from you."

"You can't prove or disprove what happens between people in the privacy of their bedroom."

"Yeah, that was your thinking on it. It's not bad. But I can prove no one who ever knew him or had business with him can corroborate your claim. I can prove you substituted a sleep aid for his nightly vitamin the morning before you left for St. Lucia. I can prove you conspired with Suzanne Custer in a scheme where each of you agreed to murder the other's spouse. I can prove you approached at least two other women, fishing the idea before you settled on Suzanne."

"It means nothing, none of it means—"

"Not done," Eve commented. "I can prove your father-in-law—whose murder I'm also going to hang on you given a little more time—was annoyed with the way you were allocating funds earmarked for the program."

"Ridiculous." But her body jumped. "Insane."

"You keep thinking that," Eve invited. "Reginald Anders's murder opened the door to your long-term plans. I can prove you not only spoke with, not only contacted Suzanne after Custer's murder, but drove to a lot several blocks from her home—reserved slot again—and met her on the street where you were seen by witnesses. Black coat, fur trim. We've got that in evidence now, too. I can prove you drove her to a rest stop off the Turnpike, where you were seen by witnesses."

"She was blackmailing me."

"Oh please."

"After she killed her husband, she blackmailed me. She said she'd call the police, that she'd tell them I was having an affair with her husband, and that she knew he was meeting me that night. I was terrified. I met her that day, outside her building, to give her the last payment. I drove out of the city to that rest area, and I gave her the last payment. I told her it had to be the last, and she was angry. That must be why she killed Tommy."

"How much she sting you for? Quick, quick," Eve said when Ava hesitated. "How much?"

"Two hundred thousand dollars."

"See, you should've lowballed it. That's too much for her to hide, too much for you to skim without leaving crumbs."

"I sold some jewelry."

"No, Ava, no." Heaving a sigh, Eve leaned in. "Now you're disappointing me. I gave you more credit. We can check that. First, going back, Suzanne doesn't have the brains or the balls to blackmail anyone. Going further back, not only wasn't she in the room when Ned bought it, but she's too short to have executed the killing blow. This is basic forensics, and juries are pretty savvy there. Got you cold on that one. Witnesses, forensics, your own statement putting you there."

"She didn't come. She didn't come as arranged, and he attacked me."

"Who? Let's be specific since we've got such a winding road here."

Ava picked up her cup again, drank. "Suzanne's husband."

"Ned Custer attacked you?"

"Yes. He wanted sex, and I told him Suzanne was

coming, and he was furious, and attacked me. I was terrified; you have to understand. He was going to rape me, so I grabbed the knife."

"From where?"

"From . . ."

"Quick!" Eve snapped and had Ava jolting again. "Where'd you get the knife?"

"From him. He had the knife. He threatened me with it, and we struggled. I lashed out, in fear for my life."

"You killed Ned Custer."

"Yes, yes, but in self-defense. He was a madman, waving the knife, shouting. He tore at my clothes. I was terrified."

"I'll take the admission of guilt, but not the plea. And neither will a jury. Basic forensics again, Ava. You took him out from behind."

"We were struggling."

"With one, clean slice. No defensive wounds, no signs of struggle on him or in the room. You did a damn good job of it."

"I want a lawyer. Now."

"Sure. While we're taking care of that," Eve said as she began to gather the evidence bags and files, "I'll go have a little chat with Suzanne. She should be here by now."

"It was her idea."

"I'm sorry, Ava, you've invoked your right to counsel. I can't take any further statements from you until such time as—"

"Fuck the lawyer. I don't want a damn lawyer. I need your help. Aren't you a public servant? Isn't it your duty to help someone in trouble? Isn't that what I *pay* you for?"

"So I'm told. For the record, you're again waiving your right to counsel?"

"Yes, yes, yes. It was her idea. I was upset with Tommy for some silly thing, and I'd been drinking. She came to my room, at the retreat, and we started to talk."

Ava's breath came fast. Eve imagined her thoughts came even faster.

"She said we'd both be better off without our husbands. I was in a mood, I agreed. Then she hatched this idea about how each of us would kill the other's. It was foolishness, or so I believed. We talked and talked, plotting it out. Laughing about it. It was just a *joke.* I was awfully drunk, just feeling blue and ridiculous, and it made me laugh to speculate on how we'd do it.

"But then weeks later, she came to me and told me it was time. I was horrified, of course. I told her she had to be out of her mind to think I'd do such a thing. Out of her mind to believe I actually wanted my Tommy dead. She was . . . fierce. If I didn't do what we'd agreed, she *would* kill Tommy. I wouldn't know when or how, but she would kill him. She meant it. The more I argued, pleaded, protested, the more vicious she became. I did it to save my husband, I did it to save his life."

"You're scraping bottom now, but thanks for the 'I did it.' And the confession of the initial plot."

"Hers! Hers! It was her plot."

"She couldn't plot her way out of her own apartment. Look at this." Eve tapped the evidence bags. "Didn't you *tell* her to get rid of this stuff? But no, she hauls it home and stuffs it in her closet. You picked a moron for a partner, Ava—or a patsy, depending on your view of it. But you screwed up plenty. Both of your husbands killed in sex-related murders? I'm not the moron here. You're too stupid to pull it off, too hyped on giving your own statement enough juice to put you into media spotlight. It's that PR training. Any story's a good story. You fucked this up, all the way back to your father-in-law."

"You'll never prove it. None of it. Everything you have is speculation."

"Oh, lots more than. And there's the little matter of your confessions."

"You twisted my words around. You tricked me, put words in my mouth. And you didn't advise me of my rights before the interview."

"Officer Trueheart did—on record. Covers us both, Ava."

Eve smiled broadly. "Oh, and you may not have recognized the guy talking to Roarke outside. But he's the kind of businessman who takes precautions. You had one of your volunteers pick up the remote—but I've got a solid witness who followed her all the way to your house, where it was delivered. It's just icing on my cake. But, upside for you? You're going to get hours and hours of screen time over this."

Eve shook her head, picked up her files and bags. "You stupid, pitiful murderer."

Ava came up like a tidal wave, heaving the table aside. That tight skin she'd worn for years was split into shreds now, Eve noted.

"Stupid? We'll see who's stupid at the end of the day, you *bitch.* Nobody's going to believe any of this. I have friends. Powerful friends and between us we'll eat you and your ridiculous *interview* to bits."

"Lady, you've got no one. You did have. You had a good, decent man who loved you."

"What do you know about it? What do you know? Sixteen years of my life invested in a man who obsessed about golf and box scores, and children that weren't his own. I earned everything I have."

"Marrying it isn't earning it."

"You married money. Who are you to talk?"

"I married a man. The man. You'll never get that. Your kind isn't capable of it. On the door."

When it opened, she passed out the files and bags to the officer outside, then turned back. "Ava Anders, you're under arrest for the murder of Ned Custer, and for conspiracy to murder Thomas A. Anders. Other charges include—"

"Get me a fucking lawyer. Get the Prosecuting Attorney in here. Now, goddamn it. He'll make a deal for my testimony against that twit."

"You can have the lawyer, but the PA already made a deal with Suzanne Custer this morning." Eve grinned. *"Psych."*

She saw it coming. God, she'd been praying for it all

through the interview. Anticipating it so that the cop on the door, and those in Observation stayed back, as she'd ordered, when Ava charged her.

She turned away from the nail swipe so those long, pretty nails barely broke the skin under her jaw. And she took the first shove that bashed her into the wall.

The rest would look better on the record that way. Eve stomped on Ava's instep, plowed an elbow into her gut, then finished with a solid uppercut.

She studied the woman sprawled unconscious at her feet. "Guess we'll get into those other charges when you wake up. On the door." Eve stepped over Ava. "You and another officer take her down through Booking when she regains consciousness. She wants a lawyer, see that she's allowed to contact one."

"Yes, sir. Lieutenant, you're bleeding some."

"Yeah." Eve brushed her fingertips over the nail marks. "All in a day's. Interview end."

Reo was the first out of Observation. "Good enough for you?" Eve asked her.

"And then some. I'm going to make her lawyers cry like babies. Fun for me now. You've had yours."

"Showed?"

"To those of us who know and love you. You should've decked her before she scratched you."

Eve angled her head, tapped just below the marks. "Jury's going to love it, if it goes that far. Wrap her up, Reo. I want to take a moment out of my day now and then to think about her rotting in a cement cage off-planet."

"Anything for a pal. I'd better get to it."

"Peabody, get the paperwork on this, will you?"

"Sure, it was fun to watch, so writing it up's fair as the price of admission."

She started by, but Baxter stepped in her path. And held out a hand. A bit baffled she took it, shook. "It's a good day," he said, and she nodded.

"Yeah, it's a good day. You're back off the roll until Monday."

"I'll see this through, then I'm off."

She cut through to her office for a quick boost of coffee. Thinking of Tibble—and more important, his wife—she decided she'd contact Commander Whitney, give her oral. And let him pass it on. Just in case.

"Sit," Roarke ordered as he walked in with a small first-aid kit.

"Look Nurse Studly—"

"We'll play Nurse Studly and Patient Sexy later. Now sit so I can doctor those scratches. Nasty cats like that have nasty germs."

"She is pretty nasty." Eve sat, tipped up her head. "I should've just knocked her back. If I get slapped for knocking her out, I've got it coming."

"I don't think so."

"The instep was for Suzanne's kids, the elbow in the gut was for me. The knockout, that was for Tommy Anders."

As he cleaned and medicated the scratches, Roarke met her eyes. "She deserved each, and the rest you've seen to she'll get. You strung it out quite a bit."

"Yeah, that was indulgent. But I liked how she kept twisting herself up, changing her story. And all the tinglies were tough to resist. She's good at planning, but she's crappy at thinking on her feet. Makes it tougher for her lawyers when she gives so many conflicting statements in one interview. Plus, she's not going to be able to afford a bunch of fat lawyers now."

"Oh?"

"She can't use anything coming from the death of her spouse, as she's charged with conspiring to murder same. That cuts it back. And if I can pin down the Hampton case, she'll lose what she got from the father-in-law's death. She's going to have a lot less to spend on fancy lawyers. Anyway."

"Anyway." He leaned down, brushed his lips to hers. "You're done." He set the first-aid kit on her desk. "Any thoughts to going home?"

"Yeah, as soon as I contact Whitney and run it for him. And I figure I'll give Nadine a heads-up. Maybe you can buy me a fat, juicy steak."

"Maybe I could."

"Roarke."

"Eve."

It made her smile, but her eyes stayed serious on his. "What she said about me marrying for money?"

"You answered it, and quite well."

"Yeah, but we know some people think that."

"Eve—"

"Some people think it sometimes, some people think they know it all the time. You and me, we know different."

"We do, yes." He drew her to her feet, and this time the kiss was long and deep and just a little dark. "We both know you married me for the sex."

"Well, yeah, which is why I don't mind if some people think it was the money, because that's less personal. Thanks for the first aid."

"I'd say anytime, but it so often is."

She grinned, then sat down to contact her commander.

Roarke settled in her visitor's chair. He took out his PPC and amused himself by checking the stock reports on Anders. He thought it might be quite fitting to buy up the shares formerly owned by Ava Anders.

And put them in Eve Dallas's name.

And now a special excerpt from

Salvation in Death

J. D. Robb's next exciting novel
featuring Lieutenant Eve Dallas and Roarke!

Available in hardcover from G. P. Putnam's Sons!

At the Mass of the dead, the priest placed the wafer of un-leavened bread and the cheap red wine on the linen corpo-ral draping the altar. Both paten and chalice were silver. They had been gifts from the man inside the flower-blanketed coffin resting at the foot of the two worn steps that separated priest from congregation.

The dead had lived a hundred and sixteen years. Every day of those years he'd lived as a faithful Catholic. His wife had predeceased him by a mere ten months, and every day of those ten months he'd grieved for her.

Now his children, grandchildren, great- and great-great-grandchildren filled the pews of the old church in Spanish Harlem. Many lived in the parish, and many more returned to it to mourn, and to pay their respects. Both of his surviving brothers attended the rite, as did cousins, nieces, nephews, friends, and neighbors, so the living packed those pews, the aisles, the vestibule to honor the dead with the ancient rite.

Hector Ortiz had been a good man, who'd led a good life. He'd died peacefully in his bed, surrounded by photographs of his family and the many images of Jesus, Mary, and his favorite saint, Lawrence. St. Lawrence had been grilled to death for his faith and in the way of irony became the patron saint of restauranteurs.

Hector Ortiz would be missed; he would be mourned. But the long, good life and easy death lent a flavor of peace and acceptance to the Requiem Mass—and those who wept shed the tears more for themselves than for the departed. Their faith assured them, the priest thought, of Hector Ortiz's salvation. And as the priest performed the ritual, so familiar, he scanned the faces of the mourners. They looked to him to lead them in this final tribute.

Flowers and incense and the smoking wax of candles mixed and merged their scents in the air. A mystical fragrance. The smell of power and presence.

The priest solemnly bowed his head over the symbols of flesh and blood before washing his hands.

He'd known Hector, and in fact had heard his confession—his last, as it came to be—only a week before. So, Father Flores mused as the congregation rose, that penance had been the last Hector had been given.

Flores spoke to the congregation, and they to him, the familiar words of the Eucharistic Prayer, and through to the Sanctus.

"Holy, Holy, Holy Lord, God of power and might."

The words and those following were sung, as Hector had loved the music of the Mass. Those mixed voices rose up, tangling in the magically scented air. The congregation knelt—a baby's fretful wail, a dry cough, rustles, whispers—for the Consecration.

The priest waited for them to quiet, for the silence. For the moment.

Flores implored the power of the Holy Spirit to take the gifts of wafer and wine and transform them into the body and blood of Christ. And moved, according to the rite, as representative of the Son of God.

Power. Presence.

And while the crucified Christ looked down from behind the altar, Flores knew he himself held the power now. Held that presence.

"Take this, all of you, and eat it. For this is my body," Flores said, holding up the host, "which will be given up for you."

The bells rang; heads bowed.

"Take this and drink it. This is the cup of my blood." He raised the chalice. "The blood of a new and everlasting covenant. It will be shed for you and for others for the forgiveness of sin. Do this in memory of me."

"Christ has died, Christ has risen, Christ will come again."

They prayed, and the priest wished them peace. They wished peace to each other. And again, raising voices, they sang—*Lamb of God who takes away the sins of the world, have mercy on us*—while the priest broke the host, placed a piece of it in the chalice. The ministers moved forward, stopping short of the altar as the priest lifted the chalice to his lips.

He was dead the moment he drank the blood.

St. Cristóbal's Church in Spanish Harlem knelt quietly between a bodega and a pawnshop. It boasted a small gray steeple and was innocent of the graffiti that tagged its near-neighbors. Inside, it smelled of candles, flowers, and furniture polish. Like a nice, suburban home might smell.

At least it struck Lieutenant Eve Dallas that way as she strode down the aisle formed by rows of pews. In the front, a man in black shirt, black pants, and white collar sat with his head bowed and his hands folded.

She wasn't sure if he was praying or just waiting, but he wasn't her priority. She skirted around the glossy casket all but buried in red and white carnations. The dead guy inside wasn't her priority either.

She engaged her lapel recorder, but when she started to climb the two short steps to the platform that held the altar—and her priority—her partner plucked at Eve's arm.

"Um, I think we're supposed to, like, genuflect."

"I never genuflect in public."

"No, seriously." Peabody's dark eyes scanned the altar, the statues. "It's like holy ground up there or something."

"Funny, it looks like a dead guy up there to me."

Eve walked up. Behind her, Peabody gave a one-legged bounce before following.

"Victim has been identified as Miguel Flores, age thirty-five, Catholic priest," Eve began. "The body's been moved." She flicked a glance up to one of the uniforms securing the scene.

"Yes, sir. The victim collapsed during Mass, and there was an attempt to revive him while the nine-one-ones were placed. A couple of cops were on scene attending the funeral. That guy's funeral," he added with a chin point at the casket. "They moved people back, secured. They're waiting to talk to you."

Since she'd sealed her hands and feet before coming in, Eve crouched. "Get prints, TOD, and so on, for the record, Peabody. And for the record, the victim's cheeks are bright pink. Facial injuries, left temple and cheekbone, most likely incurred when he fell."

She glanced up, noted the silver chalice on the stained white linen. She rose, walked to the altar, sniffed at the cup. "He drink from this? What was he doing when he collapsed?"

"Taking Communion," the man in the front row answered before the uniform could speak.

Eve stepped to the other side of the altar. "Do you work here?"

"Yes. This is my church."

"Yours?"

"I'm the pastor." He rose, a compact and muscular man with sad, dark eyes. "Father López. Miguel was officiating the funeral Mass, and was taking Communion. He drank, and he seemed, almost immediately, to seize. His body shook, and he gasped for air. And he collapsed." López spoke with the faintest of accents, an exotic sheen over rough wood. "There were doctors and other medicals here, and they tried to revive him, but it was too late. One said, one thought, it was poison. But I don't believe that could be."

"Why?"

López merely lifted his hands. "Who would poison a priest in such a way, and at such a time?"

"Where did the wine come from? In the cup?"

"We keep Communion wine locked in the tabernacle, in the anteroom."

"Who has access?"

"I do. Miguel, Martin—that is, Father Freeman—the Eucharistic ministers serving the Mass."

A lot of hands, Eve thought. Why bother with a lock? "Where are they?"

"Father Freeman is visiting family in Chicago, and expected back tomorrow. We have—had—three ministers today due to the large attendance at the Requiem Mass."

"I'll need their names."

"Surely you can't believe—"

"And this?"

He actually paled when Eve lifted the silver disk holding the wafer. "Please. Please. It's been consecrated."

"I'm sorry, now it's evidence. There's a piece missing. Did he eat it?"

"A small piece is broken off, put in the wine for the rite of fraction and commingling. He would have consumed it with the wine."

"Who put the wine in the cup and the . . ." What the hell did she call it? Cookie? Cracker?

"Host," López supplied. "He did. But I poured the wine into the receptacle and placed the host for Miguel before the Consecration. I did it personally as a sign of respect for Mr. Ortiz. Miguel officiated, at the family's request."

Eve cocked her head. "They didn't want the head guy? Didn't you say you were the head guy?"

"I'm pastor, yes. But I'm new. I've only had this parish for eight months, since Monsignor Cruz retired. Miguel's been here for more than five years, and married two of Mr. Ortiz's great-grandchildren, officiated at the Requiem for Mrs. Ortiz about a year ago. Baptized—"

"Just one minute, please."

Eve turned back to Peabody.

"Sorry to interrupt, Father. ID match," Peabody told Eve. "TOD jibes. Drink, seize, collapse, die, red cheeks. Cyanide?"

"Educated guess. We'll let Morris confirm. Bag the cup, the cookie. Pick one of the cop witnesses and get a statement. I'll take the other after I have López show me the source of the wine and the other thing."

"Should we release the other dead guy?"

Eve frowned at the casket. "He's waited this long. He can wait a little longer." She turned back to López. "I need to see where you keep the . . ." Refreshments? "The wine and the hosts."

With a nod, López gestured. He walked up, turned away from the altar to lead Eve through a doorway. Inside cabinets lined one wall, and on a table stood a tall box, deeply carved with a cross. López took keys from the pocket of his pants and unlocked the door of the box.

"This is the tabernacle," he explained. "It holds unconsecrated hosts and wine. We keep a larger supply in the first cabinet there, also locked."

The wood gleamed with polish, she noted, and would hold prints. The lock was a simple key into a slot. "This decanter here is where you took the wine for the cup?"

"Yes. I poured it from here to the vessel, and took the host. I brought them to Miguel at the beginning of the Eucharistic Liturgy."

Purplish liquid filled the clear decanter to about the halfway point. "Did the substances leave your hands at any time before that, or were they unattended?"

"No. I prepared them, kept them with me at all times. To do otherwise would be disrespectful."

"I have to take this into evidence."

"I understand. But the tabernacle can't leave the church.

Please, if you need to examine it, can it be done here? I'm sorry," he added, "I never asked your name."

"Lieutenant Dallas."

"You're not Catholic."

"What gave you the first clue?"

He smiled a little, but the misery never left his eyes. "I understand you're unfamiliar with the traditions and rites of the church, and some may seem strange to you. You believe someone tampered with the wine or the host."

Eve kept both her face and her voice neutral. "I don't believe anything yet."

"If this is so, then someone used the blood and body of Christ to kill. And I delivered them to Miguel. I put them in his hands." Beneath the misery in his eyes, Eve saw the banked embers of anger. "God will judge them, Lieutenant. But I believe in earthly laws as well as God's laws. I'll do whatever I can to help you in your work."

"What kind of priest was Flores?"

"A good one. Compassionate, dedicated, ah, energetic, I'd say. He enjoyed working with young people, and was particularly good at it."

"Any trouble recently? Depression, stress?"

"No. No. I would have known, I would have seen it. We live together, the three of us, in the rectory behind the church." He gestured vaguely, as if his mind was crowded with a dozen other thoughts. "We eat together almost daily, talk, argue, pray. I would've seen if he'd been troubled. If you think he might have taken his own life, he wouldn't. And he would never do so in such a way."

"Any trouble with anyone? Someone with a grudge, or a problem with him—professionally or otherwise?"

"Not that he mentioned, and as I said, we talked daily."

"Who knew he'd be doing the funeral today?"

"Everyone. Hector Ortiz was a fixture in the parish. A well-loved and well-respected man. Everyone knew about the funeral Mass, and that Miguel was officiating."

As she spoke, she crossed to a door, opened it. The May sunlight beamed through the exit. The door had a lock, she noted, nearly as simple as the one on the wooden box.

Easy in, easy out.

"Were there any masses earlier today?" she asked López.

"The six o'clock weekday Mass. I officiated."

"And the wine, the host came from the same supply as the funeral Mass?"

"Yes."

"Who got it for you?"

"Miguel. It's a small service, usually no more than a dozen people, maybe two. Today, we expected less as the funeral would be so well attended."

Come in, Eve mused, attend Mass. Go back, poison the wine. Walk away. "About how many did you bring in this morning?"

"At morning Mass? Ah . . . Eight or nine." He paused a moment, and Eve imagined him going back, counting heads. "Yes, nine."

"I'll need that list, too. Any unfamiliar faces in that one?"

"No. I knew everyone who attended. A small group, as I said."

"And just you and Flores. Nobody assisting."

"Not for the six o'clock. We don't generally use a minister for the morning weekday service, except during Lent."

"Okay. I'd like you to write down, as best you can remember, the vic's—Flores's movements and activities this morning, and the times."

"I'll do that right away."

"I'm going to need to secure this room as part of the crime scene."

"Oh." Distress covered his face. "Do you know how long?"

"I don't." She knew she was brusque, but something about all the . . . holiness made her twitchy. "If you'd give me your keys it would be simpler. How many sets are there?"

"These, and a set at the rectory. I'll need my key to the rectory." He took a single key off the chain, gave Eve the rest.

"Thanks. Who was Ortiz and how did he die?"

"Mr. Ortiz?" A smile, warmer, moved into his eyes. "A fixture of the community, and this parish, as I said. He owned a family restaurant a few blocks from here. Abuelo's. Ran it, I'm told, with his wife up until about ten years ago, when one of his sons and his granddaughter took over. He was a hundred and sixteen, and died quietly—and, I hope, painlessly—in his sleep. He was a good man, and well loved. I believe he's already in God's hands."

He touched the cross he wore, a light brush of fingers. "His family is understandably distressed by what happened this morning. If I could contact them, and we could complete the Requiem Mass and hold the Commitment. Not here," López said before Eve could speak. "I'd make arrangements, but they need to bury their father, grandfather, their friend. They need to complete the ritual. And Mr. Ortiz should be respected."

She understood duty to the dead. "I need to speak to someone else now. I'll try to move this along. And I'll need you to wait for me at the rectory."

"I'm a suspect." The idea didn't appear to shake him or surprise him. "I gave Miguel the weapon that may have killed him."

"That's right. And right at the moment, pretty much anyone who walked into the church and gained access to this room is a suspect. Hector Ortiz gets a pass, but that's about it."

He smiled again at that, just a little. "You can probably eliminate the infants and toddlers, of which there were scores."

"I don't know. Toddlers are pretty suspicious. We'll need to take a look at Flores's room at the rectory. As soon as I can, I'll see about moving Mr. Ortiz from the scene."

"Thank you. I'll wait at home."

Eve led him out, locked the door, then told the closest uniform to bring in the second police witness.

While she waited, she circled Flores again. Good-looking guy, she mused. About six feet—hard to tell body type with the funny robes, but she'd scanned his official ID. That had him weighing in at a trim one-sixty.

He had even features, a lot of dark hair with a few glints of silver running through it. Smoother, she thought, than López. Leaner, younger.

She supposed priests came in all types and sizes, just like regular people.

Priests weren't supposed to have sex. She'd have to ask somebody the root of that rule, if she found it could apply. Some priests also ignored the rule, and got their jollies, just like regular people. Maybe Flores didn't care for celibacy.

Who would?

Maybe he'd diddled the wrong person. Angry lover or angry spouse of lover. Worked particularly well with young people, she mused. Maybe he liked to poke into the underage well. Vengeful parent.

Or—

"Lieutenant Dallas?"

Eve turned to see a hot number in sedate black. Petite would be the word, Eve supposed, as the woman hit maybe five-five in her black dress heels. Her hair was jet-black as well, sleeked back into a quiet knot. She had huge, almond-shaped eyes in a kind of simmering green.

"Graciela Ortiz. Officer Ortiz," she added, almost as an afterthought.

"Officer." Eve came down from the altar. "You're related to Mr. Ortiz."

"Poppy. My great-grandfather."

"I'm sorry for your loss."

"Thank you. He lived so well, and long. Now he's with the angels. But Father Flores . . ."

"You don't think he's with the angels?"

"I hope he is. But he didn't live long, or die peacefully

in his bed. I've never seen death like that." She took a breath, and there was a shudder in it. "I should have acted more quickly, to preserve the scene. My cousin and I— Matthew is with Illegals—should have acted sooner. But I was closer. Matt was in the back of the church. I thought—we all thought—Father had had some sort of attack. Dr. Pasquale and my uncle, who is also a doctor, tried to help him. It happened very quickly. In minutes. Three, four, no more than that. So the body was moved, and the scene compromised. I'm sorry."

"Tell me what happened."

Graciela relayed the events, set the scene as López had. "Did you know Flores?"

"Yes, a little. He married my brother. I mean to say he officiated at the marriage of my brother. Father Flores also gave time to the youth center. I do the same, when I can, so I knew him from there."

"Impressions?"

"Outgoing, interested. He seemed to relate to the street kids. I thought he'd probably been there and done that in his time."

"Did he show any interest in any particular kid or kids?"

"Not that I noticed. But I didn't run into him there often."

"He ever move on you?"

"Move . . . No." Graciela seemed shocked, then thoughtful. "No, no moves, no sense he considered it. And I never heard of him breaking that particular vow."

"Would you have?"

"I don't know, but my family—and there are a lot of them—is very involved in the church and this is our home parish. If he was going to move on someone, odds are the someone would've been related or connected to the Ortiz family. And family gossip runs pretty hot and strong. My aunt Rosa housekeeps for the rectory and not much gets by her."

"Rosa Ortiz."

"O'Donnell." Graciela smiled. "We diversify. Is it homicide, Lieutenant?"

"Right now it's suspicious death. You might talk to family members, get their impressions."

"Nobody's going to be talking about much else for days," Graciela commented. "I'll see what I can find out from those who knew him better than I did."

"Okay. I'm going to have your great-grandfather released from the scene. You and your cousin should take that detail as soon as we're clear."

"We appreciate that."

"Where's your house?"

"I'm with the two-two-three, here in East Harlem."

"How long on the job?"

"Almost two years. I thought I wanted to be a lawyer, changed my mind."

Probably change it again, Eve thought. She just didn't see a cop in those sizzling green eyes. "I'm going to get my partner, and we'll clear the casket. If anything regarding Flores occurs to you, you can reach me at—"

"Cop Central," Graciela finished. "I know."

As Graciela clicked out on her funeral heels, Eve took one more scan of the crime scene. A lot of death for one small church, she mused. One in the coffin, one at the altar, and the one looking down on both from the really big cross.

One dies in his sleep after a long life, one dies fast— and the other gets spikes hammered through his hands and feet so they can hang him on a cross of wood.

God, priest, and the faithful, she thought. To her way of thinking, God got the worst deal of the three.

"I can't decide," Peabody said as they walked around to the rectory, "if the statues and candles and colored glass are really pretty or really creepy."

"Statues are too much like dolls, and dolls are creepy. You keep expecting them to blink. And the ones that smile, like this?" Eve kept her lips tight together as she curved them up. "You know they've got teeth in there. Big, sharp, shiny teeth."

"I didn't. But now I've got to worry about it."

The small, unimposing building that housed the rectory had flowers in a pair of window boxes—and, Eve noted, minimum security. A standard lock, those flower-decked windows open to the spring air, and no palm plate, no security cameras.

She knocked, then stood on long legs in simple trousers, on feet planted in worn boots. The pale gray blazer she'd shrugged on that morning covered her weapon harness. The frisky May breeze fluttered through her short, brown hair. Like her legs, her eyes were long, a whiskey brown. They didn't sizzle like Graciela's—and were all cop.

The woman who answered had an explosion of dark curls tipped with gold around a pretty face. Her red-rimmed eyes scanned Eve, then Peabody. "I'm sorry, Father López is unable to take visitors today."

"Lieutenant Dallas, NYPSD." Eve drew out her badge. "And Detective Peabody."

"Yes, of course. Forgive me. Father said to expect you. Please come in."

She stepped back. She wore a red carnation on the lapel of her black mourning suit—and both over a beautifully curved body. "It's a terrible day for the parish, for my family. I'm Rosa O'Donnell. My grandfather . . . It was his funeral Mass, you see. Father is in his office. He gave me this for you." She held out an envelope. "You asked him to write out what Father Flores did today."

"Yeah, thanks."

"I'm to let Father know if you need to see him."

"No need at this time. You can tell him that we've released Mr. Ortiz. My partner and I need to see Father Flores's room."

"I'll show you upstairs."

"You cook for the rectory," Eve began as they moved from the tiny foyer to the stairs.

"Yes, and clean. Some of this, some of that. Three men, even priests, need someone to pick up after them."

The stairs rose straight to a narrow hallway. The walls were white and adorned here and there with crucifixes or pictures of people in robes looking benign or—to Eve's eye—sorrowful. Occasionally annoyed.

"You knew Father Flores," Eve prompted.

"Very well, I think. You cook and clean for a man, you come to know who he is."

"Who was he?"

Rosa paused outside a door, sighed. "A man of faith, and humor. He enjoyed sports, watching them, playing them. He had . . . energy," she decided. "And put much of that into the youth center."

"How did he get along with his housemates? The other priests," Eve explained when Rosa looked blank.

"Very well. There was respect between him and Father López, and I'd say they were friendly. Easy with each other, if you understand."

"Yeah."

"He was friendlier, well, closer, you know, with Father Freeman—they had more in common, I'd say, outside the church. Sports. He and Father Freeman would argue about sports, as men do. Go to games together. They ran together most mornings, and often played ball at the center."

Rosa sighed again. "Father López is contacting Father Freeman now, to tell him. It's very hard."

"And Flores's family?"

"He had none. He would say the church was his family. I believe his parents died when he was a boy." She opened the door. "He never had calls or letters from family, as Fathers López and Freeman often do."

"What about other calls, other letters?"

"I'm sorry?"

"Who was he connected to? Friends, teachers, old schoolmates."

"I . . . I don't know." Her brows drew together. "He had

many friends in the parish, of course, but if you mean from outside, or from before, I don't know."

"Did you notice anything off—in his mood, his routine, recently?"

"No, nothing." Rosa shook her head. "I came in to fix breakfast for him and Father López this morning, before the funeral. He was very kind."

"What time did you get here?"

"Ah . . . about six-thirty, a few minutes later than that."

"Was anyone else here?"

"No. I let myself in. I have a key. Though, as usual, Father López forgot to lock up. The fathers came back from Mass shortly after, and I gave them breakfast. We all talked about the service, then Father Flores went into the office to work on his sermon."

She pressed her fingertips to her lips. "How could this have happened?"

"We'll find out. Thank you," Eve said, by way of dismissal, then stepped into the room.

It held a narrow bed, a small dresser and mirror, a night table, a desk. No house 'link, she noted, no computer. The bed looked to be neatly made, and over its head a picture of Christ on the cross hung next to a crucifix. Seemed like overkill to Eve.

There were no personal photographs in evidence, no loose credits scattered over the dresser. She saw a Bible, a rosary of black and silver, and a lamp on the bedside table, a comb and a pocket 'link on the dresser.

"That explains why he didn't have a 'link on him," Peabody commented. "I guess they don't take them when they do a service." As she turned, the sassy little flip at the ends of her dark hair bounced. "Well, I guess this won't take long, considering he didn't have a whole lot."

"Take a look in the other rooms. Just a scan from the doorway. See if they're the same as this."

As Peabody went out, Eve opened a dresser drawer with her sealed hand. White boxers, white undershirts, white socks, black socks. She pawed through, found nothing else. Another drawer held T-shirts. White, black, gray—some with team logos emblazoned on the front.

"They've got more stuff," Peabody announced. "Photographs, man junk."

"Define 'man junk,'" Eve said as she drew out the bottom drawer.

"Golf ball on a display tee, pile of discs, a pair of boxing gloves, that kind of thing."

"Check the closet here." Eve drew the bottom drawer all the way out, checked the bottom, the back.

"Priest's suits, two sets with pants, and one of those dresses. A pair of black shoes that look worn, two pairs of high-tops, one pair looks shot. Shelf . . ." Peabody paused as she rummaged. "Cooler-weather gear. Two sweaters, two sweatshirts, one hooded sweat jacket—Knicks."

After checking all the drawers, backs, bottoms, sides, Eve pulled the small dresser out from the wall, checked the back of the mirror.

With Peabody, she moved to the desk. It held a date book, a few memo cubes, a short stack of brochures on the youth center, the Yankees' schedule, and another for the Knicks.

Eve checked the last entries in the date book. "Vigil for Ortiz at the funeral home last night. Yankees game Wednesday. Let's see if anyone went with him. He's scheduled for FHC—need to find out what that is—for a week from this coming Sunday at two. Got a few games and sessions at the youth center on here. Pre-C counseling. Need to get the meaning of that. Two of those—last Monday and Tuesday. Names of whoever he was counseling in here. We'll run them down. The funeral's on here. A teaching gig at St. Cristóbal's Friday, a baptism a week from Saturday. All priestly, except for the Yankees."

She bagged the date book. "Take a look at the 'link," she told Peabody, then began on the little night table.

She flipped through the Bible, found a few small pictures of saints. In Hebrews, she read an underscored line:

<u>And thus, having had long patience, he got the promise.</u>
And in Proverbs: <u>With me are riches and honor, enduring wealth and prosperity.</u>

Interesting. She bagged the Bible for evidence. Inside the drawer were a couple more community flyers, and a mini-game player. She found a silver medal taped behind the drawer. "Well, well. Why does a priest tape a religious medal behind a drawer?"

Peabody stopped her own search. "What kind of medal?"

"It's a woman, with the robe thing, hands folded, and it looks like she's standing on a pillow or something with a little kid holding her up."

"It's probably the Virgin Mary, and the Baby Jesus. And, yeah, weird place for a medal."

Carefully, Eve peeled the tape away, turned the freed medal over. "*Lino, May La Virgen de Guadalupe watch over you—Mama.* Dated May 12, 2031."

"Rosa said she thought his parents died when he was a boy—and he'd have been about six at this date," Peabody commented. "Maybe Lino's a nickname, a term of affection in Spanish?"

"Maybe. Why tape it to the back of a drawer instead of wearing it, or keeping it *in* a drawer? Are priests allowed to wear jewelry?" Eve wondered.

"Probably not big honking rings or chains, but I've seen them wearing crosses and medals and stuff." To get a closer look, Peabody squatted down. "Like that sort of thing."

"Yeah. Yeah. So why is this hidden? You hide something so nobody sees it, and you hide it close when you want to look at it in private now and then. This mattered to him, whether it was his, a friend's or relative's, or he picked it up in a secondhand store, it mattered. It looks like silver," she murmured, "but it's not tarnished. You have to polish silver to keep it shiny."

After another study, she bagged it. "Maybe we can trace it. What about the 'link?"

"Logged transmissions, in and out from Roberto

Ortiz—that would be the late Mr. Ortiz's oldest surviving son. A couple to and from the youth center, and the oldest last week to Father Freeman."

"Okay, we'll have a look and listen. Let's call the sweepers in for a pass, then I want this room sealed."

She thought of the two underlined passages, and wondered what riches and honor Flores waited for.